FOX HUNTER

FOX HUNTER

A CHARLIE FOX THRILLER

ZOË SHARP

PEGASUS CRIME

NEW YORK LONDON

FOX HUNTER

Pegasus Books Ltd.
148 W 37th Street, 13th Floor
New York, NY 10018

First Pegasus Books cloth edition August 2017

Interior design by Maria Fernandez

Library of Congress Cataloging-in-Publication Data is available.

ISBN: 978-1-68177-438-1

10 9 8 7 6 5 4 3 2 1

Printed in the United States of America
Distributed by W. W. Norton & Company

For Jean Melling
mother of my childhood second home
1947–2017

ONE

THE DEAD MAN HAD NOT GONE QUIETLY. IF WHAT HAD BEEN done to him was any indication, he had died begging, cursing, screaming, or a mix of all three. There was a time when I would have given everything I owned to be the one responsible for that.

Not anymore.

At least, that's what I told myself when I looked down at what remained of his body. A part of me even believed it.

The dead man had not gone quickly, either. Most people will cling to life long past the point of logical expiry. I had a feeling that for Michael Clay, his final moment could not have come soon enough. I kept my expression bland, neutral, by pure effort of will.

"I understand you didn't like the bloke much," Garton-Jones said from the doorway in the cut-glass tones so at odds with his skinhead appearance, "but the poor bastard certainly didn't deserve to go out like that."

1

He'd led me as far as the makeshift mortuary but left it to the medics to pull back the sheet. Not squeamish, I judged, just tired. He'd seen it all before, and didn't need to see it again.

I glanced across at him.

"No," I agreed, without being more specific.

In truth, saying I hadn't liked the dead man much was wildly understating it. I reckoned that under the circumstances my opinion on the manner of his demise was probably better left unvoiced.

Garton-Jones seemed to guess anyway. He shifted his weight as if to make an issue, then decided it wasn't worth the effort. He was a big man leaned down by heat and tension until the body armor he wore like a business suit fit slack on his frame.

"How long had Clay been out here?"

"About eighteen months, on and off." A shrug. "So he claimed."

Something in his voice nudged me. "Oh?"

"Streetwise International has only recently picked up the contract, as I'm sure you're aware," Garton-Jones said levelly. "Clay worked for our predecessor. He wanted to stay on. We needed local knowledge."

I studied him for a moment, head on one side, decided, "You didn't like him much, either."

"I'm not running a popularity contest, Ms. Fox. I didn't have to like the bloke. His experience was solid, and he came recommended. As long as he could be trusted to do the job, that's as much as anyone can ask."

"And could he?"

"What?"

"Be trusted to do the job?"

There it was again, that fractional pause, the stiffness in his voice when he answered. "I expect everyone here to give a hundred and ten percent," he said at last. "Sometimes I got the

2

feeling Clay's mind was not altogether on the task at hand, that he might have had a little something extra going on the side. I kept a close eye on him, but he knew how to toe the line—there was never anything actionable."

"It's an unwritten rule in any business that you hire people for their professional qualifications," I said, "and fire them for their personal failings."

"If you're asking would I have fired him if I'd had cause, then the answer's yes, I would have done so." He sighed, eyes flicking to the dead man. "He was a decent enough soldier, I suppose."

I felt my lips twist. "That has the ring of consolation praise."

"There are worse ways to be remembered."

As a treacherous coward, I thought. *As a monster.*

I turned away, nodded to the medic, who drew the sheet back over the man's mutilated face.

"*Ex*-soldier, surely? I thought both Gulf Wars were officially over. That you and your people were here simply in . . . how did you once put it? A cleanup capacity."

For a second he stilled, and I knew he remembered those words—they were his own repeated back at him from our first encounter years before. Another country, another time. We had parted with a grudging respect for one another that I had not mistaken for friendship.

His lips widened into a mirthless smile, but when he spoke his voice was cold.

"Reminding me of my roots, are you, Ms. Fox? Trying to rub it in that the last time we met I was in charge of a bunch of glorified security guards trying to bring a degenerate sink estate in the north of England to heel?"

"Not at all." I waited a beat. "They didn't have enough finesse to be security guards."

He grunted. I eyed the pair he had standing just outside in the corridor. A man and a woman. Like Garton-Jones they

3

wore tan cargo pants and black polo shirts with the Streetwise company logo on the left sleeve. But the equipment strapped on top was all high-grade military spec, and from their eyes, their hands, their stance, I judged this was not their first time at the fair.

I didn't recognize the faces but I knew the look all the same. I made a mental note not to turn my back on any of them.

I shifted my gaze pointedly back to Garton-Jones. "More like glorified thugs."

The lines around his eyes tightened minutely. "Well, I seem to recall that *you* were little more than an interfering do-gooder whose only income derived from prancing around in a leotard part-time at the local gym."

It was no lie that I'd been drifting in those days, still lost after the army, but the gym where I'd worked had been more spit-and-sawdust than leg warmers and aerobics. I'd nearly died there. And again when Garton-Jones's heavy-handed methods had turned that "degenerate sink estate" into a battleground.

But I smiled back, mainly because I knew it would annoy him, especially when we were both aware he'd been asked to afford me every courtesy.

"And yet here we are, Ian, both of us. Who'd have thought it?"

He gave another grunt that could have meant anything or nothing and turned on his heel, jerking his head in a kind of universal "follow me" gesture. I took my time complying, let my eyes roam over the shrouded figure one last time.

"Rot in hell, Clay," I murmured. "You earned your place there."

And I walked out of the morgue without looking back.

Garton-Jones was waiting for me a little farther along the corridor, impatience apparent in the set of his shoulders. The couple flanked him like a pair of Sphinxes. The bare blockwork walls showed more expression than their faces.

4

In the entrance to the building they paused just long enough to slip on their Wiley X antiballistic sunglasses. Oh yeah, they had all the right toys. They did a vehicle check on the Streetwise up-armored SUV before waving us out.

It was showy and unnecessary, in my view. One look at the group of street kids who crowded round them with outstretched hands should have been enough to tell them nobody had planted any nasty surprises. Otherwise, those kids would have stayed well outside the blast radius. You grow up fast and canny in southern Iraq. Or you don't grow up at all.

Maybe the performance was for my benefit. Or rather because the two of them knew I worked for the prestigious Armstrong-Meyer private security agency in New York and hoped I might be talent spotting. Just in case, each had their name helpfully embroidered into their shirt above the left nipple, complete with blood type. Tasteful.

Out in the street it was 104°F. The kind of dry-bone heat that sucks the spit off your tongue and cracks your lips in the space between heartbeats. The SUV had dark glass all around, but even with the air-con going full blast, for the first few minutes it was like sitting inside a fan-assisted oven.

I'd studied the maps of Basra before I landed in neighboring Kuwait only twenty-four hours ago. I knew we should have been heading nominally south, even allowing for a circumspect route. It was now just past noon local time. The sun was flaring from the oversize side mirror back into my eyes, when it should have been somewhere ahead of us.

I glanced at the guy alongside me in the rear seat. The sleeves of his polo shirt were tight around overdeveloped biceps, his hair close cropped without having the same razor-cut as Garton-Jones. According to the needlework on his company polo, his name was Bailey (Type O positive). I was sitting on his right, directly behind Garton-Jones.

The woman was at the wheel. Her name was Dawson (Type A positive). She had a smaller, compact figure—the type that tends toward hourglass shape if left to its own devices—kept rigorously in check. I suspected they both spent a lot of time in the hotel gym when they weren't on duty.

Their positioning made sense, to a point. The driver's hands would be full controlling the vehicle, so Bailey had field of fire to the left. Garton-Jones had the right. They had not seen fit to offer me a weapon, and I hadn't asked for one. Maybe they'd checked out the bandage on my left forearm and decided I wasn't capable of holding it anyway.

"Excuse me, folks, but where are we going?"

"Back to base," Garton-Jones said without turning in his seat. *Lie.*

Outside the shaded windows, the traffic was chaotic. Donkey carts mingled with overloaded trucks, new pickups, and elderly Japanese saloon cars not imported into the UK or America. The traffic lanes were only a suggestion. If a gap opened up, at least two or three vehicles attempted to surge into it. Most flew pennants I had yet to learn the meaning of and suspected I would not like when I did.

The buildings lining our route were mainly low-rise, dirty, and dust-blown, some just a bare concrete framework where construction had long ceased. The tallest structures by far were the ornate towers of the mosques.

I leaned toward Bailey to peer at a particularly grand one going past on his side of the car, pointed across him at the window.

"Sorry, but do you know what that—?" I began.

As he automatically twisted to follow my sight line, I hit him in the throat with a clenched backfist, ignoring the spike of pain that jolted through my left arm as I did so. Then I picked the Glock pistol off his hip while he thrashed, gasping.

I yanked on Garton-Jones's seat belt and shoved the muzzle against his ear, leaned in close.

"*Where* did you say we were going?"

Dawson almost sideswiped an ancient minivan with decals of what looked suspiciously like Bin Laden on the side. She stood on the brakes and was nearly rammed from behind by a truck towering with cement blocks. She hit the accelerator again. Horns sounded all around us.

Garton-Jones roared, "Jesus Fucking Christ, woman. Will you calm down before you kill us all!" and it wasn't clear which of us he meant.

"I *am* calm. Tell your boys to stand down, and then—for the last time—tell me: Where. Are. We. *Going*?"

For a second he considered stubbornness, just for the hell of it. It was to his credit that he jettisoned the idea as fast as it arrived. He nodded to the driver, who hunched her shoulders and scowled into the rearview mirror.

I let go of Garton-Jones's seat belt, reversed my grip on the Glock, and surrendered it to him, butt first. It seemed a better option, at that moment, than giving it back to Bailey. Garton-Jones looked down at the gun and flicked me a glance. There was the glimmer of a grim smile flirting around his lips.

"That's not the first time you've pointed one of these at me. I do hope it will be the last."

"That depends more on you than on me," I said. "And you haven't answered the question."

"We're going to the scene."

"The scene?"

"Of the crime, Ms. Fox. I'm taking you to the place where Clay died. The place where Sean Meyer tortured him to death."

TWO

"WE DON'T KNOW WHERE SEAN IS NOW, BUT WE KNOW WHERE HE was yesterday," Parker Armstrong told me less than forty-eight hours ago. "And you're not going to like it any more than I did."

We were in the cargo bay of a Lockheed Martin C-130 Hercules transport plane. Normally, trying to carry out any kind of conversation over the roar of four massive turbo-props would have been a nonstarter, but Parker had managed to commandeer a couple of headsets for the pair of us with comms built in. The crew told us we were on a separate channel and would not be overheard. Conversation was still difficult, but it was better than shouting.

We were both a long way from New York, which Parker had called home since birth. I'd adopted it when Sean and I moved over from the UK to work for him, only a couple of years previously. Plenty of roads traveled since then.

Right now, though, I was straight off a job that had come close to killing me. Just how close, Parker didn't know, and I wasn't about to tell him. If I did, I suspected there was no way he'd even brief me on Sean, never mind send me after him.

"Just spit it out, Parker. You already told me he crossed from Kuwait into Iraq. What then?"

Parker was leaning forward with his forearms resting on his knees. His close-cropped hair had turned gray early, according to all the photographs I'd seen, but he looked suddenly older, and tired to the bone.

"A man's body turned up in Basra," he began, caught my expression and rushed on. "No, no, it's not Sean. They've ID'd him as a guy called Michael Clay. Ex Special Forces, working for a private military contractor out there. You know him."

That last could have been a question, but it wasn't. Parker did his homework too well for that.

The moment he mentioned Clay's name, I was hit by a rush of images, rapid snapshots of a big, sandy-haired guy with the flattened nose of a boxer. A neck like a bull and strength to match. He had a tendency toward silence, so that some mistakenly took him for the average bone-headed squaddie. A mistake. He had a quick brain and a good grasp of strategy. And if he didn't say much, when he did it was usually worth listening to.

Right up to the point he'd said to the others, "Hold her down . . ."

The familiar litany unfurled inside my head.

Donalson, Hackett, Morton, and Clay.

Morton was dead. That I knew for certain. Now Clay. Perhaps I should have felt something. All that came up was emptiness.

I cleared my throat. "Yes, I knew him. What does this have to do with Sean?"

ZOË SHARP

Parker's gaze settled on me before he answered. In that brief look I read a whole host of meanings. He knew what had happened to me in the army, and he knew the names of the four men responsible. If we'd had a more intimate setting for our conversation, maybe he would have pushed it. I was thankful we did not.

"I discovered that before Sean left New York, he'd been in touch with Madeleine Rimmington. As you know, she took over Sean's old close-protection agency in the UK. She'd been running searches for him on some of the guys he served with—Clay was among them."

I shrugged. "So? He could have been planning a reunion."

"With the guys who ended your army career. Yeah, sure," he said flatly. "What was he gonna do—buy them a beer for old times' sake?"

I sat back against the vibrating airframe, momentarily closed my eyes. "The way he is these days, Parker? Your guess is as good as mine."

"Look, I know he's been . . . changed, since the coma. C'mon, a gunshot to the head? We were lucky to get him back at all."

"But we didn't get all of him back, did we?"

He sighed. "No, we didn't."

"To be honest, I've been wondering how long you're going to leave his name over the door in the hope there's more of him still in there."

For a time Parker said nothing. We swayed in our canvas seats as the air throbbed to the beat of the engines and the big plane thumped into occasional pockets of turbulence like a truck hitting potholes on a dirt road.

"I know to some people I must look like a lucky guy—sit back and let the world owe me a living," he said then. "But I work hard for what I have. And you know what? The harder I work, the luckier I am. I can't let anyone ruin what I've built up single-handed."

In truth, the Armstrong-Meyer private security agency had offices on a prestigious Midtown block, in a swanky building owned outright by Parker's family. When it came down to it, he probably could have lived off his trust fund and made a career out of country club lunches and tennis parties and rounds of golf. Instead, he'd served his time in the Marine Corps and then put that knowledge to good use in the private sector.

Strip away their shared military service and their similar code of ethics, and he couldn't have come from a background more different than Sean Meyer's.

Sean had originally joined up because it had been a choice between that and prison. His mother still lived in a rented house on a run-down estate in the northern English city of Lancaster. It was the kind of area where you kept your tires spinning as you drove through to stop the local toe-rags from undoing your wheelnuts along the way.

He'd thrived in the military, made his way up to sergeant, and earned his place in Special Forces on ability and sheer bloody-minded determination.

It wasn't until he got together with me that things began to go wrong for both of us.

"PMC work can be dangerous," I said. "And Iraq's a dangerous place. Who's to say that Clay didn't simply—?"

Parker silenced me with a slitted stare.

"Let's just cut to the chase, shall we? Sean tracks down Clay, and within a few days of him arriving in-country, Clay's dead. *Slow* dead."

"Meaning?"

"Whoever killed him made him suffer first."

There wasn't much I could say to that. So I said nothing.

"I came out with all the same arguments when I got the report, Charlie, trust me on that. Sean met with Clay, argued with him. Next thing, the guy turns up dead. It . . . doesn't look good."

"How soon can you get me out there?"

He shook his head. "You're in no state to go into a highly unstable country. You're injured. Left arm and ribs, at a guess. Oh, you hide it pretty good, but I know you well enough by now—the way you move."

"I wasn't planning to get into a fistfight with anyone."

He flashed a wry smile. "Since when did that ever stop you?"

"I'm right-handed. So it won't stop me shooting anyone, either."

"You're not going to talk me round on this. I'm telling you now because you have the right to know. Doesn't mean I'm prepared to sanction you going in after him."

"You think I need your sanction to go after him?"

"You're not up to it." He caught my expression as I started to rise, held up a hand. "And before you tear me a new one, just hear me out first."

I subsided, not without effort, gestured for him to go on.

He met my eyes. "I know, better than most, what you're capable of, Charlie, injured or no. You think I'd say something like that lightly?"

His words stung enough that I said nothing.

He sighed. "Look at the facts. Sean has gone off the grid in a war zone. A man he has very good reason to hate is dead—killed in a way that suggests there was something real personal about it. What conclusions would you draw?"

"Sean knew the names of those guys—what they'd done—long before he was shot in the head," I said, which was both answer and avoidance. "If he'd wanted to go after them, he had plenty of opportunity back then." *When he still knew me for who I am. When he still loved me.*

"Exactly. And he didn't," Parker said, as if that proved a point. "So something's unbalanced him, set him off on this course. Care to shed any light on what that might be?"

I hesitated for a moment, then shook my head. I counted Parker as one of my closest friends, but I'd lied to him about what had happened in the aftermath of Sean's injury, about the real circumstances surrounding the death of the man who'd put him in his coma.

I might have told myself I'd done it to protect Parker, but that was a lie in itself. I'd done it so he wouldn't think less of me, of what I'd done.

"So, *if* there was no precipitating event," he said, gaze steady as if daring me to come clean, "then he's gone clean off the rails."

"You've nothing more than circumstantial evidence that he is in any way responsible for Clay's death. I thought you, of all people, would give him a fair trial, Parker."

"That's just it, I can't afford to. You know as well as I do that in our line of business we succeed or fail on reputation alone. The whispers have already begun about Sean. Hell, I've been hearing them for months. Ever since he went back into the field."

"You mean since we lost a principal—since I lost him."

"Yeah, since then." Parker scrubbed his palms up and down his face as if to clear the grit of weariness. "Either way, if it gets out that Sean's gone on some kind of murderous rampage— regardless of the truth of it—it could well be enough to finish us. I just . . . can't let that happen."

"All the more reason for me to go after him as soon as possible. Find him, find out what really happened and—"

"And what? Talk him in? That's just it, Charlie. If Sean *has* gone after this guy for revenge, it's a one-way deal. You know as well as I do he can't come back."

"You'd turn him in?" I demanded, aware that the kick in my chest was not only for Sean but for me, too.

"I couldn't do that to him. Prison would kill him. Better to give him another way out."

"One round in the chamber and tell him to do the honorable thing, you mean?" The acid in my stomach leached out in my voice.

"If he'll take that option."

"And if he won't?" I demanded. "After all, this is a man you think has gone 'clean off the rails.'"

"If he can't be reasoned with, then he has to be stopped. Like you said—Iraq's a dangerous place."

"Jesus, Parker. You're talking . . . assassination."

A pause, then he nodded, his face bleaker than I ever remembered it. "And *that*, Charlie, is the part I don't think you're up to."

THREE

❖

GARTON-JONES SHOVED OPEN THE DOOR TO HELL AND GESTURED me in.

I paused a moment before complying. Not least because the three of them climbed out of the SUV with weapons drawn. It might have been standard operating procedure for this area of Basra, but I couldn't ignore the possibility they were planning to use them on someone a little closer to home. Bailey, in particular, looked desperate for the excuse.

We were to the west of the city, in the sprawling outskirts. The building we were about to enter was constructed of bricks sloppily laid in no discernible pattern. Between each one mortar had squidged out and set like worm castings. The gothic-arched windows on the ground floor were boarded from the inside. Above, an intricately carved and decorated Ottoman balcony appeared ready at any moment to slide down the front façade.

15

The detritus of modern man littered the roadside—tattered plastic flapping languidly, rubble and crap. The heat was overwhelming and the smell almost as bad. Even the usual begging children were absent.

Further out I could see the roiling dirty-orange smoke from the gas burn-off at the West Quma oil field. Oil was being sucked out of the ground as fast as the derricks could handle it.

There was an air of hurry and fear as Western eyes looked to the trouble in the north, scared that control of southern production might be lost to militants, as it had in the supergiant field of Kirkuk. Greed saturated the place like a layer of grease.

Lucifer, I reckoned, would feel very much at home here.

"After you," I said to Bailey.

He thought about arguing. I fixed my eyes meaningfully on his throat. Garton-Jones jerked his head, and Bailey scowled but went in. He moved light on his feet, passing through the doorway at an oblique angle to reduce his exposure to a minimum.

Dawson followed suit. One automatically went left, the other right. Two people who'd operated together for a long time. Who knew what was needed without asking or being asked. I was suddenly, sharply, reminded of working with Sean.

Inside, the building was dim and marginally cooler. It was difficult to tell its original purpose. The walls of the structure had once been decorated with care, but the days when it commanded any pride were long past. The only furniture was a foldout plastic table and a metal chair. I guessed they had survived only because they could not be burned.

I stepped through debris and fallen plaster to the archway leading to a larger, darker space at the rear, which I peered into but did not enter. The smell of old meat and dried blood was rank. I could hear the buzz of flies echoing against the bare walls. Their whine rose in pitch and volume at the disturbance, intensifying the darkness there.

I turned, found the Streetwise crew watching my reaction. If they were hoping for shock, or disgust, they were disappointed. There was nothing here I hadn't seen before.

"So, you want to talk me through it?"

Both looked to their boss as if for permission. Garton-Jones stood near the doorway, his attention apparently on the street. Nothing seemed to pass between them, but after a moment Dawson said, "We found Clay still tied to the chair. He'd been dead about four hours. Meyer was long gone."

"How do you know Sean had been with him at all?"

"He came to the hotel before we shipped in-country, got into it with Clay there."

"Oh?"

"No idea what it was about, but whatever it was, Clay didn't like it much. He was pissy the whole day, wouldn't spill what Meyer had to say, or what was bugging him."

I could imagine most of what Sean had to say. And why Clay would not have liked it. It was not something I felt inclined to share.

"If they met at the hotel, why would they need to meet again here?"

"Look around you," Dawson said. "You could scream forever in a place like this and nobody would bat an eyelid."

"I agree that as somewhere for an interrogation it's sound," I said. "But Sean could hardly have found such a location within forty-eight hours of arriving. More likely it was Clay's choice. So, if he'd already met with Sean, and they'd had . . . words, why on earth would he agree to meet with him a second time—alone—somewhere like this?"

There were further exchanged glances I couldn't read—beyond a reluctance to see the logic in anything I had to say. Dawson shrugged.

"Clay's last incoming call was from a burner phone—a new number. His regular contacts don't use 'em. And he wouldn't have agreed to come out here to meet with someone he didn't know."

"All I'm getting from you is hearsay. To describe it as thin is putting it mildly." I paused. "I'm assuming Clay was armed?"

It was Garton-Jones who nodded. "Standard issue M4 carbine and .40-cal sidearm. Clay carried a Glock. His choice."

"Were they taken?"

A fractional pause, then a shake of the head. "No."

"Sean's unarmed." *As far as we know.* "If he shook Clay down for information, why not take his weapons, too? Got to be easier to grab what's on offer right in front of you than trying to source it in a hostile environment."

I turned away, but not before I caught the frown from Garton-Jones. *At last, a bit of doubt.*

I crouched, looked at the dusty floor. It was a mess of boot prints.

"Before you ask, no, we didn't take casts of that lot," Bailey sneered. "We're not CSIs."

I twisted, glanced up at him. "You don't need to be in order to glean information from these. The fact they're clear prints, for a start."

"Meaning?"

"Meaning they were left by people walking about in here."

"So?"

"Jesus H. Christ, do you really need me to spell it out? OK, they were *walking and standing.* Not fighting, not scuffling, not grappling and pushing and shoving and beating seven bells out of each other. No, Clay walked in, and—at least to begin with—everything was hunky-dory. These are full prints, sole and heel. If anyone had been moving fast, they'd be toe prints, scuffs, scrapes. It also means that whoever he met with, they weren't alone."

"Oh c'mon! How do you work that one out?"

"Clay was a big guy, and he was fast on his feet. He must have a couple of inches and thirty pounds on Sean. Even if Sean had pulled a gun on Clay, as soon as things went south, Clay would have chanced his arm."

I didn't add that the last time Clay tried going hand-to-hand with Sean, Sean had taken him apart without breaking sweat. Garton-Jones didn't need to know that, and besides, there still would have been physical evidence. "And yet they were able to subdue him without leaving any signs of a struggle. I assume your guys ran a tox screen on Clay?"

"Of course."

"Any barbiturates, tranquilizers? Midazolam or ketamine, perhaps? Rohypnol even?"

"Not those, no," Garton-Jones said. "But he was positive for Dexedrine—in his bloodstream rather than his stomach, so it was injected, not ingested."

"You're sure he didn't take it himself? Using Dexies is common among squaddies. The go-to pill for combat fatigue."

Garton-Jones skimmed his gaze across Dawson and Bailey. Bailey shuffled his feet and wouldn't meet his boss's eye, which I took as an answer in itself.

"Unlikely he would have gone to the trouble of distilling and injecting it, even so."

"Unless whoever gave it to him didn't want to wait for it to take effect," I suggested. "It would have helped keep him conscious while they worked him over, made him more inclined to be talkative."

"Oh, I think he would have been talkative, looking at what was done to him. Whatever they wanted to know, I'm sure he told them."

I noted the *"they"* rather than *"he"* without comment. Progress, of a sort. And once I had them on the back foot, I pressed home the advantage.

"Are you sure that was the sole point of the exercise—getting information out of Clay, I mean?"

"Hardly a fucking exercise!" Bailey snapped. "You know what they did to—"

"That's enough." Garton-Jones had sufficient control over his people that he didn't have to raise his voice. He swung his attention back to me, and his voice was icy calm. "As opposed to . . . ?"

"I've read the postmortem examination report, as Mr. Bailey points out." I matched his tone. "Clay was a tough bastard, but he wasn't a martyr. They yanked his teeth out, sliced him to pieces, cut off half his fingers, and scooped out his *eyes*, for God's sake. Whatever they wanted, if he had it, he would have given it to them way before then. This doesn't look like interrogation to me, it looks more like punishment—or a message." I skimmed my gaze across the three of them. "So, what have you guys been doing since you got here to warrant that?"

FOUR

WE CLIMBED BACK INTO THE STREETWISE SUV IN SILENCE. BAILEY and Dawson had swapped places—Bailey behind the wheel and Dawson alongside me in the rear. From the look on her face I guessed she'd lost some kind of toss. Even behind those expensive sunglasses, I could tell she was keeping a watchful eye on me.

I ignored her, tilted my head so I could check out the dusty street through the front screen as we retraced our route. It had been a long couple of days, and I wanted nothing more than to close my eyes for the return journey to the hotel back in Kuwait. *Once we get over the border*, I promised myself. The landscape there was dull and flat and largely featureless anyway.

Staying awake now meant trying hard not to scratch at the sweaty dressings on my arm and stomach. At the same time, I didn't fancy any more surprises over our destination.

Bailey drove bullishly, not stopping at intersections. Speed had both advantages and disadvantages. Made us a faster moving target, more difficult to hit, but gave him less time to check out the terrain.

"What's that?" I pointed between the seats at a lump by the nearside of the road.

"Just a dead dog or a goat," Garton-Jones said. "These are not a sentimental people."

"Neither am I," I said. "But it wasn't there when we came past on the way in."

Bailey had been ignoring me, determined not to be distracted again. But, give him credit, as the import of what I'd said sank in, he stamped on the accelerator. There was a moment's pause while the transmission kicked down, then the SUV's V8 engine delivered a surge of power and the heavy vehicle lurched forward.

It was almost enough.

There was an almighty crump of sound that shoved into my back, my kidneys, like a punch from a massive fist. The same giant's hand grabbed the back corner of the SUV and flipped it into the air. The vehicle slewed, Bailey grappling uselessly with the wheel.

We slammed down onto the driver's side, accompanied by the splinter of glass and the graunch of buckling metal. The engine was revving to the limiter.

For maybe a second I hung suspended on my seat belt. Then I braced hard against the center armrest and unclipped. Above me, my door was stuck. I swiveled, gripped both headrest supports, and jacked my legs up, kicking the door open. Immediately, rounds thudded into the outside of the panel, coming from dead ahead of our position. The armor held.

Below me, Dawson was groaning. I glanced down, saw blood in her hairline. One arm was crumpled under her. Concussion and a busted collarbone—she was out of the fight.

I reached down, pulled her M4 carbine loose, checked the mag, and charged a round into the chamber. In front, Garton-Jones was fighting his way free. He and Bailey jammed the muzzles of their own weapons through the crazed screen and fired in coordinated short bursts. Ejected brass pinged around the interior.

My ears still pulsed from the initial explosion, leaving a dull, muffled clanging inside my skull. I took a deep breath and launched upward through the door aperture, leading with the gun.

As soon as I had eyes on the scene, I caught a figure working his way to our rear, trying to flank us. He was twenty meters away on the other side of the street, a *keffiyeh* headscarf concealing his face, a long gun in his hands. I didn't stop to consider, couldn't afford to hesitate. I fired a three-round burst. He returned fire and ducked into the nearest doorway. I held my nerve, rolled my shoulder into the stock. Half a second later he dodged back into view, square into my sights.

I squeezed off another three rounds, aiming center mass. He fell back inside the building. Right at that moment he was no more to me than a targeting problem.

I covered my arc of exposure, both eyes open, looking for movement, for muzzle flash. Waiting for the zing of incoming rounds. Nothing showed.

To our front, Garton-Jones and Bailey were still laying down fire. I hoped they'd brought plenty of spare clips.

"Fox—you hurt?" Garton-Jones's voice shouted up.

"No, but Dawson is out. Shoulder."

"Damn," came the calm response. "I've radioed for backup. My blokes are less than a klick away."

I risked a quick glance under the curved edge of the rear door, saw a dirt-covered Nissan Patrol. It must have bowled out of a side street the moment the IED exploded—they probably remote-detonated it from there.

Two guys were using the Patrol for cover. All I could see of them were bobbing glimpses of their *keffiyeh*-wrapped heads above the open doors and their booted feet below. They were firing sporadically.

I ignored them, sprayed the Patrol's front grille with two quick bursts. It made a large static target. I hardly had to aim.

Whatever their original plan, the two X-rays decided on a tactical retreat as soon as their getaway vehicle came under specific attack. They jumped into the Patrol and reversed back into the side street. I vaulted out of the SUV and ran to the corner just in time to see them execute a professional J-turn. I had the satisfaction of putting half a dozen rounds through the rear screen before they swerved from sight.

By the time I'd turned back, the Streetwise men were out of the SUV and had taken up defensive positions, front and rear. There was no movement at all along the street. It was eerily quiet, but that wouldn't last long. The news of hostage-ready sitting-duck Westerners was no doubt already being relayed.

I jogged over, aware of the trembling in my limbs from the adrenaline hangover. Garton-Jones gave me a hard stare and nodded to the M4. "Dawson's?"

"Well, she wasn't using it."

"That your blood or hers?"

Confused, I looked down, realized the stitches had blown on the wound in my abdomen. Blood had seeped through both dressing and shirt. I pressed a hand to it. Damp but not sodden. Until then, I hadn't felt a thing. Now it began to throb like a son of a bitch.

"I'll live. How's Dawson?"

"She'll live," Garton-Jones echoed. His eyes still scanned constantly. "We got off lightly."

Behind us, the improvised explosive device had left a modest crater at the side of the road. Big enough to have pulverized us inside our armored tin can if it had caught us square on. It was why some squaddies were happier patrolling in open-top vehicles. If you were caught by a roadside bomb, you tended to get blown out instead of up.

Leaving the two of them with the SUV, I started across the street.

"Hey!" Bailey yelled. "We're not fucking sightseeing here!"

I didn't answer, moved cautiously along the front of the building where the third of our attackers had sought cover. When I reached the doorway, I could see the sole pattern of his combat boots. The rest of the body lay sprawled beyond on the dirt floor.

I'd put two rounds high into his chest. More by luck than judgment, the third had taken him in the throat, angled upward.

An AK-47 with a folding stock lay close to his out-flung arm. I toed it further out of reach, knelt over him and unwound the red-and-white *keffiyeh* from his head. Nothing pulsed below a face I didn't recognize. Under his jacket he wore body armor. My first two rounds were lodged in the Kevlar weave of the vest. The third had got the job done.

I pulled out my cell phone and took a picture of the dead man's face. Maybe Parker could ID him later. I patted him down one-handed, keeping the M4 at the ready. He carried no ID. I pulled open his shirt, checked the labels, untucked it and unzipped his fly.

"Oh for fuck's sake—" Bailey's disgusted voice came from behind me. I ignored him, took a cursory look at the under-wear, the boots. There was nothing in his jacket except a cell phone, a couple of spare clips for the AK in the leg pockets of his cargos.

I would have liked more time with the body, but Garton-Jones shouted, "Bailey! Fox! Transport—let's go."

I picked up the AK, pocketed the rest, brushing past Bailey. He jerked back as if afraid of contamination.

Another Streetwise SUV came roaring into view, kicking up clouds of dust and grit. As soon as it braked to a halt the men inside were out, weapons ready. Garton-Jones had clearly briefed them on our situation. They immediately began extracting the wounded Dawson, dragging her out through the buckled tailgate. They were being speedy rather than careful, but she was too unconscious to object.

"What about their guy?" I asked, nodding to the doorway.

"What about him?" Garton-Jones shrugged. "They'll come back for their own." A trickle of blood dripped down his cheekbone from the outer corner of one eye, like a prison tattoo, where a glass sliver had nicked him.

"Long way to come."

"What?"

"He's not an Iraqi," I said. "If I had to guess, I'd say he bought his underwear at Okhotny Ryad—in Moscow. He's Russian."

FIVE

I WOKE WITH HANDS GRASPING MY SHOULDERS AND A KNIFE AT MY throat. Panic ripped through me. My body gave a convulsive heave that threw me half out of bed in bucking reflex. I dragged myself upright, pulse thundering in my ears. The hands, the knife, were gone.

I fumbled for the bedside light, clicked it on and sat alone in my Kuwait City hotel room, shivering, breathing hard, until the residue of the nightmare faded.

I'd intended only to patch up my stomach and grab a shower when we got back to the hotel. Instead, I'd made the mistake of lying down.

In the half-light between waking and sleeping, images of Michael Clay flared through my mind. I met him the first day of Special Forces training. There were twenty-five of us. We'd all passed Selection, but some of the guys were not pleased to find three female trainees on the same intake.

Clay didn't immediately show his dismay. As I was to discover, one of his traits was to play dumb. To sit back and wait and take it all in before he made his feelings known. He fooled me back then. I hoped I was no longer so gullible.

The others were easier to label. Morton was a joker. Cruel jibes with acid at their core, chipping away under the guise of banter. Hackett was just plain nasty. Donalson gave me the creeps.

But Clay, I didn't see him coming.

Not until it was too late, anyway.

I wobbled out of bed on shaky legs, stripped, and set the shower running. My abdomen looked angry, but when they'd pulled me out of the ground they'd pumped me full of enough broad-spectrum antibiotics that it wasn't infected. Or it hadn't been. I cleaned the area thoroughly with antiseptic wipes, just to make sure, re-closed it with strips of micropore tape, and stuck a waterproof dressing over the top so I could shower. If it split open again, I might have to risk gluing it.

My father, an eminent British consultant surgeon, would not have approved.

In theory my arm should have been the worse of the two injuries. I'd been impaled on a length of rebar, straight through my left forearm and into my torso, working security after an earthquake. Maybe the arm was just easier to strap up.

The knock on my room door as I was dressing made me start. I stepped back into the bathroom, away from the door itself, and called, "Who is it?"

"Garton-Jones."

"Give me a minute."

I buttoned my shirt, tucked it in, and pulled on my boots. Whatever he had to say, I'd take it better fully dressed.

I checked the Judas glass, moving fast, then kicked away the doorstop I'd wedged under the door. Garton-Jones stood alone in the corridor. He was in his regulation company polo shirt and tan cargos, but neatly pressed. Maybe several sets of each were all the clothes he'd brought in-country with him. As a concession to being indoors, and this side of the border, he'd forgone body armor.

"What can I do for you, Ian?"

"We need to talk, and what I have to discuss would be better said in private than in front of the men."

As I moved aside, gesturing him in, I wondered if he included Dawson in that coverall description. He took his time looking around, but my room would have told him little. A book-marked novel on the nightstand, together with a flashlight. He couldn't see the knife hidden in the bedside drawer, but I doubt it would have surprised him. He watched me tap the doorstop back into place with my toe. I never traveled without one.

"Today's experience unsettled you, Ms. Fox?"

"Not particularly. I'd take the same precautions if I was staying in Croydon," I said. "Take a seat and tell me what's on your mind."

He sat in one of the two easy chairs near the curtained window, rested his elbows on the high arms, and steepled his fingers. I stayed on my feet.

"I've had my people back in the UK do something I prob-ably *should* have asked them to do quite some time ago—run an in-depth background check on you."

Uh-oh.

"And?"

"You've been busy since last we met."

"Likewise."

"And before we met—you'd had quite a past then, too."

Saying nothing seemed the safest option. I took it.

He sighed. "Look . . . Charlie, I now know Michael Clay was one of the men who raped you back when you were in the army."

29

His use of my first name unnerved me more than the revelation. Sarcasm and hostility from him I could stand. Sympathy might just be my undoing.

"I told you I didn't like him much."

"The mother of all understatements, I would say."

"Yeah, well, we all have our cross to bear."

His face ticked at the flippancy, but we all have our coping mechanisms, too.

"You and Sean Meyer were . . . involved back then. He was your training instructor. Is that why they went for you?"

"Very probably." My face felt stiff. "Look, I'd love to reminisce with you all evening, but I—"

"There's been a new development. One that makes things . . . difficult, now that I understand your position—and that of Meyer—more fully."

"Oh?"

"A witness has come forward. He claims he saw Meyer leaving the building where Clay was found, right around the time we judge Clay to have been killed. There was blood on him."

My heart cramped in my chest, stuttered, and then began to race. "You know this for a fact? That it was blood, I mean."

"The witness is another contractor, an ex–Royal Marine medic. He's seen enough of the stuff to recognize it, and he picked Meyer's photo out of a selection without any prompting. No connections to Clay, before you ask."

Shit.

"OK, so Sean was there. Still doesn't mean he killed him."

Garton-Jones regarded me for a moment, and when he spoke his voice was tired rather than angry. "Look at the *way* the man was killed, Charlie—the way he was tortured. His genitals were mutilated. Man alive, he was practically castrated. That speaks of it being something . . . personal—*very* personal. Wouldn't you agree?"

"Sure, it sounds personal. But Sean wouldn't ever have allowed it to get *that* personal. Not for him."

"I understand he suffered a considerable brain injury not so long ago. When someone recovers from such an injury, the brain often rewires itself in ways we don't expect, let alone understand." Garton-Jones paused, added almost diffidently, "My brother suffered a stroke in his forties. Part of his brain was damaged as a result. He recovered, more or less, but he was never the same again. Even his temperament altered." He paused again. "Can you be certain you know how Meyer's mind works now?"

No, I can't. And that's half the problem.

"Of course," I said, looking him dead in the eye. "One of those changes you speak of is that Sean doesn't remember much about our relationship except the bad things. He certainly doesn't feel enough for me anymore to mutilate and murder a man on my behalf."

"That must be . . . hard for you." He gave me a shrewd study. "You were prepared to die for him once."

"I would have said the feeling was mutual—once."

"But not anymore?"

"No, not anymore."

He nodded, as if I'd confirmed something he already knew rather than told him something startling.

"You asked me earlier who might want to send us a message— besides the entire local population, of course," he said. "I could ask the same of you."

"I've only just arrived. Even if I was trying really hard, I doubt I've had time to piss anyone off enough to want me dead." *So far.*

"And yet . . . you just so happened to be in a vehicle that was hit by a targeted IED. Coincidence?"

"Far more likely, surely, that the bomb was intended for your people," I pointed out. "Our attackers might have been wearing local headgear, but they weren't Iraqis."

"You got a good look at only one of the three. How do you come to that conclusion?"

I put my head on one side, trying to work out if he was being intransigent, or just testing me. "Their boots. They were all wearing combat boots—you could see them under the doors of their four-by-four. How many times have you seen a group of three Iraqi insurgents who all had decent boots? Most of the time they're in ordinary shoes, trainers, or sandals."

He didn't respond to that, but by the way he got to his feet, the conversation was over. "You handled yourself well out there today. I think I see why Mr. Armstrong sets such store by you."

There was a host of undercurrents lurking beneath his words, hints of favoritism and something altogether unsavory about my relationship with Parker. I offered him a bland smile.

"My boss chooses all his people very carefully. And he's prepared to go to the wall for them."

I hoped the message, such as it was, went in and stayed there.

I also hoped, with more fervor, that it was true.

SIX

◈

DAWSON OPENED THE DOOR TO HER HOTEL ROOM WITH HER LEFT arm in a sling, jerked her head to beckon me in. She stepped past, threw a quick glance up and down the corridor, then ducked back inside.

"Your note was cryptic," I said, "but I don't think I was followed."

Her smile was brief. "You must know what it's like working with a bunch of Neanderthals. If you're seen coming here, half of them will have us down as a pair of lesbians before you can spit."

I watched as she bolted the door. She was a couple of inches shorter than me, and in a sleeveless vest top I could see hard-won muscle around her upper arms and shoulders, a narrow waist, and flared hips. Below loose jogging pants her feet were bare, the toenails painted orange.

Her accent might have been pure London, but her coloring had hints of Mediterranean, Greek or Italian maybe. Dark hair, cut choppy and short, dark eyes with long, thick lashes. There was a dressing over her collarbone, visible above the sling, and a line of Steri-Strips closing a gash on her forehead. The left side of her face was peppered with small cuts from the SUV's side glass. They were already scabbing over.

I nodded to her shoulder. "How is it?"

"I've had worse. They plated my collarbone—very efficient. But my six months' stint is going to end early, worse luck. The boss is packing me off home in the next day or so."

"How early is 'early'?"

"Three months. Bit of a pisser, but not much I can do about it." She managed a tight smile. "My bastard of an ex cleared out the joint account when he scarpered. Left all his debts behind, of course, and the maxed-out credit cards. So . . . I need the money."

"Ah."

An awkward silence fell. I wasn't sure if Dawson had invited me here to ask for a loan, or a job, or to sell information. She knew something, I just wasn't sure what—or what it was worth.

I folded my arms, leaned against the corner of the bathroom wall, and waited. Her room showed signs of longer occupation but was identical in layout to mine, although two floors higher. I always asked for something on the third. High enough to make outside access difficult for the nefarious; not so high that the ladders of the local fire service couldn't reach it in an emergency.

Eventually, she said, "The boss is making out there isn't a reason for anyone here to go after Clay . . . the way he was killed. But there is. And with what I know about him now . . . well, what he did . . . back when he was still in the army . . ."

I froze, realizing belatedly what lay behind her hesitation.

"Who told you that?"

"The boss."

"And what did he tell you, exactly?" If she heard the frozen note in my tone she gave no sign.

"That he and some of his buddies were charged with raping a fellow trainee and got off on a technicality. Hell, I'm not surprised you didn't like the guy . . ."

So, Garton-Jones didn't . . .

I shook my head to clear the sudden buzzing that filled my ears with static, had nothing to lose by playing it down.

"Ancient history. I mean, he wasn't on my Christmas card list, that was for sure, but I'd still like to know who killed him."

Especially if I can prove it wasn't Sean . . .

"Yeah, well, I've always had a bad vibe from him. Like he was laughing at me for some joke I wasn't in on—and wouldn't like even if I *was* in on it. Didn't take Bailey long to follow suit. Fucking pair of apes."

"I think you're being hard on the apes."

She gave a short bark of laughter. "Partly, it's the way they trash-talk about women, even when I'm there, as if I'm *not* there. Or like I don't count."

"I agree he was less appealing than a ladleful of slime, but you mentioned someone else having a specific reason to go after him . . . ?"

"Yeah, well . . . During the time Clay's been out here there have been four women raped. In Iraq, I mean, not Kuwait. Young women, kidnapped off the streets, all wearing full-cover *burqas* or *niqabs*—you know, just with the eyes showing—rather than the *hijab*."

"The significance of that being . . . ?"

She looked at me blankly, as though I was asking about the color of the sky or grass. "Apart from in the areas controlled by the extremists, most Iraqi women cover only their hair with a simple headscarf, or *al-Amira*. The percentage who go for the full *burqa* is tiny. It's like this guy has been seeking them out."

"You think the rapes were all committed by the same man?"

"Men, plural, not man. But the MO's the same. All taken in broad daylight, thrown into the back of a van, locked up until dark, blindfolded, raped, dumped back on the street."

"I suppose it's useless to ask if local law enforcement has made any progress?"

She shook her head, then stiffened, her eyes closed for a moment, as something spiked through her injuries. I could sympathize there.

"Very few cases like that would ever get reported. Female victims of rape are 'deemed to have brought dishonor onto their families' and . . . well, you can guess what happens to them."

I could, even if I didn't want to.

"You suspected Clay?"

"He was in-country when all of them took place." She saw my look and rushed on. "I know, I know, but just hear me out on this. There was more to it. He was AWOL for the nights of the rapes. And the following couple of days it was like he'd taken something—drugs, I mean. First time, the boss ordered a random dope test on him. He's shit hot on stuff like that. Drink, too, while we're out here."

"But the Dexie was Clay's, I assume?"

She hesitated, then nodded. "We all pop a few pills to keep us going on a long slow duty, but I've never seen him inject."

"So other than the speed, his drug test came back negative."

"Clay claimed he was 'high on life' or some such shit. But the way he looked at me . . . ." She shivered. "I made sure not to be alone with him after that."

I wasn't sure Dawson's gut instinct was admissible in court, but I was inclined to trust it, even so.

"So you think this—the way he was killed—might be locals meting out some kind of rough justice? Taking his eyes for seeing what he was forbidden to see—"

"—and his dick for sticking it places it was forbidden to go," she finished for me.

It broke the tension. She smiled, waved me further into the room. I leaned my hip on the desk–cum–dressing table while she perched on the edge of the bed.

"I think you might have something there . . . What do I call you apart from Dawson?"

"Luisa," she said, holding out her right hand. We shook.

"And I'm—"

"—Charlie. Yes, I know. Your reputation precedes you."

That threw me. "Are you sure that shouldn't be *exceeds* me?"

"Don't think so, if what the boss said about your performance today is anything to go by. Took out an insurgent with a head shot, moving target, under fire, right after being blown up by an IED. Wish I'd been awake to see it."

"He wasn't an insurgent—not of the home-grown variety, anyway. Not if his clothing was anything to go by."

"So who was he?"

I shrugged. "He didn't have any ID on him, but his clothing was Russian, from the looks of it. And he was trying to blend in—carrying an AK and wearing a *keffiyeh*. I've sent his photo to my boss to see if he can put a name to the face."

"Russian?" She frowned, shifted her position, easing her injured arm in her lap. "Well, I've no idea what we've done to piss off anybody from that neck of the woods. The last few months have just been reporting on supply routes, a bit of convoy work, and security for some Dutch engineers working on a sabotaged pipeline just north of Basra."

"Garton-Jones tried to hint that they might have been after me rather than your team."

"Yeah, well. He would, though, wouldn't he?"

"You like him, as a boss?"

She gave a one-shoulder shrug. "Had worse. Better than the army, but not as well-funded as the Yank outfit I worked for in Sierra Leone. Still, at least he gives us medical cover, eh?"

I thought again of the dead Russian. The skills I'd used to kill the man were not something I could feel proud of. I couldn't prevent a twinge of . . . regret that there hadn't been another way. "I wonder who's going to be shipping today's body home."

"You mentioned you'd sent a photo to your lot. Don't still have it, do you?" she asked. "I just wondered—if it's someone in the same game, I might recognize him."

I dug out my smartphone. I thumbed through it until I came to the snapshot I'd taken of the man who'd been part of the ambush, then handed it across.

Luisa Dawson studied the picture for a moment, gave the screen a flick with her forefinger and thumb to enlarge part of the image, and peered closer.

"Ring any bells?"

She shook her head slowly. "Not the face, no . . . but there's something about his *keffiyeh* . . ."

She handed the phone back. I'd peeled the red-and-white cotton scarf away from the man's face to get a clear shot of him, but it was visible in the immediate background of the picture.

"It's the tassels around the edges. They're not really the local style. You tend to find that kind of thing more in Jordan than Iraq." She pulled a face. "Not much help, is it? I'm sorry."

"Don't be," I said. "Believe me, when you're operating in the dark, any little chink of light that isn't tracer fire is a help."

SEVEN

⬨

IN VIEW OF LUISA DAWSON'S CLOAK-AND-DAGGER ATTITUDE THE
night before, I confess to mild surprise when she made a beeline for my table at breakfast the following morning.

"Mind if I join you?"

I gestured to the chair opposite with the coffeepot in my
hand, completed the move by pouring into the cup in front of
her as she sat down.

"Pointless to ask this time if *you* were followed," I said,
noting the heads already turned in our direction. It might have
had something to do with the fact that the testosterone in the
room was utterly overwhelming the estrogen. Having most of
it clustered at one table was causing a hormonal imbalance in
the atmosphere.

She grinned as she added milk and sugar, stirred.

"Got a proposition for you," she said, "and if you say no, well,
I'm supposed to be on a flight out of here this evening anyway."

I refilled my own cup, wary now. Dawson had admitted she was in this line of work for the money. That, I considered, was likely to make whatever she had to sell more expensive than it was worth. She didn't seem in any hurry to get down to it, either, but took her time enjoying the scent and taste of her coffee.

The hotel restaurant was a twenty-four-hour buffet, serving a wide-ranging, if slightly bizarre, selection of food it classified under the one-size-fits-all term *international*.

Mind you, it was worth eating there if only for the view. Plate-glass windows stretched from tiled floor to double-height ceiling, looking out onto palms and marble columns surrounding an immaculate water feature—the ultimate in swank for a country that was mostly desert.

"I'm going to miss the scoff in this place if nothing else," Dawson said at last.

I set down my cup. "If you don't cut to the chase, you're going to miss your flight as well."

That earned me another flash of smile. A dimple came and went in her cheek. And as quickly as it appeared, the humor was gone.

"There's a women's clinic I know of. Been helping out there whenever I've had some downtime—I was a medic back in the army. Originally set up by Médecins Sans Frontières, but now it's locally run."

"When you say 'locally' . . . ?"

"Here—in Kuwait, I mean, rather than over the border. One of the . . . women I mentioned to you. She's there, at the moment, having treatment. She *might* be prepared to talk to you."

"Providing that *you* act as go-between?" I guessed.

"Not necessarily." She gave a casual one-shoulder shrug. The arm with the plated collarbone was held close to her body by the sling. "You speak Arabic?"

Ah.

I shook my head. "Not enough for that kind of conversation."

"Well then, how about you talk your boss into hiring me for my brains instead of my brawn?" She reached for the coffeepot and helped herself. "Only make your mind up soon, 'cause otherwise—like you said yourself—I've got a plane to catch."

I sighed, plucked the starched square of linen from my lap, dumped it by my plate, and got to my feet.

"All right. Give me ten minutes to call New York. And if you're going to guzzle all the coffee, at least order another pot before I get back."

Not much of a snappy parting shot, but under the circumstances it was the best I could manage.

❖

Parker, needless to say, was dubious.

"Unless we think Sean had anything to do with these attacks—which I don't," he added quickly before I could jump in, "then I don't see what this gains us."

"Reasonable doubt," I said. "Not as far as I'm concerned, but the people on the ground here—Garton-Jones at Streetwise, for a start. If I can show motive for somebody *other* than Sean wanting Clay dead in the manner in which he was killed, it gets us reasonable doubt and buys me a little more time."

"Wait . . . you reckon you might be running out?"

"If for *'time'* you read *'cooperation,'* then definitely. Garton-Jones knew before I got here that I wasn't exactly impartial, but since I arrived he's carried out some extra background checks on both Sean and me that make things look worse rather than better. At the moment he's toeing the line. Can't say how much longer he'll continue to do so."

"Ah."

That was one of the nice things about working with Parker. He caught on fast.

I was up in my room, partly to stay away from flapping ears, and partly so I didn't let all and sundry know I'd brought an encrypted satellite phone with me as well as my standard cell.

Garton-Jones wasn't the only one who kitted out his people with all the best toys.

"OK. Just as long as it's not a personal safety issue." His voice softened unexpectedly. "I need you back in one piece, Charlie."

I spoke lightly, trying to ignore his use of the word *need*. "That *is* the condition I was aiming for."

And if not, then at least in no more pieces than I am already.

I did not tell him about the Kalashnikov I'd won from the dead Russian. There were some things he was better off not knowing. Besides, he might try to insist I hand over the weapon—although who to was another matter.

He sighed.

"Look, I know this is hard for you. Not just because of Sean, but now there are other . . . aspects to this. Disturbing aspects. If you—"

"You can say the word *rape* without me going to pieces on you, Parker."

"I know, but . . ."

"It's something that happened to me, OK?" I said gently. "It's not all of who I am."

"I know," he said again.

I hadn't expected to speak with him directly when I called the office in Manhattan. Kuwait was eight hours ahead of the East Coast, which made it a little after midnight over there. Parker had a duty officer manning the phones around the clock—especially when he had anyone in the field—but I was both relieved and a little apprehensive to hear his voice on the other end of the line.

I could picture him at his desk in the corner office with its fabulous views of the glittering Midtown skyline. I used to wonder about the fact that he sat with his back to the windows, until I found out he had antiballistic glass installed.

"So . . . any ID yet on the Russian from the ambush?"

"The name he used to enter the country was Kuznetsov, but don't get your hopes up on that score. In Russian *kuznets* means 'blacksmith,' so . . ."

I could almost see the shrug. "And do we even know if Comrade Smith might have been working for a PMC out here?"

"If he was, nobody's claiming him yet."

"Hardly surprising, when you think about it. Either the attack on us was authorized, in which case his bosses would have a lot of explaining to do, or—"

"—or it wasn't, in which case there would still be awkward questions," Parker finished for me.

"Not to mention the shame of having to admit they couldn't control their own guys."

"You got it."

He was smiling now. I could hear it in his voice. There was a moment's comfortable silence between us. Too comfortable.

Parker cleared his throat. "Anyway, I guess if you feel it's necessary, I'll OK Dawson. Send her details through, and Bill will handle the paperwork."

"Will do, boss."

"And if this Garton-Jones guy does stop cooperating, let me know, OK? You need backup you can rely on out there." He paused. "I meant what I said before: I need you back here safe and sound."

I heard the longing, however much he thought he'd buried it. "No, Parker," I said gently. "You might *want* me back safe, but please don't confuse that with *need*."

EIGHT

❖

I DROVE, DAWSON NAVIGATING FROM THE PASSENGER SEAT. THE
vehicle was a new-model Range Rover whistled up by the hotel.
With one of his vehicles destroyed in the ambush, Garton-
Jones claimed he didn't have another to spare. I wasn't about
to argue the toss. Not when there might be something more
important I needed from him later.

Dawson chattered most of the way, far more relaxed than
she'd been on duty for Streetwise. I learned she had joined the
military more or less straight from school—mainly to escape
the boredom and unemployment of her hometown.

"Didn't fancy either working the checkout at the local
supermarket, or giving birth to hordes of little brats to get
myself moved up the waiting list for a council flat," she said.
"Wanted to *do* something. Y'know—get out there and see the
world."

"I think they showed me that brochure, too, in the recruiting office. Travel to fascinating places. Meet interesting people. Kill them."

She laughed.

I glanced at her. "And now that you have . . . ?"

She leaned forward a little. "You'll want to be turning right at the next main intersection."

We were heading into the outskirts of Kuwait City itself, a modern high-rise metropolis that seemed more Mediterranean than Middle Eastern. The roads were wide, fast moving, the shoulders crammed with parked cars. The buildings, a mix of contemporary and traditional, carried occasional battle scars still left over from the Gulf War. Strange pinks and browns contrasted with high-tech green glass. Poverty lived alongside extreme wealth, jostling for space under the relentless sun.

"Most of the world I've seen is not quite what it's cracked up to be," Dawson went on. "There were a few places that took your breath away, but mostly it was shit-heaps and slums. There were a few diamonds among the bastards, too, don't get me wrong. But I don't count my ex as one of the diamonds."

"So, what happened with him?"

"Oh, the usual, I s'pose. Met him in Cyprus, decompressing on the way back from Afghanistan. My first tour, his second. Thought he had a bit more about him than the average grunt. We got together that night, as I recall. Well, when you've made it out of 'Stan, the first thing you want to do is prove to yourself that you're still alive. Still human, y'know?"

"Yes, I do," I murmured. "So he was army, too."

She held up her free hand in protest. "Yeah, yeah, I know. We shouldn't have got it on. Especially with us being different ranks."

Sean and I had been different ranks—he a sergeant, me an ordinary soldier. We shouldn't have "got it on," either. A creeping feeling of déjà vu made the hairs riffle at the back of my neck.

I glanced over. "Different ranks?"

"Oh, um, yeah. He was a corporal. I was a freshly minted second lieutenant, actually. Should have known from the outset it was never going to work."

"Get you," I said, surprised. "A Rupert."

"Nobody was more gobsmacked than me when I came through square-bashing with P.O.M. stamped on my report." Another shrug. "In the end, I liked the job, just couldn't stand all the bullshit that went with it."

With the kind of background she'd painted, the way she spoke, for Dawson to come through basic training singled out as Potential Officer Material made her something out of the ordinary, by my reckoning.

"Your ex was OK with you outranking him?"

"To begin with." She frowned. "I think he maybe even quite liked the idea of giving me the 'benefit of his vast experience' and all the rest of the macho crap. That was all right until first I didn't *need* his advice anymore . . . and then I didn't *want* it, either."

"You said he left you in debt?"

"Yeah, well, I should have seen that one coming. You think it's going to make life easier—being with somebody who's in, I mean. You think they're going to understand what it's all about . . . what you see, what you have to do. But it doesn't, not really. Hey, we're turning here!"

I braked hard and just made the corner, checked my mirrors in time to see another car carry out a similar maneuver without causing alarm. I got the feeling such driving was the norm around here. Either that, or . . .

One eye still on the mirrors, I said, "We all cope with our experiences in our own way. There is no one-size-fits-all solution."

"In the end, I think he couldn't cope with the fact that I could handle the way the job messes with your head sometimes, and he . . . couldn't."

"Drink? Drugs?"

"A little of both—more booze than was good for him, and too much wacky-backy—but his real problem was gambling. Those bastard online sites hoovered the cash out of his pockets faster than the army could put it in. I nagged, pleaded, yelled, cut up his credit cards. I even contacted the sites he was on and asked them to block him. He'd just open accounts with new ones. He promised he'd quit. Next thing I know he's disappeared and I'm left to pick up the pieces."

"I'm sorry," I said.

She nodded, turned her head away to stare at the dusty buildings without seeing anything outside her memories.

For the most part Sean and I had coped with what we'd seen and done without coming adrift in any noticeable way, at least. And in the end it wasn't our differences that had driven us apart.

It was our similarities.

NINE

◈

THE WOMAN DID NOT WANT TO GIVE US HER REAL NAME. I COULDN'T blame her for that.

"She says the doctors here call her Najida," Dawson said, her voice soft and respectful as we sat alongside the bed. "It means—"

"—'Brave,'" I said. "Yes, I know. It suits her."

The woman was, in truth, little more than a girl. She was in her late teens or early twenties perhaps, and had once been beautiful. Dark, thick hair, dark eyes with an almond tilt to them, eyelashes with no need for cosmetic enhancement, good bones.

But the arrangement of her features was distorted by the wound to her face. It had ripped open her cheek, now bloated and discolored, leaving the corner of her mouth torn, as if by a giant fishhook. Dressings and strips of micropore tape held the damage together. How well it would all heal was another matter.

But she met our gaze without arrogance or shame, just a calm acceptance of what had happened to her, of what might be still to come.

I made sure to maintain eye contact while her words were translated. I could follow a little of what was said, enough to know that Dawson's Arabic was nuanced and fluent. And also that she was giving me the story straight.

"She was going to the market," Dawson said. "With her mother and her sister."

"Do they wear the *burqa* also?"

"Not the veil. Just the *hijab*. Her sister is younger. She would like to dress more . . . Western. But now she is confused . . . and frightened."

"Did you feel unsafe before this? Uncomfortable to be out?"

Without translating first, Dawson glanced at me. "Are you asking why she wore the *burqa*?"

"Yes."

She relayed the question, put more directly than I would have done.

Najida hesitated, then began to speak, looking at me rather than Dawson, as though she knew I was the dubious one. One eye was clear, the other bloodshot and swollen.

"When she was younger she didn't mind the stares of men," Dawson said, her tone bloodless, slightly hollow. "But after she went to university she started to resent them looking at her. They had no right. And she wanted to be judged not for how she looked."

I nodded, didn't quite trust myself to speak.

The undamaged half of Najida's face gave a twitch approaching a sad smile. "You do not agree," Dawson said. It was not a question.

"It is not my place to agree or disagree," I responded. "Your culture is far different from mine . . . but not your experience."

Out of my peripheral vision I saw Dawson's head snap around, but I kept my eyes on Najida as the translation was made.

She let her own gaze drop away and nodded, as if that made sense. As if no Western white woman would have bothered coming to see her without such a connection.

Knowing my arguments would not persuade her otherwise at this stage, I said nothing. After a minute or so she let out a breath and started into her story.

They grabbed her without warning, she said. One moment she was walking along the side of the street. Her mother was in front. Her sister had dropped a little way back—something on one of the stalls had caught her eye. Najida stopped to wait for her.

The next thing, she was taken. Not hard to bind her hands, to gag and blindfold her. They used her own clothing—the very clothing she wore to give her a feeling of safety, of privacy.

They were very fast—practiced, even. They shoved her into a van that had stopped beside her before her sister looked up or her mother looked back. The van did not hurry away but moved off slowly. So slowly the two women paid no attention to it, even as their surprise at Najida's sudden vanishing act turned to alarm.

Her abductors drove with her for what seemed like a long distance. There were many turns, and the road was rough—she was thrown around on the floor of the van. The man who had grabbed her stayed in the back of the van with her throughout the journey. He held a knife at her throat. She was too frightened to struggle, but she pleaded, over and over, for them to let her go unharmed.

"Even though she knew it was probably too late for that already," Dawson reported.

"Is that your opinion or hers?"

"Hers."

I nodded to Najida. "Tell us only what you feel able to."

The one with the knife, she said, was a big man—tall and muscular. They both smelled . . . foreign. When I queried this, she came back with:

"Of foreign food, maybe? Different spices. He did not smell like her brother or her father."

And their voices were foreign, too. They spoke English. She knew enough to recognize a few words but couldn't say if they were Americans or Brits.

Eventually they stopped the van. The driver climbed into the back. Between them they stripped her, cutting away her clothes. They secured the blindfold in place with tape.

Then they raped her, taking turns. And while they did so they laughed and goaded each other. It seemed they were more . . . excited if she cried out. She did her best to keep silent. It was not always possible.

When they were finished, they took her to within half a kilometer or so of where she had been abducted. There they dumped her, naked and bleeding, on the roadside. She had been a virgin.

"Was there any kind of investigation?" I asked. "If these men were indeed foreigners, surely the police—"

"*La alshshurta!*" Najida said.

I got that without any need for Dawson's language skills. *No police.*

"Whose choice was that—yours? Or your family's?"

"Her father said she had brought great shame onto the family name, that she must have done something to provoke these men. He told her she was . . . soiled, that no good man would ever want to take her as his wife." Dawson's voice was flat, level, but still betrayed the barest hint of her contempt. "Her mother wept and said she now had only one daughter. They would not let her into the house."

I stared at the woman, saw the untold sadness in every line of her body, in the acceptance of her disfigured features, and said slowly, "The men who attacked you did not do that to your face, did they?"

"She would not leave the family home. She was distressed, crying for her mother," Dawson said. "So her father and brother took up their guns, and they chased her away. And when she fell, still crying, her father walked up to her where she lay and shot her in the head. She flinched at the last minute, and the bullet hit her in the face—knocked her unconscious but didn't kill her." Dawson swallowed as if her mouth was suddenly dry, or to combat a rising nausea. "And when she came to, she had to dig her way out of her own shallow grave."

TEN

OUTSIDE, DAWSON SAID, "YOU'RE ANGRY."

I stuffed the Range Rover's keys into the ignition, cranked the engine, and sat back as the air-con sent a blast of heat into our faces. It took a moment before I trusted myself to speak.

"Aren't *you*? Not just at what was done to her, but the treatment by her own family?"

She cocked her head on one side. "There's more to it than that. It's the *burqa*, isn't it? It was her own choice. Why does it bug you so much?"

"Why *doesn't* it bug you?" I shot back. "Just because men are not taught to respect women enough not to hassle them in the street, spit or stare at them, or pinch their arses, or just *take* whatever the hell they want, it's the *women* who have to drape themselves from head to foot, leaving only a mesh slit to see out through."

"It made her feel safer."

"Safer? What kind of awareness of her surroundings, freedom of movement, or peripheral vision did it give her? What kind of ability to fight back? Absolutely fucking none. And because of that, and the fact she was already wearing the equivalent of a sack to tie her up in, she was such an easy target it's unbelievable."

"Girls in the UK choose to go for a night out in dresses too tight to let them run, and heels they can only totter about on, and then drink themselves halfway to oblivion," Dawson pointed out. "Does that make them any better prepared to fend off attack?"

"No, it doesn't, and it's stupid in the extreme," I agreed, "but in both cases, why should it be the woman's responsibility to do the fending? Why can't it be the bloke's job not to let his little brain do all the thinking for him instead of his big brain?"

"Define 'big' there, would you?" Her dry tone was enough to break the tension.

I let out a long, pent-up breath and threw her an apologetic smile. "Sorry. Pet peeve of mine."

"I noticed."

"What will happen to Najida now?"

Dawson shrugged. "Nothing. Her father and brother will be seen as upholding the family honor and be respected for doing so. As for the men who raped her, they will most likely never be identified, let alone held to account. The feeling is that foreign soldiers in Iraq do as they please."

I put the Range Rover in gear, turned out of the gates of the clinic, and accelerated toward the end of the road.

"Things don't seem to have advanced much since the Middle Ages as far as civilization goes, do they?"

I thought back to my own attack, the assumption that I must in some way have given the men encouragement. Unwitting at best. At worst, a deliberate act I'd then regretted and tried to escape the consequences of.

My character—the number and frequency of my sexual partners, the way I dressed, what I said and the way I said it—had been dissected and scrutinized in court, in the newspapers, while theirs seemed to have escaped close inspection. Were all victims treated that way?

If I had died, as had been the plan, would they still have unpicked my life to the same degree? Or was an accusation of rape seen as an attempt by the woman to tarnish men she'd had sex with, out of little more than spite? It had to be upgraded to murder before the woman was truly seen as the victim.

Men were not expected to control their urges, but a woman—any woman—had to be chaste and modest, and offer no provocation. Provocation was justification. It made choosing to wear the *hijab* and the *burqa* more understandable, but as Najida had discovered at great cost, doing so provided little defense.

"You think Clay was one of them?" Dawson asked.

"Well, he was certainly a big guy. And the knife to the throat is his style, but it's hardly unique."

"What you said to Najida, back there . . . about shared experience," Dawson said at last. "That wasn't just a line to get her to open up to you, was it?"

I was silent for a moment, using the excuse of crossing traffic to turn out onto a busy main road to gather myself.

I'd thought when Garton-Jones found out about my past, he'd told Dawson, but now I realized he'd been more discreet than I'd given him credit for. Her questions were more general, I recognized, and I was grateful for that, at least.

"No," I said at last.

"Shit."

"Yeah, I would say that about sums it up."

"Did they ever . . . catch him?"

It was, simultaneously, both not enough of a question and too much of one. I settled for leaving out all the ifs and if onlys and answering the least of it.

"Yes. They caught him."

"Well, that's something, I suppose. I hope the bastard suffered for it inside."

I thought of Clay's corpse, of what had been done to him.

"He did," I said. *Eventually.*

I felt her stare but kept my eyes on the road, my expression neutral, daring her to follow up.

Wisely perhaps, she did not.

For the next few klicks, silence filled the big car's interior. It still smelled of polish and new leather. How long would it be before that wore off and it just smelled like the inside of any car?

I glanced in the mirrors again, said to Dawson, "We're being followed."

To her credit, she didn't twist in her seat, just ducked her head a little to check out the side mirror. "The tan Toyota two cars back?"

"Uh-huh. He trailed us to the clinic, picked us up again when we hit the main road."

"Not unusual. Two foreigners, women, traveling on our own. They like to keep their eye on such things around here."

"You carrying?"

She shook her head, regretful, lifted her slung arm a little. "Couldn't use it even if I was. You?"

"No, but I did take out all the extra insurance on this thing, so if necessary I'll use it as the world's most expensive battering ram."

She laughed, a short bark betraying the tension, snuck another look in the side mirror. "Just out of interest, did you tell anyone about today?"

I changed lanes. Two cars behind us, the tan-colored Toyota copied the maneuver.

"My boss in New York."

"I didn't even tell G-J." She gave a taut smile. "Not officially in his employ right at this moment, so it's none of his damned business."

"But I'm assuming you might want to work for him again in the future?"

"'Course." The smile became a grin. "He's not bad to work for. Tough, but tough on everyone, and he doesn't seem to have the usual problem with us lumpy jumpers. In fact . . . he talks about you, you know."

"He . . . ? Why?"

"He mentions you as this girl he met a few years ago. Back when he was running security teams in the UK. Said you took a bullet for someone. Just stepped in front of this guy and took two in the chest. That right?"

Discomfited, I pointed out, "I *was* wearing body armor."

"Still . . . they could have gone for a head shot."

I shrugged. "If they had, I wouldn't have known much about it, so it makes no difference now."

But it might have.

I will never forget the sense of helplessness, of impotence, on a very different day—the day Sean took a round to the head. I'd been there and watched it happen . . . watched his life change forever.

Mine, too.

"The Toyota's still with us. Looks like two of them in the car," Dawson reported. "How do you want to handle this?"

"Not much we *can* do besides hope it's just a watching brief and head back to the hotel. At least there we might have some backup on hand."

Dawson gave a snort. "I wouldn't count on it."

As soon as we cleared the densely populated streets, the Toyota moved up directly behind us, not making any pretense of a covert tail. I stuck to the speed limit but bullied my way through traffic, making sure to leave myself an escape route, not allowing us to be boxed in.

Dawson spent her time half-twisted in her seat, openly watching behind us.

"Here they come," she said, a moment before I caught the glint of lights coming up fast on our outside.

"Face forward," I told Dawson. "If they *do* ram us, with you like that, you'll break your spine."

She pulled a face. "No thanks, I've broken quite enough this trip already." She dropped back into her seat, pulling her lap belt tight across her hips.

But they didn't have ramming us in mind.

As the Kuwaiti police cruisers came barreling up behind us, I pulled over obediently into the inside lane. The first car whizzed past, then swerved directly in front and hit the brakes.

I had to stand on the Range Rover's brake pedal to avoid rear-ending them. While I was wrestling to maintain control of the big vehicle, the second car moved up alongside. With the unmarked—but undoubtedly police—Toyota close up behind us, we were in a rolling box. I had to admit it was smoothly and efficiently done.

I jammed my foot back onto the accelerator. The Range Rover's automatic transmission kicked down in response. Just for a second the cruiser alongside pulled a touch too far ahead. Our front end was level with his rear door.

I gripped the steering wheel, knowing all it would take was a twitch of my hands to sideswipe the rear quarter of his car into a deadly fishtail slide. I'd practiced the maneuver on every offensive driving course I'd ever taken until I could do it blind.

But if I did, at this speed, the cruiser was likely to end up across the central reservation and head-on into approaching traffic.

It might save our lives.

Or it might see me spending the rest of mine in an Arab jail.

I relaxed, allowed our car to be slowed and forced over onto the sandy shoulder of the road.

And I hoped like hell I didn't live to regret it.

ELEVEN

❖

I PULLED OVER ONTO THE DUSTY SHOULDER, WELL CLEAR OF THE ROAD. As soon as I did so, the black-and-white police cruisers swerved across our front and rear, lights still strobing. The tan-colored Toyota sped on without a pause. Being seen taking part in a police stop would do its value as a surveillance tool no good at all.

Two men climbed out of the forward car. They were wearing dark uniforms and military-style berets with police insignia where you'd expect to find a regimental cap badge.

One man carried an M4 carbine, the shortened version with the ten-inch barrel mounted into the Close Quarter Battle receiver. Easier to handle in the confined space of a car. He sighted on us over the rear end of the cruiser, resting on his elbows and using the bulk of the vehicle as cover. His movements were relaxed and steady, his forefinger lying outside the guard rather than curled around the trigger. It smacked of well-worn routine rather than high alert.

In the mirrors I saw that the other two officers had also exited their vehicle. Again, one stayed behind with an M4, covering Dawson's side. The other was standing behind the open driver's door of the cruiser, radio mic in hand.

Not the best tactics in the world if they were expecting trouble—far better to keep both police vehicles behind us to avoid blue-on-blue crossfire. I didn't know whether to be insulted or relieved by their attitude, settled on the latter.

I forced myself to take in air, deep and slow, let any coalescing sense of panic out with the expelled breath. I dropped my window halfway, then put both hands on the top of the steering wheel, in plain sight.

The driver of the forward car had not immediately drawn a weapon. But he approached with his right hand hovering meaningfully over the sidearm holster on his hip.

"Your license," he said. He had regulation short-clipped hair and a wide mustache that hid most of his mouth. His eyes were covered by a pair of gold-framed Ray-Bans with mirrored lenses. He wore a nametag on the breast pocket of his shirt, but I couldn't read the Arabic script.

I dipped carefully into the center console for my international driving license. I'd shifted it there from my back pocket as soon as I'd made the decision to stop for them. No point in giving anyone an excuse to get trigger-happy.

He barely did more than glance at the document when I handed it over. Instead he took it back to the cruiser, got on the radio. His eyes never left us as he spoke to whoever was at the other end. The mustache and the Ray-Bans made it impossible to gauge the conversation from the language of his facial muscles. The guns never wavered.

"We look that dangerous, huh?" Dawson said past a clenched jaw.

"You read and write Arabic as well as speak it?"

"Uh-huh."

"In that case, make a note of all the names and ID numbers you can remember, as soon as possible. Just in case."

Just in case I don't come back.

"Won't be easy if they've taken away everything including my bootlaces."

"Somehow, Luisa, I don't think they've come for you."

"Oh," she said, her voice dry. "I feel so rejected."

The officer put down his radio mic and returned. He did not bring my license with him. Good job I only ever carry copies.

"It would seem that you are wanted for questioning by our esteemed colleagues across the border," he said in classless, almost accentless English.

"Questioning with regard to what?"

He opened my door, hand now resting on the grip of the gun. "You will please step out of the vehicle, Miss Fox," he said. "You will come with us."

"My colleague, as you can see, is injured and will find driving herself difficult. Perhaps I could return her to her hotel first and accompany you from there."

"One of my officers will drive this vehicle." He jerked his head to the men behind us. "Perhaps it is not your . . . colleague you should be concerned about."

I shrugged and climbed out. He gestured me to walk ahead of him and fell in behind my shoulder. By instinct too ingrained to give up, I gauged the height and weight of him, the likely level of his skills, his reactions, and the location of his sidearm, even as I logged the positions of his men, their fields of fire.

Last resort . . .

It was not much comfort.

He opened the rear door of the cruiser for me, but at least he didn't put a hand on my head to help me on my way as I slid inside. The rear of the car was caged off with reinforced

Plexiglas. As the door shut with a prison-cell clang, I tried to reassure myself that at least he hadn't cuffed me as well.

The officer and his M4-toting buddy got back into the front. As we rejoined the road I twisted in my seat to check on Dawson. One of the men from the rear car was just climbing behind the wheel of the Range Rover. As we moved rapidly away, she stared after me from the passenger side, as if she couldn't quite believe what had just happened.

I leaned forward slightly in my seat, spoke through the small slot in the acrylic screen that separated me from the two policemen.

"If you're going to take me over the border, shouldn't I have my passport with me?" I asked, even though it was safely tucked away in the leg pocket of my cargo trousers. They hadn't patted me down, or they undoubtedly would have found it, and that omission bothered me.

Still, they hadn't found the folded Ka-Bar knife shoved down the side of my boot, either.

Some you lose, some you win.

TWELVE

IT TOOK ME LONGER THAN IT SHOULD HAVE TO REALIZE WE WEREN'T
heading for the border.

Being so slow off the mark was entirely my fault. I'd had
little more than the duration of a long-haul flight to prepare
for this assignment, if that's what it was. So I'd focused on Iraq,
to the extent that my familiarity with the geography of Kuwait
in general—and Kuwait City in particular—was superficial, to
say the least.

I sat locked in the back of a police cruiser, silently cursing
at such a foolish, basic mistake—and at finding myself being
driven, for the second time in as many days, to an unknown
destination. Unlike my trip with Garton-Jones, however, there
was no easy way to coerce cooperation out of my kidnappers.
I didn't even try.

The two men in the front might or might not have been
genuine officers. Although they were noted for enforcing the

law with reasonable reliability, the Kuwaiti police also had a reputation for not being above taking bribes. And they had a noted bias toward their own citizens rather than foreigners when it came to disputes.

This country was supposed to be a staging post, nothing more. I hadn't anticipated needing anything from Kuwaiti nationals. Question was, what did somebody here want with me?

I closed my eyes a moment, tried to picture my safe room— the place into which I could mentally retreat under . . . robust interrogation. It was a long time since I'd needed to adopt such a construct. I hoped I could still remember how.

The last time was when I went undercover into an organization called Fourth Day in Southern California, considered by the security services to be a dangerous cult. I thought my backstory was sound, that it would stand up to the kind of pressure-testing it was likely to encounter. Instead, I discovered that Fourth Day's leader, Randall Bane, had a way of getting inside your head, under your skin. He could cut to the heart of memories and emotions with an accuracy that was almost surgical. In the debriefings that followed, I did not admit to anyone—least of all my boss, Parker Armstrong—how much the man had unnerved me.

And before that?

Before that was the army. Or, more specifically, during my all-too-brief stint in Special Forces. Resistance to interrogation exercises were all part of the training. Ironically, it was during a particularly realistic and nasty one that Sean Meyer first allowed me a glimpse of the human being beneath that hard-bastard exterior. Up to that point, I think all of us had begun to suspect that he might not be human at all.

As one of our training instructors, he'd kept his distance from the group, never let his guard drop as though to do so might expose a weakness we'd exploit. But, unlike the others,

I never got the impression he despised the women who'd made it through Selection. He looked down equally on all of us.

He also didn't have the same predatory air as one or two of the other sergeants, who would lag behind so they could offer us a helping hand—in return for certain . . . considerations, of course.

On the whole, I'd thought Sean a cold fish. I found out the first night we spent together how wrong I was about him. He had formidable self-control, almost as if he dared not let himself go for fear of what we might do to each other.

He watched my every response, allowed me nowhere to hide, both taking everything and giving everything in return. I believe it was that ruthless streak I found most attractive. The quality about him that started my fall . . .

The cruiser slowed and swung off the main highway onto a side road leading to what looked like a run-down industrial area. The driver took his corners fast enough that any contemplation of jumping from the car was a nonstarter. And that was discounting the fact there were no handles or window winders on the inside of the rear doors. The glass had a discolored quality to it that spoke of some kind of reinforcement.

I conserved my resources for a more promising opportunity.

It was stifling in the back of the cruiser. The men in the front had the air-con wound up to maximum, but little made its way through the slot in the Plexiglas screen between us. I hoped that, wherever we were going, we got there soon, otherwise I was going to lose half my body weight in sweat.

There were no people on the streets. The parked cars and the buildings we passed were coated with a layer of dust, as if forgotten.

Eventually, we turned sharply to the left through an open roller shutter door into the ground floor of an empty warehouse building. The contrast between the acid glare outside and the dim interior left me momentarily blinded.

As my eyes adjusted, I saw a Cadillac Escalade with dark paint and darker glass. It gleamed with polish, as if they'd spent the time waiting for us giving it a full valet. Around it stood three guys in combat-style fatigues and body armor. They all carried automatic weapons—a couple of M4s and a compact H&K. I did not take this as an encouraging sign for my continued health.

The cruiser stopped and both men got out. The officer who'd done all the talking went across to them. His body language was cautious, but less than during our traffic stop. Either these were men he trusted, or they were ones he'd dealt with before. The second officer stayed behind his open door, fingers flexing on his own weapon.

One of the trio detached and came forward, letting his MP5K dangle on its shoulder strap. There followed some talk and much gesticulating. I gathered the officer was trying to play on how difficult I'd been to apprehend and therefore up the price. The newcomer wasn't having any of it.

Neither he nor the other men with the Cadillac looked like Iraqis, or Kuwaitis, come to that. They were all hardcases, though; that tends to be a universal type. I studied their faces, each in turn, just as I'd studied the two men in the front of the cruiser during the drive. I'd recognize those two again by the shape of their ears, clearly visible below their sloped berets. The human ear is unique in shape. I believe someone was once caught and convicted by the print of his ear left pressed against a window.

I sat and sweated in the residual heat during the brief negotiations. Even out of direct sunlight I could feel it dripping down the indentations of my spine.

After a moment, the two men reached some kind of agreement. A package—money? drugs?—changed hands. Then it was all smiles.

The officer beckoned to his colleague, who turned far enough to open one rear door. He jerked the barrel of his weapon to indicate this was the last stop and I should vacate the train.

"No thanks," I said cheerfully. "I think I'll pass."

He didn't follow all the words, but he got the meaning clearly enough. His eyebrows bunched together, and under his breath he called me and my mother something that was both uncomplimentary and, I thought, probably physically impossible. Strange how the first words you always pick up in any language are the insults.

The officer glared at me, gave a more emphatic command. I smiled at him and didn't move.

He glanced to his superior and gave a shrug. This was not how captives behaved. He leaned in, awkward with the M4 in one hand, and made a grab for my wrist.

I let him get hold of me, then broke his grip easily enough and rotated his hand into a simple lock. He grunted, tried to yank free. I tightened the lock, feeling the torsional twist of bone and tendon, knowing that his arm from the elbow downward must feel like it was on fire.

He started to bring his weapon to bear. I kept hold of his wrist, pivoted on the seat, and booted the receiver up against the forward edge of the door jamb, trapping his other hand. Then I rolled backward and kicked him square in the throat.

He fell away, choking. I let him go just as the opposite rear door was yanked open behind me and the other officer loomed furiously into the car. I saw his arm come up. There was a flash of movement, something hard traveling very fast toward me. My vision cracked into light and pain.

Then everything went black.

THIRTEEN

THE BLOW STUNNED ME ONLY FOR A MOMENT. JUST LONG ENOUGH for the senior officer to drag me bodily out of the back seat of the cruiser. The thump as I hit the concrete floor brought me out of it.

Fighting.

He had me by the back of my collar and was dragging me toward the men with the Cadillac. I grabbed his hand, dug thumb and forefinger viciously deep into pressure points I could find in my sleep.

He yowled, whirled with his nightstick raised. I swiveled on my backside as if break-dancing, hooked one leg behind his, and scissored the heel of my boot into his kneecap as hard as I could manage.

He'd clearly received some kind of unarmed combat instruction as part of his training, but either that was a long time ago or he'd been a very poor student. With no idea of how to break his fall, he sprawled heavily on his back.

I spun again, still on my arse, and wrapped my legs around the arm that held the baton. The elbow joint is remarkably fragile when overstressed, and I had his locked up within an inch of needing surgical reconstruction. I placed the sole of my boot against his neck to keep everything tight, and dug in deep again with clawed fingers. After a moment's resistance that was down to pure obstinacy, the baton dropped from his nerveless hand.

"*Kuchi sin!*" said a guttural voice from above us. "That is enough."

I looked up, squinting against the ceiling lights. The man who'd done the negotiating had the stubby MP5K back in his hands and was pointing it at the pair of us.

I screwed the lock on one last quarter turn, evoking a muffled gasp from the officer, then let go and rolled quickly to my feet—and out of his reach. The room swayed, steadied. I shook my head to clear it.

As soon as I released my captive, he grabbed for the nightstick baton, started to scramble in my direction with blood in his eyes. The guy with the machine pistol stuffed it unceremoniously into the officer's face. It was probably the only way to get his attention.

"I said *enough*," he repeated. "You have your money. Go."

The officer hesitated, loss of face warring with common sense. Eventually, he spat at my feet and stalked back to the cruiser, trying not to limp, brushing the concrete dust from his uniform as he went. I was tempted to point out the big patch of it on the seat of his pants, but I restrained myself.

His colleague was on his feet again, also, by then. The pair of them gave me the evil eye as they climbed back into their vehicle and reversed out of the warehouse with little regard to wear on tires or transmission.

"That . . . performance will cost me," the man said heavily as he watched them go. "Our next dealings will be much more . . . expensive. This is . . . unfortunate."

"I don't see why it needs to be." I shrugged. "After all, I am only a *woman*. How could a mere woman cause trouble for two such experienced officers of the law?"

And when he glanced at me with a scowl, I added, "Play your cards right and *they* will pay *you* never to speak of this again."

He gave a grunt that could signify amusement or contempt, take your pick, and ushered me toward the back of the Cadillac.

I stood my ground. "What makes you think, after all that, I'm going to do as I'm told now?"

The man with the machine pistol turned back with a sigh, as if about to speak. Instead, he rabbit-punched me, short and sharp, in the solar plexus. My diaphragm went into instant spasm. I bent over, struggling to pull air into paralyzed lungs, making horrendous death-rattle noises. The man walked on, opened the rear door of the Cadillac, and gave a slight bow.

"Because, even though you are 'merely a woman,' you are not a stupid one," he said. "Now, please, Miss Fox. We have gone to a considerable amount of trouble to arrange this . . . opportunity to talk. Let us both make good use of it, yes?"

FOURTEEN

THE ENGINE WAS RUNNING ON THE CADILLAC. ENOUGH TO KEEP THE air-con ticking over and the interior cool as glass.

The man with the MP5K settled into the far corner of the cavernous rear seat, the weapon cradled on his lap like the fluffy white cat of a Bond villain. For a few moments we sat and weighed each other up without speaking.

He had high, slanted cheekbones with deep hollows beneath, so that in the vehicle's interior lighting his face looked more like a skull. His hair was shaved down to stubble, showing the outline of a high forehead and widow's peak. There were the small odd-shaped voids of old scars on his scalp. His short-sleeved shirt showed muscled forearms. On the back of his right wrist was a tattoo of a frog inside the outline of a bat.

"Do we start with introductions? Clearly you know who I am, so . . . ?"

The man smiled. "It is not necessary for you to know my identity. In fact, I would prefer you did not attempt to discover it."

His English was excellent, formal and precise. Hardly a trace of an accent . . . but it lay underneath like a coat of old paint, just the same.

"Oh, you 'would prefer'?" I repeated flatly. "Of course you would."

He inclined his head and smiled again. It was not reassuring.

"I am merely a messenger—a go-between—and therefore being aware of my identity will not add to your knowledge."

"What kind of messenger?"

And what kind of message?

"Please, Miss Fox, have patience. Know only that I have gone to a good deal of trouble and expense to engineer this opportunity to speak with you."

I gave a short laugh. "You could have saved yourself all that by simply coming to my hotel and walking up to me in the bar."

"Perhaps. But this way you have some idea of the . . . extent of our influence here."

"That you know which cops to bribe, you mean?"

"Exactly."

"OK, so let's hear it—this message."

"Go home."

"That's it?"

"That is it," he agreed. "Go home and do not concern yourself with affairs that are none of your business."

"I see. And if I choose to disregard this . . . advice?"

"I would ask you not to regard this as mere advice. That—with respect—would be a mistake."

Rarely had I encountered someone so well armed and yet so politely spoken.

"Also *with respect*, it is difficult to reach that conclusion for myself without knowing exactly who is sending me this message."

"A friend. Someone who knows you. Someone who has your best interests at heart."

Did he mean Sean? I eyed the man opposite. Ex-military without a doubt. And Russian. The kind of man Sean would have encountered many times both during his own army career and afterward.

The fact he was a stranger to me didn't necessarily mean a thing. I had not been Sean's keeper during the time we'd been together, any more than he'd been mine. He had made and developed his own contacts across many countries. I trawled my memory for anyone he'd mentioned, however casually, who he might trust to deliver this warning. I came up blank.

And surely he wouldn't feel the need for all the cloak-and-dagger rigmarole, anyway. Hiding behind intermediaries? Having me grabbed off the street by corrupt cops, for heaven's sake? It was not his style.

I shook my head. "You'll have to give me more than that."

His face gave a tic of annoyance, and he sighed. I guessed that despite his apparent eloquence, he was not a man for whom negotiation came as a first choice. Disagreements were no doubt settled quickly and with violence.

"Ask your questions. If I can answer them, I will do so. If not . . ." A shrug.

"How well does this man know me?"

If he noticed I was actually asking two questions in one, he didn't make anything of it. But when he answered, there was something sly in his voice I didn't like.

"Oh, yes, he knows you . . ."

So it is a man. Apart from that, you're no help.

"Why does he want me to leave Kuwait?"

"Not just Kuwait. Iraq also. Because there is trouble on the way, and he does not want you to become . . . enmeshed in it. He is trying to do you a favor. Why not accept it and move on?"

What kind of trouble? The fallout from Clay's murder? From whoever Sean might be after next? There was still a possibility Sean was indeed behind Clay's death, although it felt all wrong. What had been done to the man was almost gleeful in its savagery. Sean would have found a more effective way to make him suffer, and he would not have enjoyed the process.

But Clay was tortured for a purpose. If Sean needed information from him—and needed it badly, urgently—how far would he really go?

Or was this all about the attack on Najida? For all their shameful, barbaric treatment of the girl, was her family now looking to take revenge on the men who, in their eyes, had ruined her?

"Has your employer considered that it might be too late for that? That I might be enmeshed already—and have been so for a very long time?"

"Of course. But he is hoping that you can be . . . persuaded to stand down."

"And if I can't be . . . 'persuaded'?"

"Then that would be most unfortunate."

"Define *'unfortunate'* for me, would you? And just give me a straight answer for once. I'm getting bored to tears of dancing with you on this."

Another shrug. An "if you insist" one this time. "I would be compelled to . . . incapacitate you, which I am sure you would agree would indeed be unfortunate," he said, very matter-of-fact and utterly without regret. "Not difficult to arrange just across the border. Your coalition forces did not leave Iraq in a better state than they found it. Not impossible to arrange here, either. As you have seen for yourself, we have friends in many places."

"Well, you've made one attempt already. Didn't go so well for Comrade Kuznetsov, did it?"

To my surprise, he looked almost embarrassed. "That was an . . . unauthorized action. It should not have happened."

"What makes you think you'll be any luckier if you try again?"

"You were a soldier, Miss Fox, and you are now a bodyguard. There is an old saying that is true in both cases: To survive— to protect a life—you have to be lucky every day. But your enemies, they have to be lucky only once."

FIFTEEN

✦

POLITE TO THE LAST, THE RUSSIANS DROVE ME BACK TO WITHIN a klick of my hotel. That still left me farther to walk in high heat than I would have preferred, but there were any number of worse alternatives.

As I trudged the last few hundred meters toward the hotel's shady portico, my shirt glued to my back, all I wanted was a glass brim-full of any kind of liquid so long as it also contained a *lot* of ice. They served a very refreshing mix of sweetened lemon juice and chopped mint leaves in the hotel bar. During the walk I'd started to fixate on it just a little.

Before I'd even made it to the portico, the glass doors swished open and Luisa Dawson hurried out.

"Charlie! Hey, I wasn't sure I'd ever see you again, except on a mortuary slab."

"Sorry to disappoint you."

"No joke. Those guys meant business."

"But they brought you back here all right?" I asked as we walked into the blissful cool of the lobby.

"Yeah. I kept my mouth shut and my ears open as much as I could. The one who did all the talking was called Al-Hasawi. The others were a bit pissed off that they didn't get to escort you to the drop-off point—worried about him cheating them on the split of the money, I think."

"Nice to know there's no honor among policemen, never mind thieves."

"Isn't it just?" She paused, looking uncomfortable. "And, um, you need to call your boss—let him know you're OK."

"Parker? How did . . . ? Ah, you called him."

She shrugged. "Wasn't sure what else to do. No idea if you were coming back, and thought if they were intending to throw you in an Iraqi jail for shooting that guy who ambushed us, you'd need someone on the outside making plenty of noise A-SAP to get you released again."

"Good thinking. Thank you."

She grinned. "You're welcome. After all, we *do* work together, however temporary that arrangement might be."

Faces I'd come to recognize drifted into the lobby with studiously casual expressions. Groups of women might have a bad reputation for gossiping, but they have nothing on squaddies, or ex-squaddies for that matter, who seem to thrive on inference and rumor.

I stepped in a little closer to Dawson, asked quietly, "Did you tell anyone else?"

"No. But . . . Bailey saw me arrive back here with a police escort. Made a point of grilling me to find out what it was all about."

"And you told him . . . ?"

"Jack shit," she said with another quick grin. "Which made him come over all shifty."

"Hmm. Actually, it might be worth mentioning to him in passing who we went to see this morning, just to see if he gets shiftier still."

"You don't think . . . ?" She swallowed her distaste, added reluctantly, "He *was* pretty tight with Clay, I suppose. I just don't like to think I might have been working with not one but *two* of the perverted bastards."

"I'll go upstairs and check in with Parker without the flapping ears. Meet you in the bar in ten." I flicked my eyes to a spot over her shoulder. "Meanwhile, how about you start spreading unrest among the troops?"

Dawson glanced up and spotted her erstwhile colleague lurking by the entrance to the bar. Good job Bailey was employed more for his obvious muscle than his abilities in covert surveillance.

Dawson grinned again, suddenly reminding me of the Russian with the MP5K.

"It would be my pleasure."

◈

It was two thirty in the afternoon in Kuwait, which made it six thirty in the morning back in New York. I called Parker's office line from the satellite phone, knowing if he was at home it would redirect there or to his cell.

No surprises when he answered in three rings.

"Can't tell you how good it is to hear your voice, Charlie. You OK?"

"Fine," I said. While I filled Parker in on what had happened, I took advantage of the fact we were using voice-only communication to stand in front of the mirror and lift up the front of my shirt. Where the Russian had punched me, just below my sternum, was a fist-sized, bluing mark, already starting to spread. Fortunately, it was far enough away from the taped-up wound that he'd done no additional damage. "They wanted to emphasize how they had the local cops in their pocket, and tell me to go home. Other than that it was amazingly amicable, all things considered."

Parker knew there was more to it than that, I could tell by his momentary pause. He chose not to call me on it. "Any ideas who they were?"

"My guess would be Russians again. But to be quite honest, I don't really know. The guy who did all the talking said something in what sounded like Russian which translated to 'that's enough'—I think."

"Kuchi sin?"

"Something similar. And he had a tattoo of a frog inside a bat on his arm, which signifies some kind of naval operations division of Spetsnaz, I believe?"

"Frogman," Parker agreed. "The equivalent of the UK's Special Boat Service or our Navy SEALs."

"His English was excellent. No contraction of words, so he sounded a little wooden, but hardly any trace of an accent."

"Hmm, Spetsnaz operate outside the Soviet Union, just like our own Special Forces guys. They probably crossed paths. No surprises he speaks a second language."

Something jogged at the back of my mind. I tried not to grab for it, knowing if I left it alone, whatever it was, it might just float free.

"Charlie—?"

"Just a sec."

What was it? Something Parker said . . . or something I said . . . ?

"English," I said. "He was speaking *English*. Not American-English, *English*-English."

"So?" Parker sounded nonplussed. "Doesn't mean much on its own. In fact, it kinda makes things look worse for Sean. If an ex–Special Forces Russian speaks with a Brit accent, it increases the chances he had contact with the British SAS. And *that*—"

"Yeah, I know. That brings us back to Sean—maybe."

"And I guess one of us has to say it, Charlie. The fact they didn't kill you when they had the chance points in Sean's direction, too."

"Trust me, that had not escaped my notice."

"What was it the guy said if you didn't comply? He'd 'incapacitate' you. That doesn't necessarily mean injure."

"Or it could mean they're going to break all my arms and legs."

"OK. But who else would claim to know you well and want to keep you out of danger?"

"That's not quite how he put it, Parker. He said 'trouble' was 'on the way' and he wanted to prevent me becoming 'enmeshed' in it. But trouble for me, or trouble for them? And what kind of trouble?"

"It may be time to call in a few favors with some of the three-letter agencies." Parker's voice was grim. "I'll get back to you if they have anything."

By "three-letter agencies" I knew Parker was referring coyly to the CIA or some similar black-site setup. I'd had dealings with them in the past. It rarely ended well, and every time we came into contact I had the uncomfortable feeling they owned another chunk of my soul.

"There's something else you might want to get onto—if you haven't already," I said, reluctance like a bad taste in my mouth. "And that's the current location of Donalson and Hackett."

I heard his indrawn breath, heard the questions he wouldn't—couldn't—ask.

I swallowed. "I'm hoping Clay's death is nothing to do with Sean, but . . ."

Silence hung expensively between us. After a moment or so, Parker sighed. "Dawson filled me in a little on your visit this morning to the Iraqi girl who was attacked. I guess she couldn't make any direct connections to Clay?"

"No, but I don't think it's a dead end. Not quite yet, anyway."

"Oh?"

I gave him a brief précis of the conversation I had with Dawson when I arrived back at the hotel, as well as her present task of spreading disinformation in the bar.

"It might shake something loose, you never know."

"Sure," he said, but I heard the doubt in his voice.

"I know it's not exactly in my remit, but if testing a theory that someone else might have been gunning for Clay means Sean moves down the suspect list, I'll do it."

"I know you will. But . . . the Russians turning up kinda splits this thing in different directions. Sure you don't need me to send you some help out there?"

"Bearing in mind the possible outcome . . . ? I'd prefer to work solo. Besides, I have Dawson."

"Yeah, but she has only one arm that works."

"Doesn't stop her being able to speak Arabic. And occasionally it really does make sense to ask questions first and punch someone later."

SIXTEEN

BY THE TIME I GOT DOWN TO THE BAR, LUISA DAWSON HAD CLEARLY unnerved Bailey to such an extent that he'd beaten a hasty retreat. I found her staring moodily into a small tonic water with a fruit cocktail on a stick floating on top.

"Why is it, when the guys order something nonalcoholic, they get it in a plain straight glass. I do the same and end up with a fancy thimbleful and a bloody side salad?"

I took the chair opposite. "Just luck, I guess."

She pushed the offending drink away and sat back in her chair, unconsciously supporting the wrist of her injured shoulder with her good hand.

"I never *ask* for special treatment anywhere. I just want to be treated the *same*." It was both frustrated and heartfelt at the same time.

"I'll drink to that."

"How do *you* manage it?"

I glanced at her in surprise. "What on earth makes you think so? I don't, always."

"Well, you seem to have more luck than I do."

I shook my head. "Optical delusion. I just learned that making a big thing of it achieves nothing other than emphasizing the differences I'm trying so hard to play down."

Dawson was quiet for a moment, watching her male counterparts as they cheered a football game on the huge flat-screen TV hanging at the far side of the bar. None of them, I noticed, had been given fruit salad in their glasses. I wondered if they ever thought it unfair that female patrons were.

"Did you manage to get anything out of Bailey?"

She pulled a face. "Not much. I laid it on with a shovel about the state the poor girl was in, and how they take the whole 'dishonoring of women' kind of thing so seriously in Kuwait that when they catch a perp, he's likely to get bits chopped off in the traditional style."

"How did he react to that?"

"He's too much of a macho man to *actually* wet himself in public, but I suspect it was a pretty close-run thing," she said with relish. "Then I asked him, all sober and 'I'm-only-telling-you-this-because-I-know-I-can-trust-you' bullshit, if he thought there was any possibility Clay might have been involved."

"You have a real talent for the believable lie," I said. "At which suggestion he no doubt pretended to be shocked and stunned?"

"Oh, completely so. Couldn't believe his mate would have had anything to do with something like that, et cetera."

"Which is, sadly, the obvious response—innocent or guilty."

"Uh-huh. And that's when I warned him it might not be a good idea to play up how matey he was with Clay, because from what the victim told us, her attackers obviously knew each other. And if—big if—it turns out Clay *did* have something to do with it, the first thing they'll do is have a nice little chat with his pals."

I laughed out loud. On the TV across the bar, one side or another scored, and half the assembled men performed some kind of victory dance that reminded me very strongly of a tribe of baboons. Only noisier and more vulgar.

I caught Dawson's eye. She grinned and mouthed, *"Vive la différence."*

A waiter came over. I ordered two lemon juices with mint. He inclined his head and went away again.

"When the boss told me Clay had raped a fellow trainee in the army, and we talked this morning about you being assaulted . . . well, I didn't realize it was you . . . that Clay . . ."

Her voice trailed off. I didn't answer, but she nodded as if I had.

"Is that how you got those scars?" She gave a jerk of her chin toward my open collar.

I put my hand up automatically. It was almost as if I'd forgotten the thin jagged line that circled my throat. I resisted the urge to button my shirt up another hole. Pointless now anyway.

Cursing inside my head, I wished the drink I'd ordered was spiked heavily with gin.

"No, that came later."

"Unlucky," was Dawson's only comment.

"Not really. I survived. That time, the man who attacked me didn't."

We fell into silence, punctuated by the raucous shouts from the sports watchers at the bar.

"Najida's not likely to see any kind of justice for what was done to her, is she?" Dawson said at last. "Not for any of it."

"Realistically? No."

"So, what do we do about it?"

I considered pointing out to her that it wasn't our job to do anything about it, but somehow I couldn't bring myself to simply shrug off responsibility. The same way everybody else had.

"Well, we're hardly likely to get a confession, are we? We've no forensics, no crime-scene photos, no means of tracking the van they used. And even if we *did* manage to identify the vehicle, we can't process it or link it back to the men responsible. And if they'd any sense, they nicked it beforehand and torched it afterwards anyway."

The waiter reappeared with our glasses—tall and plain—of lemon and mint that tasted almost like sherbet. Dawson waited until he was halfway back to the bar before she spoke.

"So, what it boils down to is that we've no way to tie in Bailey—or Clay, for that matter—to the rapes unless we just beat a confession out of him."

I picked up my glass, took a long drink. It was cold enough to stab me between the eyes, make my teeth shiver, even if it did lack the gin I'd craved.

"Appealing though that is, I've never found the information you extract that way to be terribly reliable."

"Which brings me back to my last question: what do we do?"

"What *can* we do?"

Her eyebrows rose sharply. "You want to leave it at that?"

"That's not what I said. How would Garton-Jones react if you took this to him?"

She shrugged. "It might be better if *you* took it to him. If I do it, there's always the possibility he'll accuse me of having some other axe to grind."

"Better still, how about I get Parker to put it to him as a working theory?"

"Yeah, that might work." Her smile faded. "Although even if G-J keeps an eye on Bailey, unless the man's an idiot or he's caught in the act, there's no chance of making anything stick, is there?"

I nodded toward one of the huge tinted plate-glass windows offering a view of blazing blue skies and potted palms.

"Realistically?" I said again. "I think I've more chance of inviting you out into the car park for a snowball fight . . ."

SEVENTEEN

I WOKE THE FOLLOWING MORNING IN RESPONSE TO LOUD HAMMERING on the door of my room. When I checked the Judas glass, Dawson stood impatiently outside. She brushed past me as soon as I opened the door.

"If the hotel's on fire," I said dryly, "then somebody forgot to sound the alarm."

She was wearing running clothes. Judging from the state of them—and her—she was on her way *back* from exercise rather than on the way out to it.

"He's gone."

"Who?"

"Bailey," she snapped. "I've just seen him on the airport bus. He arrived about a fortnight before I did for this tour. He's not due to leave for months. Bastard's trying to sneak off early."

I glanced over at the clock next to the bed. It was a little after 5:00 A.M.

"You're not kidding about the 'early' part."

"I always run at this time. It's too bloody hot once the sun comes up, and I can't stand treadmills—boring."

"Have you checked with Garton-Jones?"

She shook her head. "Thought I'd best let you know first. What d'you want to do?"

"How long ago did he leave?"

She checked her watch automatically. "Five minutes, maybe. I was on my way through the car park when I saw the bus go. But it stops off at a couple of the other big hotels on the way to the airport. If we head straight there, we can probably beat him to it."

I wasn't quite sure what exactly we could do once we got there, but doing anything seemed better than letting Bailey skip the country without challenge.

"OK, although if he's already gone through security we don't have a leg to stand on. We've nothing concrete we can use to have him held at the gate."

"I know, I know, but better to try *something* than sit here wringing our hands, don't you think?"

I learned a long time ago to lay out the next day's clothes before climbing into bed at night, just in case of emergency. It took me only a few moments to throw them on and grab the keys to the Range Rover and my phone. As we jogged down the stairs, I wished I'd made time to brush my teeth.

The sun was on the rise, the air temperature still cool. The airport was almost close enough to walk, but the roundabout route taken by the transfer bus meant I had time to drop Dawson by departures and find some short-stay parking before the bus pulled up at the terminal.

We waited inside, out of obvious sight of the automatic doors. The space was vast. The tented effect to the ceiling, supported by massive columns, gave it the feel of a modern cathedral.

The air-con inside was aggressive. I added a jacket to my wish list. Dawson shivered in her running gear, shoulders hunched.

The doors slid open and the first of the bus passengers spilled through in dribs and drabs. Their luggage was largely carried by porters who squabbled over the right to do so. No Bailey.

I caught Dawson's eye. She scowled and pointedly went back to checking the faces coming past.

Just when I thought we'd missed him, Bailey came sauntering through, carrying a khaki duffel bag. We saw the reason for the delay at once. He was walking slowly alongside a big guy who was on crutches. I'd spent some time on them myself and could sympathize. I took in the awkwardness of his progress and recognized they were a recent occurrence.

The lower half of the guy's left leg was in an external fixator, caged and pinned like someone had gone all out with a medical Meccano set. His shin was streaked iodine yellow where the pins pierced his flesh, holding his bones back roughly where they should be. I'd seen plenty of ex-fixes on fellow motorcyclists who'd been through the whole ground-sky-ambulance sequence and not come out ahead on points. I guessed this guy hadn't acquired his injuries falling off a bike.

He was a big man, not tall, but wide and muscular, with blond hair close cropped around a square, tanned face, and a mustache that didn't suit him. He wore laceless running shoes and a pair of old sweatpants with one leg cut away to allow for the mechanical support. The sweatpants looked out of place against his upper body, dressed in Oxford shirt and sports jacket.

Dawson and I let them pass, then converged at an angle from the rear in a pincer movement.

"Hello Bailey," I said, loud enough to be heard over the background chatter. "Didn't know you were skipping the country."

He turned with a start, eyes flicking from me to Dawson and back again. The other guy paused, too. His gaze tracked over the pair of us, and his eyebrows rose toward his hairline.

"Not that it's any business of yours, but I'm not going anywhere." Bailey jerked his head in Dawson's direction with the faintest suggestion of a curled upper lip. "Ask *her* if you don't believe me. She knows I've got another ten weeks to run."

"That's funny, what with you being *in an airport* and everything," Dawson said meaningfully, eyeing the duffel.

Bailey swung the bag off his shoulder with enough force to make her step back to keep it from thumping her injured arm.

"The bag's mine," the guy on crutches broke in.

His accent was London, shades of Cockney softened down by time and distance. He rested the heel of his busted leg lightly on the ground for balance and folded his arms on top of the crutches. He wore a huge wristwatch with all the extra dials you could probably have used to calculate the return trajectory of a space shuttle.

"Look, ladies, I don't know what's going on here, but I'm the one who's flying out this morning. Dave just offered to come along and help me get through check-in."

"Speaking of which, mate, I'll go see if I can rustle up a wheelchair for you," Bailey said, dumping the bag at Dawson's feet. "To be honest, it's starting to smell a bit fishy around here, know what I mean?"

I ignored the insult. Dawson glared enough for both of us.

"So, what's with the intercept?" the blond guy asked as Bailey stalked away.

"False alarm," I said shortly. "Sorry about the ex-fix. What happened?"

"Fell through a roof chasing a kid who'd been taking pot-shots at our convoy. Compound fractures, tib and fib."

"Nasty."

"Tell me about it. Worst thing was, I'm the team medic, so I had to tell the lads how to pull my leg straight again without passing out halfway through."

Team medic . . . Something twitched along my spine. "You didn't happen to be in the Royal Marines at one point, did you?"

"How did you guess?" He straightened, looking surprised and not a little pleased. "Still shows, eh?"

"Something like that . . . Look, do you have time for a quick chat before you catch your flight?"

He looked around, but there was no sign of Bailey. "Sure, why not?"

I held out my hand. "I'm Charlie Fox. This is Luisa Dawson."

"Osborne—everyone calls me Ozzy."

We found a couple of unoccupied seats within easy hobbling distance, and Ozzy lowered himself carefully into one, hooking the crutches over the arm.

"That's better. Good to take the weight off, y'know? Now then, what's Dave done to get you two so hot and bothered? Trying to avoid a paternity test or something, is he?"

There were so many things wrong with that question I hardly knew where to start. It seemed best not to try. And not knowing how much time we had, I jumped straight in.

"Were you the one who told Ian Garton-Jones at Streetwise about seeing someone leaving the place where Clay died?"

"You don't go much for small talk, do you, Charlie? Yeah, that was me."

"Want to tell me about it?"

He shrugged. "Not much more than that to tell, to be truthful. I was rolling by when I saw him come out, so I stopped."

"You stopped? Why?"

"An obvious Westerner, on foot, in that area? I thought he might be in trouble, eh?"

"Did you speak to him?"

"Sure. I saw the blood on him, asked if he was OK."

He said it so matter-of-factly that it took a heartbeat for the effect to hit home.

"How much blood?"

"Enough for it to look serious. He played it down, said he'd just helped some local who'd been hit by a car, but somehow it just didn't ring true, know what I mean?"

"In what way?"

The ex-Marine frowned. "He looked a little . . . spaced, is the best way I can describe it. Seen it before with guys who've just been under fire. Shocky, but pissed off, too."

Shocked and angry . . . Because he'd just found Clay tortured and either dead or dying? Or because Sean himself had done those things to him?

"And you left him there."

Ozzy flushed a little at the flat tone in my voice. "Hey, he insisted he didn't want help. What was I supposed to do?"

I shrugged, suddenly tired. "You just said it yourself—he was spaced, maybe in shock, and on foot in a dodgy area. So, you tell me?"

The mustache bristled as his mouth compressed. "Hey, it's not like he was on his own out there—"

"Wait a minute. You never mentioned there being anyone else with him."

"They weren't exactly *with* him. But I saw the car waiting further along the street."

Dawson must have sensed how close I was to making permanent and painful adjustments to the scaffolding around the guy's leg, because she butted in with, *"What* car?*"*

"I don't know the guy's name, all right? He's some kind of local fixer-cum-guide. Drives a beat-up old Toyota Land Cruiser the color of bad diarrhea. I've seen him touting around the hotels, but as for what his name is, or how you get hold of him, I haven't got a clue."

EIGHTEEN

WE FOUND THE FIXER THAT AFTERNOON AFTER STOPPING IN AT the major hotels used by outside contractors and asking at the front desks. At the fourth one, the concierge said he knew the vehicle we described, that the kid who ran it had taken some journalists over the border into Iraq. I left a business card, and he promised to send the kid over when he dropped them off again. He couldn't guarantee when that might be—a few hours or a few days.

Instead, it was later the same day when a skinny teenage boy appeared in the entrance to the bar at our hotel. One of the staff made a beeline to chuck him out, but he ducked lightly under the guy's arm and waved something the size of a ticket at him, grinning broadly. The man scowled but didn't pursue it.

I watched the exchange idly until the kid swaggered over toward where Dawson and I were sitting. He was, I saw then, holding my business card. It was now slightly crumpled.

"Please excuse me, pretty ladies. Are you Miss Charlie?"

"That's me."

His grin became even wider. "I am told you want the services of the best guide in all of Basra."

"Perhaps," I agreed, which dented his smile only a little. "And you are . . . ?"

"I am the one you are looking for." He bowed with something of a flourish. "I am Moe. Like from the Three Stooges, yes?"

Dawson was grinning. I had to admit the kid's smile was infectious, revealing very white teeth. He wore a football shirt for a team I didn't recognize—broad horizontal bands of black and red—low-slung jeans, and the ubiquitous sandals. He barely looked old enough to drive, never mind remember a comedy act from the 1940s, the last member of which died several decades before he was born.

I scrolled through my phone for a picture of Sean and showed Moe the screen.

"I understand this guy hired you a few days ago to drive him over the border."

The kid's face turned wary. He peered at the picture for a long time, gave a theatrical shrug. "Maybe yes, maybe no. It is hard to know if I can remember this man."

I reached into my pocket and retrieved some dollar bills, which still seemed to be universal currency. Moe's eyes locked on the money. This time when he shook his head, his sorrow was palpable.

"I am very sorry, pretty ladies, but I cannot discuss my customers with anyone but themselves."

It took me a moment to unravel the double meaning of that.

"Ah, so if I were to hire you . . . oh, for the next couple of days, for instance . . . that would make me also one of your customers, would it?"

The smile returned in a flash. "Of course!"

I agreed on a rate with only minor haggling. Dawson—and even Moe himself—seemed disappointed that I didn't put up more of a fight.

When the formalities were over with, I brought up Sean's picture again. "*Now* will you tell me where you took this man?"

Moe shook his head, his expression tragic. "I cannot speak of it," he said, then his grin was back, flicking on like a high-wattage bulb. "But I can take you there . . ."

❖

Moe's Toyota Land Cruiser was considerably older than he was. It had rolled off the production line some time in the '80s with metallic gold paintwork, to which an early owner had added fairly tasteless vinyl graphics in orange and brown. More recently, the body had been touched up with paint that did indeed resemble the aftermath of a truly upset stomach but was most likely the result of mixing all the odds and ends of leftover colors into one tin. It was now mostly two-tone beige and rust.

To be fair to Moe, however, even the splodges of rust had been waxed over and polished. The noxious smoke that poured from the exhaust when he cranked the engine might have felled a passing camel, but the motor caught and ran without a hitch. The side and rear windows had been coated with mirror film, now peeling badly. It still kept the outside world from looking in, and the whole effect was a lot less obvious than traveling in one of the brand-new SUVs usually favored by foreigners.

"What's the point of this? After all, we *know* where he took your guy," Dawson murmured as Moe trotted out to retrieve his vehicle before I changed my mind.

"*I* know that, but *he* doesn't," I told her. "If he takes us straight to the place Clay died, he might just come clean about where else he took Sean, too. If he tries to give us the run-around, we know we can call him on it."

"Ah. Devious. I *like* that about you."

It was a long and featureless drive to the border crossing into Iraq. Moe had acquired a tacky solar-powered plastic daisy in a flowerpot that sat on top of the dashboard. It bobbed and waved its leaves, in a manner that was as hypnotic as it was irritating. This was but one of the reasons I let Dawson have the front seat.

She and Moe chatted about football—European-style soccer rather than the US version—for most of the journey. She'd recognized his shirt as the one worn by the winning German team from the last World Cup, apparently. The two of them argued the merits of various aspects of the game. I tuned it out, stared unseeingly through the patchily tinted window.

Instead, I went back over the story from the injured Royal Marine, Ozzy. About seeing Sean leaving the building where Clay died. About the blood on him. *"Enough for it to look serious."* About the obvious lie that was Sean's explanation.

I think what worried me most was his description of Sean's state of mind—that he seemed spaced and shocky. Sean had seen things that went beyond my experience, both in the military and after. He hadn't forgotten that part of his past. He'd done things, too, that I would have shied away from . . . once. I would almost have said he was unshockable.

So, what had he seen or done in that grimy building in a run-down suburb of Basra that had affected him so much?

NINETEEN

"THIS IS THE PLACE!" MOE ANNOUNCED PROUDLY AS WE PULLED UP at the side of a dusty street.

I leaned across the rear seat and squinted out of the glass on the far side of the vehicle. The buildings had the same semi-derelict air, abandoned not through danger or the fear of danger but through sheer apathy. They were empty because nobody could be bothered to live in them.

In the front of the Land Cruiser, Dawson twisted to face me. As I straightened, she caught my eye with a questioning frown.

"This is where you came?" My flat tone did not dim Moe's brilliant smile.

"With Mr. Sean, yes. This is where I bring him." He pointed across the street to a doorway standing open. A beaded curtain swayed gently in the aperture, keeping out the flies. "My uncle, he serve *chai* there. That is his house."

"You brought Sean here . . . to have tea with your uncle?"

"My uncle's *chai* is the best in all of southern Iraq. He keeps a samovar brewing all day."

I took a long breath in through my nose, let it out slowly, and tried to keep my voice reasonable. "Moe, listen to me. I need to find Sean. It is very important that I do so. And I don't have much time. You understand me?"

He nodded. "This is why you hire me. Best guide in city!"

"And because you claim to be the *'best guide in city'* I agreed to pay you very well for your services, yes?"

"Yes, Miss Charlie. Very fair price."

I rubbed my hands across my face, aware of a dull throb beginning to build up behind one eye.

"What Charlie is saying," Dawson broke in, "is that if you do a good job for us, she will recommend you to all the foreigners at the hotels, so they will all want to hire your services, yes?"

He beamed and nodded again.

"But if you lie to us, or try to misdirect us, we will give a description of you and your truck to every head of security at every hotel in Kuwait City, and you will get no more work there," Dawson continued. "You still following me, Moe?"

"Of course." Suddenly he did not sound quite so upbeat. "But—"

"So, last chance to save your livelihood—where did you take Sean the day he hired you?"

He threw up his hands. "Here! I bring him *here* to drink tea at the house of my uncle. I swear!"

She passed me a resigned look. *I tried.*

"I am telling you truth," Moe insisted, sounding close to tears. "First morning, Mr. Sean ask me for place where he can meet his friend. Quiet place, away from foreign eyes. I tell him about my uncle. He ask me for address so he can tell his friend, and I bring him right *here*." He slapped the top of the sun-cracked dashboard to stress his point. The plastic daisy jiggled its leaves in response.

"Did you see this friend?"

"No, when we arrive, his friend already gone. My uncle say someone call Mr. Sean's friend on cell phone. He ask my uncle how to get to someplace else and he go. He walk."

"And what did Sean do?"

"He follow. He walk, also." From the way he said the word *"walk"* I gathered Moe thought anyone who chose to do so, when they could drive or be driven instead, was touched in the head.

"Alone? You didn't drive him?"

Moe looked embarrassed. "I have flat tire. Roads here are very bad. Spare is flat tire, also. But I have uncle who owns motor garage—best motor garage in all of southern Iraq. So, I go get tire retreaded."

"Doesn't he mean repaired?" Dawson queried.

"Probably not," I told her, eyes still on Moe. "So, he was telling the truth when he said he brought Sean here that morning. He brought Sean *here*, yes, but he picked him up again from the 'someplace else' where he went to meet his friend."

"Yes!" Moe was jubilant that I'd finally got it.

"How long was it before you picked him up?"

"A very little time only. Two hours . . . maybe three?"

"Can you take us to the place where you picked him up?"

"Of course."

We careered through alleyways and narrow side streets of crumbling buildings, most of which didn't seem much wider than the Land Cruiser itself. Their doorways opened straight into the roadway, making stepping out of your house a hazardous occupation. I guessed that it had been that way for some time if you lived in Basra, regardless of actual address.

This time, when we pulled into another street and Moe stood on the brakes, it was one I recognized. We pulled up only a few meters from where the Streetwise SUV had parked on the opposite side of the road.

"Here," Moe announced. "My timing was most excellent, because Mr. Sean call me on my cell the very moment I arrive, and tell me to go around the corner into the next street, where he will be meeting me."

More likely that Sean had been keeping a covert watch for the kid from someplace unseen. It seemed a shame to burst his bubble by telling him so.

"How was he when you picked him up?"

"He is OK. Everything is OK."

Despite the words, I heard the faint edge of desperation in Moe's voice, and I realized that Sean's reaction to whatever had happened in that dingy place had scared the kid far more than adolescent bravado would ever allow him to admit.

"Where did you take him from here?"

"Back to hotel."

"That's it?"

"Of course."

He fired up the engine, which farted another cloud of sooty smoke behind us, and swung the four-by-four into a U-turn without seeming to check for traffic. I caught glimpses of the now-familiar oilfields off to the west.

"Sean went somewhere else after here, Moe, because he checked out of his hotel, and he's gone."

The kid gave a shrug that was close to a squirm. "Maybe he go to the airport. Maybe once he has met with his friend his work is done, and he can leave—he can go home?"

Because he was driving, only glancing back over his shoulder occasionally, I was concentrating on Moe's voice. There was something just a little too artful in the way he spoke, a little too hurried. And at the same time, a little too practiced.

I shook my head. "Sean didn't take the bus to the airport, and he didn't get onto a plane. So he must have gone by vehicle." I paused. "The only thing is, I thought *you* were the best guide in all of southern Iraq."

"This is true!"

"But if you just took him back to his hotel, and you say you didn't take him anywhere else, who did? And why would he use another guide if you are supposed to be the best?"

"I–I—"

"Why not just tell us, Moe?" Dawson cut in. "We'll ask around, and somebody will tell us who really *is* better than you. Sean must have gone with them instead."

"There is nobody who is better!" Moe's voice had risen almost to a howl. Everybody had their weak points, and it hadn't taken much to learn that vanity and pride were his.

"So, he paid you not to tell anyone where you took him, didn't he?" I suggested gently.

Moe bowed over the steering wheel as if trying to hug it closer to his body. We came perilously close to sideswiping a broken-down truck in the process.

"He pay me, OK?" he admitted mournfully. "Mr. Sean pay me not to say—not to anyone. He trust me."

"That's all right. He didn't want his enemies to know where he was going, but I'm not Sean's enemy. And you haven't broken your word," I added quickly. "You haven't actually *said*."

I nudged Dawson's good arm and pointed to the maps stuffed into her door pocket. She handed one over without a word. I unfolded it, thrust it between the seats practically onto Moe's lap.

"Point. You don't have to say the place out loud. Just point to it."

He took his eyes off the road for longer than I was happy with, but I gritted my teeth and said nothing. After a few moments' study, he stabbed toward the map with a finger, jerking away again as if to touch it burned him.

Dawson marked the place with her thumb, took a glance, and passed the map back to me with her eyebrows raised.

I took a look myself . . . and wished I hadn't.

TWENTY

"SEAN HEADED NORTH," I TOLD PARKER.

"Define 'north' for me."

"His fixer drove him as far as Karbala."

I heard Parker's sucked-in breath. "You do know that's a stone's throw from Baghdad?"

"Uh-huh. About a hundred klicks. Moe's agreed to take us up there. We leave first thing tomorrow morning."

"Charlie—"

"Don't say it," I warned. "You won't be telling me anything I haven't already told myself. It's bloody stupid, given the current situation, but what else can I do?"

"What does Dawson have to say about it?"

"She's willing to come." I glanced across my hotel room to where Luisa Dawson was sitting tensely in the single armchair near the window, eyes fixed on me. "In fact, she insists on it."

"Be realistic. She's only just had her shoulder pinned back together. She's in no fit state to go into a war zone."

"I don't speak Arabic well enough to get by. She does."

"Two women, traveling alone to a part of the country largely controlled by religious fanatics? If you're caught by the wrong people, it won't matter *what* language you speak."

"And if Sean is caught by the 'wrong people,' they'll claim he's a foreign spy, hack off his head with a blunt knife, and stream it live on the internet. Which would you prefer, Parker?"

"That's a low blow, Charlie."

"Yeah, well, I never promised to fight by the rules."

"Can you at least give me another twenty-four hours? I called in those favors we talked about. I think they may have something, but I just need a little more time."

It wasn't hard to work out which favors he meant—with one of the "three-letter agencies" that lurked in the shadows of any conflict. Not just the ordinary shadows, in my experience, but always the umbra—the darkest, most opaque part.

"Can you be more specific? Either on the 'something' or the timing?"

"Right at this moment? No, I can't."

"By my reckoning, Sean's already got a four-day head start on us. If I wait any longer, the trail will be stone cold—if it isn't already." *Or he might be dead.*

"Please, Charlie. Wait just one more day."

"Moe's picking us up first thing in the morning, and I'm sorry, I'm sticking to that schedule. *But,*" I added, when he would have argued again, "it will take around six or seven hours to drive up-country. That doesn't take into account any delays en route or stopping for food or fuel. So, more likely eight or nine. Another half a day. If that doesn't give you enough time to chase up your contacts, they probably weren't going to give you anything worthwhile anyway."

There was a long, static silence on the other end of the line, then Parker said grimly, "OK. I'll work on it. But when you get back to New York, we are going to have a *serious* talk about the chain of command in this organization, you hear me?"

❖

The next morning, Moe was late.

We'd arranged for him to pick us up at seven. He'd agreed to this cheerfully enough, even though it meant leaving his bed practically before he would have a chance to climb into it.

By seven thirty, even allowing for the kid's possibly relaxed attitude to timekeeping, I was concerned. As we hung around waiting in the hotel lobby, I tried the cell number he'd given us but received only a garbled message from the Arabic network. Dawson translated that the number was out of service. "Whatever *that* means."

"Nothing encouraging—either for us *or* for Moe."

If the phone had rung without reply, gone to voice mail, or told us it hadn't been possible to connect the call, that would have been one thing. Out of service implied something more . . . permanent.

I recalled the threat from the Russian who'd had me picked up and hand-delivered by the Kuwaiti police. He had threatened to "incapacitate" rather than kill me if I didn't leave. Did putting our fixer and guide out of action fall into that category?

Just when I'd given up on him altogether, there was a flash of dirt brown and Moe's Land Cruiser swung under the hotel portico. He was full of smiles and apologies, bowing and grinning, but no explanations other than there being "Someone you must meet! We go, yes?"

Dawson and I loaded our gear into the back of the Land Cruiser, thankful to finally have it hidden away. The AK-47

I'd taken off the dead Russian after the ambush had a folding stock, which made it easier to conceal inside a bag. Easier to use within the confines of a vehicle, too, if it came to that.

I placed the bag on the rear seat, well within reach. Dawson seemed happy to take the front again alongside a cheery Moe on the drive to the border. I didn't join in. Instead I watched the desert flow past outside my window, kept an eye behind us, too.

"Everything OK?" Dawson had twisted in her seat. She'd abandoned her sling but was still keeping a supportive hand under her right forearm.

"Hmm. I thought we might have another tail, but if so, they're better at it than the last lot."

Dawson didn't respond, but I noticed she kept a wary eye on her door mirror after that.

Out of the side glass I saw nothing more interesting than a couple of guys herding camels. We crossed the unremarkable border, delineated only by a compound stacked with dusty shipping containers.

Moe had the radio on in the background. He drove slapping his hands on the steering wheel in sloppy time to the music. I took his relaxed state as a good sign. Whatever had delayed him earlier took on less sinister overtones.

Until, that is, he swerved off the main highway and started heading east for Basra.

"Hey, Moe, we're supposed to be heading north."

"Yes, yes, of course, Miss Charlie. But first you must see my uncle."

"We haven't time to drink *chai* today. It's a long way to Karbala."

"Not the same uncle. He is brother of my mother. Very wise you see him first. Then we go north, yes?" His hands, I noted, had stopped beating time on the wheel, were now gripping more tightly.

"Where is he?"

"In Zubayr. Not far."

"OK," I said, receiving a raised eyebrow from Dawson. I reached across and quietly unzipped the bag next to me, got a flicker of a smile in response.

She nodded to the scarf I wore around my neck. "I'd cover your head if I were you. Blondes are not the norm around here." Despite her darker coloring, she did the same, pulling her own scarf expertly around her face.

Zubayr was a sprawling town of squat square buildings in shades of mud and terra-cotta. Like Basra, it was punctuated by the ornate minarets of mosques. In the distance were the oilfields and refineries that dominated this area of the country. A constant reminder of what the wars had been all about.

Either Moe's truck was known there, or it didn't look as if it had anything worth begging for. The local kids hardly paused in their games of street football as we drove through. One or two—the older ones—paid a little too much attention for my liking, but there wasn't much I could do about it.

It was just a case of letting Moe take us where we were going and hoping we could deal with what we found there when we arrived.

TWENTY-ONE

AS MOE DROVE US DEEPER INTO ZUBAYR, I FOUND MYSELF MENTALLY running escape and evade scenarios. None of them looked promising if the kid was setting us up.

Eventually, he turned into a narrow alleyway with barely enough room for the Land Cruiser's mirrors to clear the rough-rendered walls on either side. At the end was a pair of studded wooden doors like the barred gates of a fortress.

As we reached them, he slowed and leaned on the horn. For a minute or so nothing happened. Then the gates swung slowly open and Moe drove through into a walled compound.

Two men carrying Kalashnikovs closed the gates behind us. They both wore black-and-white *kaffiyeh* scarves with the tails draped around the lower halves of their faces. I checked their hands, the set of their shoulders. Their stance was tight, close to jittery. Not a promising sign.

Ahead was a smallish courtyard. A woman in a *niqab* headscarf was hurrying inside the main building to the left, herding a couple of small children ahead of her. Was that a natural wariness of coming into contact with strangers, I wondered, or did she have a good idea what might be in store for us?

Moe was talking fast through his open window—too fast for me to follow. One of the guards crowded him, arguing and gesturing with one hand while the other stayed firmly on the pistol grip of the gun. I kept an eye on Dawson for her reaction.

When Moe climbed out, telling us, "Is all OK. Please stay here, pretty ladies," I gave her a nudge.

"He's explaining that he called his uncle about us, that they are insulting his honored customers by not treating us with more respect, yada, yada," she said without moving her lips or turning her head.

"Yeah, but has he said *why* he called—or why we're here?"

"Your guess is as good as mine."

After some more heated to and fro between Moe and the gate guards, he came back to the driver's window.

"Is all OK," he repeated. "Please, come meet my uncle."

I slung the strap of my bag over my shoulder before climbing out, keeping my hands in plain sight. One of the gate guards immediately barred my path. I didn't need Dawson to translate that he wanted me to leave the bag behind. Reluctantly, I did as I was ordered.

Still, he hesitated. Through the folds of his *kaffiyeh* I saw the confusion in his eyes. Clearly he had orders to pat down visitors for concealed weapons. This was probably the first time those visitors had been women—and Western women at that.

After a beat, I lifted my jacket and turned a slow circle so he could see I had nothing tucked into my waistband. Dawson did the same. I still had the folded Ka-Bar knife down the side of my boot, but I didn't fancy my chances if I had to use it.

The guard jerked his head to Moe. We followed him through the doorway where the woman and children had disappeared. Inside, the building was cool and dim. It took a moment for my eyes to adjust. By that time we had been led along a narrow corridor and into a living room. The walls were bare plaster, hung with intricately woven rugs. Cushions and similar faded rugs covered the stone floor. A few items of furniture—a couple of cheap wooden cabinets, one holding a TV set—lined the walls.

There was one armchair, in which sat an old man with a luxurious beard, threaded with gray among the black. He wore the traditional *keffiyeh* headgear and baggy trousers beneath a white *dishdasha* that reached almost to his ankles. Almost at odds was the black suit jacket he wore over the top. But the thing I noticed most were his shoes; they looked English, leather, handmade and highly polished.

Moe shook the man's hand and kissed him on both cheeks, marking him as family. Dawson and I bowed and murmured the stock Arabic greeting, *"Salaam aleykum."* (Peace be upon you.) We received the stock response, *"Aleykum salaam."* (Upon you, peace.) I was careful not to make eye contact beyond a brief glance.

The old man gestured us to pull up a cushion and sit. I didn't like the idea. It was too difficult to rise quickly, too hard to do so without telegraphing the move in advance. It wasn't until the two gate guards withdrew that I felt some of the tension begin to ease. The old man called through to a back room for *chai*. Even I could follow that.

I looked at Moe, who was smiling at me.

"You brought Sean here, didn't you?" I guessed.

"Mr. Sean? Yes indeed."

I was about to ask him why, when the curtain was shoved aside and a young boy entered, carrying the ubiquitous AK-47. I tensed. The kid must have been about ten. He handled the weapon with a familiarity I found more scary than any armed adult.

The old man spoke briefly.

"His son," Dawson murmured.

The kid bowed a fraction to me, his face stiff with disapproval, and offered me the AK. I glanced at Moe.

"Please to inspect."

Finally it hit me—his uncle was an arms dealer. Moe had brought Sean here for weapons before he'd headed to Karbala, which made me think perhaps Sean hadn't *completely* lost all common sense.

Not that I thought for a second they'd hand me a loaded weapon, I opened the bolt to check, keeping my finger off the trigger. I unclipped the magazine and, sensing this was some kind of test, fieldstripped the AK, laying the receiver, recoil-spring assembly, and bolt carrier neatly side by side on the rug.

As I added more components, I surreptitiously checked their condition, trying not to be obvious about it. No point in insulting the man in his own house. Not when he had so much firepower at his disposal.

The weapon was in remarkably good nick, compared to some I'd seen. Not that it mattered too much. It was simple and robust, designed to be operated by just about anyone, just about anywhere, from broiling jungle to ice-cold tundra. I recalled once being told that they'd trialed the originals by dragging them through sand behind a pickup truck. Afterward, technicians had roughly shaken loose the dirt and immediately test-fired the weapons. None had failed.

This was an AKM, with the stamped sheet-metal receiver. Less weighty than the older models, the AKM had the advantage of a mechanism that prevented the gun firing when the bolt was not fully closed. I'd seen the disadvantages of not having such a safety mech on the body of a would-be kidnapper using a cheap AK copy in South America. The results of a breech explosion in close proximity to the man's face had not been pretty.

When I finished stripping the weapon, I put it straight back together again. I had just reseated the receiver when the curtain was pulled aside a second time and a woman came through with a tray of black *chai* in small glass cups. It might have been the same woman I'd seen earlier, but in light of visitors she'd put on a *burqa*.

I slotted the magazine home and let the bolt run forward to close the breech, then put the weapon down carefully on the rug in front of me.

"It's good," I said.

Moe was grinning so widely now it was like he had a flip-top head. He switched the beam of it across onto his uncle.

"I told you! I told you. Miss Charlie is a professional, yes?"

For an elongated moment, the old man showed no expression, then he allowed the faintest smile to curl one corner of his mouth. Blink and you would have missed it. He reached out and ruffled the top of Moe's head as if he'd been a child.

The *chai* was handed round. I took a cautious sip. It was hot as hell, the tannin furring my tongue like iron filings on a magnet.

Then the old man looked directly at me for the first time and said in cultured, BBC English, "You are ex–British Army, I presume?"

TWENTY-TWO

◈

ALONGSIDE ME, DAWSON INHALED A MOUTHFUL OF SCALDING TEA and ended up choking. I had to thump her on the back. It gave me time to gather my own thoughts.

"Yes sir, I was in the army," I agreed sedately. "And you—I'll take a wild guess and say . . . Oxford?"

It seemed to be my day for speculation. There was just something about him that hinted not only of intelligence but also the privilege such intelligence must always have afforded him. He reeked of education among the highest echelons of the social elite. The kind undertaken in an atmosphere where knowledge can be absorbed almost through the pores.

And then there were those shoes.

Now the old man smiled more fully, showing teeth as straight and as white as his nephew's.

"I studied law at Magdalen College," he said, pronouncing it 'maudlin' as one should if one has been properly brung up.

115

As, indeed, my father would have said it. "Probably before you were born, young lady."

I glanced again at the assault rifle lying on the carpet in front of me, shook my head. "So, tell me—how does a distinguished Oxford scholar get from the proverbial dreaming spires to dealing weaponry out of a fortified compound in Iraq?"

"By having one's homeland devastated by war, civil war, and chaos," he said simply. "What Saddam Hussein did not plunder for himself, your coalition forces destroyed with ground attacks and air strikes, and now it would seem Daesh intends to obliterate what little remains to clear the way for their accursed caliphate." He shrugged, a delicately weary gesture. "What use is a lawyer in a land with no rule of law except that imposed by . . . barbarians, in the name of all that is holy?"

"But you are a Muslim, sir?"

"So? If you were a good Catholic, would you long for a return to the days of the Inquisition?"

"That wasn't my point. But I *am* curious how it fits with your beliefs that you sell guns to whoever comes to your door."

"My door, as you have seen, is not easy to find for those who do not have an . . . introduction."

"And for those who do?"

His hand, with those long pianist's fingers, twitched into a "maybe yes, maybe no" motion.

"I sell to those I believe are willing to fight to defend their homeland. Not to those who wish to add to its state of . . . perdition."

He chose the word deliberately, I judged, for its Christian overtones. If he hoped to get a rise out of me that way, he was disappointed.

"If I might ask, sir, why did you agree to sell to Sean? This is not his homeland and, whatever his reason for being in Iraq, it was not to become a freedom fighter. And Moe would not have brought *us* here without your agreement. Why did you give it?"

For a time the old man sipped his *chai* and didn't speak. It was as if the Oxford academic had disappeared beneath the surface of the elderly warlord, like a whale slipping beneath the waves. So smooth and so seamless was the transition that you could begin to doubt you saw it in the first place.

"I spoke to . . . Sean, at some length," he said at last. "We discovered that we had a certain . . . commonality of purpose. Before he left here I provided him with various . . . items of merchandise, and the name of a man in Karbala—Jahmir Lihaibi." He smiled faintly. "Someone whom I thought it might be educational for him to meet."

I frowned. I had no idea what goal Sean could possibly have had in common with the cagey old man before me. Surely he hadn't gone to join the fight against the militants overrunning northern Iraq and Syria? What did Clay's death have to do with that? Or this curious contact in Karbala?

"Why would Sean want to meet this man?"

"It is not my place to explain. That would be breaking a confidence. Perhaps when you next see Sean, you might ask him yourself."

"Your . . . acquaintance," I said carefully. "Where do I find him, exactly?"

His gaze rested on me for a moment. I felt the weight of it.

"I would not claim his acquaintance. In fact, mention of my name would gain you nothing, I fear. He is someone I know of merely by . . . reputation." He motioned casually to Moe. "My nephew can take you to him, but first I think it might be wise to ascertain the . . . purpose of your own undertaking."

I took a breath. "I don't know exactly what you and Sean discussed, but I suspect his reason for being here might be to extract a kind of . . . vengeance."

In my peripheral vision, I caught Dawson's head snap in my direction. Cursing inwardly, I realized that maybe this conversation was telling her rather more than she needed to know. *Ah well, too late to worry about that now.*

I kept my eyes resolutely on the old man.

"Vengeance?" He pursed his lips. "Some might refer to it by another name: justice."

I was suddenly tired of this verbal fencing with someone whose vocabulary was probably substantially larger than my own and held at least twice as many long words.

"Justice restores a balance," I said flatly. "Vengeance just tips you further into the void."

"There are some who would argue the extraction of that justice has to be commensurate with the original wrong, or where is the balance of which you speak?"

"In this case, I'm more concerned with the effects on the extractor than with justice itself."

"Little of value can be achieved without sacrifice."

"Of value to whom?"

"One might hypothesize that . . . justice should hold some purgative value for the victim of the original wrong."

"And what if it doesn't? What if the 'victim' believes that two wrongs do not make a right? What then?"

"Then one has to postulate that perhaps the seeker of justice has . . . their own agenda?"

"Indeed."

The old man finished his *chai* in silence, set down his glass, and spoke briefly to the child who'd brought the AK. The boy slid quickly behind the curtain. When he ducked back into the room, his arms were filled with a stack of cardboard ammo boxes, a spare standard AK magazine perched on top. He put them down carefully next to the old man's chair. Each box contained fifteen 7.62 x 39mm cartridges, made in Yugoslavia—back when Yugoslavia was still a unified country.

Until the boy returned, I wasn't entirely sure if my argument—such as it was—had succeeded or failed.

The old man glanced across at me. "How many rounds do you think will be sufficient," he asked, "to prevent this second wrong being committed?"

TWENTY-THREE

WE REACHED KARBALA JUST BEFORE THE SUN WENT DOWN. THE SKY started to turn burnt orange as the imams called the faithful to prayer.

The journey itself passed without incident. At our first fuel stop, we came across a convoy heading north for Baghdad— fuel tankers with well-equipped private contractors riding shotgun.

Although I was aware that the tankers made a tempting target, I reckoned the firepower the contractors were wielding should prove a reasonable deterrent. And they didn't seem too full of themselves, which was always a plus. There's a type who joins the PMC circuit just for the chance to shoot a live human target and get away with it. These guys were older, had the air of people who'd served their time with the military and seen enough of the pink mist to last a lifetime.

We told them we were journalists, hinted that we'd mention their outfit in a favorable light if they watched our backs on the road. Fortunately, they didn't ask to see our press credentials. They just warned us that another convoy of tankers had been hit a week or so before, and to be ready in case it all went bad.

Dawson and I rode in the back seat of Moe's Land Cruiser. It fit better with local custom regarding separation of the sexes. It allowed us to divvy up the ammo and load the AK magazines between us as well. With the pair from Moe's uncle we now had two each, holding the standard thirty rounds apiece. I'd asked for—and got—two hundred rounds, still in their original packaging. If we didn't blow it all on full-auto bursts, it should be enough to get us out of immediate trouble.

Or get us deeper into it.

Dawson reckoned she'd be up to firing the AK I bought in Zubayr. Not to any kind of sniper standard, but enough to keep the bad guys' heads down if it came to that. Moe just grinned at me and pulled out an Uzi machine pistol with an extended magazine, which he kept hidden under his seat. "For emergency, yes?"

Unfortunately, sitting alongside Dawson for the seven-hour journey gave her plenty of opportunity to quiz me about Sean Meyer and his real reasons for being in Iraq.

"I'm putting my neck on the line here," she said quietly. "The least you can do is level with me."

We had stopped for Moe to complete his midday prayers. He had parked in the shade of a building by the roadside, but we sat with the rear doors propped open to allow what little breeze there was to blow through.

"No, the *least* I could do would be to keep my mouth shut."

"You know what I mean, so stop stalling!"

I sighed. "OK. What do you want to know?"

That threw her. She floundered for a moment, then said, "I don't know! Why not start with why this Meyer guy might be out for vengeance on your behalf?"

"We were in a relationship," I admitted. "Back when we were both in the army. Bit like you and your ex, I suppose, except *Sean* outranked *me*, not the other way around. Plus, he was one of my training instructors."

"When you first joined?"

I shook my head. "I made it through Selection into Special Forces. I was in the middle of training for that role when I got . . . chucked out."

Her eyebrows shot up, then flattened into an angry line. "Because of Clay?"

"He was . . . one of the reasons, yes."

She shook her head, made a noise of disgust through her teeth. "Wait a minute, how long ago was all this?"

I had to think. Some days it seemed like ancient history. Other days it might have been just a few weeks ago. "Seven years, I think—maybe eight? It's not something I try to remember."

"I know revenge is supposed to be a dish best served cold and all that crap, but why on earth has he waited all this time to go after the guy? I mean, has he only just found out or something?"

How to answer that? There was only so much soul baring I was prepared to do with a comparative stranger. Besides, officially Dawson worked for Parker, not me. And I've found people's loyalty tends to rest, however temporarily, with whoever signs the paychecks. If my boss took it into his head to ask her some pointed questions about what had happened in the field with this job, who knew how much information she'd volunteer.

"Something like that, yes," I murmured. I wasn't entirely lying. Sean had indeed only recently found out what I'd done for him, unrequested and without seeking his consent. Rather than offering reasoned explanation, I'd told him in a fit of temper. I hadn't had the chance to lay out how the thing had gone down. How I'd never set out with the intention of killing the guy who'd shot him. But the way the game had unfolded, at the time it had seemed the right—the only—thing to do. And even though it might have sent Sean down the path he was now following, I couldn't bring myself to regret the act itself.

"So he might have been the one who did . . . all that to Clay?"

"I don't know," I said. "Sean can be ruthless, but he's never been a psychopath. What was done to Clay was downright evil. And I speak as someone who had more motive than most for wanting him dead, but even so . . ."

"One thing I have to ask, Charlie," Dawson said, thumbing a final round into her second magazine, "is why didn't you go after the bastard yourself? I think I would have been more than tempted, given the circumstances."

"Because for the first few years after I was booted out, I didn't want to think about what I'd lost, about what they'd taken away. And, if I'm honest, I was afraid of getting caught. One of them getting bumped off might have passed unnoticed, but all four and the cops would have been banging on my door before the bodies had time to cool."

I didn't tell her that what I'd been afraid of most was what it might do to me. Killing because your life—or that of another—is in immediate danger is one thing. I'd been trained to accept that possibility right from the start of my army career. But appointing yourself judge, jury, and executioner is quite another. As is doing it anyway, only to discover that it doesn't trouble your conscience nearly as much as it should.

"Aren't you worried they still might—come after you, I mean?"

"Depends on how fast we catch up with Sean. And what he has to say about Clay's death when we do."

Whatever she might have said to that was curtailed by Moe's return. He was smiling as he climbed back behind the wheel, his prayer mat neatly rolled, and we hit the road again. We passed the hulks of burned-out vehicles that had been shunted off the side of the highway and abandoned to the mercy of the desert. Stripped of anything of value, they were now being slowly eroded by the wind-driven sand. I wondered if they were left there as a lesson to the others.

We must have gone another three or four klicks before Dawson sat back and swore under her breath. "Nothing like changing the rules on me halfway through the game, is there, Charlie?"

I glanced across, met her gaze and held it. "If you want to call it a day, I won't think any less of you, Luisa. Moe will be going straight back to Basra tomorrow morning. Nothing to stop him taking you back with him."

Her chin came out, mulish. "I said I'd do this, and I don't go back on my word. But if you lie to me again, I'll punch your lights out."

"Try it," I said dryly, "and you may find you need the other shoulder pinning back together as well."

I spoke lightly, but she studied me without expression for a moment. "You would, too, wouldn't you?" She gave a rueful smile. "I'd say Sean Meyer is not the only one who can be ruthless . . ."

TWENTY-FOUR

◈

IN KARBALA, MOE TOOK US TO THE HOUSE OF YET ANOTHER "UNCLE." I was beginning to wonder if he claimed kinship with anyone who was either a good contact or had connections he thought we might need.

The man lived in a compound slightly less fortified than that of Moe's arms-dealing relative in Zubayr, but the layout was roughly the same. An outer, walled courtyard surrounded a squat, flat-roofed building within. Once again, the state of the blockwork had me speculating that any half-decent builder would never be out of work in this country.

The uncle who greeted us was younger. There were no gray threads among his hair or luxurious mustache. He was short and rather stout, in baggy khaki trousers and an open-neck shirt, and bore a remarkable resemblance to the deposed former president, Saddam Hussein. Any celebrity-double work must have dried up over recent years.

He introduced himself simply as "Yusuf" and greeted us with every appearance of warmth and an apparent lack of curiosity. That could simply have been down to his almost nonexistent grasp of English. Or, Dawson told me, it was traditional to offer hospitality for three days before asking when guests were likely to leave, or even why they were here. I couldn't see it taking very long, what we had to do.

There were several other men who could have been friends or more relatives. It was hard to tell. They were clearly curious about the pair of us but didn't feel able to ask who we were or what we were doing.

We were obviously not local, but we were not easy to pigeon-hole, either. If we'd been Western men, I think they would have been more cautious, not to mention more openly hostile. But as Western women we took on a strange, almost sexless third gender. We mixed with the women without restriction, and the men treated us with exaggerated courtesy but gave us far more freedom of movement than if we'd been local.

Yusuf's wife welcomed us with cautious nods and smiles. She showed Dawson and me to a spare room containing narrow twin beds separated by a small table. The only other furniture was an empty wardrobe with an outlandish flat-screen TV hidden inside, as though they considered owning such a symbol of Western decadence something to be ashamed of.

We were offered food with the family: mixed *mezza*—hummus and pita bread, rich eggplant baba ghanoush, tabbouleh salad—then a one-pot stew of rice and lamb cooked long enough to fall apart on the tongue. All washed down by copious quantities of thick black tea.

Afterward, the men brought out hookah pipes and sucked down *shisha* tobacco until they'd all but disappeared in cloying clouds of smoke.

I politely made my excuses and escaped upstairs. First to my room to grab my sat-phone, then up onto the roof. The night was colder now, the stars clear almost to the horizon. Karbala was considered a holy city. In the distance I could see the twin towers and dome of the memorial to Shia cleric Imam Husayn Ibn Ali, dazzlingly lit up against the muted cityscape. I vaguely recalled being told that Daesh regarded the Shia Muslims as heretics. If the insurgency spread this far, would the shrine meet the same destructive fate as much of the ancient Syrian city of Palmyra?

Up there in the darkness, I smelled nearby hot meat, heard traffic, music, and rapid voices. I could have been in any city, almost anywhere. It was hard to remember that I was a few miles from a bitter war zone.

I thought of the men downstairs. The forces fighting to take control of their country, and of Syria, did not look kindly on the hookah pipe, or cigarettes, if what I'd been told was true. They were burning by the truckload tobacco of all kinds. I wondered if local nicotine addicts simply lurked on the downwind side and inhaled.

I couldn't reach Parker on his office, cell, or even his home number. I rang the office main line, reached Parker's major-domo, Bill Rendelson.

Bill, sadly, had never been my biggest fan, nor Sean's come to that. He agreed readily enough, although without noticeable enthusiasm, to check out Jahmir Lihaibi and report back. But when I asked to speak to Parker, he would only say that the boss was "in a meeting" and not to be disturbed by anyone, least of all me. "Any message?" he asked.

"Just tell him we arrived safe and that he's got until the morning, OK?"

I disconnected before he had a chance to repeat any instructions that we were to stay put until further orders.

The delays so far were making my teeth itch with frustration as it was.

❖

Uncle Yusuf made his move the following morning, before the heat of the day got a grip. I'd woken early, left Dawson sleeping in the next bed, and padded downstairs on bare feet. The ever-present samovar was steaming gently. I poured a cup of stewed black tea and took it to the sunny side of the courtyard, sitting under a brightly colored awning.

I'd barely taken my first sip before I realized I was being watched. I kept the cup raised to obscure my face as much as possible, kept my shoulders soft and my eyes sharp. It wasn't long before I glimpsed Yusuf lurking at the back of the shadowed doorway.

In no mood for games, I sketched him a brief salute, and after a moment's hesitation he crossed the courtyard toward me. His hands were empty, but that didn't mean he was unarmed. I altered my grip on the cup in my left hand slightly, just in case I needed to use it as anything more.

As he neared me, he faltered, as if he'd set out with a purpose in mind and was now losing the nerve to complete it.

"Good morning, Yusuf," I said sedately, touching my right palm to my chest. *"As-Salāmu Alaykum."* (Peace be upon you.)

Good manners compelled him to respond, even to someone who was so obviously non-Muslim. He bowed, mumbled, *"Wa alaykumu s-salāmu wa rahmatu l-lāhi wa barakātuh."* (May peace, mercy, and blessings of God be upon you.) His eyes were everywhere but on my face.

"My friend and I are very grateful for your hospitality, sir," I ventured, playing for time to let him get his tongue unraveled. "Do you wish to speak with me?"

He gave a twitch that could have been a shrug, nod, nervous twitch, or headshake. It was hard to tell.

"You and . . . Mr. Sean . . . ?" he began. "You in . . . same business?"

No surprises that Moe had brought Sean here, too, but *were* he and I in the same business any longer? That rather depended on what Sean was doing here in the first place, and the jury was firmly still out on that one.

But I reasoned that any kind of denial would not get me anywhere. I found myself nodding. "Yes. We are in the same business."

He paused a moment, pursing his lips so the mustache bristled like fur along a cat's spine.

"This good," he said at last. "Then, perhaps . . . *we* do business also, yes?"

"What kind of business?"

He smiled, and there was something sly about it. "Same kind."

Damn, no clues there, then.

"Perhaps, if we are to . . . do business together," I suggested slowly, "we should ask Moe to translate for us? So there will be no . . . misunderstandings."

He shook his head vigorously, scowling as he searched for the right words. They evaded him. Eventually, he let his breath out on an annoyed huff and gave a theatrical shrug, face filled with regret.

I had no intention of getting into any kind of deal with the man, but the fact he assumed I *might*, solely because Sean had apparently done so, intrigued me.

"Please, wait," I said when he would have turned away.

He stopped, eyes hooded.

I pointed to my own eyes, swept my hands wide.

"Can you . . . show me?"

He hesitated a moment, then nodded, beckoning me to follow. We went through the house. I stopped, indicated my bare feet, and smiled apologetically. He caught on right away, folding his arms while I jogged up to our room for my boots. Dawson was still a huddled mound under the blankets.

Briefly, I considered waking her, but we'd made a point of not revealing her facility with Arabic. To do so now would be to invite suspicion.

And besides, if Sean was into something . . . *awkward*, shall we say, the fewer witnesses to that the better. I tiptoed around her and left her a hastily scrawled note on the bedside table.

Then I descended and followed Uncle Yusuf through a side door into the street. Dawson had already proved herself a capable safety net, but I was hoping that this time I wouldn't need to use it.

TWENTY-FIVE

WE DIDN'T GO FAR. JUST A COUPLE OF TURNS ALONG DEEPLY shadowed alleyways choked with rubble and bitter odors. Then Yusuf was fumbling with a padlocked door, the paint peeling to reveal the layers beneath like bark on an old tree. Inside was a long, low room with no windows, little more than a cellar, lined with sagging shelves.

Yusuf beckoned for me to enter ahead of him. It might have been courtesy, but I felt this was a country where chivalry was a concept rather than a custom. My instincts told me to walk away.

I went in.

Yusuf reached sideways and clicked on a single low-wattage overhead bulb, half its output dimmed further by dust and fly shit. What light remained didn't have the energy to reach all the way to the back of the room. It lost heart and petered out about halfway along the rows of shelves.

What it did reveal was clutter. A stacked jumble of objects that at first sight wouldn't have been out of place at a flea market or a yard sale. Brightly colored statues of crude design, fragments of rounded tablets covered with faint scratchings that could have been half-formed hieroglyphics, dumpy urns and vases that might have had a certain charm if it hadn't been for the lurid paint job they'd been given. There was also a smattering of gold coins far too shiny to be anything but fake. They were deformed at the edges, so I was tempted to pick one up and see if the outer foil unwrapped to expose melting chocolate beneath.

A noise alongside me brought my attention back to Yusuf. He was chuckling at my reaction.

"Is good, yes?" he demanded.

"Is certainly . . . *different*," I murmured.

He reached down, picked up a small statuette of what was possibly a woman and child, but it was hard to tell. It had been given a layer of blue paint so thick it looked more like wax. Highlights—if that's what they were—had been picked out in gold and red by someone who was clearly being paid on the quantity rather than the quality of the end result.

He handed it over with a slight bow. Nonplussed, I turned the statuette in my hands, half expecting to see MADE IN CHINA stamped on the base. It was heavy enough to double as a doorstop. Maybe they filled them with sand? After all, this was a country not exactly short of the stuff.

Yusuf seemed pleased by my lengthy inspection.

"So . . . we do business *also*, yes?"

I didn't miss his use of the word *"also,"* or the emphasis he placed on it.

Jesus, Sean, what in hell's name were you up to?

When I continued to stare, he heaved a theatrical sigh. "Take," he said. And when I would have thrust the ugly object back at him, he flapped both hands, shooing away any objections I might make as if he was scattering chickens. "Take for *duktur jamaeaa*. Then we do business, yes?" He smiled. It was not reassuring. "Just like Mr. Sean . . ."

❖

Both Dawson and Moe were waiting for us when we got back. Moe was his usual smiling self. Dawson regarded me with narrowed eyes.

"Got your note," she said. "Strange how you couldn't wake me, seeing as I'm a really light sleeper."

"Yeah, that *is* strange," I agreed blandly.

"So where did you get to? I thought you were in an all-fired hurry to get a move on this morning."

"I am, but Yusuf wanted to show me his . . . wares. And, as he's our host, it would have been rude to refuse."

"Wares?"

I shrugged, indicating the cloth bag slung over my shoulder. Yusuf had been at some pains that I should not walk the streets carrying my prize openly. On the grounds of taste alone, I was in agreement with him there.

Dawson took a step forward, pulled back the edge of the bag, and peered inside with all the enthusiasm of a reluctant aunt getting her first peek at a particularly ugly new baby.

"It's . . . um . . ."

"My thoughts exactly, but Yusuf seemed to be trying to tell me that he'd given Sean something similar to show to someone." I tried to remember the exact phrase he'd used, failed to recall more than a fragment.

Across the courtyard, Yusuf was talking to one of the other men who hung around the place. They were taking pains to act casual, but their eyes flicked constantly in our direction. Without moving my lips, I murmured, "I don't like this."

"Me neither," Dawson said around a fake smile. "What say you we grab our gear and head for the hills?"

"Sounds like a plan."

We sauntered upstairs to the room we'd shared and I threw the few belongings I'd brought with me into my bag, giving her a rough précis of my excursion. Dawson had already packed, and she took the time to unwrap the gaudy statue Moe's uncle had foisted on me so she could inspect it more closely.

"Well, what it lacks in style it makes up for in pug-ugliness," she said at last. "What do you want to do with it?"

"Well, we can't just leave it behind—I get the feeling Yusuf would be very offended, and who knows if we might need to make use of his hospitality again."

"Good point. S'pose there's always eBay when you get home."

"I doubt I'd even get an opening bid. And like I said, he was emphatic that Sean had accepted one of these things, so . . ." I shrugged, thought suddenly of Bill Rendelson's glowering features back in the New York office. "Could always give it away, though. I know just the right recipient."

Dawson grinned and handed me the statue. I shoved it in the top of my bag, wedged a T-shirt between it and the folded-stock AK so they didn't clank together, and closed the zipper halfway.

Without thinking, I hefted the bag off the bed with my left hand, sending a sharp buzz of pain through my forearm down into my wrist as the extra weight bit.

Dawson raised her eyebrows at me briefly, but for once she didn't press. I guess when it came to being physically below par, she didn't feel she could make an issue of it.

❖

Downstairs we found Moe with his Uncle Yusuf and one of the other men, drinking tea. Moe was crouched on his haunches in that relaxed way men can manage more easily than women. They were on the shady side of the courtyard, sheltered from the already fierce sun. Yusuf and his pal regarded us as if they suspected we were about to make off with the furniture.

Moe got to his feet, his face arranged into an expression of sorrow.

"So, pretty ladies, tomorrow I go home. But today I can be of service to you, yes?"

"Do you remember your uncle in Zubayr telling us about a man here he thought we should meet?" For some reason I was reluctant to mention names in front of the other men.

"Of course!"

"He also said you knew where to find him."

Moe spread his hands and smiled broadly at the suggestion that I might doubt his capabilities. "We go?"

I nodded. "We go."

As if summoned by a hidden bell, Yusuf's wife appeared with the children shepherded in front of her. The children shook hands with each of us, solemn concentration on their faces. Their mother bowed with a hand pressed to her heart. We thanked her profusely for her hospitality, and she bowed again but said nothing. I like to think she was pleased by the praise. It was hard to tell.

Outside, as we climbed into the back seat of Moe's Land Cruiser, Yusuf put his hand on the car door and said pointedly, "*Ila-liqaa.*"

It was a standard form of *good-bye*, meaning, much like *au revoir* in French, 'until we meet again.' The emphasis Yusuf used gave it meaning far beyond the throwaway conventions, however.

Knowing any vague promise would be taken literally, I opted for compromise. "When we have found Mr. Sean."

He scowled, from which I gathered that was not the answer he'd been hoping for. After that, the traditional words of peace and safe travel were somewhat grudgingly delivered.

Then Moe cranked the engine, and the belch of smoke from the Toyota's exhaust had Yusuf quickly stepping back.

Dawson and I pulled scarves around our heads as we launched into traffic. I risked a last glance back toward Yusuf's house. He was still standing outside, watching us, a cell phone pressed to his ear.

He might have been booking his car into the garage or ordering takeout, but somehow I very much doubted it.

TWENTY-SIX

JAHMIR LIHAIBI WAS ONE OF THE FATTEST MEN I HAD EVER encountered. A fact which I might have been better prepared for, I reflected, had I yet received any report about him from Bill Rendelson.

As it was, we had to walk into the meeting set up by Moe without any forewarning, which was never how I liked to approach things.

Moe had been able to tell us only that Lihaibi worked at the university; he claimed to know little more than that basic fact. The man could have been the dean or the janitor for all I knew.

I'd contemplated trying to contact Parker again, but I knew he'd tell me to postpone the meeting until we had reasonable intel on the man. And all the time I was aware of the head start Sean had on me, of how fast he might be moving, and that I had no idea of either direction or intent. It made me more willing than I might otherwise have been to take the risk.

Now Moe ushered us into a private back room in what appeared to be an internet café set up in an old store, not far from the university on the western side of Karbala. In some ways, the number of students occupying the place was reassuring.

As I peered through the curtained doorway, I saw teenagers of both sexes, mixing with apparent ease. Nobody was armed, that I could tell. They were just ordinary kids. Although a few of the girls wore a headscarf with what was otherwise Western garb, some slouched in jeans and trainers like the boys. They wore T-shirts bearing the same slogans I'd expect to see on students the world over.

Some drank tea from the traditional glass cups, but more were slurping Coke straight from the can, eyes fixed on the computer screens in front of them. A pall of cigarette smoke billowed around the ceiling fans. The music playing in the background grated on my ears, so I assumed it must be trendy.

Moe caught my expression and grinned. "Is very modern, yes?"

I nodded, admitted, "I didn't think there'd be such free access to the internet here."

"Oh yes, we have much freedom now to say what we think." His face dropped a little. "But . . . who listens?"

The back room was high ceilinged, splashily painted the shade of magnolia usually found in army barracks. It was furnished with mismatched oddments. Half the lightbulbs were bare, making the ornate chandelier at one end seem more out of place. Moe had told us on the way over that it had come from one of Saddam Hussein's looted palaces. It hung low over the single dining table, at which Lihaibi sat.

He did not rise as we approached, but I realized such a maneuver would require notice and probably mechanical assistance. Instead, he ducked his head and offered a pudgy hand, fingers distended like the twisted balloon-animal of a children's party entertainer.

"Greetings, ladies," he said, popping another date into his mouth and washing it down with turgid black coffee from a thimble-sized cup. "Please, be seated."

We sat. I pulled my chair out at an angle first so I could see both doorways leading into the room. Dawson did the same. Lihaibi nodded, as if recognizing the automatic gesture for what it was.

"So, ladies, what can a humble man such as myself do to assist the esteemed Western press?"

I avoided glancing at Dawson, just pulled a suitably journalistic-looking notebook out of the bag I'd placed at my feet.

"Perhaps we could start with a little of your background, sir."

The fat man beamed. I had, I guessed, just prompted him about one of his favorite topics. He eased his bulk from side to side, as if shifting his weight from one giant buttock to the other. The chair creaked beneath him in protest.

"Ah, I received my degree at your King's College London, which is, as I'm sure you are aware, one of the finest universities in the world. Then I took up a post at the University of Baghdad. And, although my work here is of the *greatest* cultural importance, currently I am in discussions with regard to a place with the Department of Anthropology at the most prestigious Smithsonian Institution in Washington."

"In relation to which collection, sir?"

His eyebrows climbed a little. "Excuse me?"

"I like to be precise—in the articles I write." I smiled in apology. "I understand the Department of Anthropology at the Smithsonian comprises several different collections. To which does this offer relate?"

"Ah . . . you are most well informed. Archaeology, of course. And I wouldn't yet say we have quite reached the *offer* stage

139

of our negotiations. But as one of the *foremost* experts on the artifacts and antiquities of this region, I am a natural choice when the present curator retires."

Artifacts and antiquities . . .

"Of course." I scribbled a meaningless hieroglyphic I hoped he'd mistake for the shorthand my mother had always pined for me to learn. "Please, go on."

He took another sip of his coffee, eyes darting brightly between Dawson and me. There was something a little more wary about him now, I noted, wondering how much of what he'd just told me held any truth.

"Perhaps it might be *easier* if you simply asked your questions." He pointedly tipped his wrist upward to display the face of his gold watch and gave a shrug that was not as regretful as it was intended to appear. "Sadly, my time is not *unlimited.*"

"What are your feelings on the extremists in the north?" Dawson asked. "After what happened in Palmyra . . . ?"

She gave a casual flip of her hand to indicate that the destruction of the ancient Neolithic city in Syria was well known enough not to need repeating here. It was a neat way of covering a lack of detailed knowledge.

Lihaibi's expression drooped into mournfulness. There was something spongy about his features that lent a certain exaggeration to their every move, like a rubber caricature. Or maybe he felt he had to boost his emotions so they might show more clearly through to the surface.

"A *tragedy*. Treasures that are beyond price, utterly irreplaceable, have been stripped away and may have been lost forever."

"When you say 'stripped away' . . . I thought they blew up or bulldozed most of it?" I queried.

"Ah, yes, of course, but looting of important sites has been a terrible problem in my country for many years," Lihaibi hurried on. "And as you will be aware, the original *location* of a piece is so important. As soon as it is disturbed—maybe even badly damaged if *amateurs* are employed during its removal—then the *provenance* of the artifact is lost and its archaeological significance is greatly reduced."

I dutifully made more squiggles on my notepad. Lihaibi craned forward a little, as if making sure I was accurately recording his words. I don't know what he thought he read there, but when I underlined the last part twice, as if for emphasis, he gave a grunt of approval.

I dredged my memory for old news items I should have paid more attention to at the time.

"I understand that the National Museum of Antiquities in Baghdad was badly looted during the second Gulf War."

"Sadly, this is true. Many of these treasures were plundered when the Americans invaded our country in 2003. It is said perhaps as high as *ninety percent* of the inventory was taken. It was another *tragedy*—one that should have been foreseen and prevented."

I seemed to recall that it was the Iraqi people themselves who did much of the looting but didn't think pointing this out would gain me favor. I glanced at Dawson, grasping for anything that might keep the fat man talking.

"*Ninety percent?*" she repeated incredulously. "How much of that has been recovered?"

Lihaibi hesitated again, then gave a lurching shrug. "It is hard to say. Our Department of Tourism has been working most *rigorously* with UNESCO for the safe return of stolen objects and the prosecution of perpetrators, but it is *very* difficult when artifacts turn up in auction houses *right across* Europe and *the Americas*." The accusatory note in his voice swelled as he got into his stride. He seemed to hear this for himself. He stopped, took a breath, and smiled in such a way it made my skin shimmy. "My apologies. I am a *passionate* man, and this is a subject which *arouses* me."

He glanced at his watch again. As if on cue, the door from the front of the café opened and a young man in a *keffiyeh* and a Nike sweatshirt stuck his head through.

"Duktur jamaeaa, yjb 'an nnatruk alan."

Lihaibi waved him away and placed both hands flat on the table as if about to rise.

"Ah, it is with much regret, ladies, that I—"

"What did he just say?"

Both Dawson and the fat man looked taken aback by my interruption. "That was my driver. He merely told me that it is time we were leaving."

"But that wasn't all, was it? What else?"

"Nothing else, I can assure you."

"Charlie, he's telling the truth!"

"So, what does that first part mean—'*duktur jamaeaa*'?"

Dawson stared at me as if I'd lost a good chunk of my mind. "It just means 'professor'—the guy's title. It's nothing sinister."

"Maybe not," I agreed. "Maybe it's just a coincidence and Yusuf was talking about somebody else entirely. But, just in case . . . he told me to show you this."

As I spoke I leaned down, reached into the open bag at my feet, and pulled out the ugly statuette, plonking it into the center of the table and twisting it to face the startled professor.

TWENTY-SEVEN

LIHAIBI REARED BACK IN HIS SEAT HARD ENOUGH FOR ME TO fear for its structural integrity. I watched him quickly run through an assortment of emotions before he settled on outrage.

"What is this? What is the *meaning* of this? I come here, spare my most *valuable* time—in *good faith*—and you accuse me of . . ."

His voice trailed away as he seemed to realize we hadn't actually accused him of anything. Not yet, anyway. He took a deep breath, his chins wobbling with the effort of control.

"A man gave me this specifically to show to you," I said with careful deliberation. "It's not the first time, is it?"

Yusuf had given something similar to Sean with the same instruction. Was it a message, or some kind of token to prove my own provenance?

143

Lihaibi's eyes strayed to the doorway where his driver had made his brief appearance, as if contemplating making a run for it. His mouth straightened into a mulish line.

I reached for the heavy statuette. Once again I made the mistake of using my left hand and didn't quite get a grip on it. Only because my eyes were locked on the fat man's face did I see the flicker of alarm that crossed his features as I momentarily fumbled, letting the base slip back onto the table.

The mental fog parted and I caught a glimpse of *something* on the other side. I looked again at the statuette with its ungainly shape and garish hues, and saw it suddenly not as an object in itself but as a disguised gift in lumpy Christmas paper, waiting to be unwrapped.

"Be careful of what you are asking. Journalists are not always made *welcome* in my country."

"We are not journalists," I said.

For a moment I saw him waver. But whatever the temptation, it didn't last.

"I am *furious* at this deception and shall be making my displeasure known at the very *highest* levels." He flapped both hands as if to shoo us away. "That is all. Good day to you both. Please go now."

He did manage to haul himself to his feet then, reaching for a sturdy cane that was hooked over the back of his chair. When I stepped in toward him, he brought the cane up sharply. I don't know if he actually intended to use it to defend himself, but I didn't give him the opportunity.

A long weapon like a bat or a cane is dangerous because it extends your attacker's reach, allowing them to engage you at a distance. The answer is to close that distance as fast as possible. Maximum damage is usually inflicted by a section about two-thirds of the way along the length of the weapon. Stay outside that range, or get inside it, and what starts as a tactical advantage for your aggressor now becomes a hindrance.

Much as I disliked the idea of getting closer to Lihaibi's sweating bulk than I had to, I crowded into him, shoving upward on one elbow to tip the cane out of his hands. Dawson nipped in and seized it before it had the chance to clatter onto the floor.

Lihaibi tried to take a step back, lost his balance, and began to fall. He made a grab for me, purely as a reflex, I think, but I swatted his fingers away. There was no chance I could have kept someone of his size on his feet even if I'd wanted to. This was one instance where, if I'd been asked to act as the man's bodyguard, I would have passed in favor of a six-foot-plus ex-squaddie. Preferably a knuckle-dragger who could bench-press twice his own body weight.

Someone like Clay . . .

I clamped down on that line of thought before it could take hold, stood over the professor as he sat splayed on the ground, mouth open and fear in his eyes.

"Who are you?" he asked then, bluster deflating. "What do you want?"

I moved the statuette closer to the edge of the table, where he had an unrestricted view, and patted the top of its head. "I want to know everything you can tell me about this."

He wriggled on the concrete floor, clearly unhappy to stay where he was and unwilling to beg us for the assistance he needed to regain his feet. We made no moves to offer it. After a few moments he sighed and tried for nonchalance, folding those plump hands into his lap.

"It is impossible to tell under all that . . . cheap veneer."

"Then take your best guess."

"I *never* guess."

145

"Humor me."

Another sigh. He reached up, flicking his fingers impatiently when I didn't hand him the statuette quickly enough, and gave it a cursory inspection with pursed lips. "As I said, it is very hard to express an expert opinion under all this . . ." He indicated the artifact's outward appearance with a dismissive gesture and a moue of distaste. ". . . but if you insist . . ."

I didn't miss the way his eyes drifted to the doorway. "Less stalling, more talking."

"If I must . . . then I would suggest this might very well prove to be a Mesopotamian representation of a mother and child, most probably carved from calcite alabaster, and dating back to, ah, 3000 B.C.—approximately, of course."

Dawson's eyes widened. "And . . . valuable?"

He grimaced. "If it was offered for sale to the right *buyer* . . . in the right *place* . . . naturally so."

"And would *you* be that buyer, by any chance?"

"Most certainly not! This artifact is a part of the *cultural heritage* of my country and as such it is *priceless*. It should not—"

"Spare me," I said. "So why were we told to bring it to you?"

"Ah, perhaps so that I might *return* it to the site from which it was taken."

I moved in until I was looming over him, close enough to smell the oil in his hair, the spices exuding from the pores of his skin. He tried not to cringe away from me and only half succeeded. Intimidation I could do in my sleep. Forcing an avaricious calculation into my voice was harder.

"We didn't risk our necks coming here with this just so you could give it away."

"Then why *did* you come, when you did not know what you had?" He was aiming for confusion but wasn't entirely convincing.

"To find out." I remembered what Yusuf had said, took a guess and a chance. "And then to do business."

"Ah, you wish to sell?"

"Why? Are you in a position to buy?"

"Not me *personally*, no. But I may be able to *arrange* an introduction . . . for a small commission, of course."

"How about we pay you an introductory fee, you tell us the name of your buyer, and we deal direct?"

"That will not be possible." Flat and final.

"Is that because we're Westerners?" Dawson demanded. "Or because we're women?"

"Because the sky is blue and the grass is green," the fat man said, which I gathered was his way of saying both answers were so obvious they didn't need stating.

He took a last, almost affectionate look at the statuette, even camouflaged as it was, before reluctantly offering it back to me.

As I took it, I saw the way his gaze lingered.

"How about if I were to give you that piece," I said, "in return for information."

"What *kind* of information?"

"We're looking for someone," Dawson said, and just when I would have silenced her, she added, "someone who owes us, big time."

It was as good a story as any.

"Ah. He must be *greatly* in your debt, this man, that you would follow him here."

"Did anybody say it was a man?"

"No, but . . . you are *women* . . ."

I narrowly avoided punching him repeatedly in the face. "OK, yes, it's a man we're looking for. We believe he came to see you about three or four days ago."

"A man of my reputation sees *many* people."

"Not Westerners, and not like this man. You would not have forgotten him. Possibly he brought with him similar . . . merchandise?"

Merchandise. The same word Moe's uncle in Zubayr had used. He'd advised us against mentioning his name in introduction, but considering how vehemently he'd expressed his opposition to the insurgent uprising and lawlessness that followed, why had he directed us to Lihaibi at all?

And what the hell was Sean *doing* in all this?

"It's him we want to find, more than we want to find your contact."

"You say he owes you money . . . ?"

I shook my head before Dawson could answer, knowing by the gleam that had suddenly appeared in the fat man's eye he was about to bring up the subject of commission again, and this time it would not be small. "She said he owes us, *big time.* She didn't mention anything about money."

His disappointment was palpable.

"Just suppose, for a moment, that I *do* remember this man you speak of . . . ? Even if he does not owe you *money*, he must be of no small *importance* to you, yes?"

I stared him down and said nothing.

Lihaibi cleared his throat. "I . . . may be able to use my *influence*, my *connections*, to make some inquiries on your behalf regarding this man."

"That's very generous of you, but of course you *are* getting a 'priceless part of your country's cultural heritage' in return."

"Ah, yes, yes . . . It will take a few days—perhaps a week. And there may be some *expenses* incurred, naturally, which you will need to meet—"

"No."

"No?"

"No delays. No expenses. No influence or connections required," I said. "Just tell us what you told the guy—where you sent him. Then take the statue, and we all leave happy. Surely that's worth more than a small commission?"

Haggling was a ritual so ingrained for Lihaibi it was now almost a muscle memory. He was clearly loath to deviate from the habit.

"Two days. Three at the most. And a mere *five hundred* US dollars. No more—on that you have my word—"

Aware that we were fast running out of time, I stepped in and backhanded him across the face, hard enough to get his attention rather than do him any serious harm. He jerked back with a squawk. A thin trickle of blood began escaping from one nostril, which I put down to stratospheric blood pressure rather than impact. Still, I was glad I hadn't really put my weight behind the blow.

"I'll give you two hundred and fifty dollars, plus the statue, but you tell us right now, or you will be carried out of here on a stretcher."

"You would not *dare*! I have friends in the *highest* of places. You do not have the *least* idea *who* you are dealing with!"

"Two hundred dollars and the statue. The more you argue, the more the price goes down."

"And the more she hurts you," Dawson put in. She pulled the neck of her shirt away just far enough to reveal the puckered scar over the plate holding her collarbone together. "See this? Last time *I* disagreed with her."

I thought that was pushing the bounds of credibility a little too far, but the fat man looked as if he had no trouble believing it. I didn't know whether I should be flattered or insulted. Besides, I'd always found that greed was a far better motivating factor than fear, which tended to fade the moment you walked out the door. With greed at least they had something shiny to look at after you were gone.

"Very well! Two hundred and fifty, and the piece, and I will tell you exactly what passed between us," Lihaibi said sourly, mopping his upper lip. "But there will be *consequences*, of that you can be quite certain."

I waited. He raised an eyebrow and smoothed the pad of one thumb across his fingers in the universal gesture for money. Without a word I went to my bag and fished into the pouch containing the bribe allowance Parker had provided, counting out the amount by touch alone, just so he didn't get any fancy ideas.

I put the stack of notes on the table, next to the statuette.

"Talk, Professor."

Eyes on the money, he said, "I told him that I could not help him. Sometimes I know the *origination* of the artifacts brought to me, and often I am able to verify their *authenticity*. But that is all."

"So this 'introduction' you offered . . . ?"

"I await to be contacted when they are ready to trade." He gave an apologetic shrug. "Not the other way around."

"What else did he want to know?"

"He wanted to know where they were going when they left Iraq, how they were transported. *That*, I do *not* know. There has been much *upheaval* in recent months. The situation in the north of my country has . . . changed." He gave a shiver that was not feigned. "So that I do not *wish* to know."

I couldn't see Sean going away satisfied with so little. "What else?"

"Nothing, I swear!"

"So, he came to see you, brought you a similar artifact, concealed in a similar way?"

"Yes!"

"What did he bring?"

Lihaibi looked puzzled at the question. "A . . . piece of tablet—most likely made of clay—covered in early pictographic writing."

"Cuneiform?" There was something about being patronized that brought out the show-off in me.

"Ah . . . yes. Very old—possibly dating back to the fourth century B.C., and of *considerable* archaeological value."

"What happened to this tablet?"

"He . . . took it away with him when he left."

"And he gave you no indication of where he might be going?"

The fat man shook his head, winced, and dabbed at his nose again.

Damn. A dead end.

"Did he say anything else to you? Anything at all?"

"No."

Unable to think of another useful question, I moved back, leaving the money and the statuette on the table. I nodded to Dawson. We both shouldered our bags, and she approached the fat man with his cane.

Lihaibi shied away from her until he realized she was simply handing it back. He glanced again at the contents of the table and slowly reached for the cane as if expecting it to be snatched from his grasp at any moment.

We were almost at the rear door before he spoke again.

"Your friend—" he began.

I stopped, unsure if he meant Dawson or Sean.

"—he said something as he was leaving. Something about having come too far now to turn back. I did not understand, so I paid it little attention. He said it quietly, under his breath. I did not think he was talking to me."

TWENTY-EIGHT

◈

MOE WAS WAITING FOR US OUTSIDE. HE HAD THE ENGINE RUNNING, not so much playing the getaway driver as keeping the air-con going. He was drumming his hands on top of the steering wheel in time to the music blasting from the stereo. It sounded like the same thing the kids in the internet café had been listening to.

We strolled across the street, trying to make it look as if we weren't running away from anything.

"How the *hell* did you know all that stuff about the Smithsonian," Dawson demanded. "And cuneiform writing, and all that shit?"

"Parker always has *National Geographic* magazines in the waiting area at the office. I flip through them when I'm bored."

We jumped into the back of the Land Cruiser. Moe took off into traffic like a new cop on his first emergency call. Rather

152

than watching the road, he was grinning over his shoulder at the pair of us.

"All is good, yes?"

"Maybe," I said. "Or maybe not."

"She knocked the fat professor flat on his arse," Dawson explained.

Moe gave a delighted crow of laughter. I let Dawson deal with his questions, instead twisted in my seat to keep an eye out through the rear screen. Just before we reached the end of the street, I saw a figure dash out of the internet café. It was too far to recognize his face, but from his clothes I guessed it was Lihaibi's driver. He gesticulated after our disappearing vehicle, waving his arms.

"So, where to now, boss?" Dawson asked.

"Anywhere away from here would be a good idea for the moment."

"OK. You want I should take you back to the house of my Uncle Yusuf?"

"Er, no," I said. "Just drive, Moe, and we'll work it out."

"Will we?" Dawson said quietly. "Because I don't know about you, but I'm more confused than I was before we went in there."

"Yeah, I know what you mean . . . Sean went to Lihaibi looking for answers, and I'd say he failed to get them. So, what did he do next . . . ?"

"Well, he hung onto his bargaining chip—the tablet—so maybe he went looking for another way to contact a buyer."

"Or maybe he didn't trust Lihaibi to do the right thing with it."

"Like you have, you mean," she shot back. "You know that statuette's going to be up on the black market as soon as Green-peace rolls the professor back into the water, don't you? So why *did* you leave the damn thing with him? We could have used it."

"In the meantime we had to carry it, and we're trying to travel light." I shook my head. In truth, I wasn't sure myself.

"I'm just looking for Sean, but as to what Sean's looking for . . . who knows?"

"Hey, Moe," Dawson said. "Did you take Mr. Sean to see the professor?"

Moe rotated in his seat again to face us. "To my great sorrow, no. I took him to the house of my Uncle Yusuf, and then I returned to Basra."

"Do you take *all* your passengers to the house of your Uncle Yusuf?" I asked.

"Oh no, Miss Charlie," Moe said, his face serious. "Only those I bring to Karbala."

Dawson laughed, but something about the comment niggled at me. "So, your other uncle—the one in Zubayr—he would have known you would take us there?"

Moe scowled in furious concentration for a moment, still not watching the road. The Land Cruiser drifted to the right until the front wheel bumped the curb. He was forced to saw at the steering and actually look where he was going. Must have been the first time in half a kilometer.

"Yes, he did!" he said then. "Before we leave, he told me to be sure to show such honored guests the hospitality of the family."

I glanced at Dawson. "Are we being set up?" I murmured. "And if so, by who, and for what purpose?"

"We're Westerners in Iraq," she said dryly. "Like they *need* a reason."

We were driving past a park bordered by spindly trees. In the center were wooden swings and a slide. Children played, surrounded by parents, single fathers, mothers chatting in groups. Apart from the modesty of their clothing, we could have been anywhere. Even the patchy khaki-colored grass was reminiscent of England during an unexpected heat wave, with the hosepipe bans in full force.

Moe kept driving. I began to realize the scale of the city, the contrast between immaculate open plazas, the white stone-work dazzling in the sun, intricately decorated minarets, and abandoned construction sites. Rusting rebar poked skyward from the upper stories of buildings that could be finished next month, next year, or never. Paved roads suddenly gave way to dirt, then back again. Moe took it all in his stride.

And because we were heading in no particular direction, perhaps it made the tail that much easier to spot.

I nudged Dawson's arm. "We've got company—again."

"Oh joy," she muttered, peering behind us. "The white pickup?"

"Uh-huh. At the moment, anyway. If I'm right, they're also using a silver SUV and a black Merc."

"Three teams? That doesn't sound good."

"The pickup picked us up first—no pun intended—and the others have been playing tag ever since. If there was more traffic, I probably would never have spotted them."

"Locals, do you think?" she asked tightly, and I heard the unspoken question.

"Not sure. Somehow it feels a bit too . . . slick."

Dawson nodded and reached for her bag, sitting between us on the rear seat. She slid out the AK we'd bought from Moe's uncle in Zubayr, checked the magazine was seated, and rolled her injured shoulder. "What do you reckon they're going to do this time—pull us over or try to blow us up again?"

"Your guess is as good as mine." Carefully, I retrieved my own weapon and the spare magazine, keeping it low. "You ready for trouble, Moe?"

"Always, Miss Charlie," Moe said cheerfully, and before I could stop him he fished out the Uzi from under his seat and waved it in front of us, as if to prove it.

To the vehicle following, the silhouette of the machine pistol must have been clearly visible through the glass. Dawson yelled at him to put it down.

I saw the pickup's front end lift as the driver stamped on the gas. The vehicle leaped forward, closing up fast.

Moe tried to replicate the move. When he stood on the ancient Land Cruiser's accelerator pedal, all that happened was the engine note rose to a tortured howl and belched sooty smoke from the exhaust. Still, at least it stopped the pickup's occupants leaning out of the windows to take a bead on us. I doubt they would have survived their first lungful.

Instead the driver swerved wide a moment before he would have rammed into us. The nose of the pickup drew level with the rear quarter on my side.

It was a double-cab model with a rear seat. I caught a flash of black-clad figures inside with covered faces, stubby weapons, and tactical vests, saw the driver shift his grip on the wheel, arms bunching.

I just had time to mutter, "Shit!" under my breath.

Then they hit us.

TWENTY-NINE

THE GUY DRIVING THE PICKUP WAS A PRO—AS IF I HADN'T WORKED that one out already.

He sideswiped the back end of the Land Cruiser just behind the rear axle, using the reinforced bull bars wrapped around the front corner of his vehicle to take the brunt of it.

Having rammed us, the pickup kept coming, sinking its teeth into our haunches like a wolf on a lamb refusing to let go. I caught sight of the driver wrenching at the wheel again as he tried to separate us, ripping off our back bumper in the process as he finally broke free.

The maneuver launched us into a vicious broadside skid—exactly what it was designed to do. I'd practiced the same move on every offensive driving course I'd ever taken part in. So I knew full well that nine times out of ten, with a civilian behind the wheel, that should have been the end of us.

What I hadn't counted on was the fact that Moe must have been driving on desert sand since he was old enough to reach the pedals. Suddenly finding himself skittering sideways clearly held no surprises for him. He wrestled with the wheel, all feet and elbows, calling out prayers and whoops of encouragement to the old Toyota in a voice turned squeaky with adrenaline. Dawson and I were holding on for grim death, unable to take aim even if we'd wanted to.

Whatever Moe entreated, either his God or his vehicle, it had the desired effect. The elderly Land Cruiser shook off its attacker and came back to hand with a last wallow. We were almost at ninety degrees to the carriageway by this time. A side turn had opened up in front of us and Moe didn't hesitate, sending us barreling off down it.

I glanced over my shoulder. The pickup was going too fast to make the turn. It overshot the junction in a cloud of kicked-up dust and stones, already braking hard. We pulled out a marginal lead, which I knew couldn't possibly last.

"Where you want we go?" Moe asked over his shoulder.

"Some place there'll be plenty of cops or army."

Dawson threw me a doubtful look. "For all we know, these guys *are* cops or army." And I knew she was remembering that traffic stop in Kuwait.

I shrugged. The pickup bounded back into view and began rapidly reeling us in again. Now, though, two of the occupants were leaning out of the double cab's rear windows on either side, assault rifles at the ready. They wore combat black with no insignia.

I remembered the Russians who'd arranged for my abduction, and what they'd threatened to do if I didn't get straight on a flight home. Suddenly the word "*incapacitate*" took on all kinds of unpleasant and painful connotations.

Moe yelled, "Hold very tight, please!" and threw the Land Cruiser into a sharp left bend. I swear both inside wheels lifted through the turn. This time, however, the pickup was ready for us. If anything, they made the corner more easily than we had and gained another meter.

The crack of automatic-weapons fire started up behind us. I caught the flare of twin muzzle flash and ducked down even though the thin foam and fabric of the rear seat was unlikely to provide much protection. The glass in the tailgate shattered, showering us with fragments.

"We don't have a hope in hell of outrunning them," Dawson said grimly.

"Or outgunning them, either. I know."

"So, do we stand and fight now . . . or wait until after we've crashed?"

I leaned forward in my seat. "Moe, get as far ahead of them as you can, then turn off, stop, and run for cover before they see you, OK?"

"But Miss Charlie—"

"This is not your fight, Moe."

"But—"

"You run, for fuck's sake, or I'll shoot you myself."

He hunkered over the wheel as if I'd slapped him. I slid back, was almost thrown into Dawson's lap by the next violent turn. She shoved me roughly onto my own side.

"You, too," I told her.

"What!"

"Take it as an order if it makes you feel better. Soon as Moe stops, take off and don't look back. I'll do what I can to keep them occupied. Get hold of Parker. Tell him . . ."

I broke off. I had no idea what she should tell him.

More incoming fire from the pickup strafed across the back of the Land Cruiser. I flinched as one of the tires blew out, the steel and rubber remnants flailing against the underside of the arch. I felt suddenly naked and wished heartily we'd asked Moe's uncle in Zubayr for body armor as well as guns.

Keeping tucked in as far as I could to the side of the vehicle, I wedged the barrel of the AK against the leg of the headrest, sighted, and fired a short burst into the front grille of the pickup.

I saw the driver react to the hit, swerving slightly. For a moment I thought I'd missed anything vital, then I caught the first jet of steam hissing from the front end.

"Now's your chance—before they call for backup and the others arrive."

For once, neither of them argued with me. The pickup had dropped back. We were in a half-built industrial area of what seemed to be abandoned warehouse projects, the roads between them little more than dirt tracks marked out with fluttering plastic tape tied to rebar stakes in the ground.

Moe stood on the brakes and the Land Cruiser slewed to a stop. I clung onto the headrest and maintained my sight picture, covering our rear, felt and heard the doors open and the two of them jump down.

Heard them hesitate, too.

"Go!" I shouted.

They didn't need to be told a second time, and I didn't watch them leave. I didn't need to know the direction they'd taken. It was enough to know they were clear.

I could hear the pickup coming, the engine note harsh as it overheated rapidly, on its last legs. The idea they might sacrifice their dying vehicle in a last-ditch ram raid occurred to me.

I jumped out into the brutal heat, keeping the gun up into my shoulder as I backed around the front of the Land Cruiser and crouched, making sure to keep my body blocked by the front wheel and shielded by the bulk of the engine. The four-wheel drive had enough ground clearance that I could peer underneath it.

The pickup limped into view, steam billowing from the busted grille now. It must have been on the verge of seizing. As soon as the driver saw the Land Cruiser, abandoned with the doors thrown wide, he pulled up fast.

The next thing, rounds were punching into the Land Cruiser—through it in places. I dropped flat, face in the dirt. Above me, the vehicle lurched and sank as another two tires were blown out. Only the one I was directly behind was still intact.

When I raised my head fractionally, the four men in the pickup had debussed and moved behind their own vehicle for cover. Two checked the rooflines on either side of the street, while one covered their rear and the driver kept his weapon trained in my direction. I guessed he'd done the shooting, maybe just getting his own back.

Heart hammering against my breastbone, I stayed down, waiting for them to make their move. I had no desire to make a suicidal last stand until there was no other option. And the longer I kept them guessing, the longer Dawson and Moe had to make their escape without pursuit.

The driver held up his fist in a "hold" gesture to the others. It took me a moment to work out what he was waiting for. Then, above the thunder of blood in my ears, I heard another engine approaching, something big and powerful, revving hard in low gear.

Shit!

I inched forward until I had a clear line under the Land Cruiser. One of the men scoping the rooftops took a step out of cover. I sighted center mass, then remembered the body armor the dead Russian had been wearing. I let the AK's muzzle lower a fraction and shot him through the fleshy part of his right thigh. He dropped as his leg bucked out from under him, and went down yelling.

I fired one round only, on the grounds that a wounded man would tie up at least one of his colleagues but the dead could be left to fend for themselves. Besides, I didn't have ammo to spare.

One of the others grabbed the shoulder strap of the wounded man's equipment harness and dragged him back into cover while the forward pair raked the Land Cruiser with rapid fire.

I was fast running out of viable options. The nearest building was not close enough for me to get to without being shot in the back long before I reached it. The Land Cruiser was disintegrating around me, and the enemy were rapidly encroaching.

As the assault eased, the big Mercedes that I'd seen tailing us earlier hove into view. It came roaring in closer than the pickup and disgorged another four guys, dressed and armed the same.

Can things get any shittier?

Then two from the rear seat moved around to open up the trunk and heaved something out. It landed with a dull thump in the dirt. They dragged it into view, and I saw at once it wasn't a some-*thing* so much as a some-*one*, zip-tied and bloodied.

And I got the answer to my question.

Yes, they most certainly can.

THIRTY

"LUISA!"

For a moment, I couldn't tell if Dawson was alive or dead. I was still struggling to process how they'd managed to catch her so fast. Then I saw her head lift and turn, almost blindly, toward the sound of my voice. There was blood down the side of her face.

"Charlie?"

Her voice was thready, with a hint of desperation. I said nothing, just took a bead on her mouth, where I knew a single shot would penetrate the brainstem and be instantly, painlessly fatal. *Better than being burned alive or beheaded.*

But was that what our attackers had in mind for us?

It was only the sliver of doubt that kept my finger resting lightly on the curve of the trigger, rather than squeezing it home.

"Fox!" shouted the driver of the pickup, almost jerking me into the shot from surprise alone. "Give it up and come on in, and nobody else has to get hurt."

It took me a moment to realize that his accent was American, not Russian.

Doesn't mean he isn't working with them, though . . .

"Give me some incentive."

"Apart from you being entirely surrounded and us having got a hold of your girlfriend, you mean?"

"Yeah, apart from that."

"Hah! Well, he said you had balls. Got *that* right."

"Who said?"

"Your boss—Parker Armstrong. Who d'ya think?"

I hesitated. Who I worked for wasn't a secret. If somebody knew my name, they were likely to know Parker's name, also. Enough to toss it into the negotiations, at any rate.

"Nice try," I said. "What else you got?"

Even across the distance between us, and with gunfire still ringing in my ears, I caught his heavy sigh. "Don't make us do this the hard way, Fox. You know we got you. Just put down the weapon and we can all—"

He probably finished the end of his sentence, but I didn't hear him. All my concentration was suddenly focused on what felt distinctly like the muzzle of an assault rifle pressing into the back of my neck.

I froze. A gloved hand reached down and peeled the AK out of my slack fingers. When I tried to turn my head, I received a sharp jab against the back of my skull that rammed my face into the dirt. Rough but efficient hands patted me down, yanked my hands behind my back and zip-tied them. Then a voice above me called, "Clear."

The pickup driver approached. "You took your goddamn time. Thought I was gonna have to keep talking to this limey bitch forever."

I squinted up at him as he loomed over me but couldn't see much detail against the bright sky. A big guy, full of swagger, who held his weapon slanted across his body like he rarely let go of it. Not a good combination from my point of view.

After a moment's study, he kicked me hard in the long muscle of my left thigh as I lay on the ground. Half my leg burst into flames and the other half went utterly dead. I curved around the pain, fought not to make a sound.

"That's for Dan, bitch. Think yourself lucky you don't get the same as you gave him."

Two of them picked me up by my upper arms, like I weighed nothing. They must have been stronger than they looked. I got my first chance to glance behind me, saw the silver SUV I'd spotted tailing us earlier now parked about two hundred meters away. The obliteration of the Land Cruiser had effectively masked its approach.

Still, the two guys who'd been inside had had plenty of time to take me out while I'd been lying in the road. Instead, they'd crept up on me and disarmed me instead. It went toward this being a capture mission rather than kill.

So, what happens now?

Before I could voice that thought, the two guys who'd picked me up dropped me onto my knees alongside Dawson. She still looked dazed, and when they pulled her up into a half-sitting position, she swayed drunkenly against me.

The pickup driver moved in front of us, still cradling his weapon. He was carrying an M4A1 carbine, with the underslung grenade launcher. It was sobering to know they could have blasted us to bits at any time.

I looked at the remains of the Land Cruiser, listing heavily to one side, its body pockmarked with bullet holes.

One of the men from the Mercedes pulled our bags out of the back, checked inside, and threw them into the still-open trunk of the car.

"All set," he told the pickup driver, who nodded to the men alongside Dawson and me.

"Get them loaded."

"Where are you taking us?"

"You'll find out when you get there. Don't press *your* luck and *my* patience."

Dawson seemed to come out of it enough to put up a token resistance when they brought up the silver SUV and swung open the rear door.

One of the men hit her, almost casually, in the fleshy vee under her rib cage with the butt of his M4. It knocked the wind and the stuffing right out of her, and she collapsed, gasping. He pulled a black hood over her head as he loaded her.

"Hey, she could suffocate under there!"

He ignored my protests, came at me with a similar hood. I reared back instinctively, and he grabbed my hair.

A sudden hoarse cry jerked them all around. From one of the unfinished warehouses on the other side of the street a slim figure dashed out, machine pistol spitting rounds in a continuous stream as he came. I recognized him at once.

"Moe! Don't!"

"I will free you! *Allahu akbar!*"

"*No!*"

What happened was inevitable. One teenage boy against half a dozen well-armed and well-drilled soldiers. They dropped him before he'd gone more than a few meters, and kept firing long after they needed to. His body continued to dance in the dirt as every round hit until his clothes were tattered with blood and bone.

"Stop, for fuck's sake!" I yelled. "Stop firing, stop firing."

When they did, all that was left was a pathetically small heap of sticky rags. I scrambled closer before a hand grabbed my shoulder, close enough to see one chocolate-brown eye, open and staring out of the carnage. There was nothing left behind it.

The lust for life, the enthusiasm, the cheek, guile, and sheer *promise* that had been Moe, were gone.

THIRTY-ONE

WHEN THE HOOD CAME OFF, THE LIGHTING WAS SO INTENSE I screwed up my eyes in response. But all I could hear inside my head was Moe's voice drowning in gunfire. All I could see imprinted on my memory were his eyes, his tattered body. It was less painful to face reality.

I found myself in an artificially lit, artificially chilled room. Bare walls, bare floor, a scarred table, and a pair of hard chairs. The same interrogation suite décor I'd come across more times than I was happy to count.

I was pushed into one of the chairs with my hands still zip-tied. There was no sign of Dawson.

Whoever removed the hood stayed behind me, lurking. When he shifted his weight, I tensed. He was close enough for me to smell stale sweat through clothes badly laundered and worn a day too long. I beat back the fear with anger, stoked it to sustain me through what was to come. I reminded myself that I'd been here before and survived. I *would* survive it again.

What other choices did I have?

Out of my sight line, a door opened and closed, fast enough to indicate anger or purpose—or both. A thin woman strode into view, dressed in black. Loose trousers and a high-collar sleeveless jersey, which showed off sinuously muscular arms. Her hair was cropped short and peppered with gray, making it seem older than her face.

She was holding my battered passport, which she slapped down onto the tabletop as she walked to the far side, slumping into the chair.

"So you're Charlie Fox," she said. Another American accent, West Virginian this time, deep and slightly husky. "Care to tell me what in hell's name I'm supposed to do with you?"

There wasn't an answer to that—not one that she wanted to hear and I wanted to give. I said nothing.

After a moment or two's study, she let out a long, aggravated breath. Her eyes flicked to the man standing behind me, the one who'd brought me in and removed the hood.

"What's the word on Dan's leg?"

"He'll make it. Through and through—missed the femoral as well as the bone. He's one lucky bastard."

I recognized the voice as the driver of the pickup. One of the men who'd butchered Moe. Unconsciously, I braced my wrists, testing the tensile strength of the zip-ties. There was little give to them. I tried to relax my shoulders but couldn't entirely override the fight reflex.

When I refocused, I saw that the woman on the other side of the table had noted my every twitch. The narrowed eyes told me she correctly identified my motivating desire and didn't like it much.

"Do you have *any* idea the trouble you've caused us here?"

"No," I said. "Is it worth the life of a teenage boy?"

"Damn straight it is," she shot back. "It's worth a dozen of 'em."

"In that case, I'm sorry."

"Well, that's something, I guess, although it's kinda late in the day for an apology."

"No . . . I'm sorry I didn't aim higher."

There was a momentary pause while the meaning of that permeated the skull of the man behind me. I heard the scuff of his boots on the concrete floor, had a flash-recall of which hand he'd had on the trigger of his assault rifle. I swayed left just far enough for the punch to my right temple not to knock me cold.

As it was, he hit me like he meant it. The blow rocked the chair off its legs. It toppled slowly enough that he could have caught it if he'd had the urge. He did not.

I landed hard on my side, the air thumping out of my lungs and a rush of pain pulsing through the impact points of my body in gut-churning waves. I turned inward, blind to everything but regaining control, to not throwing up.

By the time I came back to myself, my hands were cut loose and I was propped with my back against the wall. The room tilted wildly when I tried to move. Sweat coated my forehead in a clammy film.

The woman in black crouched just beyond striking distance, which I judged was no accident. The pickup driver stayed farther back, between me and the doorway. Not that I was in any shape to make a break for it—even if there had been a handle on the inside.

"Dammit, I thought you told me she wasn't injured," the woman said sharply.

"She wasn't." There was something defensive in the pickup driver's tone, and I knew both of us remembered him putting the boot in. "We picked this one up clean."

"That's your idea of clean, is it?" I demanded, my voice a raspy mumble. "I dread to think about the state of your underwear."

He glowered but wasn't about to be provoked a second time.

"So why is she bleeding?"

I looked down at my shirt, saw a glistening stain on the left side that had spread onto the sleeve. The pain arrowed down into a deep throb, enough to make me gasp in time to the rhythm of it.

Somebody was dimming the lights in the room, starting in the corners and working toward the center. I tried to concentrate on holding onto the bright spots, but they kept shifting sideways. I closed my eyes.

The last thing I heard was the woman shouting for a medic.

❖

When I opened my eyes I was lying in a hospital bed with a raised frame around the mattress to keep me from rolling out. This was further ensured by the fact that my left wrist was handcuffed to the side rail.

I inspected it with enough care to prevent the steel cuff jangling. Attaching it to my weak arm was a clever move, and I doubted it was by chance. Experience so far of these people led me to believe they did little that wasn't calculated and planned.

My forearm had been neatly redressed and bandaged, and they must have known I'd be reluctant to undo all that good work by useless struggling.

I was alone in the room, as far as I could tell, but I had few doubts they'd be monitoring me from somewhere nearby. It had the feel of a military medical bay rather than a civilian hospital, and not just because of the drab color scheme. It would have raised too many questions to take me too far from their base of operations.

Was that why the woman in black dressed that way, I wondered hazily. She seemed to be in charge of black ops run from a black site. It had a certain uniformity of style.

I slid my free hand under the hospital gown and touched a large dressing now taped to my abdomen, probing gently. The surface felt numb, the underlying tissue overly sensitive, maybe inflamed. I could only hope I had not managed to give myself septicemia and Parker further reason to doubt my fitness—in all senses of the word—for this undertaking.

I lay back and stared up at the shadows elongated across the industrial cream ceiling by a lamp in the corner. It was stark and utilitarian, and I felt more at home here than I did in any Manhattan apartment or five-star hotel. What did that say about me?

When I closed my eyes, Moe's face appeared. Like a coward, I tried to push his image out of my head, tried to think instead of the Russian I'd shot in the ambush in Basra, but I couldn't remember *his* face at all, and the guilt of that was heavier than the act of killing him in the first place.

I could see the way he moved, had a clear picture of the weapon in his hands, the way it swung toward me. My right index finger tightened in response, the kick of adrenaline pushing my heart rate up now, just as it had then. But for the actual life I'd taken, I felt . . . nothing.

I went over the checking of his body again, as though that might make it more real, might provoke some kind of emotional reaction. Instead, I had only a detached matter-of-factness about the whole exercise. I'd been thorough and professional. Wailing over my own actions seemed pointless, when they'd been caused by his. He was the one who'd fired first.

It was down to his bad luck—and my own skill—that I had been the one who'd fired last.

But when I replayed the end of that scene, unwinding the *keffiyeh* from his head, the sight made me suck in a terrified gulp of air.

The face underneath was Sean's.

THIRTY-TWO

THE NEXT TIME I WOKE, THE WOMAN—HER CLOTHES FRESH BUT still black—was sitting alongside my bed with a manila folder open in her hands.

"Welcome back," she said, but her tone was dry as dust.

I lifted the cuffed hand slightly. "There wasn't much danger of me wandering off, now, was there?"

"Standard operating procedure," she said but made no moves to unlock me.

I made a show of raising my head and looking around. "Where's the gorilla?"

"Woźniak? Don't worry, I put him back in his cage. At least for now."

"Yeah, well, he looks the type to be happy enough with a tractor tire on the end of a rope."

"He's a tool," she said, and just when I thought she was offering a slang insult, she went on, "a specialist tool designed to do one job, and one job only, and he does it exceptionally well. But multitasking is not on his résumé."

"Neither are people skills."

"You goaded him deliberately, knowing how he would react. He was behind you—you couldn't see him—but you were braced for that punch before he even threw it." She regarded me. Her eyes were blue-gray, sharp with a shrewd intelligence. "Why bring that on yourself, knowing you were already injured?"

I carefully eased myself more upright, used that as an excuse to put off answering a little longer.

"Maybe I felt I deserved it—for putting Moe in danger. For getting him killed."

"I'm sorry about the boy, but c'mon—you point a gun at a bunch of guys with that kind of training, you *know* you're taking your life in your hands. But you *fire* a gun at them, well," she shrugged, "it was always going to be game over."

"What did they do with his body, by the way—leave it for the flies?"

Her face tightened. "They put him back in his truck and lit it on fire, covered their tracks. That's SOP, too. But you already knew that, didn't you?"

I stilled on the pillows, eyes straying to the folder, but refused to question what else she might have uncovered.

"What about Dawson, what have you done with her?" I asked instead. "Did she take her life in her hands, too?"

"She's been attended to, and besides, she's a contractor, Charlie, just the same as you. If she didn't know the risks when she started out, she sure as hell does now."

"I work in close protection," I said automatically. "I'm not a contractor."

"Yeah? So who, exactly, are you supposed to be protecting right now?"

"I'm looking for somebody," I said, which was probably not telling her anything she didn't know already. "When I find them, I'll do my best to take care of them." *However* that *works out . . .*

"Nice try, but from what I know, I'd say Sean Meyer neither wants nor *needs* any protection from you. In fact, I'd say he pretty much knows how to look after himself."

I would not let myself react to that, other than a raised eyebrow and a short, "Meaning?" Even so, I got the feeling I'd told her what she'd been fishing for.

"Meyer's AWOL. You're Search and Rescue."

It was close enough to the truth—for now.

"And what's your interest?"

"Damage limitation. Right now, I'm trying to stop the pair of you screwing up a six-month operation with millions of dollars at stake."

"Let me guess," I said. "CIA? NSA? Homeland?"

She shook her head. "Now, you *know* I can't tell you that."

"Can you tell me your name, at least?"

"Hamilton."

She held out her hand, and, after a pause not quite long enough to be outright insulting, I slipped my unchained hand out from under the bedclothes and we shook. It seemed somewhat incongruous, considering the circumstances. She had a grip that could have turned golf balls—or any other kind of balls, for that matter—to powder, and probably did on a regular basis.

"Just Hamilton?"

"Oh, we don't know each other *nearly* well enough for anything more than that, so just be happy with what you got."

"You mind if I call you 'Hammy'?"

"Oh, for—!" She gave a sigh that was more weary than exasperated. "Take things seriously for just one damn minute, will you? The only reason you're not in jail right now is because your boss has called in some favors with my boss. That, and we don't know what effect the stunts you've pulled over the last week will have long term. Sometimes you only find out you've blown your chances when the next meeting doesn't happen or turns into a full-on shitstorm. You would not believe the amount of ass-kissing and ass-*kicking* I'm gonna have to do."

She rose, began to stalk away down the ward.

"Tell me," I called after her, "do you really have enough pull to get him a job at the Smithsonian?"

She jerked to a halt, half turned. "Who?"

"Professor Lihaibi. He's got to be one of yours."

"How d'you work that one out?"

"A few of the things he said. His threats of having friends in high places, the fact you picked us up as soon as we left our meeting with him. The fact he's still in business. But I suppose it's mostly because it's not just *my* run-in with him that pisses you off but Sean's as well. 'Over the past week' you just said. You want more?"

She paced back toward me, braced her hands on the rail at the foot of my bed. "This is a classified operation," she said on a growl. "Any mention of it outside of these walls will win you deportation and some *serious* jail time."

"I'll take that as a yes, then, shall I?"

"You can take that any way you damn well please."

"Look, I need to find Sean—"

"Oh, I think you can leave that to us from here on in."

Something in her tone prodded me. "What do *you* want him for? Not simply for hassling your tame professor, surely, so what else has he done . . . ?"

Her face ticked, cheekbones taut under the skin, but just when I thought she was going to tell me to go to hell, she said, "We had someone under surveillance—someone we thought might be part of the smuggling supply chain. He died under I guess what you'd call suspicious circumstances, even for here. Meyer had contact with the guy. We want to talk to him about that."

"Michael Clay," I said immediately, watching her eyebrows rise and knowing I'd hit on the right name, surprised she'd given me that much. "I want to talk to him about that, too."

"Yeah, well, I'm afraid you'll just have to get in line." She paused, as if taking her last look at me. "There's a Royal Jordanian flight out of Baghdad at nine tomorrow morning. With a couple of layovers it'll get you into Newark sometime tomorrow evening."

"Hang on, you can't just pack me off—"

"Wanna bet? That flight leaves tomorrow and you will be on it." The lack of emphasis was, in itself, emphatic.

"And Dawson?"

"She'll be joining you—at least as far as London Heathrow. You realize, I guess, that you and your pal are lucky you didn't end up coming out of this the same way as your driver?"

"Define *'lucky.'* I still have to go and tell his family what happened to him." *Or a version of it, at any rate.*

She made a noise that might have been a snort, or a sigh. It was hard to tell. When she spoke, the dry tone was almost enough for me to miss the haunted look that passed briefly across her features.

"Yeah, that *always* sucks." She hesitated then, as if about to say something she wasn't sure was altogether wise. "I guess I should thank you—for not killing my guy. I thought it *was* just luck, at first—until I read your file . . . So, why *didn't* you kill him?"

I shrugged, washed over with weariness. "I didn't know who I was dealing with. It seemed prudent not to do anything I might regret later."

"Prudent, huh?" She gave a tight smile. "My guess is you were evening up the odds some, too."

I shifted in the narrow bed, feeling the tight spasm in my thigh where the pickup driver, Woźniak, had kicked me. I kept my voice even.

"Killing a member of a tight-knit team brings on a certain bloodlust in the others. At the time, I didn't want *them* to do anything I might regret later, either."

THIRTY-THREE

THE DOCTOR RELEASED ME—BOTH IN MEDICAL AND PHYSICAL terms—early the next morning. They told me I'd picked up only a mild infection and packed me off with antibiotics, painkillers, and advice to wear my left arm in a sling for a couple of days.

I dutifully accepted the sling but decided to ditch the painkillers at the first opportunity, too wary of their addictive lure. Besides, the wounds I'd sustained prior to this assignment were not bad enough to have slowed me down much as yet, and a little pain was a useful reminder not to take things too far, too fast.

I shook the doctor's hand and thanked him for patching me up. The smile he gave me in return was a little weary, as if he'd sent too many injured soldiers back to the battlefield to believe his repairs would be allowed the time they needed to take hold.

An unsmiling squaddie knocked and entered, then stood by the doorway, waiting.

I picked my bag off the chair Hamilton had used, next to the bed. They'd left me my sat-phone, but by my reckoning the bag was light by one Kalashnikov and several boxes of ammunition. He still took it from me as I neared. Maybe it was the sling doing the talking.

"Are you really just here to help, or to make sure I leave the building?"

He didn't reply. No surprises there.

As we stepped into the corridor someone called my name, and I turned to see Dawson hurrying toward me. She, too, had her arm in a sling and a minder in tow.

"Snap," I said. I indicated my own sling. "And isn't it embarrassing that we've both turned up at the same party wearing the same dress?"

She barely cracked a smile. "Charlie, about—"

"I know," I said, cutting her off before she could mention Moe's name, not sure I'd hold it together if she did. "We'll talk later. There's nothing we can do right now."

She shut up, nodded, but didn't look appeased. I couldn't blame her for that. I wasn't exactly ecstatic about it myself.

The two men didn't quite march us to the main entranceway, but it wasn't a morning stroll, either. The sun was barely thinking about rising, and the air was bitter with the dry cold of the desert. I shivered in my thin shirt, wondering briefly what happened to the bloodied one I was wearing when I passed out. Incinerated, probably.

"Wait here," said the guy who'd collected me, dumping my bag at my feet. I took the opportunity to fish inside for my jacket, then had to dispense with the sling to put it on.

I straightened when I heard Dawson swear under her breath. Following her gaze, I saw the same big Mercedes that had been involved in our ambush pull up. The driver climbed out. The compound was floodlit like a football stadium, so he wasn't hard to recognize, even in civilian guise of jeans and a lightweight shirt. That recognition made me want to curse, too.

Woźniak.

Had he volunteered to drive us, I wondered, or did Hamilton have a perverse sense of humor? It was about a hundred and twenty klicks to Baghdad—a good two hours' journey in the company of a man whose face I'd never get tired of kicking.

He left the engine running, twin wisps rising from the exhausts, and moved around the car, opening one of the rear doors with a mocking bow.

"Ladies."

"Last time you tried to get me into a vehicle with you, you had to beat me up and cuff me first," I said. "What makes you think I'll do it willingly this time?" And as I spoke I was suddenly reminded of a similar conversation I'd had with the ex-Spetsnaz Russian after the Kuwaiti cops picked me up.

"Either you ride in the back seat, or you ride in the trunk." He shrugged. "Makes no difference to me."

I glanced at Dawson. Her jaw was set tense enough to crack teeth, but she passed me a resigned look and slid in quickly, leaving me to walk around and climb in on the driver's side.

I didn't think anything of it until the doors closed behind us. She gave me a hard stare, shifting her eyes meaningfully to the back of Woźniak's neck as he got behind the wheel. I blanked for a moment, then realized she was remembering the way I'd taken Bailey's Glock away from him and jammed it under Garton-Jones's ear, that first day.

If I get the chance, don't worry—I will . . .

She nodded as if I'd spoken the words out loud.

But just before we left, the front passenger door opened and another man in civvies got in. He didn't bother with an introduction and sat twisted in his seat to keep an eye on us in the rear.

Damn.

Woźniak took off at speed, peeling out through the compound's gates and powering along the street beyond. The Merc's engine was a barely audible background purr compared to the more agricultural vehicles I'd been traveling in recently.

"You OK?" I asked Dawson.

She eased the sling from under her seat belt. "Yeah, I s'pose so."

"What happened?"

That earned me a slightly wan smile. "I split in the opposite direction to Moe when we all bailed out," she said. "Took off down a service road behind one of those warehouses. Next thing I know, a car—*this* fucking car—pulls straight across me and I run full tilt into the front wing."

"You haven't done any more damage to your shoulder?"

She shook her head, then grabbed at the door pull as Woźniak made a hard right without slowing.

"Just a mild concussion and banged myself about a bit, nothing more—as yet, anyway. You should see the dent I put in the bodywork, though."

"Good—to both."

"I wouldn't be none too happy 'bout that if I were you," Woźniak said over his shoulder. "Uncle Sam *has* been known to charge for damage to government property."

"Oh yes?" I said mildly. "I would have thought that was the squad leader's responsibility."

He gave a twitch, hands tightening momentarily on the wheel, then said abruptly, "Hamilton tried to tell me you wounded my guy on purpose, 'stead of just plain killin' him. Told her that was bullshit. No such thing as 'shoot to wound.' In the field it's kill or die, no question."

"Your prerogative to believe what you want. Of course, if I'd intended to kill him, I would have aimed center mass and kept firing until he went down. As it was, I fired . . . how many shots, was it?"

It took him a while to answer, and when he did it was with great reluctance and, in response, my knee thudding into the back of his seat.

"OK, OK. It was one. One shot."

"Of course, if I'd known you were going to slaughter my driver, maybe I would have played things differently."

"Your *driver* attacked my guys with an Uzi, yelling a war cry as he did so."

I shook my head. "Oh no, don't you *fucking dare* try to paint him as some kind of insurgent radical. Moe was just a good kid who believed in his God. He also believed he had a duty to protect those in his care."

Beside me, I heard a soft intake of breath from Dawson.

"'*Allahu akbar*' is not a war cry," she said, sounding surprisingly calm. "It simply means 'Allah is greater.'"

"Greater than what?" Woźniak demanded. "Us?"

"Greater than everything. Greater than fear. It's like a Christian saying 'Praise the Lord.' Not, in itself, a battle cry."

"It damn well is if the *kid* shouting it is charging you with a machine pistol."

"So that's why you shot him into enough pieces that his own mother wouldn't recognize him?" I demanded. "Get off on that kind of thing, do you?"

He paused, then lifted his chin and met my eyes in the rearview mirror, smiling the way a shark might show its teeth to the divers in the cage.

"If you've seen your buddies blown into enough pieces that *their* mothers wouldn't recognize them, either, by a teenage kid with a Koran in one hand and a remote detonator in the other, you'd keep shooting till the little bastard wasn't getting up again, too."

There was nothing I could say that was going to change either the outcome or the big man's small mind, so I said nothing.

Instead, I leaned back against the headrest and closed my eyes. It was going to be a long trip.

THIRTY-FOUR

✦

THE AMERICANS HAD BOOKED DAWSON AND ME INTO ADJOINING seats in coach for the first of our westward flights from Baghdad to Amman in neighboring Jordan. There, I was due to board my connecting flight for Newark via Tel Aviv, and she was on another for Heathrow. Needless to say, Dawson would be home quite some time before I was.

As we reached Baghdad International and climbed out of the Merc, Woźniak ducked his head in our direction and said dismissively to his mate, "The one with the sling goes to London, the one without goes to Newark. Make sure they don't miss their flights." He pinned me with a vicious glare. "Especially that one."

The man—who I mentally tagged as Lurch—nodded briefly and dogged our footsteps into the airport terminal. Even so, I expected him to leave us at Security, but he showed some kind of official ID to the staff there and was ushered through.

The airport was crowded and modern, with gleaming white tiles everywhere underfoot, and a complicated lighting array that produced the effect of a vaulted ceiling overhead. There were all the usual luxury shops you'd find anywhere, and most of the necessary signage was in English as well as Arabic script.

"I'm sure we can find our own way," I said to Lurch. "Or is it that you don't trust us to actually board the plane?"

"I have my orders," he said. "And you will be met at Amman."

"What about on the flight? How will we find the toilet without you there to guide us?"

He didn't respond to that jibe but waited with us, expressionless, until we shuffled in line to the gate and handed our tickets to the Royal Jordanian crew there. For a moment I thought he was even going to walk us along the jet bridge. He drew the line at that.

As I pulled the strap of my bag onto my shoulder I glanced behind me, found him stationary amid the flow of other passengers, eyes not leaving us. Any thoughts I had of sneaking back off the plane before the doors were closed and locked faded right about that point.

Catching my gaze, Dawson murmured, "I guess this means we really *are* going home, eh?"

"Looks that way."

But as soon as we were out of sight, I fished for the sat-phone and hit the power button. The cabin crew greeting us at the aircraft door frowned at the sight of it but didn't insist I switch it off right away.

As soon as the phone had gone through its start-up routine and acquired a fix, I scrolled through the contacts to Parker's number, but my thumb hovered over actually dialing.

I'd called Parker before Karbala, and the last thing he'd told me was that he was calling in favors with one of the cloak-and-dagger agencies—like the one Hamilton worked for. So, why had he told them Sean was missing and I was searching for him? Surely, dropping any kind of hint that Sean had gone rogue would not put his agency in the best light. Had Hamilton dug deep enough to find out anyway and dropped it into our conversation to unsettle me, to make me doubt? For what reason, I wasn't clear, but it was enough to stay my hand a little longer.

We reached our assigned seats. A male flight attendant smiled at Dawson and offered to put her bag in the overhead locker. He didn't offer to do the same with mine. Maybe he didn't approve of the phone, either. Or maybe I should have put my damn sling back on. I dumped it on my seat instead, still holding the phone.

"What's up?" Dawson asked.

"I was going to call Parker, but the more I think about it, the more I don't know if that's a good idea."

"Why not?"

"I'm not sure, to be honest. Just a feeling."

She glanced forward along the plane. The flow of passengers hadn't lessened, and the flight was starting to fill. The flight attendants were shoving bags up to make space in the overhead bins, latching them when no more could be squeezed inside.

"Well, make your mind up, because they'll be taking that off you shortly if you don't."

I canceled Parker's number and began to key in another, one that wasn't in my regular contacts but which I could still remember by heart.

It had once belonged to Sean.

As soon as the call was picked up, I said quickly, "I need to speak to Madeleine, right now. It's—"

"Yes, I know," said Madeleine's calm, cultured tones. "Hello, Charlie. How are you?"

"Listen, I don't have much time. I'm about forty-eight hours behind Sean, and I'm being more or less thrown out of Iraq. I need to know where he is, and I need to know now!"

She hesitated. In front, the cabin crew hustled the last few passengers on board and pulled the aircraft door into place. I heard the mechanical clunk of the jet bridge being disengaged.

"Madeleine, if I'm going to fake a medical emergency to get off the plane, I've got about sixty seconds to do it, so—"

"He's not in Iraq any longer."

"He . . . ? Where did he go?"

Again, I was met with agonizing silence. The female flight attendant who'd frowned at my phone was walking down the aisle toward us, checking to see that the passengers were belted in. I turned away from her approach, ducked into my seat, and made like I was bending over my bag, speaking low and fast.

"For fuck's sake, I know you're being loyal, and any other time I'd admire the hell out of you for it, but I'm not the only one who's looking for him, understand? I've *got* to find him before they do."

"What flight are you on?"

I told her, gabbling the information as the first safety announcement blared over the speakers and the plane began to roll back from the gate.

"OK, got you. Via Jordan, yes? Call me as soon as you land."

"Madeleine—!"

But she'd already gone, and the flight attendant was standing over me, glaring while I not only powered down the phone but zipped it into my bag, which she shoved into an already-full overhead locker, just to be on the safe side.

"I don't think *you're* getting any free pretzels on this flight," Dawson observed. She leaned closer, face sober. "Now, you going to bring me up to speed?"

I did so, quickly filling in my encounters with Hamilton and leaving out the one with Woźniak in the interview room. It didn't take long.

"So who's this Madeleine?"

"She used to work for Sean when he ran his own close-protection agency just outside London. When we went to the States, she took over the UK operation. Parker said Sean was in touch with her before he disappeared. That's how he tracked down Clay—or rather, she did it for him. She always was good at that kind of thing."

"What did she say just now?"

"Nothing that helped, other than telling me Sean isn't in Iraq anymore."

"She must have heard from him then. Maybe she even knows what he's up to. Be nice if somebody did."

"I would say so. But she didn't want to share, more's the pity . . ."

"Give me her address." She grinned. "When I get back to London I can go round there and make a bloody nuisance of myself if you like—see what she has to say face-to-face."

"It might come to that."

She eased the sling around the back of her neck, carefully rolled her stiffened shoulder. "Charlie, when we left Basra you were afraid Meyer might have killed Clay as some kind of weird revenge kick, but now we find out Clay was being watched because of antiquity smuggling, and Meyer seems to have taken it up as a new hobby, too. What the hell is going on? Where do a load of looted relics and US spooks come into it?"

"I don't know how Sean got involved with the relics, unless it was something he picked up on from Clay," I said, keeping my voice too quiet to be heard by the rows behind or in front. "Hamilton more or less admitted that the good professor's on their payroll."

"Ah, so as soon as Meyer buttonholed Lihaibi, Hamilton and her bunch of cowboys took an interest." Dawson nodded. "Explains why they jumped on us so fast, I s'pose."

"Yeah, and she said they wanted to talk to Sean about Clay. It sounded more like they don't know what happened to Clay, but they think Sean might. If he was involved in any kind of illegal trafficking, that opens up the field of suspects quite a bit." I shrugged helplessly. "Then again, I don't speak much spook."

That earned me the vestige of a smile. "You and me both. Just enough to order a beer."

"From what Madeleine just told me, Sean must have left the country before Hamilton's merry band managed to catch up with him—*if* the information she gave me was true, that is. And I don't see why she would lie about that."

"Uh-huh," she agreed, somber. "I wish they hadn't caught up with us, either."

We sat in silence through more cabin announcements as the plane taxied out onto the runway and lined up for its takeoff slot. As the big jet finally lumbered into the air, I glanced across Dawson at the view out the window, watching the burned landscape drop away beneath us.

I was not sorry to be leaving.

THIRTY-FIVE

❖

AS SOON AS WE TOUCHED DOWN AT QUEEN ALIA INTERNATIONAL IN Jordan, I switched the sat-phone on again. I'd retrieved my bag as soon as we were able to move about the cabin in midflight and shoved it under the seat in front of me.

It took a while for our plane to crawl to its assigned gate, by which time the phone had acquired a satellite. I redialed Madeleine's UK number.

Her first words were not the ones I expected.

"I've spoken to Sean," she said. "Look, Charlie, he . . . wants you to stay out of this."

"Tough. I'm already in it." *Up to my neck and sinking fast.* "You know Michael Clay is dead?"

"Yes . . . yes I do know."

"Do you know how he died?"

"I . . ." Her voice trailed away. I could picture her slim figure behind a sleek modern desk, manicured fingers gripped white

192

around the receiver. She had never been a field operative and didn't have the stomach for it. Since she'd taken over Sean's agency, it had progressed more toward cybersecurity than real-world. Profitable, certainly, in these times of mass hacking attacks, and it meant she didn't have to risk breaking a sweat, never mind a nail.

There had been times when I'd found Madeleine's innate sense of calm irritating. To misquote Kipling, if you can keep your head when it all goes to shit around you, the chances are you don't have a clue what's really happening.

"He was tortured, Madeleine. Drugged, burned, ripped, sliced—"

"I know what 'tortured' means, thank you very much. You don't have to spell it out for me." Was that a hint of temper I heard in her voice? "But there's no way Sean is responsible for something like that. It's unthinkable."

Madeleine claimed to know him well. Clearly, not as well as she thought.

"Just because *you* can't think it doesn't mean nobody else can." And when she would have protested further, I added, "Our friends at . . . let's call them Croydon Internal Auditors, shall we? They're looking to bring him *to account* for this, so to speak. And they're hunting for him right now."

A slight exaggeration, maybe, but I wasn't in any doubt that Sean's interrogation would be a lot less gentle than my own, if and when Hamilton's crew got hold of him.

There was a puzzled pause for a moment before Madeleine caught on to the initials with a soft, "Ah!"

I waited. One beat became several. Impatience got the better of me. That and the fact that the aircraft had come to a halt and the jet bridge was already snaking out toward the front doorway. If Lurch's warning that we would be met at Amman was on target, his counterpart would be waiting for us as soon as we stepped off the plane. I was fast running out of time.

"Come *on*, Madeleine. He may not *want* help, but you can't deny he bloody needs it. Talk to me!"

"Look, I gave him my word *I* wouldn't tell you where he is," she said. "So, please, Charlie, *take some advice. Don't continue any further* along the road you're on, and don't ask *me* again."

She cut the connection, leaving me frowning. Not at the words, but at the oddly placed emphasis and inflection. I was still frowning when I switched off the phone and stowed it in my bag as passengers began to surge toward the exit. I eyed the crush and, almost as an afterthought, pulled out my crumpled sling again, slipping it over my head and under my left forearm.

"Well, come on, what did she say?" Dawson demanded. "Where is he?"

"She wouldn't tell me, just kept saying . . ."

But as I spoke, it hit me like one of those pulled zoom shots in the movies, where the camera rushes into extreme close-up while the background recedes. I could almost feel it physically as I was yanked out of reality, and time went into a kind of weird slow motion around me.

"*. . . take some advice. Don't continue any further . . .*"

With it came the realization that however loyal Madeleine might be to her former employer, she was also worried about him as a friend.

"Oh, Madeleine," I murmured under my breath. "You little star."

"What?" Dawson looked ready to slap me, or shake me, or both. "Charlie—!"

"He's here," I said. "In Jordan."

"She said that?"

"She didn't have to." I glanced at the passengers still shuffling past. The plane was emptying quickly, and we didn't have much time.

"Look, Dawson, I need you to do something for me . . ."

I explained, too briefly for her to be at all convinced.

"This is going to get us both into deep shit, isn't it?"

"Very probably, but me more so than you. I just have a feeling that once I set foot back inside the US, Hamilton has the kind of pull that can stop me leaving again. Otherwise I'd turn around at Newark and be straight back on the first flight."

"You do have a point there."

"And if it doesn't work, claim I threatened you."

"Now *that* they'll have no trouble believing."

I flashed her a quick grin as we slipped out of our seats and joined the stragglers. The flight attendant waiting by the aircraft exit blinked at the sight of us. I thanked her cheerily as we passed and she smiled automatically. The jet bridge was a corridor of heat after the cool of the plane.

"Of course, if there are two of them, we're screwed anyway," Dawson muttered.

"And if they haven't bothered sending anyone at all, we're home free."

"We aren't that lucky. Ah, there you go—the Arnie look-alike in the dark glasses. It's got to be him."

I followed her gaze and spotted the tall Caucasian in a pair of wraparound shades. He wore a pale blue suit that didn't fit well around his overdeveloped muscles, and he stepped forward the moment we emerged into the gate area. It didn't take much of a guess—we were the only two unaccompanied Western women on the flight.

"You must be Fox and Dawson," he said in a voice disappointingly devoid of Germanic accent. "Come with me, please."

I didn't miss the way he looked straight at Dawson as he spoke, and I began to hope we might just have a chance of this working.

When Woźniak had dropped us at Baghdad, he'd identified us to Lurch solely by the fact that one of us was wearing a sling and the other one wasn't. I assumed, therefore, that our minder in Amman had been briefed in the same offhand manner.

There was no way, under normal circumstances, anyone would ever confuse me with Dawson, on hair color alone. I was fair, she was dark. But I was gambling on the fact they hadn't bothered sending visual ID on the pair of us.

So, as we left the plane, I was the one now wearing a sling and Dawson had both arms free. It had caused the flight attendant to pause, but only for a second before she accepted that her memory of us must have been incorrect.

When people wear glasses, it becomes their identifying feature. I was hoping that in the same way, Arnie would not begin to question which of us was which until it was too late for him to do anything about it.

THIRTY-SIX

"SO, WHAT'S WITH THE ARM?" ARNIE ASKED, DUCKING HIS HEAD in the direction of my sling.

I eyed him just long enough to see the lack of guile behind the question. Maybe he was simply more of a people person than his colleagues over the border.

"Busted collarbone," I said, hoping he wouldn't ask to see scars I didn't have. I nodded toward Dawson. "And that's *before* I started working for her. Since then I've been ambushed, shot at, and hit by a car."

"Yeah, well." Dawson gave a casual shrug. "You knew the risks."

I felt my eyebrows rise a little. Was I really so offhand with the people I worked alongside?

Arnie held out a meaty paw, and for a moment I thought he was intending to shake, but he merely said, "Your tickets, if you please, ma'am."

I fished into my jacket pocket for Dawson's boarding pass—a straightforward flight to Heathrow. She in turn handed over mine for the onward leg to Tel Aviv and then to Newark.

"I just hope your boss at that snazzy New York outfit has good insurance cover," I said, meeting Dawson's eyes with a challenge in mine. "Soon as I get back to London, you can bet I'll be putting in a personal injury claim."

Dawson glared back at me. "You can try it, but it won't get you far."

"Ladies, please. Let's try to keep this civilized, huh?" Arnie stepped between us, palms raised, barely treating our paperwork to more than a superficial glance. He'd checked that the names and destinations matched those he'd been given. What more did he need to do?

I turned away so he wouldn't see my smile.

Dawson sniffed and said, "If we must."

He handed back our tickets without asking for the passports that went with them, said to me, "Looks like your flight leaves first, but if either of you wanna eat, we likely have time."

"I'd rather just go and sit at my gate," I said. I lifted my injured arm a little and gave Arnie what I hoped was a wan smile. "Who knows, maybe if I talk to them nicely, I might get a better seat."

He studied me for a moment. I could almost see him weighing up the likelihood of me doing anything unexpected. I'd already laid it on that I was injured, little more than a hired hand, and slightly resentful of what somebody else had got me into.

His eyes slid to Dawson, who was standing with her arms folded, head on one side, regarding the pair of us in a wanna-make-anything-of-it kind of way. Funnily enough, now she really did look like me.

It only took him a moment to make a decision.

"Well, I'm not supposed to, but . . . you know which is your gate, ma'am?"

"I'll check the departure screens," I promised, leaning closer and adding in a confidential tone, "I need to find a loo as well. I think my period is starting."

If he had any doubts about the wisdom of leaving me to my own devices, that sealed it. He almost jerked back from me.

"OK, well, um, you have a good flight now, ma'am."

"Thanks." I lifted my chin in Dawson's direction. "I'd like to say it's been a pleasure, but under the circumstances . . ."

"Yeah, I know. Look after yourself."

"I will. You, too."

I headed for the nearest restrooms without looking back until I reached the entrance. By that time, Dawson and her minder were nowhere to be seen. I slipped inside and locked myself into a cubicle, stuffing my jacket and the sling into my bag and rooting through it for a scarf to cover my hair. In an Arabic country, despite the tourists, anyone with pale hair still stood out too much for my liking.

A few minutes later, wearing a different color from the jacket Arnie might remember, my head covered and sling gone, I walked out of the restroom and headed for the passport control area. I didn't have a visa for Jordan, but a previous job there had taught me I could buy one at the same time as having my passport stamped. It was still a relatively cheap and easy process.

Less than half an hour after parting company with the two of them, I was outside the arrivals hall with a wad of Jordanian dinars drawn on the company credit card and a freshly purchased tourist visa. I eyed the line of pale yellow taxis nearby and checked my watch. It was at least ninety minutes before the Heathrow flight was due to begin boarding, maybe another forty-five after that while they put out calls for Luisa Dawson before they realized she wasn't coming. So, I had a good two-hour head start on Arnie and whatever backup he had at his disposal.

I allowed myself a brief regroup, walking out of direct line of the security cameras and digging the sat-phone out of my bag.

This time I had no qualms about dialing Parker's number. He picked up almost on the first ring.

"Charlie! You OK? I heard things didn't go . . . smoothly."

"You could say that. Moe's dead."

There was a pause. "Moe?"

"The kid who was driving us." He started to apologize, to sympathize, but I cut him off before he had me choking up. I couldn't afford to remember too much about Moe right now. Maybe there would be time to weep for him later.

"Listen, I don't have much time. Your agency friends showed us the door in no uncertain terms and escorted us practically onto the plane in Baghdad."

He swore quietly under his breath, a rarity in itself for my boss. "I'm sorry," he said again. "I made some calls. Next thing I know, I'm being given the runaround, and you and Dawson have been snatched off the street. If I'd had *any* idea—"

"Yeah, I know."

"Where are you now?"

"Jordan. Still at the airport. I managed to slip the shackles, but I need to get away from here before they realize and send out search parties."

"I won't ask how you did it—not yet, anyhow. Do you need me to arrange a flight back?"

"You mean back to Iraq, or back to the States?"

"Well . . . either, I guess." He sounded unsure of his ground. "Do you still want to go on?"

"Of course. And if I'd wanted to come back to the States, all I needed to do was take the ticket I was offered courtesy of Uncle Sam and save you the airfare. No, I have information that Sean is here, in-country."

There was a pause, then a cautious question: "How good is your intel?"

I shrugged, a pointless gesture unless you're on a video link. "Reasonably trustworthy, I'd say. And besides, it's not only the *best* I have, actually it's *all* I have, so what other choices are there?"

"OK, got your point. What do you need?"

More of Madeleine's words came back to me, that strange emphasis:

"*. . . I gave my word that I wouldn't tell you . . . don't ask me again . . .*"

Picking my own words carefully, I said, "Can you think of any reason why Sean would come here?"

Parker didn't reply right away. When at last he spoke, it was on a tired sigh. "I was hoping he wouldn't—go to Jordan, I mean."

"Why?"

"Because that's where one of the other guys has been working for the past two years."

I didn't need to ask him what he meant by "other guys." Of the four who'd attacked me in the army, only Donalson and Hackett still remained.

Donalson, Hackett, Morton, and Clay.

The warmth of the desert kingdom retreated like a wave from the shore. In its place was frozen air, bitter with the pinch of snow. Just as it had been, back then.

The hairs prickled at the back of my neck, along my arms, across the front of my shins. I could smell them, feel their hands on me, bruising, tearing. I had to gulp in air, force myself to ground in this reality.

"Which one?"

Please, not . . .

But whoever I might have been praying to wasn't listening.

"Hackett."

THIRTY-SEVEN

◆

I SWORE UNDER MY BREATH, SHORT AND LOW BUT NO LESS HEARTFELT.

"Still sure you want to stay?" Parker asked.

"Yes." I didn't have to think about it. "More so, if anything."

Even with traffic and planes in the background at my end, and the limitations of an international phone line, I heard his sigh. "You don't have anything to prove, Charlie, I've told you that before. Not to me."

"Maybe not, but I need to prove to myself that I can face someone I have every reason to dislike and . . ." *And not actually kill him.* "And behave like a grown-up."

I said it with a smile in my voice, but when Parker answered, he didn't sound as though he found it funny.

"Think you can make Sean behave like a grown-up, too?"

"He usually does."

If anything, since his brain injury and the coma that followed, Sean had become less instinctively violent. He'd reverted to the soldier he'd once been, for whom there were strict rules of engagement.

The game we played now had fewer rules. I wondered if that was the reason I found it easier.

My father had once expressed his concerns over my affinity with death and its delivery. He had predicted that if I followed my course to its logical conclusion, I would most likely spend the rest of my life in prison. Always a glass-half-full kind of guy, my dear papa.

So far, I had avoided the inevitable fate he'd anticipated. Sometimes, though, you don't need locks and bars to create confinement. Your own mind can do just as good a job of it.

"Hackett is in a place called Madaba," Parker said now. "It's only about a half hour by car to the west of your location."

So close? Some kind of primitive proximity alarm went off inside my head. I had to force my hand to relax its grip around the phone before I lost the feeling in my fingertips.

"Tell me."

"He runs an export company that ships locally sourced goods to Europe, the former Soviet countries, and the States—mosaics, pottery, that kind of stuff. Small scale, good quality, most of it designed and made by small coop-eratives. I had Bill run his financials. Company's doing OK, each year a little better than the last, modest profits, no blips or surprises."

"A front, then."

"Oh yeah. Whatever he's doing there, it's not making it onto the books."

I took a breath, let it out slowly. "I better go and check it out then, hadn't I?"

"I guess." It was hard to say which of us sounded more reluctant. "You be careful, Charlie. Not just of Hackett, but Sean, too."

"We still don't know for sure that he had anything to do with Clay's death."

"Maybe not. He had good reason to want him dead, though."

"Hmm. I would have said that discovering there were other . . . interested parties, shall we say, makes it *less* likely Sean was involved."

"What other 'interested parties'?"

"Hamilton admitted that Clay was under obs by her people, which means they suspected he was playing some role in smuggling antiquities out of Iraq. If that's the case, and whoever he was working for thought he was compromised, who knows how they might have reacted. Or how far they might have gone trying to get that information out of him."

"That . . . actually makes a lot of sense," Parker said, his voice distracted. "But whoa, back up. Did you say Hamilton?"

"Yeah, she seemed to be in charge of the snatch squad. You know her?"

"Describe her."

I did so, briefly, watching the other people leaving the airport. Some were met by friends or relatives, but there wasn't the same level of hugging and crying you see at Western airports. Everyone seemed a little more restrained. Maybe it was just my frame of mind.

Nobody appeared to be watching me too closely, but I didn't like hanging around here. It was asking for trouble, under the circumstances.

"She sound like anyone you know?" I asked.

"Could be. Call me when you get to Madaba. I'll update you then. There's a reasonable hotel called the Mosaic City close to the center. It's walking distance to the property Hackett's using as his business address."

"I'll have to show ID when I check in, which will make it very easy for Hamilton's people to track me down," I warned. "I may not have long."

"Leave that with me. Official channels were no damn use, so now I'll try the unofficial ones."

He gave me the addresses of both Hackett's office and the hotel. I scrabbled for a pad in my bag and jotted them down, one-handed. "Sounds fine."

"By the time you get there, you'll have a room booked. And before you go breaking and entering or anything like that, don't forget to call me, OK?"

"Parker, I don't know what you mean," I said, and rang off hoping he wouldn't notice I'd given him no such assurances.

❖

Jordan was progressive as far as Middle Eastern nations went, but that didn't mean a woman driving alone wouldn't raise eyebrows. I opted for one of the taxicabs lined up outside the airport.

The driver was a youngish man, clean-shaven with a very white smile, wearing a T-shirt and Levi's. He seemed happy enough when I told him where I wanted to go.

"You are going to see the most beautiful and ancient of our mosaics while you are in Madaba?" he asked as we pulled out into traffic. "If so, and you have need of a guide . . . ?"

"I'm meeting up with friends when I get there."

"Ah, well if your friends need a guide, also, please call me."

"We won't have much time for sightseeing."

He glanced in the rearview mirror, eyebrows climbing. "Then why are you going to Madaba?"

It was a question I couldn't answer truthfully, so I didn't answer it at all.

How could I tell him I was going there to confront a man who'd taken everything away from me in the most brutal way possible?

Hackett had been the worst of the four. I'd been wary of him from the start, but somehow amid all the testosterone and macho posturing of a Special Forces training unit, the risk he'd posed to me personally had become gradually obscured. Until it was far too late to do anything about it.

I glanced at the taxi driver. Would what they did to me mean as much to someone from a part of the world where women were not seen as equals but as property—first of their fathers, then of their husbands? I thought again of Najida, the girl Dawson had introduced me to at the clinic in Kuwait City. She'd been through a similar experience of pain, fear, and violation. She, too, had turned to people she should have been able to trust with her story. Instead of believing and defending her, she had been betrayed and left for dead.

I wondered how my life would have turned out if I'd come through my own experience and been vindicated instead of vilified. It had dropped me into a deep, dark hole it had taken years to climb out of.

And now I was heading toward a meeting with one of the men who'd put me down there.

THIRTY-EIGHT

◈

LESS THAN AN HOUR AFTER MY ARRIVAL IN MADABA, I WAS LURKING across the street from Hackett's office in a store crammed with tourist souvenirs, including a *burqa*-clad Barbie doll. It also sold leather bags and belts, cheap cigarettes by the carton, magazines, postcards of the famous mosaics, cans of watered-down exotic juices, and rather crude representations of the better-known parts of the ancient Rose City at Petra. I was reminded of the statue Moe's Uncle Yusuf had foisted onto me, although I doubted any of these were priceless underneath.

I hadn't been back to see Yusuf and his family, I thought with a flush of guilt. Did he know the fate of his nephew? Did he blame us for it? He had every right to . . .

I glanced through the overstuffed front window of the store and saw a nondescript minivan pull up outside the office. A man got out, but the vehicle was tall enough to largely shield him from my view. He unlocked the door to the building and went inside. I caught no more than an impression—slim, wavy darkish-blond hair brushing the collar of a blue shirt.

It could have been Hackett, but then again . . .

I hadn't seen the man for years. Hadn't wanted to see him, either. It was bad enough when another of the four, Vic Morton, turned up on the close-protection circuit. I always knew it was a possibility I'd cross paths with one or another of them sooner or later. The career choices for ex-soldiers of their caliber tended to be somewhat limited. If they didn't become mercenaries, they usually became bodyguards.

But Hackett was different. He'd been a public schoolboy who'd joined the army under hazy circumstances. I wouldn't have been surprised if they'd caught him torturing small animals and given him no other option.

The military machine is noted for taking ordinary men and making killers out of them. In Hackett's case, they had to try to tone him down. With his background, he might have been considered officer material, but even the army realized that giving him the power of life and death over a group of others would have been a big mistake.

I turned away from the store window, paid for the oddments I'd selected, and waited while the owner bagged them and made change. The door to the office over the road stayed closed.

It was a short walk back to the hotel in high sun, the heat reflecting harshly from the stone streets. I took a circuitous route, stopping for coffee at a tiny shop-front café on the way. I took my time over drinking it, keeping an eye on the street while pretending to skim through the magazine I'd bought, even though it was in Arabic and all I could do was look at the pictures. Still, I hadn't bought it for the content.

Back at the hotel, I called Parker again.

"You hit traffic?" was his first question, dryly delivered.

I tipped out my shopping bag onto the bedspread. One ring-pull can of papaya juice drink, two leather belts, the glossy magazine, and a traditional red-and-white *keffiyeh* scarf. Not ideal, but it would have to do.

"No, I was doing a little shopping and getting the lay of the land."

"Did you find Hackett?"

"I found his office, no problem, and spotted a guy going into the place—not a local. Could have been him."

"Could have been a customer."

"Only if they hand out keys. I didn't get a good enough look at him for a positive ID, but the chances are, if it *wasn't* Hackett, this guy works with or for him and can tell me where he is."

"Don't you want to wait—keep an eye on the place until you've gotten that positive ID?"

"And what if Sean turns up in the meantime? For all I know, he could have been waiting inside already."

"He didn't fly out of Iraq—not on his own passport, anyway. If he traveled by land, the roads in the eastern part of Jordan are not an easy route. You may be ahead of him."

"I know, and I'd like to keep it that way."

"The question is, when you find Hackett, what are you going to say to him?"

I'd spent most of the journey from the airport to Madaba trying to work that one out. If it had been anybody else, the logical thing would have been to warn him that danger was possibly on its way and then wait for Sean to turn up so I could . . . what? Reason with him? Restrain him?

Kill him . . . ?

"I'll burn that bridge when I come to it," I said.

"Well, the good news is you won't have Hamilton on your back while you're doing it."

"Wow, I'm impressed. How did you manage that?"

"Played dirty—I talked to her mother."

"Her . . . ? How the *hell* did you know where to get hold of her mother? Isn't that classified, or something?"

"All I had to do was look in the client files," Parker said. "Aubrey Hamilton is the eldest daughter of Nancy Hamilton."

Nancy Hamilton was the one who'd hired me for my last assignment; she was a major financial supporter of a disaster recovery team, and she'd asked me to look into the death of the team's security adviser. In pursuit of that truth, I'd gone into the middle of an earthquake zone with them, uncertain which of them I could trust. Turned out their biggest worry was how far they could trust me.

"Well, it's a good thing she came away from it a satisfied customer, isn't it?"

"Yeah, isn't it just?" Parker murmured.

I hadn't told him just how far I'd gone in covering for the surviving team members, but he'd guessed anyway. And he was a good enough boss never to ask me outright. I'd always been more interested in justice than the legal definition of right and wrong, anyway.

"I can't believe that, however strong her maternal influence, Mrs. Hamilton would carry enough weight to get your three-letter-agency pals to back off, though."

"Maybe not, but when we spoke, she told me she had already given her daughter a glowing report of your abilities and suggested she might make use of you. That and the fact that you've had previous contact with certain *other* agencies, shall we say, and I don't think they'll be wasting their time chasing after you."

"Hmm, well, it would be nice to have one less enemy to worry about. Did Dawson make her flight OK in the end, by the way?"

"I hope those two thoughts aren't connected," he said, a smile in his voice. "Yeah, I liaised with Madeleine, and she's arranged for someone to collect Dawson from Heathrow when she lands. Sounds like she did a pretty good job for you."

"She did. I'd work with her again."

"That's lucky, because I'm thinking of offering her a contract, effective immediately, but she can start as soon as the shoulder's mended."

"She'll be over the moon. Thanks, Parker."

"Don't thank me. Arabic speakers are always in high demand."

"Yeah, let's just hope I don't need her here."

"Well, at least you know Hackett speaks English."

"True, but with a bastard like that, I'd rather it was two against one."

THIRTY-NINE

THE MAN WHO ANSWERED THE DOOR IN RESPONSE TO MY KNOCK was the same fair-haired guy in the dark blue shirt I'd seen earlier. He was not James Hackett, although in a lot of ways he had the same cocksure manner. Was it something that could be absorbed by proximity alone?

I didn't know whether to be relieved or disappointed.

"Can I help you?" he asked, politely enough, but without undue enthusiasm. I judged that the quick visual scan of me he carried out probably estimated fairly accurately my worth, and therefore the amount of business I was likely to bring his way.

Not enough to warrant the full-wattage smile, I saw.

"I'm looking for Jamie, actually," I said with enough of a drawl for him to recalculate quickly. "Jamie Hackett. Is he here?"

"Um, no, not at the moment. He's away—business, you know. I'm not expecting him back until later. Perhaps I can help?"

"Really? Oh *damn*. I was sure I emailed him the date I was getting in. He promised me dinner and a good time," I added with a wink. "Perhaps you *can* help me, after all."

The man flushed. He was maybe in his late twenties, and had the kind of pale English complexion that burns or blushes with equal, painful ease.

"I say, I'll just pop in and leave him the number of where I'm staying, shall I? Then he can call me the *moment* he gets back."

And with that I blithely pushed past him into a tiled hallway with grim overhead fluorescents and chipped tiles on the staircase at one side. I dropped my sunglasses into the shopping bag I'd slung over my arm. "Are you down here, or upstairs?"

His head jerked toward the upper floor almost automatically, and I trotted up the steps without waiting to see if he was following.

He soon caught me up. "Um, I'm really not sure if—"

"Nonsense, he'll be delighted! Through here? Oh, how charming. I do like what you've done with the place."

That earned me a quizzical look, and I can't say I blamed him for it. I was only talking so he didn't have a chance to tell me where I could and couldn't go.

The office was a large room divided in two by an opaque glass screen. The front half had been turned into a reception area, with a pair of sofas and a smoked glass coffee table, all of which went out of fashion sometime in the 1980s. On the walls were stock photographs of Jordanian landmarks in cheap frames—the Treasury at Petra, the Roman ruins of Jerash, biblical Mount Nebo, a resort on the Dead Sea. It looked like a job lot from a travel agency gone bust.

I didn't pause there long to admire the décor but kept moving past the frosted glass divider, rummaging in my shopping bag.

"Oh bugger, I can't seem to find a pen. Do you have one . . . ?" I pulled out the magazine and scarf in my search. "I'm sorry, darling, I don't know your name?"

"Ah, it's um, Docksy."

"Really? *You're* Docksy? How very cute."

It was a game to see if I could keep the blush in his cheeks. For all his initial swagger, he seemed to be far too easy to embarrass. A Hackett-wannabe rather than the real thing.

Behind the glass screen divider were two dark veneer desks shoved together at right angles. They were a mismatched pair, one slightly higher and wider. A laptop sat open on one—sleek and slim against its outdated surroundings. The other desk had a space clear of clutter just large enough for a similar laptop, but it was missing. Hackett's, I presumed.

I headed for the empty desk, moving past Docksy's own to get there. He dived for his laptop to palm the lid shut in a way that was guaranteed to make me look at the screen, even if I hadn't been intending to do so anyway.

Instead of any incriminating file or spreadsheet marked Ill-Gotten Gains, I caught a glimpse of a half-played hand of computer solitaire open on the desktop.

I laughed. "Don't worry, darling, I'm hardly going to rat you out to Jamie for skiving on work's time, am I? Besides it must be boring, all this importing and exporting stuff you do, anyway. What did you say it was, again?"

"I didn't," he said, stony now. He grabbed a pen from a mug on his desk and thrust it at me. I took my time putting down my stuff before I reached for it, smiling brightly to turn the snub into a more harmless gesture.

"Now then, if I can just find a tiny bit of paper . . ."

I ducked to lift the wastepaper basket, rifling through and plucking out an envelope. I scribbled a near-illegible note on a square I tore out of the back, adding a phone number that had the same phone code and first two digits as the Mosaic City Hotel but was entirely fictitious after that. I signed the note "Amanda"—with a flourish.

As I handed over both note and pen, I deliberately let go a fraction before he'd got his fingers to them.

"Oops, oh I'm *so* sorry, darling. How clumsy of me."

As he bent to retrieve them, I slipped the rest of the envelope into my bag. By the time he straightened again, I was pulling out my sunglasses. I perched them on top of my head, hoping they would stay there rather than fall off and make me look even more of an airhead than I did already.

"Well, I'll let you get back to your thankless toil." I gave him another wink. Oh God, much more of this and he was going to think I had a nervous twitch. I moved out around the desk. "It's been a pleasure to meet you at last, Docksy," I said over my shoulder as I headed for the door. "I've heard *so* much about you from Jamie."

I managed to get as far as turning the handle and pulling the door open just a crack before he shouldered in and slammed it shut again.

"What's the rush? You see, the funny thing is, *darling*, I've never known Jamie not to boast about his bits of skirt, and I've *never* heard a thing about you . . ."

FORTY

◈

I LET GO OF THE DOOR HANDLE AND STEPPED BACK. POINTLESS to tug at it when he was leaning his full weight against the panel.

Forcing a laugh, I said, "Hardly my fault if Jamie doesn't like to share *everything*, darling."

"Oh, but he does—like to share, that is. Just my point. He really gets off on it, in fact. And I should know."

I gave a shudder I didn't have to fake. I knew from experience that Hackett took a vicious delight in playing to an audience. What I hadn't realized was that rather than an aberration, it was his preference.

Docksy straightened and eased away from the door. His gaze was fixed on me, his movements predatory.

I maintained eye contact, allowing the strap of the bag to slip off my shoulder as I backed up another step.

Watching me, he smiled. "Which, *darling*, is how I know *you* are lying through your teeth. Question is, why?"

"Look, no offense, but I'm really not into all that kinky stuff." As my bag dropped past my elbow, I still had hold of the cotton scarf, one end of it bunched in my hand. "Clearly, I've misinterpreted the invitation I had from him and—"

He shook his head slowly. "Uh-uh. Somehow I don't think he ever sent you any invite. So, let's start again, shall we? Only with you telling the truth this time, otherwise not being into 'all that kinky stuff' is going to be the least of your worries."

I dropped the bag entirely, rolled the scarf in my hands as though in nervous tension.

"Of course I *could* just leave and we pretend this never happened?"

"Uh-uh. No way."

"You're really going to push this?"

"I really am."

I sighed. "Fuck it, then."

I flicked my eyes past his right shoulder to the closed door, telegraphing the move as much as I dared. As I darted forward, he was already reaching for me. I put my right arm out as if to fend him off and he took the bait, grabbing my forearm. He didn't look as though he spent all his downtime in the gym, but there was an unexpected strength to him.

Instead of pulling away, I closed in fast, sweeping the hand that gripped my arm up and around behind his back. By the time he began to let go, I'd already got a lock on his hand and wrist, winding it high and tight. He went rigid from pain that drove him to his knees.

As he dropped, I looped the rolled scarf around his neck, used it to control his head. Control the head, and the body will follow. I yanked him backward, riding him down.

At the last moment he realized what I was doing and kicked out, getting a foot against one of the sofas for leverage so the pair of us went sprawling. My grip on him loosened. He wriggled free, twisted to face me, and drove his body on top of mine.

"Thought you said you didn't like the kinky stuff, huh?" he grunted.

I wrapped one arm around his neck, dragging his head down to my shoulder in a parody of intimacy and trapping his arms close to my body so he couldn't get the distance he needed for a decent punch. He got a couple of blows in anyway, but they were halfhearted affairs.

The scarf was still draped around his neck. I managed to squirm up far enough to get hold of it on either side of his head, then I crossed my forearms in front of his throat and heaved.

As the choke hold bit, he tried to rear up away from me, but I kept my face buried into his shoulder so he had no choice but to take me with him. His hands flailed at my body, already weakening.

Unconsciousness hit him in a little over six seconds. I made a slow mental count, just to be sure, then released the pressure and kicked him away.

He began to recover almost at once, but was sluggish enough that I could reclaim my discarded bag and pull out the leather belts I'd bought from the tourist store across the street. I used them to secure his wrists and ankles, buckling them together behind him. The scarf covered his mouth, knotted firmly at the back. As an afterthought, I tied the ends to the belts, too, so the more he struggled, the tighter it became.

By the time I'd finished, he was back in the land of the living, writhing as he glared furiously at me over the gag. It was a bit makeshift, but it didn't have to hold him for any longer than it would take me to get clear of the place.

I patted his cheek, not gently. He snarled at me.

"I thought you were into the kinky stuff yourself?" I murmured as I rose. "And don't look at me like that, *darling*, I offered you a way out—twice."

FORTY-ONE

THE ENVELOPE I'D RESCUED FROM THE WASTEPAPER BASKET IN Hackett's office had his name followed by an address on the front of it, in both Arabic and English.

As the address, which didn't match the office, turned out to be in a fairly new residential district, I was betting it might just be his home. I could have tested the theory by waving it in front of the captive Docksy, but I'd decided against doing so for a couple of reasons.

One was I hadn't known if I was likely to be interrupted at any moment. Short of claiming I was some kind of down-market dominatrix Docksy had hired to relieve his stress levels at work, I hadn't seen how I could talk my way out of that one, and I hadn't fancied being thrown out of two countries in as many days.

The second reason was that I hadn't wanted him to know I'd found it and warn Hackett somebody knew where to find him.

Better to let them both think it had been a failed fact-finding mission. So as soon as I made it back to my hotel, I called Parker and relayed the address for him to check out.

Even so, by the time the sun bled over the western horizon and the amplified call to prayer from the mosques died away, I still didn't know for sure. The property was a large detached villa, owned by one holding company and rented by another.

It probably explained why Madeleine had given only Hackett's business address to Sean in the first place. Or she had been disingenuous. Either way, Parker had Bill Rendelson digging through the layers.

As we spoke, I stood by the window in my hotel room on the second floor, watching the street by the front entrance from behind the gauzy curtain. The lights in my room were off, so, unless someone was equipped with night-vision gear, I was invisible from outside.

"Docksy did say that Hackett would be back later"

"And you believed him?" Parker asked. "Besides, later today, or later this week?"

"I assumed today. And at that point in the proceedings he had no particular reason to lie."

"Ah, so that was *before* you hog-tied him." I could hear the amusement in his voice.

"What can I say—I didn't have anything handy to shoot him with."

"I can probably rectify that situation and have something 'handy' with you by midday tomorrow if you want?"

"Tempting, but I need to get to him tonight."

Before Sean does.

Vaguely, I heard Parker speak again, but I had no idea what he said.

Down in the street, a Range Rover pulled up by the steps leading to the hotel and four men got out.

The way they moved would have rung alarm bells whatever the circumstances. They didn't so much climb out of the vehicle as debus. Smooth and efficient, confident yet wary. It marked them as military or ex-military, even in civilian clothing. Three of the men were strangers. The fourth I recognized even from this angle.

It was the Russian Spetsnaz from Kuwait City. The one who'd had me lifted by the local cops, just to prove he could.

The one who'd warned me to give up my pursuit of Sean and go home.

I had followed neither piece of advice.

The Spetsnaz guy paused and looked around him, checking rooflines as well as street level. I resisted the urge to jerk back further into the shadows. I'd learned a long time ago that total immobility can counteract outrageous levels of exposure if your nerve will stand it.

"Charlie? I said hold off going for Hackett until you're armed. It's too risky otherwise. You hear me?"

The Russian continued up the steps into the hotel lobby. I became aware that I'd been holding my breath. I snatched the heavy curtains across the window and clicked on the bedside lamp.

"Yeah . . . no . . . Look, the Russians have just shown up downstairs."

"What the—? How the *hell* did they find you? Were you tailed from the airport?"

"Give me some credit, Parker. Unless they were using half a dozen revolving teams, drones, or a satellite, then no, I wasn't tailed."

"OK, I'm sorry. My bad."

I pulled my bag out of the wardrobe and swung it onto the bed, shoving the few things I'd unpacked back inside. "Besides, there was something a little casual about the way they just walked into the lobby."

"Oh?"

"If you were trying to execute a covert snatch, would you arrive at the front entrance, four up, and saunter in like you had all the time in the world?"

"Why not? Last time they pulled a fake traffic stop in broad daylight." I heard him breathe out. "No, OK. I would guess they're either checking all the hotels in the area—"

"—or they're checking in," I finished for him. "Either way, I still need to vacate."

"Just be careful, Charlie. Those Spetsnaz guys have some serious skills."

"I'm not exactly a damsel in distress," I said tartly.

"No, but if Sean's called in old markers and he *has* got them watching his back while he makes his next move—on Hackett—you're gonna be outnumbered as well as outgunned."

I collected my toothbrush from the bathroom and grabbed the drinks can I'd bought earlier, which I'd washed out and left to drain on the sink. I threw both into my bag, dragged the zipper shut.

"Jesus, Parker, how many times do I have to say it? We don't know Sean killed Clay. We don't even know the *real* reason he met with Lihaibi in Karbala, and we certainly don't know he's planning to go after Hackett and rip him limb from limb. Give the guy a fucking *break*, will you?"

There was a long moment of silence. I wondered briefly if I'd gone too far this time. Then he said quietly, "So why did he have Madeleine track down the current locations of those men if he wasn't planning to do exactly that?"

FORTY-TWO

I STOOD IN THE SHADOWS OF AN EMPTY, HALF-BUILT HOUSE, watching the darkened windows of Hackett's villa on the far side of the road. The exterior lights were on upstairs, and a flashy Audi was parked in the driveway, but there were no other signs of current occupation.

I tried to analyze the faint flicker of apprehension that wove through me. The last time I saw Hackett was outside court with his three codefendants after my disastrous civil suit. I'd been stung that our former commanding officer, Colonel Parris, had put in an appearance, as if lending an official stamp of approval to the men's acquittal. Clearly, their legal team had advised them not to crow in victory, but they hadn't been able to resist a few not-so-subtle sneers. At the time, I had not been so numb that I hadn't felt every one of them like thorns in my flesh.

It took me four years to come back from it, to be able to trust in myself, and in my abilities to deal with whatever might occur. Back then, in the immediate aftermath, the ordeal had been seared so viscerally into my psyche I thought I'd bear the scars forever. Maybe I still did.

There had been many paths traveled since, some far darker than others. I had come close to death several times. Indeed, I *had* died once, although as it hadn't taken, I suppose it could be described as little more than a technicality.

And I had visited death upon others.

I thought of the Russian, Kuznetsov, who'd been part of the ambush in Basra. A man I'd never met before the day he tried to kill me. Had he awoken that morning with any inkling it would be his last?

I tried to imagine him having dinner with his family, tucking his children into bed, washing his car or mowing his lawn. Anything to make him into a recognizable human being instead of simply a live-fire moving target, something to be neutralized.

Method and distance had a great deal to do with how I felt about it. Bringing a man down with an assault rifle, forty or so meters away, is a very different thing from taking their life by some means of direct contact to the body. Up close by necessity—and very, very personal. A cliché perhaps, but clichés are usually such because of the truth behind them.

I'd experienced both ways of killing. I'd been intimate enough to feel the last breath leave the chest and to see the precise moment the shine went out of the eyes. A moment of profound reality—of no return—for all concerned. For me, it caused anguish, yes, but not soul-searching, deep regret. Not as yet, anyway.

And unlike others I'd come across, it didn't give me a thrill, either.

Again, not as yet.

What would happen when I faced Hackett once more was another matter. He was a man for whom I still carried an abiding hatred, more so than the others. He'd been the ring-leader, the instigator, the one who'd urged them on when, just perhaps, they might have faltered as the sheer barbarity of what they'd been doing hit home.

But as I stood there in the dark, waiting, I recognized the underlying cause of my apprehension. It wasn't that I feared he would once again overpower me by strength or skill alone. I'd learned some hard and painful lessons in how to fight since then—in how to kill.

It was no longer just theory.

No, what worried me this time was that if Hackett made a move on me, I might be overcome by a fatal hesitation. Not because I couldn't bring myself to kill him but because I wanted it too much.

And I admit I was shit-scared of where *that* might lead.

I took a deep breath, moved out from behind the blockwork of the unfinished house, and walked across the road, keeping it all calm and casual. I had a headscarf covering my hair and neck in the style of a *hijab*. In the dark, shopping bag slung over my shoulder, only the fact that I wore trousers rather than a long skirt would give away that I was not a local.

The road itself was little more than a sandy dirt track with makeshift ramps leading to the driveway of each house. Unlike in the UK, where developers tended to put the infrastructure in first and the buildings second, over here the roads were left until last. And often, it seemed, left altogether.

I listened hard as I neared the house. Dogs were not as commonly kept as pets here as in the West, but they were still used for outside guard duty. My initial recce of the house had provoked no unexpected barking. There were only three closed-circuit cameras as far as I could tell, positioned in the more obvious places to cover the approaches.

Whatever Hackett had been doing in the years since the army, it had not been working in security.

I sidestepped the front door and moved around the perimeter of the house, keeping to the shadows.

The footprint of the building was roughly square, with balconies jutting out in odd places. Practical rather than elegant in design.

The plot sloped down at the rear, providing an extra lower story at the back. I checked the windows and doors carefully, but there was nothing that would allow me easy access.

On the far side of the house, however, one of the French windows on the middle floor was open just a crack. I levered myself over the stone balustrade, still warm to the touch from a day's absorption of the sun, and pressed close to the glass, hoping to see what lay inside.

A huge living room, from what I could tell, with overblown cream leather sofas, ornate lamps with blocky cut-glass bases, large dramatic canvases on the wall, complicated draping curtains, and yet more glass and chrome. Not hard to guess who had furnished the office.

I nudged the French window open wide enough to slip through and ducked sideways so I was not silhouetted against the glass.

While I waited for my eyes to fully adjust to the darkness, I listened intently.

Nothing.

I moved softly across the tiled floor to the doorway. It opened out into a generous hall and open stairwell. I took a few moments to check the other rooms. There was an en suite guest room and loo, but the rest on this floor were empty spaces, still awaiting furniture and designation. I guessed the kitchen and dining room were on the lower story at the back, and the main bedrooms upstairs.

I should make for the kitchen, I knew, where I would be most likely to find something I could use as a weapon—something better than I had brought with me, at any rate.

But as I stood in the hallway, a faint noise came from above. The sound of a stiff drawer being slid jerkily out of its housing. In the time it might take me to go down a level, search for a weapon, retrieve it, and then get up there, whoever was searching might have found what they were looking for and gone.

I couldn't take the risk.

With a grimace, I reached into the bag and pulled out the drinks can I'd saved earlier. I'd emptied it and torn it in half by twisting the top and bottom in opposite directions until the metal skin had split apart. The result looked relatively harmless, but the base fit comfortably into my hand, and the exposed edges were sharp enough to rip through skin and muscle like tissue paper.

Eyes upward, I moved cautiously to the wide staircase and began to climb.

FORTY-THREE

AS MY HEAD CLEARED THE LEVEL OF THE UPPER LANDING, THERE was enough moonlight coming in from the windows for me to see the ghost layout. An extravagant space with doors off to the bedrooms. The narrow slot of light shining from under one of the bedroom doors was bright in the gloom. It flickered and moved—the beam of a flashlight rather than the overheads.

I froze, straining to hear into the room beyond the closed door. More faint noises, quiet steps, furniture being opened and closed, the riffle of papers. Sounds of a search.

Not Hackett, then.

He would not, after all, have reason to be searching his own house so covertly, even if he'd mislaid something vital. So, who *did* have reason?

I thought of the Russians I'd seen arriving at the hotel. When they'd waylaid me in Kuwait City, I'd assumed they were working for Sean. Why else would they warn me off from continuing to search for him?

But if that was the case, why hadn't they carried out their threats to "incapacitate" me when I hired Moe and headed back to Basra? Maybe it had been Clay where their interest lay. Clay and his dodgy connections to Professor Lihaibi and Moe's Uncle Yusuf. And if Clay *was* involved in whatever they were up to, it wasn't unreasonable that his old army mate Hackett might be mixed up in the same thing.

How Sean fit into that scenario, though, I'd no idea.

Perhaps the person currently searching Hackett's bedroom might be able to fill in the blanks on that for me.

I put down my bag silently, keeping the ripped can in my left hand, and moved to the door. My heart rate was up, and I took a moment to breathe, to steady myself.

Surprise was on my side. If I effected entry with enough speed and aggression, even if the man inside—an assumption on my part, but more likely than a woman—was armed, the chances were he wouldn't have time to reach for a weapon.

I softened my knees, grasped the door handle, and went in fast.

As the door crashed open, I had a fraction of a second to take in the scene in the rapidly shifting beam of the flashlight. A huge double bed with a small safe next to it, standing open. A slippery spread of papers and documents on the polished floor. And a bulky figure with the flashlight, already starting to rise and twist toward the incoming threat.

The room was big, even by the standard of the rest of the villa. Even so, I was across it and launching for my opponent before he'd had time to reach for anything useful.

I hit him low, bowling him off his feet. He crashed backward, half onto the bed, and half bounced, half fell from there to the floor, landing with a hell of a crack.

He had enough training not to let the shock of the attack immobilize him, more's the pity. Even down and winded he fought back, lashing out immediately, using the flashlight to aim for strike points on my arms and body.

I blocked as best I could, slashed with my makeshift blade and felt it scrape across flesh, heard the grunt of reaction to the pain. He went for my left hand immediately, jabbing the end of the flashlight at my elbow joint. By luck or judgment, the blow connected solidly.

The lower half of my left arm went dead below an elbow that was suddenly on fire. The can dropped from my nerveless fingers and spun away under the bed. He tried to use the opportunity to get away from me, but I hurled myself at his legs and brought him down again.

He kicked out. I spun on my backside and booted him in the side of the head, wrapping my legs around his arm while he was still reeling, wrenching his wrist into a lock. By forcing his arm out straight across my thigh, I could over-extend his elbow while I planted the sole of my boot hard across his throat. Even then, he didn't stop thrashing.

"Give it up, man, or I'll break your fucking arm!"

To my surprise, all the fight went out of him. Even so, I didn't relax until he flicked the beam of the flashlight first across my face, then up to his own.

"Hello, Charlie," he said, and although his voice was hoarse from having my foot partly crushing his windpipe, I would have recognized it anywhere.

It was Sean.

FORTY-FOUR

I SWORE UNDER MY BREATH, HESITATED A MOMENT LONGER, THEN released him. He rolled to his feet and only staggered a little on his way to switch on the lamp by the bed. I glanced around automatically, but the thick bedroom curtains were closed.

"Damn it, Sean, I . . ." I almost said, ". . . *could have killed you.*" Instead changed it to "You're a hard man to find."

"I didn't ask to be found."

He turned, studied me. He wore cargo pants and a black T-shirt that was now torn across the stomach and glistened wetly. I swallowed back the words of regret, of concern, and brought my chin up.

"Well, *tough.* I was sent to find you. And now that I have, we're on the next flight out of here."

He ignored that, asked instead, "You were sent to find me by who?"

"Parker—who d'you think?"

He looked away, lips thinned in a face less forgiving than stone. I realized, too late, that he might have been hoping I'd come for him on my own account.

Ah well, too late for that now.

He was unshaven and looked dog tired, his skin taut across his bones and his dark hair longer than I was used to seeing it, hanging raggedly over his forehead. His eyes, entirely black in the shadowed lighting, were hollowed and haunted.

The face of a man on the edge, certainly, but pushed over it? I knew Sean's face as well as I knew my own, but that I couldn't tell.

"What happened between you and Michael Clay?"

I spoke gently. He looked at me and something flashed in his eyes, almost too fast to follow, then was gone again.

"I killed him. But first I tortured and mutilated him," he threw at me. "Is that what you hoped I might say?"

I heard my own indrawn breath, but I didn't move, didn't otherwise react, while adrenaline roared into my system, flooding me with the urge to flee. I held it back and kept my gaze on his face, on his eyes.

He blinked first, glanced down and dabbed at the blood oozing slowly through his slashed T-shirt.

"Of course it isn't," I said. "If I'd wanted that, don't you think I'd have gone after them myself by now?"

"It depends—on if you knew the right one to go after."

I sighed. "They all of them played a part in it, Sean."

"So how can you stand there and tell me *they* should be allowed to escape the consequences of their actions, yet at the same time knowing *you* went after the man who shot me? I didn't get a say in that decision."

"I went intending to catch him, not kill him," I said with as much sincerity as I could manage. "And at the time, you weren't in any position to *make* a decision."

"Then you should have waited until I was."

How could I tell him that, at that point in his coma, the best doctors Parker could hire thought it was more and more likely Sean wasn't ever going to come out of it? His brain activity was slowing down, his responses weakening. It felt as if he was dying, inch by inch, right in front of my eyes.

And taking me with him.

"I—"

"Besides, who says this is all about you? You weren't the only one *affected* by what they did, back then."

I said nothing, searching his face for any inkling of emotion. My heart was pounding in my chest, a double drumbeat in my ears that made my vision pulse in time with it.

I hadn't considered for a moment that Sean might be doing this with his own agenda. True, when our relationship had become known, he'd been slammed for it hard by the army brass. I learned later that they'd put an end to any career aspirations he might have had. Not only that, but they'd done their best to send him on missions that practically ranked as suicide, one after another.

And that part of his life—that part of me—was all he remembered when he finally woke from his coma.

Half of me genuinely rejoiced at the recovery he'd made. It had been a long road back, but he'd fought his way to strength and fitness. Another smaller, meaner part of me wondered if having him back but no longer mine was worse than not getting him back at all.

"How?" I demanded.

"How what?"

"How did you torture Clay?"

"You really want to hear all the gory details, Charlie? Never had you down as a closet sadist."

"Well I'm here, aren't I? I must be more of a bloody masochist instead."

"Like it rough, do you?" he mocked. "Oh, yes, now *that* I *do* remember . . ."

I bit back the flaming retort that rose like bile. Because I remembered it, too, from the last time we were together, just before he'd disappeared from New York and surfaced again in Kuwait City. I'd seduced him, for want of a better word, without tenderness or delicacy, relying on his abstinence and lust to get me past his doubts. That and an intimate knowledge of his weaknesses, of the things he found hardest to resist.

"Just answer the damn question, will you?" I said quietly.

"You want a blow-by-blow account? Ask away."

"How did you immobilize him—did you drug him?"

"Something like Rohypnol, you mean? Where would I have got hold of that at short notice?"

I nodded, but at the same time some of the tension went quietly out of my neck and shoulders. Clay *had* been drugged, I knew that for certain—if not to restrain him beforehand, then certainly to keep him conscious during—and if Sean didn't know that . . .

"You met him at the hotel, the day before, and you argued. What about?"

"About digging up the past, of course. Not surprisingly, he wanted to let sleeping dogs lie."

"And you didn't."

"No."

"Why?" The bitten-off word hung stark between us. *It's history. Another life. Why do you care?*

He raised an eyebrow in my direction.

"You know why. What they did to you was appalling, but they took me down, too. They have a debt owing—to both of us."

I shook my head. "This is no way to repay any kind of debt. Not for me, it isn't."

"Spoken like a coward, Charlie." He was taunting me again. "Justice is always worthwhile, even if it involves making a noise and a mess to get to the truth of it."

I shied away from exploring the kind of mess that had been made of Michael Clay, instead asked doggedly, "If he wouldn't talk about it at the hotel, why arrange to meet him in Basra?"

"I sent him a message, asked if he was up to his old tricks again, and how his current employers might take the news."

"What old tricks?" I demanded. It was on the tip of my tongue to ask what he had found out about the rapes and Najida, the woman in the Kuwait City clinic.

He shrugged. "Nothing for definite, but back when he was a squaddie, Clay always had something a little shady going on the side, so it was a one-size-fits-all kind of threat."

I heard the evasion in his voice but didn't call him on it.

"Where did you pick up your Russian pals?"

"What Russian pals?" His surprise seemed real.

"The ex-Spetsnaz boys you got to warn me off—twice. Once in Basra and again in Kuwait City."

He shook his head. "Nothing to do with me. If the Russians have stepped in, they're playing their own game."

I stilled, recalling the way the Russian guy had delivered his threat. After the initial ambush failed—something he'd described as an unauthorized mistake—he'd gone to some lengths to persuade me I should quit, without resorting to actual physical violence. And if it wasn't Sean who "knew me and had my best interests at heart," who *was* behind it?

"So the fact they turned up here in Madaba, the same time as I did—at the same hotel—is just a coincidence, is it?"

"Coincidences do happen occasionally." He frowned. "They're here?"

"They were checking in via the lobby at the time as I was checking out, in a manner of speaking, via the balcony."

He went to the window, his movements steadier now, and peered around the edge of the thick curtains down into the street below.

"You're sure they didn't tail you?"

Why was it *everyone* assumed I wouldn't notice that? "I'm not an amateur, Sean."

He let go of the curtain, touched the rips in his T-shirt again, and grimaced slightly. "No, you're not, are you."

"You ought to let me take a look at that," I said, adding pointedly, "before we head for the airport."

He hesitated a beat, then came back across the room. "Yeah, sure."

I jerked my head toward a second door over to my left. "Bathroom?"

He nodded.

I took a couple of steps and opened the door. The smell hit me almost at once. I was already turning back when Sean hit me just below my shoulder blades, hard enough to knock me off my feet and send me sprawling headlong onto a hard tile floor.

The door slammed shut behind me, leaving the room in utter darkness. I groped for the door, felt my way up to the handle, and rattled it hard. He must have jammed something under it on the outside, because it wasn't going anywhere.

I slammed my hand against the door panel in sheer frustration. "Sean, for fuck's sake!"

"Sorry, Charlie, but I'm not done here." His voice, even muffled by the hardwood door, did not sound in the least bit regretful.

"You don't know what you're risking if you go on." I tried to keep the desperation out of my voice but did not succeed.

"Oh, I think I do. No more than I've already risked by coming this far. You might even thank me for it one day."

"You're a bloody fool," I yelled. "And I know you didn't kill Clay."

There was a pause. "Well, that's something, at least. Try not to let anyone convince you to think the worst of me, no matter what happens next."

"What the hell does that mean?"

But only silence greeted me. Cursing under my breath, I fumbled outward from the door frame, looking for a light switch and hoping it wasn't on the outside.

My fingers closed on it with relief. Half a dozen sunken spotlights blazed on in the ceiling, and I was forced to screw my eyes shut against the glare.

When I opened them again I found I was in an opulent tiled bathroom, but I didn't have time to take in the details.

I was too busy staring at the dead man in the bathtub.

FORTY-FIVE

***

"SO IF IT *WASN'T* HACKETT?" PARKER SAID. "THEN WHO . . . ?"

"A guy called Docksy. I doubt that's the name on his passport, but it was how he introduced himself when I met him yesterday morning," I said. "He told me he worked with Hackett."

I was in yet another hotel room, across from the Queen Alia International Airport. I'd grabbed a taxi and driven straight over here without returning to my hotel in Madaba. It was now midmorning the following day, although so far I hadn't booked a flight out. I'd wanted to report back to Parker first, see where he wanted to take this. And, if I was honest, I'd also wanted to put as much distance as possible between me and the corpse.

"And . . . Sean?"

I heard the tension in his voice and knew he didn't want to come right out and ask what he was desperate to know. I deliberately sidestepped—not from cruelty but from cowardice.

"By the time I kicked my way out, he was long gone. I grabbed all the documents from the safe, just in case, wiped down anything I'd touched, and got out of there."

I'd even fished under the bed to retrieve my improvised drink-can weapon. It still had Sean's blood on it. Not something I was eager to leave behind for the Jordanian cops.

Parker sighed. I could almost see the frustrated wipe of hand across face that accompanied the sound.

"Did he do it, Charlie—yes or no?"

"How can I be expected to answer that? I'm not a forensic pathologist."

"And I'm not *asking* for a physical autopsy—more a psychological one."

My turn to let my breath out, slowly.

"From the way it was done . . . I don't know. It wasn't Sean's style, somehow."

"Interesting choice of word to describe killing a man."

"What I meant was garrotes can be messy—especially if it's a thin wire, which is what the killer used, from what it looked like." I had a brief mental image of Docksy's bloated and discolored face, stark against the white tub, with the bloodied groove from the ligature sliced into his flesh. He'd fought, from the looks of it, clawing at the weapon with fingers that were torn and bloodied, too. I shook it off.

"Sean was more than capable of breaking the guy's neck—quick, clean, and quiet. And less chance of acquiring bloodstains he'd have to hide."

"I'm assuming there weren't any?"

I hesitated. When he'd switched on the lamp, there had been blood on Sean, but I'd taken it for his own.

"Not as far as I could tell," I hedged, and Parker seemed to accept that—for now, at least.

"I hate to paraphrase good old Oscar Wilde—being found with *one* body might be considered unfortunate—"

"—but two is carelessness," I finished for him. "Yeah, I know. But even so, I still can't quite see Sean doing something like this. Why would he kill Docksy anyway? As far as I know they'd never met. The guy meant nothing to him."

The silence hummed between us for what seemed like a long time. I stared out the hotel window at a few air-conditioning units and distant jets climbing steadily into a cloudless dark blue sky.

"And are *you* OK?" Parker asked then. The question surprised me.

"I'm fine. I got the drop on him and he came off worse for once."

"Not exactly what I had in mind, although I'm glad to hear it anyhow. No, I meant . . . seeing Sean again."

"Well, I can't say being shoved into a bathroom with a corpse was my idea of the perfect end to a romantic evening, but . . . yeah, I'm OK. You don't need to worry that I won't be able to separate my head from my heart, Parker. I know exactly what Sean's capable of, and honestly, I don't think it's this."

"OK, so let's say, for the sake of argument, Sean is in the clear," he said, and I wondered if the change of subject was to hide his doubt. "If that's the case, why would someone want to kill this guy Docksy, and what was he doing at Hackett's villa?"

"The two things could be connected. Once he got loose from the office, Docksy might have headed there to warn Hackett someone was looking for him, and was mistaken for Hackett himself. They were a similar type. If you were working from a poor photo or a brief description, in the dark, it would have been an easy mistake to make—particularly the way it was done. Usually, you would garrote somebody from behind, don't forget." With a knee between their shoulder blades for good measure.

"So it's possible the killer didn't see his face until afterward," Parker said slowly. "OK, good point."

"But Sean knew Hackett—he trained him. He would have known."

"But if it *was* simply mistaken identity, who else would want Hackett dead?"

Other than Sean, you mean? Or me, for that matter.

"How long have you got?" I asked with humor that was half-hearted at best. "What we should be asking is who else would want both Hackett *and* Clay dead. But considering Hamilton said they had their eye on Clay with regard to smuggling, and Hackett's in the export trade . . . there has to be something in that, surely?"

"Hmm, you could be right. I'll check it out. Ex-military guys do tend to stick together in civilian life."

"Speaking of ex-military guys, any more info on our Russian friends? I find it a bit of a coincidence that they arrived in Madaba around the time another body joined the pile."

"You think maybe they turned up at your hotel *after* they'd been to Hackett's place?"

"That is also a possibility. I suppose it depends on how long Docksy was dead by the time I got to him. He was still fairly pliable, although his face had started to stiffen, and from memory I think that's where rigor sets in first. But I don't know if the fact he was strangled would affect that."

"Ah, not my area of expertise, I'm happy to say."

"Either way, if the Russians aren't working on Sean's behalf, we have to rethink their involvement in all this. I have no idea who else would go to those lengths to warn me off without getting violent about it."

"Charlie, they tried to blow up the SUV you were traveling in," Parker muttered. "What's your definition of 'violent'?"

"Well, they could have finished the job when they hijacked me with Dawson in Kuwait City, but they didn't. Instead, they passed on their warning and then seemed to back right off."

"How soon after that did you hire Moe?"

I thought back, counting the days. It was incredible to realize how little time I'd actually been on this job. From the inside, it felt like years.

"The following day. I got back to the hotel, then the next morning Dawson and I followed Bailey to the airport and met an ex–Royal Marine, Osborne, who told us about the fixer. We put the word out right away, and Moe turned up that afternoon."

"Hang on, let's backtrack. You said you followed Bailey to the airport, yeah?"

"Yeah, but it was some ungodly hour of the morning."

"Nevertheless, it coincided with the departure time of a flight to the UK. If the Russians were keeping tabs on you, it might have seemed like it was *you* who'd decided to cut and run."

"OK, yeah, that would fit," I agreed. "Question is, when they delivered their 'go home' order, were they warning me off following Sean, or from following up on Clay?"

"You got me there. I don't suppose there was anything useful in the documents you, ah, borrowed from Hackett's place?"

"Something in Cyrillic, you mean? No, it's mainly shipping manifests and invoices, as far as I can tell. Nothing marked Top Secret—For Your Eyes Only, unfortunately."

"Shipping manifests . . ." Parker repeated. "Why would he keep them in his safe at home rather than at the office?"

I shifted from the window, dug the sheaf of papers out of my bag, and spread them across the bed.

"I don't know. Let me have another look through and get back to you—"

A brisk knocking on the door and a muffled call of "House-keeping" stopped me midsentence.

"What?" Parker demanded.

"Wait one."

I moved to the door, keeping out of direct line between that and the window, so the light through the Judas glass wouldn't alter. As always, my doorstop was firmly wedged underneath, and all the dead bolts activated.

I took a squint through the peephole. A woman stood alone in the corridor outside. She was dressed in black, looking less like a chambermaid than anyone I have yet to see.

I sighed, unbolting the door and nudging the doorstop aside with the toe of my boot. I opened the door, and the woman stepped inside without waiting for an invitation.

Eyes on her face, I said down the phone to Parker, "I'm going to have to call you back. I think the CIA are about to throw me out of yet another country."

FORTY-SIX

❖

FROM THE EXPRESSION ON HER FACE AS SHE CAME IN, IT WAS HARD
to tell if Aubrey Hamilton was pleased or displeased to see me.
She was very hard to get a fix on. I made a mental note never
to take up any offers to play poker against her for money.

The motivations of the man who muscled along the corridor to join her were easier to fathom, though. Woźniak—
the one who'd been instrumental in gunning down
Moe—looked like he'd rather saw off his own toes using a
blunt nail file than be in my hotel bedroom without a black
hood and a set of handcuffs. And I don't mean that in any
kind of a good way.

He covered his unease by flexing his fingers and scowling
while he carried out a brief search.

"Weapons, recording devices, or contraband?" I asked
pleasantly.

"All of the above," Hamilton said. She folded herself elegantly into an easy chair—the one farthest from the window—and propped her elbows on the side arms, steepling her fingers.

I tried, as casually as I could, to gather the papers I'd stolen from Hackett's safe, in the guise of clearing myself a space to sit down on the bed opposite.

After a few minutes Woźniak stood still and cleared his throat. When Hamilton glanced at him, he shook his head.

"Thanks," she said, dismissive. "I'll take it from here."

Woźniak moved for the door and hesitated there, his eyes on me.

"Don't worry," Hamilton told him. "If I need help, I'll scream like a girl."

He scowled at her—the scowl of a protective parent forced to leave his daughter alone with someone who was very probably on the sex offenders register. But he went out without further word. The self-closing mechanism pulled the door to softly behind him. It latched, and then it was just the two of us.

I leaned forward, resting my forearms on my knees, and we sat facing each other. I gauged the distance between us—little more than two meters.

"You do realize you'd never get the chance to scream, don't you?"

"You may be a very proficient and able killer, Charlie, but nothing I've read or been told about you leads me to believe you're psychotic." She smiled, and it almost reached as far as her eyes. "Well, maybe *borderline* psychotic . . ."

That was before I watched a kid I'd grown to really rather like slaughtered without being given a chance by men under your command.

I almost said the words out loud, but I held both my tongue and my hand, not without effort. It took more effort still to ask, "Would you like coffee? I can ring down for some."

Such pretty manners would have made my parents proud.

Hamilton accepted with an incline of her head. She'd clearly had the training that said to refuse hospitality wasn't the best way to get someone on-side. While I called to order room service, I could feel her gaze on me.

When I took my seat on the bed again, she finally spoke.

"I never thought I'd hear myself say it, but this is one time I should have listened to my mother."

I raised an eyebrow and said nothing.

"She was singing the praises of 'the young woman from the Armstrong-Meyer agency' over that whole business with the rescue and recovery outfit she donates so heavily to. I admit I didn't pay enough attention for your name to click when I heard it again." Her smile was wry, a little twisted. "Careless of me."

It was not a mistake she'd make again, I guessed. I hoped Nancy Hamilton was prepared to be grilled by her daughter over every future move she would make.

"And if you *had* been paying more attention?"

She snorted. "If I'd known you were the one who'd gotten herself swallowed by an earthquake and still came out fighting? I would have sent more men to make damned certain you got on that plane." She paused, waiting for a reaction I wasn't prepared to give. "Either that, or I would have hired you."

"Am I supposed to be flattered?"

"Not particularly, but I sure as hell didn't expect you to be insulted, either."

"Really? Considering the last time we met, you had your pet thugs snatch me off the street, killing my driver—little more than a kid—in the process? Then you accuse me of interfering with your operation, threaten me with prison, and deport me under guard. If that's supposed to make me feel all warm and fuzzy inside at the thought of you, then I'm afraid you're destined for disappointment."

She let out a long breath. "Yeah, I guess when you put it like that . . ."

There was a knock on the door. When I rose to check the Judas glass, I saw Woźniak outside with a tray balanced in one hand, having intercepted my coffee order. I opened up to relieve him of his burden, then pointedly shut the door in his face without offering him a cup. Mean, but not without a twinge of satisfaction.

The coffee was Jordanian, scented with cardamom, in a small pot with two equally tiny, handleless cups. As I poured us a mouthful each, I said over my shoulder, "I assume I'm about to get another ride to the airport, although you could have sent your boys to do that. So, why are you here, Aubrey?"

Her eyes flicked to mine at the mention of her first name. She was frowning as she took the cup I held out to her, but that could have been down to the quantity of her beverage rather than my question.

"I don't like making mistakes," she said after a moment's silence. "And I think trying to shut you down when we last met may have been just that—a mistake."

"Oh?"

"I've since found out that you're very good at what you do. The fact you used us to get you as far as you wanted to go, then gave us the slip, kinda proves it. I was impressed." She smiled into her coffee. "Mad as hell, yes, but impressed all the same."

I took a sip of my coffee and reminded myself she was a spook, and therefore manipulating people was what *she* was good at.

"Why do I have a feeling there's 'an offer I can't refuse' coming?"

"Because you've seen too many old movies?" she suggested. The smile ghosted away as she added, "I'm about to seriously overstep my authority, but I want to level with you."

"In return for . . . ?"

"Information is a two-way street, Charlie. That's how it works."

The offer surprised me, even with strings attached. And if my experience with other clandestine government agencies was anything to go by, they would be bloody big strings.

"What makes you think I can tell you anything you don't know already? After all, I'm on my own . . . now," I said with just a little bite. "You've got the might of the US government at your beck and call."

"That's just it. We've had a recent . . . change of direction at the top, if I can put it like that. I don't know how much longer we'll be allowed to do our job out here."

"And—don't tell me—you hate leaving things unfinished, too."

She nodded and drained the last of her coffee—they really were tiny cups. "You got that right."

"What was Uncle Sam doing taking an interest in looted antiquities in the first place?"

"Penance?" She pulled a wry face. "Truth is, we fucked up over here. All that planning—all the logistical analysis and projections and all the bullshit that went on for a year or more before we invaded in '03, and nobody worked out the first thing people would do, soon as the heavy hand of Saddam was lifted, was go rob their own back yard."

"Surely, after what happened in Kuwait . . . ?"

"Even after the invasion," Hamilton went on, leaning back in her chair and crossing her legs, "we had, like, two guys—reservists—who knew about archaeological remains. So did we utilize their expertise? Like hell we did. One was drafted into planning for a refugee crisis that never materialized, and the other made so much noise about what was going on, he ended up getting himself reassigned guarding a goddamn zoo.

Meanwhile, every site of significance in Iraq was being robbed six ways from Sunday. Can you believe it?"

"All too easily, I'm afraid."

"Damn right. Thing is, the Hague passed some kind of resolution back in the '50s for the 'protection of cultural property in the event of armed conflict.' It's in the rules that we're supposed to put a stop to theft, pillage, or vandalism."

Professor Lihaibi had blamed the Americans for the looting that went on after the second Gulf War. At the time I'd thought him biased. An error on my part.

"Excuse me for being a tad cynical, but it seems a little late in the day for the US government to be growing a conscience, and having met Lihaibi, I don't believe he has one, either, so what more is going on here?"

She paused, favored me with another of those sharp, assessing glances. "Smart cookie, aren't you, Charlie?"

No, if I were that clever, Moe wouldn't be dead and Sean wouldn't have got away from me last night . . .

I said nothing.

"Isis is what is going on," Hamilton said then. "They make this big song and dance about destroying ancient sites that don't scan with their view of things, but most of that's just a cover. They're clever and adaptable, and since we disrupted production at many of the oilfields they seized, and stopped them trading livestock or crops from captured territory, they've gotten a huge percentage of their funding from those looted antiquities."

"If what you—and Lihaibi—say is true, I'm surprised there's anything left for them to loot by this time."

"Ah, well, at the start, the Isis high command took a twenty percent cut on stuff others were digging up. Call it tax, call it commission—the result's the same. I guess if the IRS was allowed to chop off your hands if they caught you trying to weasel out of paying, we'd have a hell of a lot less tax evasion going on back home."

"I thought they already could."

She snorted again.

"By the end of 2014, Isis decided, 'Hey, why let somebody else take eighty percent when our need is greater than theirs?' and they brought in their own archaeologists and teams with bulldozers. Now they've taken over the business almost entirely. They even scour the online markets to find out what's in demand so they can work out what's worth digging up."

"Where did Michael Clay come in?"

"Somehow they're shifting large amounts of contraband artifacts out of Iraq and Syria, and so far we have not been able to identify the route taken, or who's responsible for shipping, but we suspect they're using outsiders rather than people from their own network."

"When you say outsiders, you mean Western contractors—people like Clay?"

"It makes sense when you stop to think. They're moving in and out of the country all the time, often with large supplies of construction materials. Because of the political situation, and the speed everything is moving, the checks and balances don't always work the way they should."

I thought for a moment, nose over my cup to inhale the lingering scent of warm cardamom. "What would make someone like Clay—someone who's spent most of his professional life shooting Isis members on sight—suddenly want to work *for* them?"

In reply, Hamilton lifted her hand and slid her thumb back and forth across the tips of her fingers.

"Money," she said. "And, oh boy, lots of it."

"It would bloody need to be. Must be a bit like making a living putting your head in a man-eating lion's mouth every night of the week, and two matinee performances on Saturday."

"Exactly. So, when Clay was killed, at first we thought he'd fallen foul of his masters. A reasonable assumption—these are not people you wanna get on the wrong side of. Then, of course, we found out about Sean Meyer—and, through him, you—and that put a whole different spin on what was done to Clay, and perhaps why."

"Not by Sean, and not on my behalf, I can assure you," I said quickly. "He might have tracked down Clay, but I'm convinced now he didn't kill him. He didn't know enough of the details."

Hamilton stared at me. "You found him?" she demanded. "Already?"

I hid a smile at her obvious consternation. "I wasn't sure how much time I might have before you caught up with me, so . . . yes, I've seen Sean and spoken with him."

"Dammit. I was right—I *should* have hired you when I had the chance. Where is he now?"

"That one's not quite so easy to answer. We didn't exactly part friends." I sighed, wondering where to begin. "There was this body, although I'm pretty sure Sean didn't kill *him*, either—"

"OK, hold it right there." Hamilton held up one hand, palm outward, rubbing the other wearily across her eyes. "I think you better start at the beginning." She rose, moved to the hotel phone on the bedside table. "But first I'm going to order up more coffee—and not in goddamn dollhouse-size amounts this time."

FORTY-SEVEN

BY THE TIME I'D GIVEN HAMILTON A REPORT ON MY ACTIVITIES SINCE arriving in Jordan, we'd got through another two trays of coffee and my brain was reeling from caffeine overdose.

I told her everything, more or less. Holding back didn't seem likely to gain me much, and if I could get her looking into who else might have gone after Clay—not to mention using her greater resources to search for the Russians—it all helped take the heat off Sean.

As soon as I'd told her about Docksy's body, she called in Woźniak from lurking in the corridor and sent him off on the trail of the ex-Spetsnaz guys. He seemed glad to have something active to do. I had a mental image of her shouting, "Fetch!" and him lolloping away with his ears flying and his tongue hanging out.

Then I remembered Moe and the image faded.

Hamilton nodded to the documents I'd piled up on the pillow. "I'm guessing these are the papers you took from the safe at this guy Hackett's place?"

"Technically, they were already out of the safe by the time I arrived."

She raised an eyebrow. "Tell *that* to the judge."

I handed them across and she put on the same heavy-rimmed reading glasses she'd worn in Karbala. Initially, she looked as nonplussed by the content as I had.

"Did Meyer say if the safe was locked or open when he got there?"

I shook my head. "It didn't come up. Why?"

"Just wondering if these were left by accident or design," she murmured. She began to sort the papers into two piles.

It only took a glance to realize she was separating out the shipping manifests.

"Parker suggested that if Hackett and Clay were still pally after the army, they might have been in business together now," I said. "And if Clay was smuggling, and Hackett is in international shipping . . ."

"Uh-huh, and if the stakes are as high as we know they are, and the risks are as great, then if Hackett thought he was in danger, would he be the kind of guy who might decide this Docksy was a loose end he couldn't afford to leave behind before he ran?"

That threw me. It took a moment to realize I had my mouth open. I shut it again quickly. "Wow. I was thinking along the lines of Docksy being killed in error, because someone mistook him for Hackett," I said. "I confess it didn't cross my mind he might have been killed *by* him."

"Ah, well, you spend a coupla decades in my line of work, you kinda get into the habit of thinking the worst of everyone. Occupational hazard."

254

"And to answer your question—yes, he was *absolutely* that kind of slimy bastard."

"Question is, where would he run *to*?"

"Parker reckoned the company Hackett was running in Madaba was little more than a front. His people are going through Hackett's financials, so they might uncover another property—something he might use as a safe house." I gestured to the papers she'd culled from the rest. "Anything useful in those?"

She shrugged, pushing back the sleeves of her fine-knit polo neck as if about to get her hands dirty. "If he lit out in enough of a hurry to have left these behind without checking them too closely, then yeah."

"But if he had more time, and took anything sensitive with him, then what we have here is worthless," I concluded.

She pulled a face and nodded.

"Still, there's something I'd like to check out . . ." She picked up her phone, speed-dialed a number, and, while it connected, showed me the sheet she was interested in. It was a manifest for a container ship called the *Dolphin*, which seemed like the kind of name you'd give a sailing dinghy or a rowboat rather than a however-many-thousand-ton cargo vessel. It had sailed from the port of Aqaba, at the northern end of the Gulf of Aqaba, yesterday morning—just about the time I was watching Docksy arrive for his last ever day at work.

Hackett's company, I noticed, had space for fourteen T.E.U.s booked on board.

"Pardon my ignorance, but what's a T.E.U.?"

"Twenty-Foot-Equivalent Unit," Hamilton said, holding the phone in place between chin and shoulder. "Standard size for a shipping container. Each one holds around thirteen hundred sixty cubic feet."

I did some fast mental arithmetic. "Is it just me, or would just shy of twenty thousand cubic feet hold a hell of a lot of mosaics?"

Hamilton threw me a distracted grin and began snapping orders to whoever picked up at the other end of the line. I moved to the window to give her space, tipped the spout of the coffeepot over my cup with more hope than expectation. What came out was closer to sludge than coffee. I put it back on the tray.

When she ended the call, I stuck my hands in my back pockets.

"Well?"

She shrugged. "Fortunately, the US Navy has beefed up its presence in the Arabian Sea to keep a check on materials destined for the Iranian nuclear program. If the *Dolphin* turns south once she reaches the Gulf of Aden, they'll head her off at the pass."

"And if she turns north for Suez?"

"Well, I do believe we just so happen to have an increased presence in the Mediterranean, also, to help with the refugee crisis. Either way, she'll be stopped and boarded."

"I have to say, Aubrey, I'm impressed you have that kind of clout."

She laughed. "Don't be fooled. The navy gets all the big guns, and those boys just love to get 'em out and play with 'em," she said. "Wanna come along for the ride?"

FORTY-EIGHT

"WHAT DO YOU *MEAN* YOU TURNED HER DOWN?"

The disbelief in Parker's voice might have been comical in other circumstances.

"Just that—I said no."

"Just like that, you said no to going aboard a United States battleship to pursue, stop, and board a suspected smuggler? You've no soul, Charlie."

"Yeah, I'm sure it would have been quite an experience," I admitted, "but stopping the flow of looted artifacts from the Middle East is Hamilton's job. Mine is to get hold of Sean again and *keep* hold of him this time."

"I guess when you put it like that, I should be congratulating you on your single-minded determination to get the job done."

"Yes you should," I agreed primly. "I expect flowers and a raise when I get back, at the very least."

"You know I'd send you a dozen red roses every day, Charlie, if I thought you wouldn't make me eat them." It might have been said lightly, but somehow I knew it was not intended to be taken the same way.

"Hmm, it probably wouldn't be a good idea, would it?" My own tone was gentle, and, though it hadn't been my intention, it contained a hint of regret.

Parker was a quiet man who did not often let his feelings show. He'd revealed himself to me while Sean had been in his coma, and neither of us had been comfortable about that. Another time, another place, maybe Parker and I might have got together, but there were all kinds of reasons why it was never going to happen, even though Sean had made it clear that he and I had very little future.

There were always going to be the misogynists and the chauvinists in the private security industry who refused to believe that female operatives could keep pace with the guys. Therefore, twisted logic dictated that any women employed in the upper echelons must have slept their way to the position. Any relationship I had with Parker outside the office would instantly add fuel to the fire.

And, one way or another, I'd been through more than enough of that already.

Parker cleared his throat into the silence that had fallen between us and said, "We haven't found any other property listed where Hackett might have gone to ground. So, what's your next move?"

"I'm not sure hanging around here is a good idea. Sean now knows I'm after him, which means he's going to cover his tracks more thoroughly, and I can't make any kind of official inquiries without having some very awkward questions to answer about Docksy's murder."

"I concur, although I think Hamilton might be able to keep some of the heat away from you."

"Ha, in a country that's mostly sand and desert, that might be a tall order." I let my breath out long and slow. "So, there's only one name left on the list."

"Donalson?"

"Uh-huh. I assume Madeleine gave you a location for him along with the others?"

"She did, but are you sure you want to do this, Charlie? I mean, I appreciate it was hard enough for you—going after Sean—without bringing back a whole mess of bad memories on top of that."

"I'm trying not to think of it as bringing back bad memories," I told him. "Instead, I'm laying ghosts to rest."

FORTY-NINE

I FLEW OUT OF AMMAN ON AN AIR FRANCE PLANE THAT LEFT IN THE middle of the night and arrived in Manchester, via Paris, before breakfast. As I shuffled through the formalities of Immigration and Passport Control, I felt weary to my bones and thoroughly secondhand.

So when I emerged through the airlock of Customs into the Arrivals hall, I initially didn't register the woman calling my name. And when I did, my first thought was that bloody Hamilton had tracked me all the way here as well.

But when I turned, it was to see Madeleine Rimmington waving from the other side of the barrier. She was dressed in what looked like a black quilted ski jacket with fake-fur hood thrown back, belted at her narrow waist, designer black trousers and boots, and she was smiling.

I suppressed a groan. Madeleine has never been anything other than pleasant to me, but something about her always rubbed me the wrong way. She was tall, elegant, clever, and articulate, as if that wasn't enough reason to dislike her. When we first met, I thought there was something going on between her and Sean—an impression not dispelled by the fact she was running interference against his matchmaking mother. Since then, I discovered Madeleine's happily engaged to a chef, but a faint antagonism lingers—on my part, anyway.

Now I wished I'd taken a moment to visit the ladies to run a comb through my hair and splash some cold water on the bags beneath my eyes. In my defense, I hadn't been expecting anyone to meet me.

"Hi, Madeleine," I said, trying to inject enthusiasm into my voice. "What are you doing here?"

She smiled at me, a high-wattage smile that made the stranger who'd been walking alongside me falter in midstride just from the by-blow. She had that effect.

"How could I let you come in alone without being here to meet you?" she said, reaching for my scruffy bag. "Is this all your luggage?"

I nodded, distracted, as I fell into step. "It must be a three-hour drive from Kings Langley. When did you set off?"

"Oh, I came up last night," she said breezily. "I'm at the Radisson Blu. Thought you might appreciate a shower before I take you on wherever you need to go."

I stopped dead. "Madeleine, you can't—" I hesitated, took a breath, and started again, trying to sound more reasonable. "I don't think it's a good idea for you to come anywhere with me."

She stopped, too, turned with nothing more than polite inquiry on her smooth features. The crowd parted and moved around us, like water diverted by stones on the bottom of a stream.

"Why, what exactly are you planning to do, Charlie?"

I shrugged, walked on. "I was going to play that one by ear."

She laughed. "Funny thing. I asked Sean the same question when he first put me onto tracing Clay for him. He said almost the same thing, and look how *that* turned out."

"I don't believe Sean did it."

At my side now, she glanced at me. "Of course he didn't. Did you ever think he might have?"

Her utter certainty threw me. "Parker was . . . concerned."

"Ah."

"What does that mean?"

"Well, I don't know Parker as well as you, obviously, but I *do* know Sean, and there was never any doubt in my mind."

The mild censure irritated me more than hostility would have done. "You *used* to know him. None of us do anymore. He's not the same person."

"Hmm, so I keep being told."

We reached the Skylink moving walkway and stepped onto it. Madeleine would have kept walking, but I touched her arm.

"You've talked to him recently. Don't *you* think he's changed?"

She frowned for a moment. "He has, but nowhere near as much as you and Parker suggest. He still seems to possess the same values, the same sense of honor and decency he always had."

To you, maybe.

I shook my head. "There are big chunks of his memory missing—important chunks, as far as I'm concerned. He doesn't view me as the same person I was before the coma."

The end of the walkway was approaching. She straightened, faced forward, and said diffidently, "I don't suppose you've ever considered that you might not be?"

❖

I stood in the walk-in shower in Madeleine's hotel room with my hands braced against the tiles, letting the water pound my neck and shoulders. I had the temperature set as high as I could stand it, and the room was full of steam despite the extractor fan's best efforts.

All the while, I tried to think back over situations I'd been in with Sean since he came back to work, conversations I'd had with him, with Parker.

Yes, I admitted privately, I *had* changed. There had been little choice. Sean had come back below par and I'd been forced to step up in his stead. But that was all I'd done, wasn't it—filled a void he'd left empty?

Or had I somehow taken it further? Further than I'd needed to in some effort to prove I was worthy of the time, expense, and trust that Parker had invested in me. Had it always been hanging around at the back of my mind that people saw me as a mere adjunct of Sean? That without him there to act as icebreaker, I would not have been considered worthy on my own merits?

Parker's interest in me on a personal level made things harder. I suppose somewhere deep inside I wondered if that was why he kept me on, even as he contemplated ending Sean's involvement with the agency.

Not just ending it, but he'd asked *me* to be the one to pull the trigger.

No, that wasn't fair. I reminded myself that even when Parker had told me where Sean had gone and what he feared he might have done, back at the beginning, he'd argued against me going after him.

Because he didn't think I was up to the job.

Looking at it from any kind of moral standpoint, I shouldn't have been.

Parker had asked me to kill for him. Not only that, but to kill the man who'd been my mentor, my lover, the father of my never-to-be-born child.

He'd put the fear in my mind that Sean had gone after Clay on my behalf, and as a result he would suffer, that he'd hate the consequences of his actions when they caught up with him. That Sean himself would rather be dead than rotting behind bars.

If Parker had tried to talk me into it, I would probably have resisted, but he hadn't. He'd tried to talk me out of it instead, and I'd jumped at the chance. Was I saving Sean from himself, or assuaging my own guilt?

Had I let my own insecurities over my work and the way my capabilities might be viewed persuade me to cross a line that should have been an absolute barrier?

Or had I, in truth, already crossed it a long time ago?

FIFTY

"DREW DONALSON CAME OUT OF THE ARMY NOT LONG AFTER YOU did, as a matter of fact," Madeleine said. "His parents died—left him some money. He bought a small farm out in the middle of nowhere on Saddleworth Moor and has been there ever since."

She accelerated the Land Rover Discovery onto the M60 Manchester ring road, flicking on the windshield wipers as she did so. An earlier drizzle had hardened into rain—big, fat droplets that scrambled for grip on the Disco's glass before whipping away in the slipstream.

"A farmer?" I queried. "Doesn't sound much like the guy I remember. He was more of a . . . city slicker."

"Well, some people *do* change." She glanced over her outside shoulder and switched lanes with smooth precision. She drove with the same neat economy of movement with which she did everything. Bitchily, I could even imagine her having sex the same way.

"Maybe he finds it easier to hide the bodies out there."

She threw me a disappointed little look but didn't speak. I stared out of the side window at the outskirts of Manchester, leafless trees, brown grass embankments, and concrete bridges dark with dirt and spray.

Donalson was one who fancied himself—a bit of a peacock, who dressed just a touch too fashionably to ever look stylish, however hard he tried. He was in the habit of dousing himself in aftershave at inappropriate moments, like on exercise, so sentries could smell him coming half a mile away, even if they never heard him. The smell of certain brands still made me flinch in visceral response.

He was so sure he was irresistible it went from self-confidence to self-delusion.

"I don't suppose," I said to Madeleine, "that you brought any firepower with you?"

"Yes, thank you," she said cheerfully.

"Ah, OK. Perhaps I should have said, 'any firepower you might be willing to share'?"

"In that case, sadly not."

"Don't you trust me?"

She grinned and didn't answer.

We came off the motorway at Ashton-under-Lyne and headed east through the suburbs. Converted mills mixed with modern industrial buildings, parks, and streets of redbrick terraced houses. All very familiar, yet distant. It seemed a long time since I had last lived in the UK. There was something small about it, but it had a messy reality that was comforting, and I realized I'd always viewed New York City as a kind of giant film set. Even living there hadn't changed that slightly romanticized image.

"How long is it since you were last over?" Madeleine asked, as if reading my thoughts.

"A while."

"Are you going to see your parents while you're here?"

"I hadn't planned on it."

"Won't they be disappointed?" She shot me an inquiring glance. "Seems a shame to waste the opportunity."

My parents lived just south of Manchester in Alderley Edge, in what had become the expensive haunt of Premier League soccer players. Manchester United was famous the world over, and I'd been asked about the team everywhere, from the Road of Bones in the far east of Russia to the depths of a Brazilian favela.

"They don't know I'm here, so why would they be disappointed?"

Madeleine frowned. "Have they got over . . . you know, what happened?"

It was a couple of years since a multinational company blackmailed my father and threatened my mother. The experience had a profound effect on both of them, leading to my father's retirement from his work as a consultant orthopaedic surgeon—something at which he'd once ruthlessly excelled—and the blossoming of my mother's self-confidence. Strange how differently people react to personal danger.

"Over it, no, but I think they've got past it, in their own way."

"And that has something to do with your staying away?"

Sometimes Madeleine was too smart for her own good.

I shrugged, said tightly, "I remind them of what happened."

"Oh, come on, Charlie, don't be so melodramatic."

"Excuse me?"

"Well, why does it have to be your fault? They're responsible adults who got themselves into a mess, and you—and Sean—got them out of it. Yes, some nasty things happened along the way, but that can hardly be blamed on you."

"They can just about cope with knowing what I do for a living, just as long as they don't have to watch me doing it.

267

By the finish, the whole thing turned into a fairly graphic demonstration."

"They ought to be proud of you."

"No, that would involve me marrying a stockbroker and spawning two-point-four kids and a Labrador."

"I think you do them an injustice. They know how far you went for them and what it cost you. If they're uncomfortable about that, it's more likely to be their own guilt playing a role, not disappointment in you."

I didn't reply to that remark. There was probably an element of truth in both arguments, but I wasn't prepared to pick them apart enough to find out.

We drove farther out of Manchester. The redbrick houses gave way to pale yellow sandstone, and I caught glimpses of the moor rising through gaps in the hedges and trees. In the summer, Saddleworth could be beautiful, but in winter it just seemed bleak and desolate. Its reputation was not improved by being forever connected with the children killed and buried there by Ian Brady and Myra Hindley in the mid-1960s.

A mist clouded the tops of the hills as we bordered Dove Stone Reservoir, its black waters choppy with the driven rain. The place suited both mood and mission. Bright sunshine would have seemed a mockery.

Ten minutes later Madeleine turned off the main road onto a narrow B-road, then onto little more than a rutted stony track with a hump of muddy grass down the center. If we'd been in anything lower to the ground than the Discovery, we would have lost most of our undercarriage along the way.

Beyond rusted barbed-wire fences, the fields on either side of the track were populated with tough-looking sheep, gorse, and thistles. The few stunted trees grew at an angle as if bowing to the prevailing wind.

We crested a small rise. A farmyard squatted halfway up the next hill, walled and gated. There was a wisp of smoke coming from the chimney of the tiny house. The roof was thick stone flags to withstand the winter gales, and it was covered with lichen. Apart from the smoke, it looked deserted.

Madeleine swung the Disco onto the grass and pulled up alongside the gate with my side closest. I peered out my window. A tan-and-white collie on a chain by an outside kennel started to bark frantically, but otherwise there was no sign of movement.

"However much money Donalson's parents left him," I said, "it clearly wasn't enough."

Madeleine looked around. "There isn't another property in sight. Some people might consider that kind of privacy to be priceless."

I cracked a grim smile. "Well, let's go and knock a few quid off then, shall we?"

We opened the doors and climbed out into the blustery rain. The gate's timbers were gray from weather and the hinges had drooped, leaving it permanently ajar.

As I stepped through into the yard itself, the back door of the house opened and a man came out. He'd clearly watched our arrival and prepared for us. He wore a camouflage boonie hat, a waxed cotton jacket with a tear in the sleeve, and old corduroy trousers.

And in his hands was a double-barreled shotgun.

FIFTY-ONE

I HALTED, GAUGING THE DISTANCE, AND RECKONED IT WAS AROUND ten meters. Depending on the choke of the gun and the size of the shot he'd loaded, it was borderline whether I'd escape serious injury if he fired. Ideally, I'd have preferred another four or five meters, but the wall around the yard prevented me from making it into a safe zone.

I took my only alternative option and sidled closer to the collie. Good sheepdogs are too valuable to waste, and this one looked cleaner and better fed than her surroundings might otherwise suggest. She lunged for me, still barking furiously, and was brought up short by the chain less than half a meter away.

"Is this any way to treat a visit from an old friend, Donalson?" I called.

He laughed, a bitter staccato burst of sound, not unlike that made by his dog.

"This how you always go visiting, is it?" He jerked his head toward the Discovery. When I glanced behind me I found Madeleine standing in cover behind the front end of the vehicle, with a semiautomatic pistol in a double-handed grip. She'd never been a field operative when I'd last worked with her. Since she'd taken over Sean's old agency, it would seem that she'd widened her skill set.

"If you're not going to play nice, children, I'll take those toys away from you," I said. "I came to talk, Donalson. If I was here to do you harm, d'you think I would have driven up to your front door in broad daylight?"

He weighed that one up for a moment or so, then let the barrels of the shotgun droop, settling the receiver into the crook of his arm.

"You'd best come inside, then, out of the weather."

Abruptly, he turned on his heel and went back into the farmhouse, leaving the door slightly open behind him.

Madeleine picked her way through the gate to stand beside me, slotting the handgun away into a small-of-the-back rig at her waistband. She noted my gaze and gave a faint, almost embarrassed smile as she straightened her jacket over the top.

"Ruger nine millimeter," she said as we started up the yard. "It's small, but it fits my hand and I like the trigger action."

"I'm just surprised to see you carrying anything at all."

She bristled. "I'm the boss now. It goes with the territory. Did you think I might be too squeamish?"

"Not at all," I said mildly. "The UK's very antigun, that's all. I didn't think you'd be allowed to carry concealed."

"Oh. Well, we do a fair amount of work for . . . Um, let's just say the authorities are prepared to make exceptions in certain cases."

Nevertheless, when we reached the doorway I made sure I went through it first. It was purely a practical decision. If

Donalson was so inclined, he could have been waiting on the other side ready to blast the first one in. Better to leave the second person in a better position to return fire.

But the first thing I saw as I pushed open the door was the shotgun standing muzzle upward, leaning against a fridge freezer. Donalson was at the far end of the room, by the window. He'd taken off his jacket and was in his shirtsleeves, rinsing a couple of mugs at the sink.

"There's tea in the pot," he said over his shoulder, dumping the mugs onto the kitchen table without bothering to dry them. It was Madeleine who plucked a tea-towel off the rail in front of the Aga and wiped them, then busied herself with the teapot and a carton of milk from the fridge.

The voice was as I remembered it, educated Edinburgh. But then, as if unable to put it off any longer, Donalson turned toward us and folded his arms. He'd dispensed with the hat as well, and now, in full light, I got a good look at his face for the first time in years.

He'd been in a bad accident or a firefight, I saw. The right side of his face was wilted as if from a stroke, although the shiny patchwork of reddened scars from temple and eye socket to chin suggested the nerves had been severed. It made his jaw hang lopsided, twisting that corner of his mouth into a permanent scowl.

He watched me closely as I took in his changed appearance, nodding at last as if I'd passed some kind of test.

"You've a stronger stomach than most, I'll say that for you."

"Did you think I'd run away screaming?"

"No. No, I didn't. If anything, I suppose I thought you'd look . . . glad at the sight of me now."

"Karmic consequences, you mean?" I offered. "What goes around, comes around?"

Madeleine glanced at me sharply but didn't intervene.

Donalson winced. "Aye, something like that."

"What happened to you?"

"Car accident," he said shortly. "Coming back from a family gathering with my folks. Freezing fog on the motorway, a jack-knifed truck . . ." His voice trailed off, and he shrugged. "They told me I was lucky. Mum, Dad, and my sister—they didn't make it."

I swallowed back the human urge to offer condolences, along with a gulp of the tea Madeleine handed to me. I scalded my tongue and forced myself to say nothing. This man did not deserve my sympathy. Not after what he had done.

There was a kitchen table pushed against one wall, piled with paperwork and clutter that had overflowed onto two of the three mismatched upright chairs. It looked rooted enough for me to surmise that Donalson lived alone. For a man who at one time couldn't wait to be out on the pull at every opportunity, it must have seemed like a kind of monastic seclusion.

Perhaps even atonement.

So we stood at the edges of the kitchen, clutching our mugs of tea like lifelines because it gave us something to do with our hands. Eventually Donalson tipped the dregs into the sink and banged the mug down onto the draining board.

"You going to say it, then?"

"Say what?"

"Whatever it is you've come all the way out here for, and then you can be on your way. Get it off your chest."

And unlike the man he'd once been, he didn't let his eyes drift across that part of my body as he spoke.

"You know Morton and Clay are dead?"

Until the words came out, I hadn't been aware that was where I planned to start.

"Knew about Morton—a while back, wasn't it? Topped himself somewhere out in the States, or so I heard."

I said nothing.

He frowned. "But Clay, no . . . when did that happen?"

"A week or so ago. In Iraq." I kept my eyes on his face, saw the flicker.

"Dangerous place. How did he die?"

"Badly," I said, succinct. "From the state of him, it looked like he crossed someone who took exception to the fact."

"You saw him?"

"What was left of him, yes."

The mobile half of his face screwed up in distaste. The rest remained slack.

"Get a buzz out of this, do you? Come to taunt me with it?"

I put my own mug down on the corner of the table and stepped in closer, inspecting his ruined face with impassive eyes. His own gaze would barely meet mine, the right eye slower to slide away.

"If I wanted to fuck with you, *Drew*, I could think of a dozen far nastier ways to do it," I said quietly. "I'm here for information. Tell me the truth—if you understand the concept—then I'm gone and you can go back to whatever passes for your life."

He ducked his head away, muttered, "Ask it."

"Clay was smuggling looted artifacts out of Iraq."

"That's not a question."

I glared at him in silence until he held up both hands, palms outward.

"OK, OK. Aye, I knew he had a sideline going. He asked me if I wanted in on it."

"When?"

"Must have been about a year and a half ago . . . something like that, anyways."

About the time Streetwise took over the contract in Basra and Clay started working for Ian Garton-Jones. Did that mean

Garton-Jones was in on it, too? Or was it simply an opportunity for Clay to get more of his cronies in place?

"How much did he tell you about the operation?"

"I turned him down, so not much."

"But?"

Donalson sighed. "He told me I'd like the setup. 'Striking a blow for freedom,' he said. And that I'd be earning really good money while I was doing it."

"What did he mean by that?"

"Whatever they were transporting, I got the impression that more set off than arrived, if you know what I mean? And he said it would be just like old times—working with some familiar faces."

"By 'familiar faces' was he talking about Hackett?"

The question surprised him, but not as much as it should have. Or maybe I was just bad at reading facial expressions from only half a face.

"Ah, from that I take it you think he is, which kinda explains why you've come calling on me," he said, almost to himself. "And he's in that part of the world, too, isn't he? Something to do with shipping? Shouldn't you be having this conversation with him instead, eh?"

"If I could find him, I would, but he's done a runner from Jordan—leaving behind his business partner, dead in the bathtub."

"And you think Hackett was the one that did it?"

"I'd be foolish to ignore the possibility. Hackett would murder his own granny—or anyone else's, for that matter—if he thought he'd profit by it. Maybe he was just clearing up loose ends."

"If somebody killed Clay and then went after Hackett, are you sure there isn't another reason behind it?"

"Such as?"

"Such as *you*, Charlie."

I shook my head. "I'm very old news."

"That's what they said about Deepcut, but it came back to haunt them, and now they're going to shut the place down."

The hazing, sexual harassment, and bullying of trainees at the Deepcut training camp in Surrey in the late '90s had now become a scandal. One that involved the shooting deaths—in highly suspicious circumstances—of four young soldiers. It had been echoed in my own case. And, much like Deepcut, what happened to me was either subject to official disinformation or swept under the carpet.

"Nobody's looking to open up my case again," I said. "You did what you did—that was never in doubt. What else is there to find?"

"Ah, well, maybe that's what you should be asking . . ."

"OK, so tell me—what else *is* there?"

Donalson shifted his feet uncomfortably, his gaze flicking to Madeleine, who was watching our exchange in silence, missing nothing.

"The colonel's back in civvy street now, too. Did you know that?"

"Parris? No, but then, I didn't exactly sign up for the regimental newsletter."

"He runs some kind of private security outfit, so I heard. Employs quite a few of the lads," he added meaningfully. "Maybe you should look him up. And don't leave it too long, eh?"

FIFTY-TWO

"THERE WAS CLEARLY RATHER A LOT GOING ON BACK THERE," Madeleine said as the Discovery bumped away from the farmhouse along the rutted track. "The majority of which went right over my head. Care to fill me in a little?"

I leaned back against the passenger headrest, aware of a banging headache beginning to build at the base of my skull. I shut my eyes briefly and squeezed the bridge of my nose. "I'm not too sure myself, to be honest."

"Then use me as a sounding board and talk yourself through it."

I glanced over at her. "Now I see why you're the boss."

She smiled. "That mention of 'the colonel'—Parris—I seem to remember he was your old commanding officer. Donalson bringing his name up like that was a little too pointed for it not to mean something."

"Mm, I thought so, too. Donalson said Clay offered him work with 'familiar faces' but seemed surprised when I mentioned Hackett. I think he may have been talking about Parris."

"But Clay was working for this Garton-Jones chap in Iraq, wasn't he?"

"Doing straightforward contracting, yes," I agreed. "But we also think he was part of the crew smuggling antiquities out of the country. Maybe Parris is involved with that side of things."

"And him both an officer and a gentleman? I'm shocked."

"He was certainly an officer. I'm not so sure about the gentleman bit. Anyway, they're usually the worst. Hence the fact they're clearly skimming."

"Not having been in the military, I'll have to take your word on that," she murmured as we turned out onto the relatively smooth main road again and headed back the way we'd come. "All the former soldiers I've dealt with seem to have a strong sense of loyalty to their old comrades, their old unit. Would that be enough to persuade men who'd served under Parris to join him in an enterprise that was totally illegal, do you think?"

"Most people will do just about anything if the money's right," I said, "but *having* served with them, he had a pretty good idea who he could approach in the first place without them turning him in. Men who felt they owed him something."

"Such as standing by them after they'd been accused of rape?"

I looked at the bleakness of the moors through the streaked side glass. The rain was now down to a miserable drizzle, herding low cloud and mist along with it.

"Yeah, something like that. Most COs would have had the men involved RTU'd as soon as the shit hit the fan. That's returned to their original unit," I added, anticipating her question. "They don't want any of the aforementioned shit to stick to their command."

"Indeed," Madeleine said gravely. "But not Colonel Parris?"

"No. He stood by them. Even had the gall to tell me the needs of the many outweighed those of the few, or some such, like that made it all OK."

"Where *is* that quote from originally?"

"Besides Mr. Spock in *Star Trek*? I've no idea."

Sean would have known. Or would have once, anyway. He had a mind for odd facts and trivia.

Before . . .

Something he'd said in Hackett's house in Madaba chewed at a corner of my mind, irritating as a dog with a squeaky toy. I couldn't quite put my finger on what it was. I shook my head, like that was going to free it.

"What?" Madeleine asked, glancing across.

"Not sure. Something Sean said in Jordan . . ." I rubbed my eyes, let my hands drop in frustration as I swore under my breath.

"Don't worry. It will come back to you when you least expect it."

"Or when it's too late to make use of. I'm constantly two bloody steps behind Sean when I need to be one step ahead of him."

"I can't help you there. He asked me to track down Hackett—and not to put you on his trail—but I haven't heard from him since he went to Iraq."

"What do *you* think he's up to?"

"He never confided in me, Charlie."

"That wasn't what I asked."

"Well, I don't think for a moment he's gone off the rails and is on some kind of Mafioso vendetta," she said. "I think he's . . . confused about the past and suspects there was more to it than he knew—even *before* there were parts he couldn't remember."

A snatch of conversation in Hackett's villa came back to me in a vivid rush: me telling Sean that if I'd wanted to go after the men who'd attacked me, I would have done it already. And his reply:

"It depends—on if you knew the right one to go after."

I recounted his words to Madeleine. She frowned as she drove, automatically slowing down a little as she processed the possible meanings.

"It sounds like he'd found out—who to go after, I mean," she said at last.

"But did he mean Hackett, as the ringleader, or Parris, as the instigator of the cover-up that followed?"

"And also the architect of Sean's own career downfall, don't forget."

"I don't suppose Sean asked you to track down the current whereabouts of Parris as well, did he?"

"No, but that doesn't mean I can't do it now."

She hit speed dial on her smartphone, in its hands-free cradle on the dashboard. The line rang twice before being answered with brisk efficiency. I listened with half an ear while Madeleine asked the well-spoken young man back at her office to get onto the trail of my old CO. When she ended the call, she glanced across at me.

"Should we have warned him, do you think?"

"Who?"

"Donalson—that Sean might be coming for him."

I shook my head. "If Sean isn't working his way through my attackers—which neither of us believes he is—then what purpose would it have served, other than to put the wind up him?"

"I would have thought you might have appreciated making him . . . suffer, just a little."

I shook my head. "I don't feel anything toward Donalson. Not anymore. He was a cocky creep, but I think those days are long gone. Even if I'd been intending to kill him, having seen the state he's in, I probably would have let him be."

"Then you *do* feel something toward him," Madeleine said. "Pity."

FIFTY-THREE

MADELEINE OFFERED TO DROP ME AT MY PARENTS' PLACE IN Cheshire, but I didn't have the energy for that kind of confrontation. Instead, I opted to accompany her back down to her headquarters in Kings Langley on the outskirts of London, just outside the M25 orbital ring road.

I'd been there before, back when Sean ran the agency. It still occupied the same modern industrial unit on the edge of town. Madeleine had improved the corporate branding, if the revamped logo and interior design were anything to go by. I guessed she'd probably had a shake-up of the staff as well. Not all of them would have welcomed a female boss—particularly one who came from logistics and cybersecurity rather than the field.

When we walked into the back office, one of the first people I saw was Luisa Dawson, now minus the sling on her arm. She was wearing dark wool slacks and a cream blouse that was smart without being flouncy. Quite a change from the last time I'd seen her, travel-worn and injured at the airport in Baghdad.

She got to her feet and stood awkwardly for a moment, unsure whether to keep her distance or hug me.

I gave her a friendly nod and held out a hand to shake, forestalling anything more intimate. "Good to see you," I said. "How's the shoulder?"

"Mending. How about you?"

"Mending," I echoed. I glanced at Madeleine. "How long have you been working here?"

It was Madeleine who answered for her. "Since she got back from Iraq. I can always use a fluent Arabic speaker—here in the office until she can get back out there again."

"I'm glad," I said, and meant it.

Dawson flashed me a quick grin. "I've been looking into this Colonel Parris bloke for you. He's—"

Whatever she was about to say was lost when the door to Madeleine's private office opened and a good-looking, rather smooth Indian guy stuck his head out. "Ah, you're back, ma'am," he said. I recognized the well-bred voice she'd phoned on the way back from Saddleworth Moor and pegged him as ex-Sandhurst military academy. "I have an American lady on hold for you—says her name is Hamilton. Do you want to take it, or shall I run interference?"

"You could try," I said, "but she has a habit of getting through sooner or later. Try not to let her get up to full ramming speed."

"Yeah," Dawson added. "She usually has a black ops team in tow who shoot first and don't bother with the questions."

"It's all right," Madeleine told him. "I'll take it—I don't think refusing to speak with the CIA would be good for business. Would you make some coffee for our . . . guest?"

He nearly bowed as he withdrew, slick as a country house butler. I turned back to Dawson, got as far as opening my mouth when Madeleine interrupted.

"Actually, I think you better sit in on this, Charlie."

"In that case, Luisa should, too," I said. "If you're talking to Hamilton, we've both been on the receiving end of her hospitality."

Madeleine shrugged. "Go through and make yourselves comfortable."

Sean's old office had changed in both décor and layout. Madeleine had brought in slightly more classic furniture that wouldn't date so quickly, but she'd stuck to muted colors to put her potential clients at ease. The old conference table had been replaced by sofas grouped around a large flat-screen TV. It was more like we were about to watch a movie than receive a briefing.

Madeleine went to the laptop on her desk and picked up a remote for the TV. When the screen came to life, Aubrey Hamilton was sitting facing a webcam. The screen was big enough that she was larger than life-size, which was faintly unnerving. As ever, she was in black. It made her face appear very stark, almost disembodied, as the limitations of the camera struggled with the contrast. From the utilitarian background, I'd say she was on a navy vessel.

"Ms. Hamilton," Madeleine greeted her, sitting down at the opposite end of the sofa I'd chosen. "What can we do for you?"

"The *Dolphin* was a bust," Hamilton said without preamble. "Legitimate goods, all accounted for and documented up the wazoo."

"Oh . . . arse," I murmured.

"Yeah, that about sums it up. Still, at least our sailor boys and girls got to play with their big guns."

"So that answers *that* question," I said. "When we got there, Hackett must have already taken anything incriminating out of the safe, so it was left open by design—not accident."

"Uh-uh. Not necessarily. I'm still not ruling out that your pal Meyer had time to open and remove whatever he needed before *you* got there."

Both Madeleine and I started to protest, but Hamilton held up a hand. "I'm not ruling it *in*, either. Just putting it out there as something I have to consider."

I nodded, then looked up sharply and asked, "How did you find me here, by the way? Did I swallow some kind of tracking bug in that last pot of coffee you ordered in Amman?"

She laughed, a husky bark of sound. "Nothing so high-tech. I called your boss. He told me Ms. Rimmington had arranged to pick you up soon as you landed in the UK."

"I'm not sure if that makes me feel better or worse."

"Occupational hazard. Get used to it."

Almost as soon as I mentioned the word *"coffee,"* Madeleine's assistant reappeared with a tray laden with a cafetière and all the associated bits and pieces. He put it down on the low table in front of the sofas and left again. Even over a webcam, Hamilton looked at it longingly.

"OK, so if the *Dolphin* was the bad news," I said only half jokingly as I poured the coffee, "I don't suppose you have any good news?"

"Don't know if you'd class it as good or bad," Hamilton said. "The Russians you ran into in Kuwait City and again in Madaba? Woźniak managed to snag some intel from immigration in both countries on a group of Russian guys who fit the profile and were in the right places at the right times. I've emailed over a couple of pictures and their passport details, although I doubt they're using the names they were born with."

I remembered Parker's explanation of Kuznetsov as "Smith" but just said, "Oh?"

"Well, you reckoned they were Russian ex–Special Forces, the equivalent of our Navy SEALs?"

"Or our Special Boat Service," Dawson put in, but Hamilton barely missed a beat.

"Well, the names kinda follow—Griorovich, Levchenko, Panteleyev, Tributs, Ushakov. All names of Russian naval vessels. The *Admiral Ushakov* is a Kirov-class battle cruiser. You can thank the fact I'm on a ship surrounded by people who know the Russian navy backwards for that one."

Over on the desk, Madeleine's computer chirruped. She moved over to it, hit a couple of keys, and a moment later the printer whirred to life.

"The *Admiral Kuznetsov*, by the way, is an aircraft carrier," Dawson said quietly.

Kuznetsov. The man I'd killed in Basra the day Dawson had busted her shoulder. The day I'd been shown Clay's body and had worried that Sean really might have been responsible.

I looked up to find Hamilton's oversize image peering at us. "I don't have a Kuznetsov listed going into Amman," she said. "What am I missing?"

"He was part of an ambush on the contractor I was working for in southern Iraq," Dawson explained. She indicated her shoulder. "They planted an IED and then opened fire on us. I snapped my collarbone, but Charlie managed to take out one of the shooters—this guy, Kuznetsov."

"Hmm, funny you didn't mention anything about wasting this guy when we spoke before," Hamilton said. "Slip your mind?"

"Ah well, maybe I'm just naturally modest."

"Yeah, or maybe you're just full of—"

Madeleine cut her off by dropping the printouts into my lap. I flipped through two or three that I vaguely recognized before

285

one jumped straight out at me. I turned the picture around so Hamilton could see it.

"That's the one—Ushakov," I said. "Definitely the guy who warned us off in Kuwait."

"You sure?"

"One hundred percent. I never forget anyone who punches me."

"I'll be sure to tell that to Woźniak so he has time to start running."

"Why run? He'll only die tired."

She snorted. "Damn, I was right. I *definitely* should have hired you."

"Too late," I said. "OK, so we know where this Ushakov *was*, but where did he come from? And where did he go afterwards?"

"Sofia," Hamilton said. "It's an easy hop from there to anywhere in Russia."

"Sofia, as in Bulgaria?" Dawson asked suddenly.

Hamilton made an impatient noise. "How many others do you know?"

"Well, apart from one in New Mexico, there are at least a couple in old Mexico and three in Cuba," Dawson said evenly. "As well as more in Moldova, Sweden, Mozambique, Portugal—"

"OK, OK, so you're a smart-ass. I get the picture," Hamilton snapped. "Yes, goddammit, Sofia, Bulgaria. Why?"

Dawson flicked her eyes to Madeleine as if seeking permission, then reached for the folder she'd brought in with her. "Because earlier today the boss asked us to track down one Colonel John Parris—former commanding officer of the Special Forces regiment Charlie was training with."

"Same one as Michael Clay and James Hackett?"

"That's the one. Turns out Parris wasn't hard to find. He handed his kit in three years ago and now runs his own private security firm. The word in the industry is that he's good, but not too fussy who he contracts to if the money is right. And as of this moment, he's working for a fairly dubious guy who has a place in the mountains, not far from Borovets, Bulgaria."

"What do you know about the guy who's hired him?"

"Not much as yet," Dawson said. "I just had a couple of pictures emailed through and was about to start a search to try and identify him."

She passed across a color print for me to show to the webcam, as I was nearest. Out of habit, I glanced at it.

And froze.

It wasn't just the sight of Colonel Parris, to the left of the shot, in civilian clothing but unmistakably military in bearing. It wasn't even the other obvious mercenaries arranged in a loose diamond formation around their principal.

It was the principal himself.

"Charlie?"

I looked up to find Madeleine staring at me with concern. I cleared my throat.

"Unfortunately, I know exactly who this is," I told her. "And so do you."

FIFTY-FOUR

"HIS NAME IS GREGOR VENKO," MADELEINE SAID. "CAME TO prominence during the Balkan Wars of the '90s, although nobody was ever quite sure whose side he was on. He supplied just about anything to just about anybody—providing they had the money—and made a considerable fortune doing so."

"Dare I ask how you and Charlie came to know this guy?" Looming from the flat-screen, Hamilton's narrowed eyes flicked between the two of us.

"Madeleine never met him, and I only encountered him professionally, so to speak," I answered. "It was in Germany, a few years ago. I made the mistake of saving the life of Gregor's son, Ivan."

"Mistake?"

"It prevented an innocent girl dying, which would have been the outcome had anything happened to the boy," Madeleine put in, sending me a disapproving glance. "And

288

to be fair, Charlie, you didn't know at the time that it was a mistake."

"On some level I did, as soon as I first laid eyes on him. Even at barely twenty, Ivan was a nasty piece of work. I doubt he's developed much of a conscience since then. Gregor was old school. At least with him you felt there was some kind of honor system at work."

"So how did Venko Senior react to what you did?" Hamilton asked. "He feel he owed you one?"

I shrugged. "He told me he wouldn't forget," I said. "At the time it sounded more like a threat than a promise."

And then he'd sent me an extraordinarily generous gift—a fact I did not feel inclined to reveal to Hamilton. Or Madeleine, for that matter. It felt too close to accepting a bribe.

"Send me what you have on this guy," Hamilton ordered. "I'll get my people to work up a full packet."

Her brisk tone was enough to make even Madeleine bridle.

"I'm sure my people are more than capable," she said pleasantly.

"Of that I have no doubt. But you're doing this pro bono. I have the Federal Reserve behind me—for the moment, at least—not to mention access to NSA files and satellite tracking. Why not take advantage?"

"All right," Madeleine said at last. "Would I be out of order to ask what you intend to do with the information?"

Hamilton paused a moment, as if considering. "We appear to have lost both Meyer and Hackett, but we assume they've left Jordan without alerting the authorities. We believe Hackett is involved with transporting stolen antiquities out of the region, but we don't know what route he's taking, or where he's headed. However, finding out he may have been working for his former CO, and that Parris is, in turn, working for this gangster, Venko, it gives us someplace to start looking."

I sat and sipped my coffee while Madeleine and Hamilton arranged the details, then the American signed off and the flat-screen went blank.

Madeleine regained her seat on the sofa and picked up her coffee. "Good work," she said to Dawson. "I'm impressed with how much you got done in the time it took us to drive south."

"Thanks, boss. Would have been better if I'd been able to identify Venko myself, though."

"Don't beat yourself up about it," I said. "I haven't seen him for years, but I know he was fairly camera-shy even back then."

She rose, gave us a slightly lopsided smile, and gestured to the folder. "Do you want me to stick with this or move onto something else?"

"Put it aside for now," Madeleine said. "Go back to the logistics on the assignment in Bahrain next month and let's see what our American cousins can come up with, shall we?"

Dawson nodded and went out, leaving Madeleine and me alone with our coffee.

We drank in silence for a few moments, then she said, "Do you think Hamilton will actually share whatever she finds out? Because, if not, I'll keep Luisa digging. The way Donalson brought Parris's name up . . . I can't help but feel Sean's gone after him."

"Yeah, I know. And, to be honest, if there was more to what happened back in the army than we realized—and Parris knows about it—I wouldn't mind having a few words with him myself."

FIFTY-FIVE

FORTY-EIGHT HOURS LATER, I FLEW INTO SOFIA AIRPORT, MY WALLET stuffed with Bulgarian leva and my luggage with hastily obtained snow gear.

Despite my protests, Madeleine and Dawson were with me.

They argued that to all intents and purposes we'd look like we were on a group girlie skiing holiday. I pointed out that I could just as easily have been on a single girlie skiing holiday, but it didn't cut much ice.

Besides, it was no bad thing to have people I knew I could trust on site as backup.

Once again, there was someone waiting with a sign in the Arrivals hall. This time the clipboard read HAMILTON PARTY rather than individual names.

That would have been no bad thing, either, had the person holding the clipboard not been Woźniak.

As the three of us approached, Madeleine was the only one who smiled in greeting. Then she turned, caught a glimpse of our scowling faces.

"Ah, I see you've all met before."

Woźniak seemed quickly charmed by her, which did not improve my mood.

He hustled us outside into the early afternoon sunshine. It was not as cold as I'd been expecting, and a welcome relief from the baking heat of the Middle East.

We loaded our bags into the back of a Mercedes minivan waiting with another of Woźniak's men behind the wheel. He hopped in the front and we spread out in the back. There was seating for six back there, so we had plenty of room.

"How long is the journey?" Madeleine asked.

Woźniak glanced over his shoulder. "An hour twenty, maybe an hour thirty," he said. "Colder, too. Borovets is around four and a half thousand feet above sea level."

"And Sofia?"

"Eighteen hundred. Hope you brought plenty of winter clothing." He was positively chatty.

Madeleine smiled at him. "Of course. Will Aubrey be joining us?"

"Ms. Hamilton is already at the resort, ma'am."

The snow was patchy in the city, huddled into dirty heaps on the shoulders of the road. Much of the scenery was unremarkable until we started to climb into the mountains, where the covering was thicker.

The road followed a river, then passed the hydroelectric dam at Pasarel and hugged the big reservoir at Iskar. The snow-shrouded mountains were permanently in view above the trees now, distant and dominating in the sharp, cool light. The trees themselves each wore a snow shroud. It was hard not to feel the thrill of a kid at the white Christmas scenery.

"How much skiing have you actually done?" Dawson asked.

"A fair amount," I said. "These days there are always people who want someone looking after them on the slopes, so I've had quite a bit of practice over the last few years. You?"

"Learned in the army, but I haven't done any since." She pulled a face. "I hope to hell I don't fall on my arse on the first day and wreck this shoulder—just when it's beginning to mend."

Dawson cocked an eyebrow at Madeleine, who gave a faint smile. "I learned as a child, then trips with school and later holidays," she said. "I'm a little rusty, too, but I daresay it will come back to me."

"Don't tell me," I said, "your family always took their winter break in St. Moritz."

She looked surprised. "Yes, how did you know?"

I suppressed a groan. "Just a lucky guess . . ."

I stared out the window after that, letting the conversation in the car float over me. I wondered where Sean was, how he was. Was he really planning to go after Parris, or was he still somewhere in Jordan or Iraq? If he *wasn't* on his way here, then I was in utterly the wrong place, and even further behind than before. I approached our imminent arrival with both impatience and a sense of dread. Once we got there, I would find out what I didn't altogether want to know.

As it was, we made good time to Borovets itself, which seemed to be entirely devoted to skiing, snowboarding, and anything else that involved sliding down an icy mountain in a semi-out-of-control state. The small town was packed with hotels, bars, and restaurants catering to tourists, or stores selling the associated paraphernalia of winter sports.

As we drove past the town center and the main ski lift, I saw a family riding in a sleigh drawn by two shaggy ponies, just passing a wooden shack with blacked-out windows and unfeasibly well-endowed Playboy bunnies on the posters outside. Something for everyone, then.

Our driver turned off the main drag, slowing for people in awkward boots and lurid jackets traipsing across the road in front of us with their skis shouldered.

We reached a sign for ski-in ski-out apartments and drove in, which gave me a moment's uneasy feeling. The last time I'd stayed in a resort like this, it had not ended well—for me or my principal.

"You OK?" Madeleine asked, frowning, and I saw she was watching me minutely.

"I'm fine," I said, forcing myself to relax.

She did not look convinced.

We pulled up in one of the spaces that had been cleared in front of a wooden chalet with picturesque shutters and a carved wooden balcony around the upper floor. As soon as I climbed out, the cold knifed straight to the bone. When I exhaled, my breath formed a cloud.

"Wow, you were right about the change in temperature," Madeleine said to Woźniak. She threw up the hood on her belted jacket and instantly looked chic.

"You're in here, ma'am," Woźniak said, nodding to the nearest chalet as he opened the rear of the Merc. He and the silent driver grabbed all our bags and carried them into the covered porchway. By the time we'd all made our way carefully over the ice, the front door was open and Aubrey Hamilton was waiting for us.

"Coffee's on. There's soup and bread in the kitchen," she said by way of greeting. "Bring your gear up and grab something to eat. Briefing in ten."

FIFTY-SIX

IN THEORY THE CHALET COULD SLEEP SIX, DEPENDING ON HOW good friends everyone was. There were three bedrooms containing a total of two double beds and two singles, decorated in a compromise between cost and style, in which style had come out marginally the loser.

Hamilton had already called dibs on one of the doubles, and Madeleine pulled rank for the second, so that left Dawson and me sharing the room with the singles. Funny how those furthest down the food chain are also usually those closest to the sharp end.

I dumped my bag on the bed nearest the door and took my wash kit into the tiny en suite shower room to brighten myself up. Feeling mildly more human with a clean face and brushed teeth, I followed the sound of voices up to the open-plan living area. There was an open log fire and French doors leading out onto the full-length balcony. I could tell nobody had ventured out there yet by the snow settled almost half a meter up the glass.

Madeleine was at the dining table, tucking into a bowl of soup that looked thick enough to eat with a fork rather than a spoon. She flashed me a smile. Hamilton was drinking coffee and reading a file that lay open across her knees. She didn't look up when I entered, or when Dawson followed me in a few minutes later.

By unspoken agreement, I dished out two bowlfuls of soup while Dawson poured coffees. The soup was a generic orange color and smelled like winter vegetable—some kind of squash if I had to guess. As we took our seats across from Madeleine, Hamilton finally came to life.

"OK, I'm guessing that because you're all female you can eat, drink, *and* listen without having someone else push your chests in and out," she said with the glimmer of a smile, "so I'll get right into it."

She laid printed-out pictures on the table next to us so we didn't have to stop feeding to take them. Clearly she'd spent a lot of time working with squaddies—never get between them and their grub if you want to keep all your fingers.

The first image was of a grandiose building that looked more like a hotel than a private home. It was mainly white, dotted with timbering, turrets, and towers, around a courtyard leveled with snow. Parked to the left of the shot were a couple of snowmobiles and some kind of large tracked vehicle, like an SUV on stilts.

"This is Gregor Venko's stronghold. Used to be a tsarist palace, although I understand they referred to it as a 'royal hunting lodge' back in the good old days. Makes you wonder what it took to really impress those guys."

"Where is it?" Dawson asked. "How far from here, I mean."

"Only a mile or so to the base of the mountain, but then you gotta climb another couple thousand feet. In the summer you can drive up. In the winter, you'd need one of those." She stabbed a finger at the vehicles pictured.

"Looks like you'd need a lot of people to run a place that big," I said. "How many staff? And how many of them class as civilians?"

"Good question. As far as we've been able to ascertain, there are eight full-time domestic staff with no military background or training."

"And those who *do* have it?"

"Maybe a dozen, working a rotating shift pattern, plus Parris. Good electronic security and camera coverage, from what we can see, and they've got location on their side. Always a major pain in the ass to storm a fortress on top of a mountain."

"How many men do you have here?"

Hamilton regarded me for a moment as if debating whether she wanted to answer or not. "Four—they're in the cabin next door."

"I hate to say this, but you won't be doing much storming without more troops."

"Yeah, well, we'll just have to work with what I got. This is not the only iron in the fire for my department."

"Who else lives up there?" Madeleine asked, as if to forestall an argument I wasn't about to start. "What about Venko's family?"

"Nobody knows what happened to Mrs. Venko. She was last seen in a sanatorium somewhere in the Ukraine, but that was years ago. But Gregor's son, Ivan—who seems to be following in Daddy's footsteps—also lives at the hunting lodge-slash-fortress."

"How about we just call it his lair and have done with it?" Dawson suggested.

"Ivan's still with him?" I murmured, more to myself than to the room at large. "I would have thought he'd got tired of being under Daddy's watchful thumb a long time ago."

I'd had one brief encounter with Ivan Venko—and not in the sense of a love story filmed in black-and-white and set in a railway station café back in the age of steam. I'd very likely saved his life, yes, but I did not expect him to remember or appreciate that fact next time we met. How his father might react to me could go either way.

"Rumor has it that Venko's been legitimizing his empire over the last few years and grooming Ivan to take over. Not much on the son besides hearsay and a couple of minor public order offenses, which Daddy's team of lawyers made all but disappear."

"Unless he's had some serious therapy in the last few years, Ivan's the one to worry about," I said, and Madeleine nodded. She'd been involved in the operation in Germany—the first step along the road to close protection for me. My first job for Sean.

"Well, Venko Senior has certainly been throttling back the past couple of years. Another reason we're here is that he's become a noted collector of artifacts from ancient Sumeria and Persia. But the guy's almost a recluse—hardly ever seen in public, and when he does venture out, he's always well guarded."

"By Parris, or the Russians?"

She passed me another shrewd glance and dug out more pictures, taken sometimes through foliage or crowds, with long lenses. They showed a heavily swathed Gregor; Gregor in a business suit; Gregor in shirtsleeves and sunglasses. He was always surrounded by at least four men, although not always the same men. I recognized some of the Russians, including, I thought, the late Comrade Kuznetsov. Parris himself was often present in the shots, within the protective formation rather than outside it.

"Parris is head of security but tends to tag along if father or son are off the property separately. Hard to say which of them is his top priority." She shrugged. "If we had more time for surveillance . . ."

"How long has Parris been with them?"

"Since his discharge from the military—which was honorable, or whatever the Brit Army equivalent of that might be. Walked straight into the job."

"Which means he and Venko probably knew each other from before."

Hamilton nodded. "Anything significant in that, d'you think?"

My turn to shrug. "Parris served in the Balkans, performing one role or another. There's a faint chance they could have met then."

Hamilton nodded. "So he's more likely to be Gregor's choice than Ivan's."

She gathered up the papers, tapped them upright on the table to line them up, and shoved them away into the folder.

"We've managed to uncover a network of holding companies owned by Venko, leading to auction houses which have been buying and selling on the antiquities market," she said. "If the quantities are anything to go by, it's the tip of the iceberg. We need more intel, and surveillance is not going to be easy. They can see anyone coming a mile away up there."

I finished the last of my soup and sat back, warming my hands around the coffee mug. "I presume all Woźniak's guys ski?"

"Sure—like pros," Hamilton said. "Not much point in bringing 'em, otherwise."

"And you yourself?"

A sneaky smile was hovering around the edge of Hamilton's mouth, because she knew I had a purpose for asking, and I think she was hoping it was one she hadn't thought of. "My mother keeps a winter house in Vail."

"Ah, of course she does." I finished the coffee, which had been lukewarm to start with, and set the mug down. "Well, that's a pity, because the first thing I think we should do tomorrow morning is hire a load of cheap skis and an instructor."

FIFTY-SEVEN

OUR INSTRUCTOR'S NAME WAS RADKO. HE WAS A NATIVE OF BOROVETS, he told us, who taught skiing here at the resort during the winter and spent his summers picking fruit in the UK. What he planned to do *next* summer, though, he said gloomily, he did not yet know.

We let the rental place fit us out with basic boots, helmets, skis, and poles, which were somewhat battered and unmistakably ski-school uniform in style and color. Woźniak's guys hated it. They'd all brought their own latest-spec gear, lovingly waxed and honed and prepped.

They had been first dismissive and then aggressive when my idea was explained to them. This had now settled into the uncooperative stage—much scowling and communicating in grunts.

But as we waited in line for the first lift up the mountain, Woźniak looked around at his guys, standing in apparent couples with the rest of us, and gave me a single brief nod.

"OK, I'll give you that one," he muttered, as though I'd had to extract his fingernails with pliers to get him to admit it. "Never thought it would take sticking out like a bunch of sore thumbs to blend in, but you nailed it, Fox."

"As long as they remember to tone down their skiing, we'll be fine," I said. "Mind you, I think most of them will trip over their egos at least a couple of times on the first run."

He made a noise that might have doubled as a short laugh or could simply have been indigestion, then shuffled through the barrier in time for the next chairlift to whack into the back of his legs before scooping him up, the way chairlifts always do.

The ride up the mountain was crystal cold, the trees below dusted with icing sugar, sparkling in the sun. The view was stunning and made half freezing to death on the way up a small price to pay. Everyone mentions the end of their nose, but I found that by the time we reached the top, it was my chin I could barely feel, despite burying it into the scarf wrapped around my neck.

Radko assembled his class and gave us all the standard pep talk. He said he would watch us on the first run to see how we went, adding, "And now we ski with good style!" and set off into the first sweeping loop.

I was a reasonable skier rather than outstanding, so I didn't make any particular effort to perform badly. The guys overdid it, until Hamilton whizzed past them, with plenty of Radko's requested style, and growled at them to behave.

Radko, annoyingly, was able to ski backward while watching his class, although once he had reassured himself that we were not imminently about to plummet over the nearest precipice, he quickened the pace a little as he led us down to the start of the next lift.

"We all OK to go up?"

He grinned at the nods and deftly hopped onto the express lift to the top. This one carried riders in pairs. I took the chair alongside Dawson, with Woźniak and Madeleine just ahead of us.

As the lift rose, gained altitude, and cleared the treetops, below us instead of landscape there was only a grayish-white layer of cloud, roiling softly like a misty sea above which the tops of the mountains appeared as islands.

On one of those islands was Venko's hunting lodge, in view for the first time. It made an impressive sight. I noticed arms extended further up the lift line as other skiers noticed the collection of buildings and pointed.

"What's he up to, d'you think?" Dawson demanded suddenly, nudging my arm. I shifted my gaze forward and noticed that Woźniak seemed to be in some kind of clinch with Madeleine. His arm was certainly around her shoulders and she was pressed tight to his side.

"No idea," I responded, "but if it was uninvited, he's going to need the rescue sled to get him back down the bloody mountain, because he won't be able to stand up well enough to ski."

As soon as we got off the lift I moved quickly over to Madeleine. She saw the look on my face and put up a warning hand.

"Easy, Charlie. It was just cover so I could take some photographs of Venko's place—nothing sinister." She unzipped her jacket just far enough for me to see that underneath she had an SLR camera on a shoulder strap, with a telephoto lens.

I let my hackles subside. "All right," I said grudgingly. "But if he starts to enjoy his work too much, let me know and I'll break all his fingers."

"Aw, thanks." She gave me a sunny smile. "That's so sweet of you."

"Any time, ma'am."

We couldn't see the hunting lodge from the lift station itself, but as soon as we skied down on a narrow trail that led through the trees and burst out into bright sunlight again, it seemed very close—as the crow flies, anyway. To get there on foot would have involved going down the mountain we were on and climbing the next, submerging and surfacing through the cloud sea like a whale.

Radko grouped us all together out on the open trail to explain the route we were going to take down. I edged closer to Hamilton.

"This is about as close as we're going to get to Venko's place without tipping off his security," I said. "We could do with someone taking a dive so Madeleine has a chance to get some more photos."

"Leave it with me," Hamilton said. She prescribed a neat serpentine through our assembled ranks and had brief words with Woźniak and one of his men. Whatever she said to them, neither looked happy about it.

The next time Radko led us off in formation, the pair was first away after him. They got onto open ground, and Woźniak made a sharp turn across the ski tips of the guy following, who couldn't put in a turn of his own in time. The two of them collided and went down, barreling into the powdery snow. Poles and skis detached and went in opposite directions. Entirely by accident, one ski found the fall line and began a rapid solo descent. Radko gave chase.

The rest of us converged on the two fallen skiers, helping them up, patting them down, retrieving skis and goggles. Completely uninjured, they stood and gave each other good-natured grief, while Madeleine lurked in the center of the group with her camera pointed toward the far mountaintop, its motor drive whirring.

FIFTY-EIGHT

✦

MADELEINE DOWNLOADED THE PICTURES FROM THE MEMORY CARD as soon as we were back at our chalet. I got a fire going in the living area, while Dawson inventoried the food laid in. Hamilton started making phone calls the moment we got in, disappearing into the privacy of her room to do so.

The light outside was fading fast now, and the piercing spotlights alongside each ski run had been switched on. The weather was worsening, too, the wind picking up. It had started to snow, dampening the sound from the bars and clubs along the main street.

"We've got the makings for a giant spag bol and garlic bread," Dawson announced as she came through from the kitchen, wiping her hands on a towel.

"Sounds lovely," Madeleine said warmly. She lived with a Michelin-starred chef, but I guess occasionally peasant food like spaghetti Bolognese had its attractions, if only for novelty value.

"I'll give you a hand," I offered, getting stiffly to my feet. Skiing gave a workout to muscles I hadn't used in a while. I swear my knee joints actually creaked.

Hamilton reappeared, not looking pleased.

"The NSA tell me it will be another forty-eight hours before we can re-task a fly-by, by which time this weather will have closed in. All their birds are on trajectories over Syria or Russia, and Bulgaria is not currently a high-enough priority."

She went briskly over to the dining table to peer over Madeleine's shoulder. "What you got, Mad?"

Madeleine was frowning. "Not much, I fear. Really just confirmation of what we knew already."

"Always good to have confirmation," Hamilton said. "We—"

Whatever she'd been about to say was cut off by her phone ringing again. It reminded me that I hadn't checked in with Parker since I left the UK. Would he be worried?

Hamilton listened to whoever was speaking in tense silence for a minute, then said, "How long before they get here?" A pause. "How come this is the first I'm hearing about it? Uh-huh. Well, in future, keep me in the goddamn loop!"

She stabbed the End Call button on her phone and threw it onto the sofa.

The three of us stood and waited without asking the obvious question. I didn't think she could keep whatever she'd just been told bottled up for long.

"I've just gotten word that James Hackett has turned up in Odessa, Ukraine," she said. "He's with a convoy of trucks that off-loaded about an hour ago from a boat out of Rize, a port in northwest Turkey on the Black Sea."

"How many trucks?" I asked.

"Five. They're listed as carrying 'reproduction antiques for use in the motion picture industry' if you can believe that."

"Is it too late for you to have the Customs people hold them—at least until they can be verified as reproductions?" Madeleine suggested.

"In Ukraine?" Hamilton shook her head. "Our influence there is pretty much zip."

"Do I take it," I said, "that they're heading here?"

"That's the theory. Unless they come nonstop, they'll arrive late tomorrow or maybe the day after."

Madeleine was tapping at the keyboard of her laptop, bringing up maps. "They would have to come through Moldova and Romania. If you think they're carrying looted antiquities, can't you have them intercepted at those border crossings?"

Hamilton shrugged. "Unlikely. Organized crime is a major problem in both countries. So is corruption. Even if we had the authority to ask for Hackett to be detained, chances are that money would change hands and the convoy would magically slip through their fingers. And then Venko would know we were coming."

"Yeah, but we're *not* coming, are we?" Dawson argued. "That's the problem. We don't have the manpower or the fire-power to attack Venko's fortress. I'd hazard a guess that we can't call on the local authorities for any kind of backup, and your people have just made it clear that anything happening in Bulgaria is 'low priority.' S'cuse me for speaking out of turn, but what exactly *are* we doing here?"

Madeleine raised her eyebrows in silent admonishment, but she kept them raised in inquiry as she turned to Hamilton, who scowled in response.

"I have requests in for a larger covert team, but after the first tip-off—the *Dolphin*—didn't pan out, my bosses want concrete proof before they make their next move."

"By which time any contraband will, regrettably, be long gone," Madeleine pointed out.

"Yeah . . . maybe."

"You mean *probably*."

"And what about Sean?" I cut in. "You have your objective, Aubrey, but mine—ours," I amended, "is to find him before he gets into anything with Parris. And at the moment we don't have any idea where he is, except he's most likely hot on Hackett's trail."

"So what do you suggest, Charlie?" she threw back. "Because right now I'm all ears."

I glanced at the photo of the former royal hunting lodge up on Madeleine's laptop screen. It did indeed look like a fortress surrounded by a moat, on that mountaintop isolated by the cloud.

"I find mostly in these situations, the simple solution is the best."

"Which is?"

"I was thinking about going up there and banging on Venko's front door."

FIFTY-NINE

AS I APPROACHED THE OUTER GATES OF THE FORTIFIED HUNTING lodge where Gregor Venko had made his home, it's fair to say a number of things went through my mind. Not least of which was whether the impressive set of studded oak doors had a bell-push.

If they didn't, I was very likely to freeze to death up here.

I'd ridden up the mountainside in what was almost a blizzard, on a rented Polaris snowmobile, with Woźniak acting as wingman. He'd peeled off without even a wave as we'd neared the edge of the final stand of trees, letting me ride in the last half kilometer alone. No doubt it was a sign of his disapproval of this latest plan—if I could call it that.

I don't know what his initial reaction had been. Hamilton had taken little convincing, mainly because her options had reached scraping-the-bottom-of-the-barrel territory, and my personal safety was not strictly her responsibility. I had not run the idea past Parker before embarking on it. I hadn't had to, to know exactly what he'd say.

Madeleine had hovered in the doorway to my room while I'd changed into my thermals and regarded me gravely. "What do you hope to achieve by this, Charlie?"

I shrugged. "Like I said—getting to Sean before he gets to Parris. Or Hackett, come to that. And who knows, I might still have enough credit left with Gregor to get out of there again without a bullet in the back of my skull."

"And if you don't?"

"Then you can tell Parker he was right—I wasn't up to the job after all."

The journey up the mountain had taken an hour, with visibility closing in by the minute and the temperature dropping until the snow had felt more like hail pelting into the exposed bits of my face between scarf and goggles.

We'd seen nobody except for the occasional flare of headlights from the big mechanical groomers high on the neighboring mountain, eerie through the snowfall, flattening the trails for the following day's skiers.

I needn't have worried about the doorbell. By the time I reached Venko's gates, hit the engine kill switch, and stiffly dismounted, security spotlights blazed on. A personnel door in one of the gates swung inward and a guard stepped through. He held a machine pistol across his chest on a shoulder strap, hand wrapped around the grip and gloved finger lying alongside the trigger guard. I gathered from this that I was not considered to present an immediate danger.

A second man was visible in the doorway, though, keeping back just in case.

"*Kakvo iskash?*" the first guard demanded, which I took to be a general inquiry along the lines of "Who the hell are you?" His voice was harsh, but that could have been a mix of language and cold rather than an actual threat. His face was hidden behind a ski mask, hat, and goggles, so I couldn't glean anything there.

"I'm here to see Gregor Venko," I said, keeping my movements slow and my hands in view.

The guard paused a moment, head slightly tilted. I guessed he was receiving instructions from a hidden earpiece. Then he flapped his hand in a universal "go away" gesture. I stood my ground.

Above me was a small security camera, tucked into the stonework surrounding the gates. I unsnapped the strap on my helmet, removed it, pulled my scarf down so my face was visible, and stared up at the lens.

"My name is Charlie Fox. Tell Gregor my name," I insisted. "If you value your job, tell him." And this time I was speaking to both the man in front of me and whoever was watching from a distance.

There was another pause. Just when I'd begun to think this really wasn't going to work and was planning some kind of exit strategy that didn't involve a long stay in hospital, the guard took a step forward. He lifted the machine pistol slightly in warning and motioned for me to put my arms out to the side, shoulder height.

I did as I was ordered, still staring into the unblinking eye of the camera. He patted me down, quick but thorough, and jerked his head that I should follow him through the gate. I pointed questioningly to the snowmobile. He grabbed the keys out of my hand and made the "follow me" gesture again, more impatiently this time.

I followed. As I stepped over the sill and through the inset doorway, I was surprised, if I was honest, that the gambit had worked, and I realized that a part of me had hoped it might not, that I would be sent packing and could return to Hamilton with a shrug and a "Well, I tried . . ." Now I was filled with the uneasy sense of taking a wrong turn, a bad road. I took it anyway.

On the other side of the gatehouse was a utilitarian Mercedes G-Wagon with snow chains fixed to the tires. I was bundled into the back seat. The first guard got behind the wheel, while the second slid into the passenger seat and twisted so he faced backward. He never took his eyes off me.

It was less than a minute up what might have been classed as a driveway. At the moment it was a narrow corridor cut between two walls of packed snow. The walls reached the top of the G-Wagon's windows on either side, limiting my view of the lodge itself until we drove under an archway and pulled up inside the courtyard I'd seen in the image on Madeleine's computer.

I wasn't given time to admire the view, just hustled across the snow and in through a side door.

Inside was a hallway, sparsely furnished, with walls painted that shade of pale cream you find in old hospitals. Either Gregor had vastly simplified his tastes since the last time we'd met, or this was the tradesman's entrance. Through an open doorway I glimpsed a room lined with banks of security monitors.

The heating must have been cranked to maximum. Within moments of stepping into the building, I was sweating. I unzipped my coat, still not making any sudden moves. The two men who'd brought me in patted me down again, just to be certain I didn't have anything they'd missed the first time. They were more thorough about it this time. It was not something I enjoyed at the best of times.

Then they unstrapped their guns and shrugged out of jackets and goggles. They did it one at a time, one always keeping watch.

As they did so, I recognized the one who'd come out to intercept me. It was the ex-Spetsnaz guy who'd had me kidnapped in Kuwait City, and turned up again at the hotel in Madaba.

"Ah, Comrade Ushakov," I said. "Or should that be *Admiral* . . . ?"

SIXTY

USHAKOV NEVER EVEN CRACKED A SMILE. HE JUST STARED DOWN AT me, the overhead lights making the widow's peak of his close-clipped hair more pronounced than I remembered it.

"Tell me, Miss Fox, what part of 'go home' did you have the most difficulty in understanding?"

"But I *did* go home," I said brightly. "And then I came here. Maybe you need to be more precise when you deliver threats. 'Go home . . . *and stay there*,' perhaps? That might have worked better."

My flippancy produced a faint twitch at the corner of his mouth but did not add even the smallest flicker of warmth to his eyes. "Next time," he promised, "I shall . . . not forget."

The words were said slowly, with enough underlying menace that I struggled to hold my smile in place, keep my shoulders relaxed, and my gait loose as he waved me toward a doorway leading further into the house. What was it about Venko and the people who surrounded him, that they prided themselves on such cold remembering?

The door led to a paneled corridor, opening out into a larger hallway clad in a rich wood the color of a chestnut horse. It had been lovingly cut to preserve the beauty of the grain, and varnished until the reflection seemed deep enough to dip your arm in to the shoulder.

The effect was like walking into an oversize cabin on a grand old yacht. Possibly owned by someone who'd spent a lot of time ashore on desert islands, skewering the wildlife. I'd never seen so many decapitated heads of wild boar and what looked like antelope stuck on a wall.

We walked another corridor. More glossy wood, more dead animals, supplemented by small dark paintings in huge ornate frames. Up a wooden staircase that would have allowed four people to walk up abreast, down another made of marble. The standard of opulence had an anesthetizing effect. The more of it there was, the less it penetrated—or meant anything.

Eventually, Ushakov stopped outside a pair of doors that were possibly ten feet tall, and still nowhere near ceiling height. He knocked, waited for a gruff order from inside, then ushered me through.

I half expected that he'd stay outside, but he and the other man followed me in and stood on either side of the doorway like sentries. Now that I looked more closely, I recognized him from Madaba, too. He'd been in the car with Ushakov, front passenger seat, when they'd pulled up at the hotel.

Inside, the room was not lined with wood, for a change. Instead it was largely gold leaf on a background that might have been pale cream or white. It was hard to tell against all that bling. Someone had gone berserk with plaster scrolls and cornices and molding, then picked them out in gold just to make absolutely sure you couldn't miss them. It was so over the top, from the antique mirrors to the fireplaces to the crystal chandeliers, that I almost laughed out loud at the sight of it.

Then I saw the figure on a deep-buttoned leather sofa at the far end of the room, and I was glad I hadn't.

Gregor Venko and I had few things in common, and I was willing to bet that a warped sense of humor did not make the list.

I was shocked by the sight of him. The man I remembered was a force of nature. Even sitting still, there had been something restless about him, something both calculated and calculating, like a coiled snake waiting for the most advantageous moment to strike. Not someone to turn your back on, even for a moment.

Now, his stillness had an air of malaise about it. There was no suppressed dominance, no more restless imagination.

The way he was dressed didn't help. Gone were the immaculately cut suit, the silk tie, the equally magnificent overcoat. The uniform of a powerful man.

Instead, he wore well-washed moleskin trousers that were too wide for his skinny legs, so his knees protruded at sharp angles in the sagging cloth.

The old Gregor had been a bull of a man, squat, wide, muscular. The type who would once have appeared, with striped bathing costume and curling mustache, bending iron bars in a circus sideshow.

The new Gregor looked simply . . . old.

He regarded me with no recognition in his eyes, which drifted back to the crackle of logs in the grate. Someone had let air out of him so his fleshy features were slightly deflated, glistening with a film of sweat. His wardrobe had yet to catch up with his frame. The open collar of his shirt gaped beneath a yellow sweater that might have been made of cashmere but which fit so poorly that it looked no better than a street-market special.

I glanced behind me, at Ushakov. He met my eyes, but his face told me that I had to cross this psychological minefield on my own. Physically was another matter, and when I moved forward, he was at my shoulder. At first I was grateful for the apparent solidarity, until I remembered he was there to keep me from harming Gregor, not for my benefit.

It seemed a long way across the Persian rugs, but only when I halted a respectful distance in front of him did the old man at last look slowly in my direction.

I waited, unsure how to break the silence. A man like Gregor had to be treated carefully at best. Here, in his domain, he wielded ultimate power. He could reward or punish on little more than a whim.

Eventually, he swallowed painfully and said, "Miss Fox. It has been a long time, I think."

"Indeed it has, sir."

His lips had been full but now they had thinned, so that when he pulled them back into a smile, it was more of a snarl. "What has brought you to my . . . home?" he asked, not quite fierce enough to be a demand, but close. "What do you want?"

"I'm here because a man died—badly—in Iraq."

"It is Iraq. Many men die badly in Iraq," Venko dismissed. "What makes this man any different?"

"He worked for you—in Basra."

Venko went very still. A trickle of sweat rolled down the side of his face, although the room was not overly warm, despite the open fire. Nerves, or something more? He leaned back and fumbled awkwardly in his trouser pocket, his hand emerging with a crumpled handkerchief, which he used to mop his face. While his features remained impassive, there was a minute tremor in the tips of his fingers.

"Michael Clay," he said, so softly I barely heard him.

I nodded. "Yes."

His eyes fluttered closed for a moment, no longer than a slow blink, and he let the hand drop back to his lap.

His gaze rose to my face, then past me to the man standing at my shoulder. I followed his sight line to Ushakov, then moved sideways slightly so he remained in my peripheral vision and was not directly behind me.

"Why did you send your man to gently warn me off asking questions," I asked Gregor, nodding in Ushakov's direction, "unless you knew Clay was dead?"

"I . . . did not know," Gregor said, eyes still boring into the Russian with something of their old intensity. "I was led to believe he had . . . absconded."

An interesting choice of word. It had connections with embezzlement in my mind. *So-and-so absconded with the payroll.* I wondered if that was why Gregor had selected it.

He'd thought Clay was on the take, and maybe he was. But if Sean didn't kill him, and Gregor hadn't had the Russians do it, who did?

Gregor finally dragged his attention back to me and swallowed again. Both actions took effort, but he was not a man short on willpower.

"What is he to you, this Clay?"

"He's nothing to me," I said truthfully. "Less than nothing. But the man on whom suspicion has fallen, he *is* something to me. And because of that I need to find out the truth."

"Who?"

"Sean Meyer."

I didn't elaborate. I was willing to bet Gregor rarely forgot a name, and certainly not the name of a man like Sean, who'd done at least as much as I had—if not more—to return Ivan to him alive.

So it surprised me when his expression hardened, tightening the jowls into a reasonably accurate facsimile of the man I'd met before.

"Michael Clay stole from me . . . something of great value. Something unique and irreplaceable which was certainly worth killing him for. *If* Sean Meyer killed him, as he is suspected, perhaps he has . . . stolen from me, also?"

Before I could deny the accusation, or work out quite where it sprang from, the double doors nearest to our end of the room burst open and a young man strode in.

I had not seen Ivan since bundling him into the back of an up-armored stretch limo in Germany, under fire, several years previously. And if the intervening time had been cruel to Gregor Venko, they had been overly generous to his son. A likeness of Oscar Wilde's *Picture of Dorian Gray* came unbidden and unwelcome to my mind, with Gregor playing the suppurating portrait, and Ivan the gilded flower of permanent youth.

Before, Ivan had been handsome to the point of pretty, with those stunning pale green eyes, blond hair, and exaggerated Slavic cheekbones. He could have been a male model rather than a gangster-in-waiting. The intervening years had filled out his body from slightly gawky to physically mature. He obviously hit the gym on a regular basis, too.

There was no getting away from it, if you looked no deeper than his skin, he really was quite beautiful.

"*Papa*, what the FUCK?" he yelled, voice ending on a high-pitched squawk that took the shine off his attractiveness somewhat. He jabbed a finger in my direction. "What is this BITCH doing here?"

Gregor ignored the outburst, just sat patiently and waited until Ivan reached him, glared down, chest heaving beneath the open collar of a silk shirt. I caught a glimpse of a gold crucifix on a chain around his neck.

"She is here because of Michael Clay," Gregor said at last. "Why did you not tell me he was dead?"

Ivan stiffened as if insulted. "Because I did not know this, *Papa*. I left him alive, as I told you, begging for your forgiveness and promising to prove his loyalty by returning what he had taken. I should not have trusted that his fear of you would be strong enough . . ." Shrugging, he let the words trail away as his eyes speared mine with pure venom in them.

And I realized then, with a sudden, startling clarity, that Michael Clay had not been alive when Ivan left him. My mind went winging back to that dirty building in Basra, to the blood and the flies. I saw again the ruined body lying on the mortuary table. The wanton mutilation that even those sterile conditions could not disguise.

I remembered the underlying viciousness that had always marred Ivan's perfect exterior, the brutality of his actions in Germany. Of being told that Ivan had been unbalanced right from the start. That Gregor had been cleaning up after him since the boy was seven.

And I knew, without a shadow of a doubt, that Ivan Venko was the one who murdered Clay.

The problem was going to be proving it.

SIXTY-ONE

MY PROBLEM WAS GOING TO BE NOT JUST PROVING IVAN'S GUILT, I considered a few minutes later, but proving it to his father. The Gregor I'd known was only too aware of his son's faults. Now, as he patted Ivan's cheek, he seemed not only willing but determined to ignore them.

Maybe the state of his health had much to do with that.

Clearly, Gregor was not well. If I had to guess, I'd say early Parkinson's disease—something neurological, at any rate. The weight loss, the slowed movements, the difficulty swallowing, the tremor in his hand that was caused by more than emotion. Indicative, rather than conclusive.

I wondered if he knew.

He must. How can he not have realized something is seriously wrong?

But otherwise-intelligent men of a certain age could procrastinate stupidly when it came to the matter of their own health.

And seeing the devious expression on Ivan's face as he gazed down at his father, I guessed Ivan had not encouraged him to consult a doctor.

Not until he was sure it was too late for anything to be done.

Gregor raised his head and looked into his son's face, into his eyes. At one time, such a direct gaze might have made Ivan quail, I thought, but while he produced a creditable impression of regret, spreading his palms, his reaction was little more than a facsimile.

"You do not believe me, *Papa*. Perhaps then you will believe the word of another." He glanced at the guard over by the door and said, "Fetch him." As though it had all been prearranged.

The man turned and went out without a word.

Ivan sat next to his father, leaning in, confidential. "I always knew *she* would be back one day, with her hand out," he said, sliding his eyes in my direction. "Didn't I warn you? Just like all the other greedy bitches."

"I want nothing more than the truth," I said without heat. "If something so valuable is missing, you should want that, too." I wasn't sure Gregor heard me. Ivan continued as if I hadn't spoken.

"We should have dealt with her in Iraq." He snapped his fingers to demonstrate how easily I could have been snuffed out. "Just like that—gone."

"As I recall, you tried," I said. I met Ushakov's impassive gaze. "I'm sorry about Kuznetsov, by the way, but I think it's fair to say you started it."

Ushakov shrugged. "He knew what he was doing. It is unfortunate that so did the mercenaries accompanying you."

From that remark I gathered he did *not* know I was the one who killed his comrade. I didn't think it healthy for me to enlighten him.

"You told me she had gone home—that she had run away," Ivan accused him. Ushakov shifted his weight in reflex, and I realized those were not quite the words the Russian would have used. Ivan was trying to divide and conquer, dripping a little poison into everyone's ear. No outright lies, just exaggerations and omissions. Enough to spin a web of distrust, with him at the center as the spider. How very Shakespearean. I couldn't suppress a smile at his lack of subtlety. A mistake. His eyes narrowed.

"I wonder now how you came to make such a mistake, when you claim to be the best money can buy," Ivan said to Ushakov. "Are you sure that it *was* simply a mistake?"

Ushakov folded his arms across a muscular chest and regarded him blandly.

Whatever jibe Ivan might have been about to make next was curtailed by the doors at the far end of the room opening again. Two men entered. One was the guard, who resumed his sentry position. The second was a man I had not seen for a long time, and had not missed.

Colonel John Parris, my old commanding officer in Special Forces. I had to compel myself not to snap to attention at the sight of him. I reminded myself we were both civilians now. In fact, if it came to a direct comparison between our employers, I could even claim to outrank him.

Time had not altered him much. A few more lines on his lean, craggy face. A touch more gray at the temples of his sandy hair. A touch less hair. I wonder if all men who spent a lifetime wearing headgear of one description or another suffered from hair loss.

"Ah, Charlie, isn't it?" he said, managing to sound both familiar and patronizing at the same time. "It's been a while."

"It has, John," I returned with a deliberate drawl. There were plenty of other comments I could have added, but I had no wish to cut my own throat with sharp words, when there were others in that room who would fight me for the chance.

Parris blinked but didn't rise to the insubordination. He angled his body away from me, as if I no longer held any interest for him, and glanced between Venko father and son. Another careful snub—polite to the lady present, and then on to the real business with the men.

"How may I be of assistance, gentlemen?"

"My father has just informed me that Michael Clay is dead," Ivan said. He made a doleful face that he must have practiced in front of a mirror. "He doubts my word that we left him in good health."

"Not quite," Parris said, and just for a second I thought he was going to tell the truth, until he added smoothly, "naturally, we impressed upon him your displeasure with his conduct. That took a little beating home, as it were, but I think Ivan put your position across . . . admirably."

"By mutilating him?" I asked.

"Of course not," Parris responded. "Clay was a damned fine soldier. He expected any breach of regulations to result in punishment. One can't maintain discipline in the ranks otherwise."

He spoke easily, taking the sofa opposite Gregor's without invitation and draping an arm along the back, crossing his legs. His face was a study in relaxation, but the foot of his free leg flapped at the ankle, betraying a nervous tension. He was, I considered, lying through his nicotine-stained teeth. Gregor nodded vaguely.

"If you didn't kill him, who did?"

"Oh, I'm sure there were plenty with a reason to want him dead. He fought in a lot of places, many of which I'm not permitted to reveal, in covert actions that had far-reaching consequences. And since his military discharge, his contracting work was not always appreciated by those he tried hardest to assist in-country."

"So, what are you trying to say—that Iraqi insurgents were responsible?"

He gave me a pained look. "Hardly, my dear. But by working with us to remove priceless artifacts out of harm's way, so to speak, he was conspiring against the interests of certain parties who are infamous for their barbaric approach."

"You're trying to claim Isis killed him," I said flatly. It didn't need to be a question.

He shrugged. "It's possible, or perhaps someone had a more personal reason for wanting him dead." His pause was artful. "Someone like Sean Meyer, for instance."

He paused, one eyebrow raised. I said nothing. There was little I could offer that would not reveal I had already spoken with Sean—albeit briefly—about Clay's death. My silence surprised him.

"I'm sure you might try to argue that Sergeant Meyer would never do such a thing, but I understand that since he recovered from a serious gunshot wound to the head recently, his personality has been affected most profoundly. And with respect, Charlie, I question the neutrality of whatever opinion you might offer on the subject."

I took a breath while I willed calm onto my accelerating heartbeat, an adrenaline rush begging for violent release.

Instead, I said with commendable restraint, "I wasn't aware that Sean's state of mind was such public knowledge."

Parris chuckled. "Oh, it isn't, my dear."

"Then there's nothing more to be discussed." I inclined my head to Gregor, almost a bow. "I'm sorry to have troubled you, sir."

Parris let me step back, begin to turn away, before he said, "Did you really think it would be that easy?"

"Excuse me?"

"Did you really expect to come into a man's home—his castle, in this case—make serious accusations, and waltz out the door again without a care in the world?"

He rose, stalked toward me, got in close, crowding me with height and muscle. My eyes were about on a level with his Adam's apple. It made an appealing target.

I glanced toward Gregor, curious about his reaction to all this, but the old man was sitting in utter stillness, his eyes closed as if in meditation.

So I lifted my chin to meet Parris's challenge, refusing to back away from him, to back down. Instead, I ran through a mental checklist of ways to hurt him. It was reassuringly long.

"I have, naturally, left word of my location with certain agencies," I said calmly. "If they don't receive a phone call in the next, oh, twenty minutes, I would say, to reassure them of my well-being, I will not be the only one waltzing into your man's castle today."

Parris regarded me without apparent unease. "I assume you're referring to the group you were with on the mountain this afternoon. I don't think we need to worry too much about them."

I smiled as if that piece of information had not just shaken me. "You think they are all I have at my disposal?"

"You will stay, Miss Fox," Gregor said suddenly, opening his eyes as he broke his silence. "I have not forgotten what you did for me. Make whatever call you need to make, but you will stay—as my . . . guest. Twenty-four hours. Then we will see."

It might have been phrased and delivered graciously, but I did not mistake the order for a mere suggestion.

SIXTY-TWO

PARRIS RELIEVED ME OF MY CELL PHONE, REMOVED THE BATTERY, then casually told Ushakov to throw it off the mountain. I was glad I abandoned, back at the chalet, the far more expensive satellite phone I'd used in the Middle East.

Parris stood over me while I made the call to Madeleine from a landline, presumably so they had a record of the number, and also so she could not trace my exact position, even if she'd had the equipment to do so.

I reported without verbal expression that Gregor had cordially invited me to stay until the following evening. We had worked out a simple code beforehand. By use of the word *"cordially"* rather than *kindly, generously,* or *hospitably,* she knew I was not under duress, exactly, but not free to leave, either. House arrest rather than maximum security, and not to plan a rescue op just yet.

That was the theory, anyway.

I was taken to a guest suite and left to my own devices. Needless to say, the door was firmly locked once I was inside. The suite was made up of a large bedroom with sitting area and fireplace at one end, the decoration leaning heavily toward the intricate plasterwork and gilt end of the scale. The fireplace was empty, sadly, and devoid of anything readily combustible. They really didn't want to provide me with any weapons I might improvise.

I explored, casually. The window offered a view down onto the courtyard, where I could see the G-Wagon that Ushakov had used to run me up from the gatehouse. The window did not open, and although the frame looked like wood, closer inspection revealed it to be disguised steelwork, the panes of glass too small for me to climb through unless I crash-dieted and was given a thorough rubdown with goose grease.

Adjacent was a bathroom—all marble and mirrors—accessible via a door that looked like part of the wall. The wardrobe contained the kind of fluffy bathrobe you'd get in an upscale hotel, and a selection of clothing that looked roughly my size, including a slinky evening dress and heels. They looked little worn, but not new. I couldn't help wondering what had become of their previous owner.

I had a sudden picture of a scene from an early James Bond movie—*Dr. No*—where the eponymous villain provides 007 with a dinner jacket, then wines and dines him before having him severely worked over. If I was going to get a pasting, I decided, I'd rather do it wearing my own clothes.

I also found a tiny camera concealed high in the corner diagonally opposite the doorway, as well as two microphones, one of which, disturbingly enough, was behind the light fitting over the sink in the bathroom. I hopped up onto the vanity unit to take a closer look, then curled my forefinger and thumb into my mouth and blew the loudest, shrillest whistle I could manage, directly into the mic. I'd been practicing, so the best I could manage was pretty bloody loud.

Childish, I knew, but anyone who wanted to eavesdrop on me while I was on the loo deserved to suffer partial hearing loss.

Having whiled away the best part of an hour, I lay down on the bed, fingers laced across my stomach, ankles crossed, and stared at the intricately carved wooden ceiling. If nothing happened soon, I contemplated taking a nap. Most soldiers—and ex-soldiers, come to that—won't pass up the opportunity to either sleep or eat. You never know when you might next have the chance. Plus it tends to alleviate the boredom caused by long periods of inactivity punctuated by short bouts of fear.

Whoever was watching the feed decided that allowing me to rest undisturbed was probably not a good idea. Or maybe it was the guy on the receiving end of my ear-splitting whistle. Either way, it was only fifteen minutes or so after I'd lain down that I heard a key turn in the lock and watched the door swing inward.

I rolled off the bed and onto my feet, knees soft, hands ready. When I saw the identity of my visitor, I was glad I had done so.

"Mr. Parris."

"I'll take '*Colonel* Parris' if you don't mind."

"I understand you resigned your commission when you left the army, *Mr.* Parris. Without being officially granted the right to continue using your rank in civvy street, you'll take what you can get."

He regarded me steadily, the same way he might once have studied a disappointing recruit.

"I would remind you that I may be your only friend here, and would advise you not to rile me unnecessarily."

"With friends like those . . ." I murmured. "Besides, I get the feeling that without Gregor's intervention, I'd currently

327

be chained to a wall in a damp cellar rather than enjoying my present surroundings."

He gave a rueful smile. "You may have a point there," he allowed. "Tell me, my dear, did you fuck the old man as well, to procure such an easy ride?"

The insult, so pleasantly delivered, knocked me sideways like a slap to the face. I felt the squirt of adrenaline as a prickling of my scalp, a beat in my fingertips. The blood dropped out of my face then flooded back in an angry, heated wave. I had to wait for it to subside before I trusted myself to speak.

"I don't believe I've ever had an 'easy ride' out of anyone, regardless of whether I fucked them or not." I paused, then, more in annoyance than wisdom, tossed out, "After all, I got well and truly fucked by you, didn't I?"

I was thinking of his support for the four men, but his next words utterly threw me.

"Oh, I beg to disagree with you there. If I hadn't taken the course of action I chose, I would have been forced to arrange some manner of training accident for you, wouldn't I? And the bureaucratic red tape attached to any kind of fatality outside of an actual theater of war was quite monumental, as I'm sure you can imagine."

His tone invited sympathy with his predicament. But his words hit me like blows from a sledgehammer rather than a modest palm cracked across my cheek. Parris watched the emotions that must have been flitting openly across my face.

And he laughed.

"Even now, you can barely comprehend it, can you? The lengths I had to go to in order to be rid of you. I never wanted females under my command. Not in training and certainly not out in the field. A damned liability, attempting to do a man's job with all their pathetic whining about gender equality, yet at the same time quite incapable of carrying the same load, and demanding constant access to sanitary products, for God's sake. But you were foisted on me from above, and, like any good soldier, I had to improvise."

"Why me?" I whispered when my voice came back to me, albeit at less than half power. I swallowed past the stone in my throat, tried again. "There were two other women who passed Selection besides me. What did *I* do to deserve being singled out? Did you just stick a pin in a fucking *list*?"

Parris didn't answer right away. He strolled to the window, clasped his hands behind his back as he stared out, although I doubt he registered the view.

"You seemed like a bright girl—you *must* have realized you were the only one I had to worry about. Those other two were never going to set any records, make any waves. But *you*, my dear—you were a different animal altogether."

He turned then, pierced me with cold and bitter eyes. "You were the one who was going to change things. *You* were the one who looked set to perform not just as *well* as the men but better than the majority of them, with the resultant appalling effect on morale. I *could not* let that happen—not on my watch."

SIXTY-THREE

THE SMALL CONVOY OF TRUCKS ARRIVED AT VENKO'S FORTRESS
around ten the following morning. Somewhere between getting off the boat and reaching Borovets, they had been fitted
with mammoth tires and snow chains. Even so, I was surprised
they'd made it.

Three of them rumbled into the courtyard below my
window, the sound booming off the stonework as it rose.
Cab doors slammed and shouts of greeting and celebration
floated up, too, along with a mist of air warmed by bodies
and engines.

It was cold otherwise, and fat flakes of snow swirled and
eddied in the vortices caused by the buildings. All the people
wore heavy coats, big hats, their faces muffled and gaits disguised by the partially frozen slush underfoot. Walking was
done carefully, arms splayed for balance. Impossible to recognize any of them.

It seemed strangely appropriate to be staring down at the tableau. I'd spent most of a sleepless night with my brain hovering on the ceiling, staring down at my own body. Now, it felt as if someone had split me apart from myself and put me back together not quite fully aligned, so everything was slightly off center, out of whack.

Disengaged, I replayed every action and reaction I could remember, from the moment I'd passed the brutal Selection process and arrived in Hereford for my training, to the collapse of the disastrous civil trial against my four attackers. Picked it all apart, analyzed and second-guessed, and then put it back together with new facts holding it all in place. Certain things made more sense than they had back then.

And, more recently, it was clear why Donalson had introduced Parris's name in that apparently random fashion in the kitchen of that bleak farmhouse on Saddleworth Moor. Snatches of Sean's more cryptic comments in Hackett's villa in Madaba came back to me—about knowing the right person to go after.

A chill rippled across my skin at the thought that they had all known, and I seemed to be the last to find out. Paranoia made me wonder if Sean had told Madeleine, if she in turn had told Parker. A whole chain of meaningful whispers that went both over my head and behind my back.

It was hard to know if I was more ashamed now of the original assault or my own ignorance of the machinations behind it.

Down in the courtyard, the trucks were backed slowly under cover, their reverse warning buzzers shrill. Unfortunately, the workshops or garages into which they disappeared were directly underneath my window. Even with my face squirmed against the glass, I could see little of the procedure, and nothing of what was happening inside.

I perched on the window ledge, aware of the radiated nip from the cold glass, and kept watch. The trucks did not reappear. Neither did the men who had been driving them. The snow continued to pile up softly on the ground, soon melding the tire tracks and footprints until they could hardly be distinguished. It was like seeing the outline of ancient foundations from the air, long after they've been reclaimed by fields. Not exactly the height of entertainment.

When I heard the key rattle in the lock again, I rubbed the windowpane with my sleeve to clear the greasy smudge left by my cheek and hopped down. I settled for leaning on the radiator below the window instead, arms loosely folded.

To my relief, it was not Parris again who entered but Ushakov. I don't know why I should have been reassured by that. After all, Parris had gone to some lengths to avoid killing me in the army, all that time ago, while I got the impression the Russian had no feelings on the matter one way or the other. If Gregor's orders for him in Kuwait had been different, I had no doubt he would have done his best to carry them out.

He stood just inside the doorway and scanned the room before he focused fully on me. A careful man with a serious expression. It was how he'd managed to live so long.

"Gregor wants you."

I raised an eyebrow and didn't immediately make any moves, mainly out of pure pigheadedness. I'd been brought supper on a tray the evening before, which I'd done little more than pick at, partly because my encounter with Parris had made my stomach churn at the thought of food, and partly because I hadn't been sure about what pharmaceutical additions might have been made to it. In the past, I'd been on the receiving end of midazolam—a pre-op relaxant that induced compliance along with amnesia. I had no desire to wake later and be unable to remember something I'd apparently been willing to do.

Not with Ivan Venko on the loose.

Breakfast had provoked the same fears, and the same response. Hunger probably made me more awkward than I might otherwise have been.

"What for?"

"When Gregor calls, you answer," Ushakov said. "You walk, or I drag you by your ankles." He shrugged. "Your choice."

I might have thought he was joking, but I reckoned any latent sense of humor had been rigorously expunged in training. It was not a quality the Russians seemed to prize.

Besides, there were a lot of stairs in this rabbit warren of a place, and I had no desire to thump the back of my head on every tread if he made good on his threat.

I pushed away from the radiator and walked toward the door.

"Gregor will expect you to . . . look nice."

He took a pointed look down at my rumpled clothes. I was not prepared to strip for the camera, so I'd slept in them, taking off only my boots and zip-up fleece.

"Good for him. Every man should have ambition—however unachievable," I said. "I am not a doll he can dress up when he wants to play with me."

Ushakov shrugged again, didn't push it. His silent companion from yesterday was waiting outside in the corridor, and the three of us walked downstairs in single file, with me the filling in the thug sandwich.

They took me back to the same room, where Gregor waited on the same brocade sofa, before the same log fire. I wondered if he'd even been to bed. His clothing was almost the same—a slight variation on a similar theme. My father, I recalled, tended to wear the same things as he got older. More so now that he had retired. A comfort zone rarely ventured beyond.

Gregor did little more than nod to acknowledge my arrival. I was not invited to sit, and I preferred to stand anyway. Harder to be pinned down that way.

A few minutes passed, during which time the only noises were the logs shifting in the grate and the tick of what looked like a Louis XV clock on the mantelpiece, all gilt and cherubs.

Then one set of doors opened and four men came in. Ivan and Parris I was expecting. And Hackett, of course, laughing a little too loudly at something Ivan had just said. He punched the man next to him lightly on the shoulder in a display of macho camaraderie. And that did throw me, both the friendly gesture and the recipient, because I never expected to see that combination outside of a really disturbed night's sleep.

The man Hackett was being so pally toward was Sean.

SIXTY-FOUR

FOR A MOMENT I COULDN'T SPEAK, COULDN'T MOVE, COULD HARDLY even breathe. I experienced the same disconnection from my body I'd had during the night, so that I viewed the scene from high above it, like a movie, with the men approaching their patriarch and the woman standing meekly to one side.

It was hard to work out if it was worse to see Hackett again, or to see him looking so at ease with Sean. A photo finish with little to decide it.

"You are later than expected." Gregor's voice, a low grumble, made them quiet but did little to actually dampen their bonhomie.

"Relax, *Papa*. The journey was long and not without difficulties," Ivan said, "but all is well. They are here now." He flopped down onto the sofa opposite as though he himself was exhausted from battling out of a war zone at the wheel of one of the trucks. A poseur, but a dangerous one.

"Not quite 'all,'" I said. "What happened to the rest of the trucks?"

"What the fuck are you talking about, woman?" Hackett demanded. Something about the question surprised me. Not the question itself, but the asking of it. I realized it was the first time he'd addressed me, looked at me directly, since we'd faced each other across a British courtroom.

"The numbers are simple enough that even you should have no difficulty understanding them," I said. "You got off the boat in Odessa with five trucks and arrived here with only three. Where are the other two?"

There was a brief silence that prickled in the air, then Ivan began to clap in slow and languorous insult.

"Oh, very good." Contempt dripped from his voice. "How long, I wonder, was your devious little mind working to come up with that lie?" He looked to his father. "See—she is a scheming bitch, like I told you. First she tries to tell you that I killed Clay, and now that we have disappeared two whole trucks. Poof!" Another overdramatic click of his fingers. "Like David Blaine."

Gregor's head turned in my direction, expression heavy. "How do you know number of trucks that landed at Odessa?" There was something reluctant in his tone, as if he felt compelled to ask but did not want to know.

"Do you think I would arrive here with no intel?" I asked mildly. "Five trucks boarded a Black Sea ferry in the port of Rize in northern Turkey and disembarked yesterday morning in the Ukraine."

"Why did you fail to mention this until now?" Gregor asked. His rheumy eyes met mine briefly and I thought I saw pain in them, but as fast as it came it was gone.

"Perhaps because I did not think any of your own people would be foolish enough to try to deceive you."

"Hah!" Ivan jacked to his feet, stabbed a finger in my face. I refused to blink at the spittle flying my way. He turned, spread his hands to his father. "If five trucks had miraculously appeared, she would have told you there should be seven, eh?"

"Well, I don't remember us shedding a couple on the road," Hackett said easily. "What about you, Sean?"

Sean had not spoken to this point, but neither had he taken his eyes off me. Now he continued to hold my gaze for several moments before he shook his head. "Three," he said.

He might as well have put on a black cap and told me I'd be taken from this place to a place of execution . . . I ripped my eyes away from Sean.

"Out of interest, how much was Clay supposed to have stolen from you?" I asked Gregor. "It wouldn't happen to be just about enough to fill two trucks, by any chance?"

"You are a LIAR!" Ivan's accusing finger was back in my face. I barely resisted the urge to grab and twist, just to feel the bones snap and the ligaments tear. Just to hear his screams drown out the ones rebounding inside my skull.

I don't know what showed on my face, but he stepped back automatically, wary. Then he scowled, furious with himself—but more furious with me—for invoking such a reaction.

"She always was one for making up stories," Hackett said. "They were good—just not quite good enough, if you take my meaning. Convincing enough to drop you in the shit, but didn't stand up to close inspection. By that time, of course, it was too late. The shit was flying and some of it stuck."

I pushed away the lies, delivered in that snide tone I remembered so well. What worried me more was the fact everyone present seemed to be taking it at face value. I hadn't felt this outnumbered, outmaneuvered, *and* outgunned since the army. But what knifed me deeper than anything else was the look of disdain on Sean's face.

"I was told she waited until I was posted, then claimed I'd bullied her into sex. Like Hackett says, that kind of shit sticks. It finished *my* chances of promotion, that's for sure."

I could hardly credit it was Sean who'd just spoken, and I struggled not to gape at him. When we'd met again for the first time since the army, he'd admitted that *was* the line he'd been sold about my behavior. He'd been posted weeks before I was attacked, hadn't been there, hadn't known.

As one of my training instructors, he should not have been involved in any kind of relationship with me, but I hadn't said a word against him. It was only later that we found out who had dropped us both in it—accidentally, it turned out—by revealing our affair to the army brass.

It had made the outcome worse, perhaps, but hadn't been the cause of it.

I would have bet my life on the fact that Sean knew that. Even now—even *after*, as I'd come to think of him post-coma.

I glanced at Parris, who'd moved to stand at ease to one side of the fireplace, his back to the grate and hands clasped behind him. Had he told Sean that he'd been the mastermind of my downfall—and ultimately Sean's, too? His face was impassive, giving nothing away.

Gregor was watching me with something akin to his old intensity. There was maybe a little expectancy there, too, as if he was hoping I would come up with some plausible denial to the accusations. He'd painted me as his son's savior, and he'd spared my life because of it. Now I could see he was expecting me to provide him with reasons not to regret that decision.

I couldn't, and didn't try.

"I don't know how many trucks could have been filled with the treasures that Clay stole from you, sir," Sean said now, addressing Gregor with deference and without apparent irony that those very "treasures" had already been stolen from the Iraqi people. His eyes flicked to mine. "I asked him to reveal that information with every means at my disposal, but he was a very stubborn man . . . right up to the moment he died on me."

SIXTY-FIVE

WHEN I THOUGHT ABOUT IT LOGICALLY, CLINICALLY, THERE WAS not much Sean could have said right then that would have discredited me more.

Gregor already knew that Clay was dead but not, as I'd suggested, at the hand of his psychotic son. Instead, Sean had freely admitted he'd been the one to torture, mutilate, and murder Clay, when I'd been prepared to swear up, down, and sideways that he was innocent. All in all, I was just about finished as far as Gregor's trust was concerned.

He made a dismissive gesture, muttered, "Get her out of my sight. I will decide what . . . later."

Ushakov stepped forward, but Parris intercepted him before he'd taken me more than a couple of steps.

"Please, allow me," he said, as if he was cutting in for a waltz.

And I did allow him to lead me from the drawing room where Gregor sat hunched in front of his log fire. I felt eyes on my back all the way to the door, but I refused to give them the satisfaction of a last, longing look back.

I didn't want to see what might be written on Sean's face. I had a feeling I wouldn't like it much.

We walked in silence up the various staircases and along the corridors. Parris opened the door to the same guest suite I'd been in the night before, then stood aside with a parody of a courtly bow.

"If you're still alive by tomorrow," he said conversationally as I moved to pass him, "I shall give you to Ivan."

I hid the shudder of instant revulsion to ask lightly, "Gift-wrapped in ribbons, with a bow in my hair?"

"Oh, I think we may have to bind you with something, but I doubt very much it will be ribbon. Meyer has been filling me in a little on your . . . exploits since the army. It seems I was correct in my assessment of your potential. You've developed quite the killer instinct."

"You sound as if you're taking the credit, John. Perhaps you should be taking the blame."

He gave a smile. It was not a heartwarming one. "I think you rely too heavily on being underestimated, my dear. People see your unassuming exterior, and they don't trouble to look past it. I won't make that mistake. And in case you have any ideas in that direction, don't worry—you won't be in any condition to do Ivan any damage."

"Two of the men downstairs have already fucked me," I threw at him, using any weapon I could think of, the first that came to hand. "Do you really think he'll want their castoff?"

"Who said anything about sex?" Parris asked, amusement in his voice now. "Ivan gets his kicks in quite another manner. After all, you saw Clay's body . . ."

He let that one drift off and watched the effect of his words as they seeped into me like rain. "The boy's an artist when it comes to robust interrogation—just doesn't know when to stop. That, and he enjoys his work a little too much. Clay gave up the location of the goods within the first twenty minutes. The rest was just for Ivan's own entertainment. I rather think I'm looking forward to seeing what he has in store for you."

I forced a shrug. "Well, he never did like me very much."

"How true. After all, you—a mere girl—had the affront to rescue him, so I understand. A real blow to his pride."

"At the time, Gregor felt it was preferable to having him taken apart by the Germans," I said. "And I think Gregor is the one you underestimate. He has an old-world sense of honor, for a mobster, and he still remembers what I did for him, saving Ivan's neck. I doubt he'll agree to let his son feed me slowly through a wood-chipper, however happy it might make the evil little sod."

If anything Parris's smile grew broader. "You really can't see it, can you?" he murmured. "The old man is sick—not quite on his last legs, but not far off. The last few years, he's been holding Ivan at bay like a lion tamer fending off a hungry big cat. In Ivan's case, he's hungry for power. It's been simmering away for some time now. And the longer Gregor clings to control, the more hungry for it Ivan becomes. We may have reached something of a boiling point. And if Gregor doesn't let the boy have what he wants, I rather think we're heading for a coup d'état."

"Which leaves you where, exactly?"

"Oh, I'm the civil service of the Venko empire, as it were. Gregor's simply a figurehead, but my men and I represent boots on the ground and are therefore essential to achieve a smooth transition of power. Ivan needs me, and he knows it."

I shook my head. "Why would you even *want* to work for a psychopath?"

"Because they're so easy to predict and manipulate. Ivan would be a piece of cake compared to his father. Gregor is a master strategist, always three steps ahead of those around him, and prepared to shake up the hierarchy every now and again, just to throw the cat among the pigeons."

"Ushakov," I realized out loud. "Gregor brought in the ex-Spetsnaz guys to keep you on your toes. And so you didn't know every detail of everything."

Parris shrugged, but there was something a little less casual about the gesture than he'd intended. Gregor had gone over his head, I thought, managing at the same time to put his nose out of joint. That required some considerable dexterity. But why had he done it . . . ?

"Gregor doesn't altogether trust you," I hazarded a guess. "That's why he hired Ushakov, and that's why he sent Ivan to Iraq to find out what Clay had been up to. Tell me, did Clay decide to cheat Gregor off his own bat, or were you pulling his strings there, too?"

Parris laughed, but there was a flush of blood to the sides of his neck, the tips of his ears, that told me I'd hit closer to the truth than he was happy to admit.

"Like I said, you always were a bright girl."

"You make it sound like an epitaph."

"In your case, my dear, it will be." He started to turn away, one hand on the door, then faced me again as if only just remembering the "one last thing" he'd been holding in reserve from the start. "Oh, if you were hoping for the seventh cavalry in the form of your American friends to ride to the rescue in *your* case, my dear, I'm afraid you're destined to be disappointed."

"Oh?" I tried to keep the single syllable noncommittal, but Parris didn't need much prompting. He was bursting to tell me.

"Ms. Hamilton has been on our radar for some time. At one point she even had us a little concerned, but fortunately that's all changed with the administration."

"In what way?" I could have taken a stab at it, but it seemed mean to deprive him of his moment of glory. Besides, you never knew what else he might let slip. "I thought President Trump was all for boosting military spending."

"Oh he is, but the budget for anything not directly connected to actual firepower has been slashed, and that is particularly so for a small department tasked with recovering foreign cultural items which *may or may not* be connected to the funding of terrorism. It's such a gray area—the cost-benefit is so difficult to prove. Hardly worth tweeting about."

"And I suppose you'd claim that, by stealing the stuff out from under the noses of Isis, you're actually behaving like a patriot."

"Quite so, my dear."

"And then, of course, by stealing two fifths of it from Gregor—because you know as well as I do there were five bloody trucks—I suppose you count yourself doubly virtuous for doing your bit against organized crime as well?"

Parris's smile this time was different from the others. It contained a genuine amusement, which faded to regret as he scanned me up and down.

"Such a shame that things had to come to this, Charlie, but that's how it goes sometimes. Do try to get some rest if you can. Ivan does rather like his victims to be in good voice . . ."

And with that he went out and pulled the solid hardwood door firmly closed behind him, as if sealing the entrance to a tomb.

SIXTY-SIX

◈

AS SOON AS PARRIS HAD GONE, I STARTED LOOKING FOR A WAY OUT. The door was old, solid, with thick panels and tight joints. No leeway in the frame, and hinge screws hidden in the fold between door and jamb. The keyhole, interestingly enough, had been blocked off so the door could not be locked—or unlocked, more to the point—from the inside.

So, Gregor did not like his "guests" wandering the halls in the wee small hours.

The window yielded nothing promising, either. I'd already established that I wouldn't fit through the glass apertures. And even if I could have somehow broken the welds on the steel frame, it was a good fifteen meters from the outside ledge to the ground. Not only that, but because there were those garages directly beneath the wing I was in, the snow had been cleared in front of them. No soft landing there.

I went into the bathroom, climbed up onto the vanity unit, and inspected the microphone. I'd expected it to be wireless, but when I picked at it repeatedly with my nails, I found twin-core wire—the kind you'd use to power a doorbell—disappearing into the wall.

The wire might have been thin, but that didn't mean I could break it without any tools. Fortunately, the mic had been attached to the end with solder. When I tugged on it, the mic came free, along with a coil of plaster that popped off the wall around the wire hole.

I'd already checked that the mirror was simply that—a mirror—rather than a hidden screen in front of another camera, so at least they couldn't see what I was doing in there.

I hopped down off the vanity. There were no plugs in the bath or sink—presumably so I couldn't block them up and flood the place. I ran some water into the drinking glass and dropped the mic into that instead.

The small piece of plaster, I noticed, had fallen into the sink, painted side down. I stared at it, frowning.

The underside was pink.

Some years ago I was living in a rented cottage, which I did some renovation work on. Well, I *started* the work, but then trouble got in the way, as it had a habit of doing. But I took down some old plaster walls, and they were usually gray with age. Pink was the color of modern gypsum plaster.

Hardly surprising, when I thought about it. Back when this place was built, it probably wasn't the norm for every room to be en suite—not even for Bulgarian royalty. The bathrooms had been added later, with stud partition walls to separate them.

The wall with the microphone wire hidden inside it was opposite the bedroom rather than backing onto it. So it was likely to be the divider between this suite and the bathroom of the next. I tried to recall if Parris had had to unlock the door before he'd put me in here that first time.

No, he hadn't . . .

I wondered if my ex-CO realized what he'd achieved by our last conversation. He must have known I was reeling from my encounter with Sean. But assuming I'd crumple when he told me I was about to end up in Ivan's sticky mitts, and that my chances of outside rescue were minimal, now *that* was a mistake. He galvanized me rather than making me give up altogether, made me doubly determined to get out of here.

I tapped the wall. It sounded thin, hollow. It had to be horrible as a guest to be able to hear the ablutions of your neighbor, as in a cheap hotel, but right now I couldn't have been more thankful that Borovets had its share of shoddy builders, just like everywhere else.

From the wardrobe in the bedroom I picked out those glitzy high heels that had been left for my use and decided to take them at their word. They seemed like good quality shoes.

Back in the bathroom I managed to hammer the stiletto heel of one straight through the wall next to the sink. It took half a dozen blows onto the shoe with the side of my fist to put a hole through the plaster layer on top of the drywall. The heel snapped off—nice to know Gregor was a cheapskate when it came to footwear. I kept going with the other.

Once I'd created a weak point, I carried on with my feet. Fortunately, they'd left me with the boots I was wearing when I arrived. They were thick-soled against the snow, heavy duty. Just right for kicking down a wall.

Stamping sideways onto it allowed me to enlarge the hole between the upright studs so I could reach the plasterboard on the other side of the framework. Then it went quicker. Far easier to break the plaster coating from behind.

In less than five minutes I had a hole large enough to squeeze through to next door. Nobody had come to find out what I was doing, or why the microphone in my bathroom had suddenly stopped recording anything more than bubbles.

I took the broken-off heel with me. The wider part that had been attached to the shoe fit nicely into the palm of my hand, and the tapered tip could be deadly. They named stiletto heels after a type of knife for a reason, after all.

The hole in the wall led through to another bathroom, a mirror image of my own, and then into another guest bedroom, this one decorated slightly differently, but laid out the same. I didn't linger, aware there was likely to be a camera in there, as well. The operators might well not bother watching the feeds from rooms they knew to be empty, but I couldn't rely on that. For all I knew, they were motion-activated.

As I passed through the bedroom, though, I scooped a copy of a magazine off a low table by the window. It was thick and glossy, some kind of Russian fashion mag, even if I couldn't read the Cyrillic print. I rolled it into a tight baton in one hand, shoved the stiletto heel into my pocket. Better to strike from a distance if I could manage it.

I admit I was holding my breath when I reached for the door handle, but it turned without resistance. I risked a moment with the door open a crack, listening and watching, but there was nobody nearby.

I slipped out into the corridor, retraced my steps down the staircases. The carpeting on one flight was secured with old-fashioned brass rods at the back of every tread, but I didn't have the necessary tools to remove them or the luxury of time to do so. None of the ornaments or artwork I passed had much weapons potential.

I kept heading down. Down led to out.

On one of the floors I almost ran into a woman carrying a tray. The startled gasp she gave marked her as domestic staff rather than combatant.

I smiled in what I hoped was a reassuring way and muttered, *"Izvinete,"* which I hoped meant something along the lines of 'excuse me' or 'pardon.' I hadn't exactly had much time to brush up my Bulgarian before this trip.

She gave me a shy smile and scuttled away. I wondered if I should borrow a drab frock and a tray from somewhere. As disguises went, it was so good she might as well have been wearing an invisibility cloak.

I made it to the lower ground floor after a couple of false starts and doubling back a few times, although without any further interruptions. There was no unnecessary expense on decoration down here. It was part of a warren of workshops and storerooms, some of which contained crates with Arabic script stenciled on the side of them. I could only guess what was inside.

Part of me was surprised that hardly anywhere seemed to be locked, but I guessed that all the security efforts went into keeping people outside the perimeter. Once they were inside, locked doors obstructed your defensive efforts as much as it delayed those who were attacking. Besides, you could always lock or booby-trap doorways as you retreated, if it came to that.

I walked briskly but didn't run, and tried to look as if I had every right to be there. Far less chance of catching the eye of whoever was watching the monitors.

The closer I got to the garaging, the colder it became. I found a thick padded jacket with a fur-lined hood hanging on a peg in what appeared to be a break room, and I shrugged my way into it. It came to midthigh, and I had to push back the sleeves so I could see my hands, but it was better than shivering. I shoved the Russian magazine halfway into one outer pocket, and the shoe heel into the other.

I was glad of the coat when I opened the final door that led into the garage itself. A blast of cold air met me like a slap in the face. Just inside the door was a row of official-looking clipboards on hooks. I took the first in line and pretended to study the Cyrillic script as if it meant something, lifting a corner of the first page to study the second. I frowned in mock concentration, keeping my head down, but my eyes constantly scanning. As far as I could tell, the place was devoid of life.

The three trucks I'd seen enter earlier stood inside a large white-painted workshop, each surrounded by a small moat of melted slush. Scarred steel workbenches were bolted in along the back wall, with the usual tool chests and storage cupboards you'd find in any mechanic's lair. Somebody appeared to have taken part of a driveshaft to bits on one of the benches and had yet to reassemble it. It glistened with gritty oil.

The trucks were unlocked, but the keys were not in any of the ignitions, sadly. I jumped down from the cab of the last in line and turned a slow circle, wondering where the logical place would be for them. Near to hand but out of the way.

I rounded the front of the truck and found another doorway in the middle of the end wall, where it had initially been hidden from view. The door itself had once been painted white, but it now bore grimy smears about chest height, where too many dirty hands had pushed it open. Alongside the door was an internal window of meshed safety glass. An untidy desk and filing cabinet were just visible in the gloom beyond.

I didn't want to go in there—it was a dead end, too far away from the main doors, too easy to become a trap. I took a last look behind me and went inside.

SIXTY-SEVEN

INSIDE, THE OFFICE WAS MUCH AS I EXPECTED. SMALLISH, A DESK covered with slightly crumpled paperwork and a sheen of oil that seemed to coat every surface. The ergonomic typing chair had rips in the seat, both arms repaired with duct tape. I guessed that the upholstery had once been some kind of dull tweed, but it was now shiny from years of greasy overall-clad bums sliding across it. I did not sit down for fear I'd stick to the surface. The whole place stank of cigarettes.

A pegboard on the back of the door held numerous sets of keys, but without being able to read the labels dangling from them, I had no idea what belonged to which vehicle.

I scanned the desk. There was a charging station for a walkabout phone, but it was empty. It took a moment for logic to tell me that they wouldn't take the phones away, lock them up, or deliberately hide them. I lifted a pile of brochures for snowmobiles, a catalogue for suspension bushes, and a hard-core porn mag—the usual garage reading fare—and found the phone handset discarded underneath.

I assumed with a place this big there would be some kind of networked phone system, but I juggled the buttons until I managed to get a dial tone. I punched in Madeleine's number because it was the only one I knew off the top of my head. She answered on the third ring, a wary "Hello?"

"Madeleine, it's me. Where's Hamilton?"

"Charlie! Are you OK?"

"Fine—for the moment, anyway."

"Glad to hear it. Hang on, let me put you on speaker . . . OK, go ahead."

"Hackett and three of the trucks have turned up. What happened to the others?"

"Five of 'em drove into Transnistria—it's a kinda autonomous region along the border between the Ukraine and Moldova," Hamilton said without preamble. "They play by their own rules when it comes to import and export charges. Anyway, five went in; only three came out. Could be simply the local tax system at work."

"So, why would Hackett lie about the numbers?" I wondered. "Surely Gregor's brought stuff in by that route before, so he must know how things are done?"

"Could be Hackett's done a deal along the way and is splitting the proceeds, or keeping them for himself."

And what about Sean? Why did he lie for Hackett? What did that achieve beyond stitching me up?

I shook my head, keeping back from the window and watching for anybody moving around near the trucks. I couldn't see the entrance to the garage from here. The feeling of sitting in a dead-end trap returned.

"How are things at your end?" Hamilton asked. "You wanna give us a sitrep?"

Where do I start?

"Gregor's losing his grip, so any safe passage I might have hoped for is up the spout," I said. "And Parris knows you're here. He says your budget's been slashed and you haven't got the clout to stage any kind of intervention to come in and get me. That so?"

Silence greeted me down the phone line. But outside the window I heard the sound of booted footsteps, the murmur of voices entering the workshop. I ducked back out of sight. The office held no places big enough to hide.

"I'll take that as a yes, then," I said quickly, keeping my voice low. "Look, Aubrey, your looted antiquities are sitting here, still in their trucks, with a load more besides in the neighboring storerooms. If you want them, come and get them. I'll make my own way out."

"Charlie—"

But I stabbed a thumb onto the End Call button and shoved the phone back under the porn mag on the desk. The bend it caused to the front cover made the unfeasibly well-endowed girl pictured there look like she was pushing her chest out even further.

A shadow passed close by the window, then the door handle rattled slightly and started to turn. I stepped to the side nearest the hinges and tucked into the corner. I had nowhere to hide, so that left only one course open to me.

Attack.

I slid the other magazine—the one where the models wore slightly more clothing—out of the pocket of my stolen coat, furled it tight in my fist. I shrugged off the coat, letting it drop. It might offer a bit of extra padding if I got hit, but it would also slow me down. And besides, I wasn't planning on getting hit.

Already, I had played through what my adversary might do as he entered. He might walk straight in. He might turn away

353

ZOË SHARP

from me, toward the desk. Or he might turn toward me, maybe reaching for a set of keys from the back of the door. I overlaid each image with a grid map of strike points, had time for one deep breath.

The door opened. A man, wearing a fleece but no heavy outdoor coat, stepped inside. He began to turn away from me. I stabbed the blunt end of the rolled magazine into his right kidney, putting weight and muscle behind it. His legs gave out on him and he started to fold, reaching for the desk as he fell.

He dragged in a breath as if to shout. I moved over him, shouldered the door closed, and grabbed a handful of hair on his crown. Yanking his head back, I slashed the magazine across his larynx, hard enough so that the only sound he could make was muted gargling.

Hands to his throat, he went all the way down. And as he did so, I got a good look at his face, and I recognized him.

Hackett.

I told myself that the reason I added strikes to his elbows, wrist joints, and knees was to temporarily disable him, but I couldn't be a hundred percent sure I was telling the truth. All I knew was that as his eyes swiveled up to mine, they widened with realization and fear, and in that moment I won back a small measure of what he'd once taken away from me.

It wasn't enough.

I renewed my grip on the magazine. Nobody ever thinks something made of paper makes such an effective weapon, but back in the days when I used to teach self-defense classes, it was something I always advised people—especially women— to carry. It looks inoffensive, unthreatening, and certainly wouldn't be taken as going equipped in a court of law. But rolled tightly like that, you could punch one through an internal door—or into an internal organ if it came to that.

Hackett was certainly going to be pissing blood for a few days from the kidney strike.

If he was lucky . . .

I readied, saw him flinch in reflex. I brought the magazine flashing down, aiming for an area just behind the temple, where four major bones meet. At one time I would have been able to name them. Now I simply knew where to aim to hit the precise spot—the weakest point of the skull, with an artery running beneath. The impact point that makes boxers bounce off the mat before they realize they've lost the fight.

I landed the blow. Hackett slumped. He wasn't getting up again.

I stood over him, breathing harder than I needed to for the effort I'd just expended, fists aching with the need to keep pounding at him.

The blood ran so fierce in my ears that I hardly heard the door opening again until I caught it in my peripheral vision.

I crouched and spun, but someone grabbed both arms and piled me back into the corner behind the door.

"Charlie!"

Even as I remembered Sean's voice, I still didn't—couldn't—let myself relax.

"For fuck's sake, don't kill the bastard," he growled. "We need him."

SIXTY-EIGHT

"NEED HIM FOR WHAT?" I DEMANDED.

"To nail that bastard Parris to the fucking wall."

He tossed the words over his shoulder as he bent toward the man on the ground, lifted one eyelid.

I gaped. "Hackett *told* you that Parris ordered . . . everything that happened?"

Sean shook his head. "No—Clay did. I found the poor sod like that. Bleeding, dying. He wanted me to know . . . like his last fucking confession."

Hackett's limbs moved in feeble circles, the way a sleeping dog still chases rabbits in its dreams. I wondered what Hackett might be chasing in his and decided I didn't want to know. And what was more, I didn't care.

Sean slapped the man's face, not particularly gently. It did not wake him. Sean swore under his breath.

"So . . . everything you said to Gregor was . . . ?"

He threw me a quick, dismissive glance. "What—you thought I meant it?"

I moved sideways so I could keep a check through the meshed glass. It also gave me a good excuse not to have to look him in the eye.

"Well, let's just say you were very convincing."

He sighed with a weariness that held disappointment rather than surprise.

"I had to be. You know how much undercover work I did back in the army—so did Parris. If he'd thought I was faking it, I'd be in a hole under the snow by now."

"He must like you then. He threatened to give me to Ivan, gift-wrapped."

Sean's glance was sharp, but he didn't comment. Instead, he slapped Hackett's face again. "Come on, soldier, snap out of it!"

Hackett groaned a little louder, legs and arms beginning to thrash, though still without any force.

"He was only in here for a second," Sean said. "What did you do to him?"

I shrugged. "Probably rather more than was good for him. But far less than he damn well deserved."

"With that?" Sean nodded to the magazine I hadn't realized was still clenched in my hand.

I nodded, dropping the weapon into the waste bin, where it uncoiled slowly and resumed its utterly inoffensive air. Only when I'd done so did I see Sean's shoulders relax slightly. I hadn't time to process quite what that meant.

Instead, I asked, "Where did you catch up with him in the end?"

"Jordan—just before he set off for the border." His mouth gave the faintest twitch. "One of his drivers was, ah, suddenly taken ill. They needed another, fast."

"And he trusted you?" I said, skeptical. "Why?"

"Because the others were hired grunts—they'd do what they were told and ask no questions. He knew that without some backup, Parris would probably have him killed after he got back here, just to make sure Gregor never found out about those two extra truckloads."

"Ah." I nodded. "And if he *didn't* come back, Gregor would have had him killed for failing to deliver."

"Yeah, so he was stuffed either way." He pinned me with a gaze I couldn't get a reading on. "He killed the guy you found in the bathroom, by the way—back at the villa. He told me that after what happened to Clay, he daren't leave anyone who might lead Ivan to him."

I glanced down at Hackett. "He deserves everything that's coming to him."

I might have moved in closer, but Sean blocked me, saying, "Look, I've told Hackett I'll keep him alive—get him out of here."

I glared at him, said with feeling, "Oh. Shit."

Hackett was still not entirely conscious, although his movements were gaining more coordination now. Still, he was in no state to get on his feet. "Well, you might have to carry him."

"Yeah, thanks for that."

On the floor, Hackett began to retch weakly onto the stained tiles. It did not make them look any worse. I jerked my head in his direction.

"How were you planning to get him out of here?"

"Snowmobiles," Sean said with a grimace. Hackett was in no fit state to stay aboard a snowmobile, even as a pillion passenger. "But I need to get some kind of confession out of Parris first."

A pity he hadn't been up in the guest suite when Parris had told me the truth of what happened, without a hint of duress . . .

"The security monitors," I said suddenly. "They record, pre-sumably—not just a live feed?"

"A rolling week, so I understand."

"In that case, we don't need to put the thumbscrews on Parris," I said. I nudged the still-puking Hackett with the toe of my boot, hard enough to elicit another groan. "Or him, for that matter . . ."

I'm not sure what Sean thought I might be preparing to do, but he grabbed my wrist. I was halfway to a countermeasure before he said quietly, "I gave him my word I'd get him out of here, Charlie."

I twisted out of his grasp. "All *right*," I said, aware my tone was sullen. "What do you want to do with him while we go find the security discs?"

If I'd been hoping he might suggest we lock him in a small cupboard, I was destined to be disappointed. Sean grasped Hackett by the scruff of his jacket and hauled him to his feet.

"He comes with us. It took me long enough to find the fucker. I'm not letting him out of my sight now."

SIXTY-NINE

WE WERE ALMOST AT THE SECURITY CONTROL ROOM WHEN ALL HELL broke loose.

Somewhere horribly close by, a siren started to screech. Even with fingers stuffed into my ears I heard echoes of others, outside in the central courtyard, elsewhere in the building.

"Bugger," I said. "I think they may have discovered I've become a fully paid-up member of the hole-in-the-wall gang."

Sean, forcing a dazed Hackett into a stumbling run, shook his head. "No offense, but they wouldn't go off the deep end for a simple escape." We caught the sound of automatic-weapons fire from outside, the chatter of a machine pistol, the answering crack of assault rifles. "I think you're the last of their worries now—we're under attack."

Hamilton?

She had gone very quiet over the phone when I'd repeated Parris's claim that she didn't have the resources to stage any kind of rescue. What if that silence wasn't because he was correct in his assessment, as I'd assumed, but because her guys were already on their way? She couldn't be sure the line was secure, so better to say nothing, even if it pissed me off, than to put her men in danger.

I didn't bother voicing any of this. Sean had never met her—as far as I knew—so it would be rhetorical at best.

As we neared the area where Ushakov had first brought me into the building, Sean shouldered open a side door and shoved Hackett through.

Inside was a break room with a couple of kitchen units and a kettle, sink, and drainer holding washed-up mugs. There was a scarred table in the center, surrounded by mismatched chairs in only slightly better condition than the one in the garage office. On the table sat a crusty bowl of white sugar and the kind of red, brown, and yellow squeezy bottles you'd get in a cheap roadside diner, each with part of its contents congealing around the spout.

Sean rammed Hackett down into the nearest chair with the command "Stay." Then he looked at me.

"Oh no," I said. "I'm not babysitting him."

"Charlie, we don't have a choice. I need to get those security discs, and I'm a hell of a lot less likely to be stopped doing it than you are. In case you haven't noticed, Venko doesn't run an equal opportunities program when it comes to personnel."

"'Cept the maids," Hackett said, voice still croaky from the blow to the larynx. He gave a raspy chuckle. "Half of 'em are hookers who go like—"

Sean gripped him by the throat, quite literally choking off what he'd been about to say. "Your life is in Charlie's hands," Sean said, giving him a shake before he let go. "Don't give her the excuse she's hoping for to finish what she started."

"Hey, you can't leave me with that crazy bitch. You promised!" Hackett broke off into coughing.

"You can trust her," Sean said, his eyes boring into mine. "She's a professional—aren't you, Charlie?"

"Sean—" I began warningly.

He stepped in closer, murmured, "Please, don't make a liar out of me . . ."

I hesitated a moment longer, then nodded. "Just be quick, though, will you? I don't know how long my resolve will last."

He gave me what might have been a smile, but it came and went too fast to be sure. Opening the door a crack, he checked the corridor outside, slipped through, and was gone.

Leaving me alone again in a room with James Hackett.

For a moment the only noise in the room was the buzz of the overhead fluorescent tube. Hackett swallowed, eyes darting into the corners as though in search of somewhere to hide.

"So, what *did* happen to those two nonexistent trucks?" I asked abruptly. "The ones that never got off the boat in Odessa."

His face showed surprise. Of all the subjects I could have chosen, I guess this hadn't been at the top of his list. He almost seemed relieved by it. Relieved enough to answer, anyway.

"We left them parked in a secure warehouse, en route," he said with a smug smile. "To be returned for at some later date."

"Why Transnistria?"

His mouth opened and closed again as surprise turned to annoyance. "How the hell—?"

"Just answer the question, Hackett."

He glowered for a moment, then said grudgingly, "It's a small state—if you can call it that. The UN reckons it's part of Moldova, but after the former USSR came apart, there was a minor civil war over it. The laws there can be more . . . *flexible*, shall we say. Ivan has been throwing plenty of money around, making lots of new friends."

"So was it ever Clay, or was Ivan stealing from his father all along?"

Hackett laughed. "Oh, he would have if he'd thought of it first."

"He's preparing the ground to take over, isn't he?"

"I would say so, yeah." Hackett nodded, put a hand to his head, which must have been still aching like a bastard. "And I doubt he's going to wait until his old man shuffles off this mortal coil from natural causes, either, if you catch my drift."

I swore under my breath.

"So . . . where'd you learn to fight like that, then?" he asked, still rubbing his head where I'd hit him. "Not in the army, eh?"

"Well, you and your pals—and Parris—saw to that, didn't you?"

"Hey, listen—"

"Don't," I said with cold precision. "No excuses. No lily-liver words about how you were forced into it. I know what being forced is all about. Nobody was holding a gun to your heads. And certainly nobody *forced* that look of fucking *glee* onto your face." I jerked to my feet, saw him flinch. "The colonel picked his scumbags well, didn't he? I bet you were halfway on board before he finished asking."

"He was *right*, though." His tone might have held a touch of belligerence now, but his eyes still skittered about the room. "Females are just not cut out for the kind of role we were training for."

"The very fact he felt the need to get rid of me speaks differently."

"I don't mean that. You were good enough. Shit, you put most of us to shame. But combat's not the same as training. You lose a teammate, and it fucking hurts, but you suck it up and get on with the job. But if that teammate is a *female* who's

363

killed, maimed, or captured, it blows a big hole in the morale of the whole unit."

"I see." I was suddenly reminded sharply of Najida, the Iraqi woman Dawson had taken me to see in that clinic in Kuwait City, who'd been betrayed first by the men who'd abducted and raped her, and then again by her family. "So, *you* were the ones with the attitude problem, but *I* was the one who had to suffer for it."

"No! Well . . . yes. OK, but—"

I held up a hand. "When up to neck in fucking hole, Confucius say, stop digging."

His mouth shut so suddenly I thought he'd bite through his tongue. Even so, he couldn't leave it alone, and after a moment's silence, he said, "I'm sorry. Not that I s'pose an apology after all this time is worth much. I've done some pretty nasty things in my time, but that . . . well, it's stayed with me. Haunted me, you might say."

With a little more practice he might even have sounded sincere.

"You're right," I said. "An apology from you—no matter how late—is worth nothing at all."

SEVENTY

LESS THAN TEN MINUTES AFTER HE'D LEFT US, SEAN WAS BACK. IN his hands was a compact machine pistol—an Arsenal Shipka, the folding wire stock extended into his shoulder. The gun was produced in Bulgaria, chambered for Russian 9mm ammunition from a 32-round magazine. It was simple and robust in operation, and exported to police forces all over Eastern Europe.

As he came in, Sean shrugged a second weapon off his arm, where it hung by its strap. Hackett reached for it, but Sean pulled it away before he could get his hands on it. Even so, Sean hesitated fractionally before he passed it across to me.

Hackett threw his hands up. "Aw, come on, mate!"

"Nothing personal," Sean said. "But she's the better shot."

"Ha, she might be able to hit a target OK, but has she ever . . . you know?"

The question of how capable a killer I might be seemed a funny subject to be coy about, all things considered. Then I remembered what they'd done to me and the fact I hadn't killed any of them—either at the time or since. Maybe it wasn't quite such a funny question after all.

I swung the wire stock out from the side of the receiver and around into place, settling the gun in my hands.

"What do you think happened to Kuznetsov in Basra?" I asked and, without waiting for a reply, turned my attention to Sean. "Did you get the discs?"

He shook his head. "Apparently Parris ordered a full wipe of everything since you arrived."

"Of course," I said grimly. "He's getting ready to deny I was ever here."

"That would be my guess."

"Did you see any of the attackers—who they are?"

"Not Bulgarian SWAT or Special Forces, as far as I could tell. Hard to recognize anyone when they're in full tactical gear and keeping a low profile."

"Numbers?"

"I don't know—small, though, otherwise we'd be overrun by now. They seem to be trying to keep everyone pinned down rather than going for a breach."

"Good enough," Hackett said. "Come on, mate. Give me a gun and we'll fight our way out."

"Slight problem with that," I pointed out. "They could be the good guys."

Hackett gave a rough laugh. "Depends which side you're on, darling."

I thought of Hamilton's man in Karbala. "Well I'm not going to shoot any of them until I find out."

"Either way, we're wasting time," Hackett said. "Are we getting out of here or what?"

"We need Parris," Sean said. "In this situation, where would he go?"

"He'll be with the Venkos—standard operating procedure if they're under threat."

A burst of gunfire sounded from outside—much closer than it had been before. I tensed in reflex, tucked my forefinger inside the trigger guard until I could be sure they weren't about to come through the doorway.

"Where?" Sean repeated.

Hackett let out a shaky breath, because he knew if he told us we'd go there—and that meant he would have to go, too. Probably unarmed. Sean took a step toward him.

"OK, OK. Secure rooms in the east wing. Blast doors more like a bloody bunker. That's where they'll be headed, if they're not there already."

"Parris will let *you* in, though, won't he?"

Hackett snorted. "He's more reasons not to. A bigger share of the haul, for a start."

Sean gave him a grim smile. "Well let's just hope you can be highly persuasive about your ongoing usefulness, then."

SEVENTY-ONE

WE CREPT BACK UPSTAIRS, FOLLOWING MUCH THE SAME ROUTE I'D taken on the way down, through the ornate rooms, passages, and open landings that were bigger than rooms in themselves. An extravagant use of space.

It sounded as if the attackers had not yet made it into the main body of the house. Venko's men were holding them successfully outside. How much longer that would be the case was anyone's guess.

Sean took point, with Hackett close behind him to guide the way. He'd clearly spent as much time in the Bulgarian mansion as he had in the sweltering Mosaic City in Jordan. He gave directions in low tones, or more often than not just a tap on one shoulder or another. Not giving him a weapon certainly made him careful about walking us into any kind of trap.

I brought up the rear, weapon ready but hoping like hell I wouldn't have to use it. I'd no desire to alienate Gregor by killing any more of his men. And still less did I want to risk Hamilton's wrath—if indeed she was behind the attacking force.

In other words, we had no clue what was going on and were trying hard not to make a bad situation worse.

In front, Sean halted suddenly, clenched fist raised in a "hold" gesture. Hackett flattened against the wall behind him. I faced rear, gripping the Shipka's polymer receiver, the wire buttstock pressing firmly, if uncomfortably, into my shoulder.

I glanced forward and found Hackett's gaze fixed on the front of my shirt where the butt of the gun was causing the sides to gape apart. I released the pistol grip just long enough to backfist him in the face, splitting his lip. He let out a muffled yelp. Sean glared at him. Hackett dabbed at a dribble of blood and jerked his head in my direction. Sean glared at me. I dragged the edges of my shirt together and glared right back.

We were at the end of a corridor where it opened out into a wide landing for yet another grand staircase leading to an upper floor. At least three sets of double doors led onto the landing, and the multiple entry points were reason for caution. The ceiling was high, and the staircase itself split both left and right at a half landing where hung a life-size portrait of some Bulgarian aristocrat on a prancing horse.

Abruptly, one of the doors on the main landing swung open and three men stepped out, heading for the stairs. The first man was Ushakov, the ex-Spetsnaz, walking softly and carrying an assault rifle with a fold-out stock. An AS Val, made in Russia, with a built-in suppressor that gave it a distinctive bulky barrel. It was the weapon he might have carried back when he was still doing black ops for the Russian government.

Shambling behind him was Gregor himself. Unarmed, he looked dreadful, his skin gray.

Bringing up the rear was Parris, alert, walking softly, with an Arsenal Shipka in his hands like those we carried. For a moment it was hard to tell if Gregor was their captive or their principal.

But when Sean stepped out into view, the way Ushakov moved quickly in front of Gregor told me the latter was the case. Ushakov stared down the barrel of Sean's weapon with cold eyes, but he did not try anything stupid.

As soon as Sean moved, I elbowed Hackett out of cover and took a bead on Parris. I aimed for his pelvis, low center mass where I could be absolutely certain of putting him down, even with a weapon I'd never fired before. Even if he was wearing body armor or made any sudden evasive maneuvers.

He didn't try anything stupid, either.

"What is this?" Gregor asked without apparent fear. "Have you turned against me, Mr. Hackett?"

"It's not you they're after," Hackett said. He pointed to Parris. "It's him."

"You little shit," Parris said pleasantly.

Hackett shrugged. "Well, needs must."

"And what do you want from Mr. Parris?" Gregor asked, and I was pleased that he didn't address him as "colonel" either.

"Same thing I wanted when I first arrived," I said before Sean could speak. "The truth."

"About Michael Clay?" Gregor asked. He tilted his head toward Sean. "You already have it, from his own lips."

"I'm sorry, sir, but we both know that isn't the case. Sean didn't kill Clay, no matter what he told you." I paused, said carefully, "I think you are well aware who did."

Gregor's shoulders slumped. He looked older, if that was possible.

"Yes," he said, almost a whisper. "I have always known it. But . . . he is my son."

"What he's become . . . it's not your fault."

He lifted his head and focused on me fully, as if seeing me for the first time. "He was with me, in the Balkans, when he was just a boy. He saw things no child should see . . ."

I wanted to say that many children had lived through that particular war and not turned into monsters, but I didn't think it would help.

We stood there without speaking for no more than a few seconds maybe, with sporadic gunfire audible outside. Ushakov and Sean never took their eyes off each other, like two circling dogs. Neither wanted to be the first to blink.

And then Parris took half a step back.

He was standing side on to me, facing Gregor, with the staircase on his right. As he moved, I saw his eyes slide up toward the top of the stairs. Mine followed.

At the highest point of the left-hand branch of the staircase, where the gap between ceiling and treads narrowed to a vee as it reached the next floor, I caught a glimpse of movement.

And the barrel of a gun.

I yelled a warning and dived for Gregor, just as the brutal crack of a three-round burst exploded down onto us.

I felt Gregor jerk as at least one of the rounds hit home. I rolled away from him and fired, using the gun as an extension of my arms, aiming by instinct.

Up on the stairs, my opponent gave a guttural cry and dropped his weapon. It clattered down half a dozen treads before coming to rest, wedged against part of the ornamental bannister. The man scrabbled to rise.

Sean was already sprinting for the stairs, taking them three at a time, keeping his own weapon on target. Ushakov stood over Gregor, scanning for additional threats. Hackett was crouched beside Gregor—more, I suspect, to use the old man's body for cover than to protect him.

I got to my knees, ears ringing savagely, and started to pat the old man down, looking for wounds. One round had torn through the flesh of his upper arm on a downward trajectory, scouring across his rib cage on the way out. It was messy, and no doubt painful, but not serious in itself. I was more worried about shock and blood loss.

"Where's the nearest medical kit?" I demanded of Ushakov.

"In the secure room. We were on our way there."

"Then let's go," I said. I threw Hackett and Parris a dismissive glare. "And seeing as I'm just a pathetic feeble *female*, you two can carry him."

Parris pinned me with an evil stare, but he slung his weapon onto its strap and bent to take Gregor's good arm. Between them, he and Hackett got him onto his feet. He made no sound of protest or pain, but he was sweating and had begun to tremble.

Sean came back down the stairs, dragging a man by the scruff of his jacket. He left a bloodied trail along the marble treads, and squealed as his injured leg bumped down each step.

When Sean reached the bottom he threw the man onto the ground at Gregor's feet, where he wrapped his hands around the blood leaching from his thigh and swore at all of us in three languages.

I didn't need to see his face to know who he was, and if I wasn't surprised, I was certainly disappointed. That must be nothing compared to how Gregor himself felt.

The gunman who'd just tried to kill him was Ivan, his son.

SEVENTY-TWO

BETWEEN THE FIVE OF US, WE GOT THE TWO INJURED MEN TO Gregor's panic room in the east wing, Ushakov leading the way. Gregor was carried with some care. The only reason Ivan wasn't dragged the whole way there was because his screaming caused his father distress and did not exactly allow us to proceed with any degree of stealth.

I got only a brief impression of the room as we got inside and Ushakov locked the steel door behind us. It was similar to the drawing room where I'd had my audiences with the old man, except there were no fireplaces and no windows, only the soft hum of an air ventilation system under the overhead lights.

Hackett and Parris gently maneuvered Gregor onto a wide couch, and Ushakov dumped a medical kit by my side. I wasn't quite sure why I was the one who had to tend to him, but I wasn't going to argue about it now.

The medical supplies were pretty comprehensive. I pulled on a pair of latex gloves and got on with it. The kit even had three or four different types of scissors, including those for cutting away clothing. I did so, slicing up the side seam of his sweater and shirt and peeling the sleeves of both down his arm. His skin was so pale it was almost translucent, threaded with blue veins and already beginning to bruise. He was also shivering.

"Somebody fetch him a blanket," I said over my shoulder. "We need to keep him warm."

The gouge across Gregor's rib cage was down to the bone, but it was clean and little more than a graze. The arm was still bleeding, at an ooze rather than a gush. I checked that the bone was intact and cleaned up the ragged ends of flesh with antiseptic wipes, then made a pad of gauze to cover the wound.

"Here," I said to Hackett. "Wrap your hand around his arm—there, almost in his armpit. Now squeeze, gently, until the bleeding stops."

Although not keen to comply, Hackett did as he was ordered. I checked Gregor again for other injuries, but only the one round had hit. By then, with Hackett pressing on the main artery into his arm, the bleeding had slowed almost to a stop. I fixed the pad of gauze in place as a compression dressing, making sure to tape it only halfway around his arm so it didn't cause swelling.

Then, between us, we laid him propped slightly on his side. Ushakov draped a blanket over the old man with surprising sympathy.

"Thank you," Gregor said as I rose, and I knew he was not referring only to the medical aid.

I nodded. "You're welcome. There's morphine if the pain is bad, but it will slow your breathing."

"Is not so bad." He gave a faint smile. "Is not first time . . . I have been shot."

I nodded again and turned away, peeling off the bloodied gloves.

Sean had dumped Ivan on the floor and was standing over him with the Shipka readied. I hesitated a moment, then picked up a new pair of gloves and approached Gregor's son.

He snarled like a cornered dog. "Get away from me, you stinking *bitch*."

I shrugged, bent to pick out a rubber tourniquet from the kit, and threw it into Ivan's lap.

"Sort yourself out then. But do it quickly—you're making a fucking mess on the carpet."

Parris straightened. "Well, everything here seems to be under control," he said. "I ought to go check on the men."

His eyes flicked between Ushakov and Sean as he spoke, as though they were the only two whose permission he needed to seek.

I swung the Shipka off my shoulder into my hands and lined up on him steadily.

"I don't think so, John. This time you don't get to walk away."

"My dear girl—walk away from what, exactly?"

"Responsibility. You're Gregor's head of security. That means you're supposed to keep him safe. But the moment you saw Ivan up there, taking a bead on his father, your only thought was to step back out of the line of fire," I said. "I'm not well up on my military history, but as I understand it, during the battle of Stalingrad the Russians executed their own men for that."

"Even if that were true . . . this isn't bloody Russia."

I glanced at Ushakov. He returned my gaze blandly enough, but his jaw was tight.

"No, it isn't," I agreed. "Or you'd be dead already."

He laughed. "Don't you think you're being a little too . . . emotional? Typical female trait. The shock of the gunfight, no doubt."

Parris looked about him, but if he was hoping for agreement or approval from the others, they gave him no response.

"I thought I saw movement at the top of the stairs and merely repositioned for optimum visibility," he said, sounding every inch the commanding officer. "Gregor Venko is my employer. Why would I wish any harm to come to him?"

"And yet there he is—shot by his own son. On your watch."

"Have you considered the possibility that perhaps *you* were Ivan's target, and by throwing yourself at his father, *you* were the reason he was injured?"

Ivan had been fumbling to secure the tourniquet around his upper thigh, holding it tight enough to stem the bleeding. At Parris's words he stopped, head jerking up.

"Yes!" he shouted, with the fervor of a drowning man tossed a life belt. "I wanted that lying bitch dead!"

"But you're a shit shot, is that what you're saying?" I demanded. "You were what—less than six meters from a static target—and you *missed*?"

He scowled, unwilling to admit to something that went so against his ego however much it might have saved his skin. "Shooting down like that, at an angle . . . is not easy," he muttered eventually.

"There we are then. Mystery solved," Parris said briskly. "Now—"

"Stay where you are," Gregor said. His voice was weaker than it once had been, but it carried no less authority for all that. It was enough to make Parris hesitate. "Did you think I would allow you to wipe security tape without first making copy?" Gregor asked him. "After all, I am 'master strategist, always three step ahead.' Was that not how you describe me?"

Parris sagged visibly. It came over me, in a hot prickle of awareness, that Gregor had seen and heard the conversation I'd had with Parris when he'd taken me back up to the guest suite after Hackett and Sean had arrived with the depleted convoy. But how . . . ?

My eyes flicked sharply to Ushakov. His face was expressionless as always, but I knew, even so, that he was the one who'd taken the discs to Gregor. Or a copy of them, at any rate.

Gregor, I reasoned, had not trusted Parris for some time. And right now the colonel must have realized he was completely and utterly fucked.

Even so, the man was not prepared to give up without a last-ditch effort to retrieve the situation.

"I know it looks bad, sir," he said to Gregor, "but you must understand I was merely playing along with Ivan in order to learn his intentions, while doing everything I could to—"

"You LIAR!" Ivan roared. It was rapidly becoming his catch-phrase. "*You* were the one who was stealing—you and *him*." He stabbed a bloodied finger at Hackett, who instinctively took a couple of steps back. "And I—" A finger to his own chest now. "—*I* discovered this, by forcing it out of Clay."

"You tortured him to death," Gregor said, almost sadly.

Ivan scuttled closer on arse and knuckles, dragging his injured leg. His efforts with the tourniquet had not been entirely successful, and it was still leaching blood through his combat pants. If someone didn't deal with that, and soon, he was going to be in serious trouble.

His eyes were wild with pain and shock and desperation. There was a kind of madness in them. I guessed it had always been there, but usually he kept it better hidden.

"He was a bad man, *Papa*. A terrible man. He was stealing from you, and his comrade, they kidnap and rape women. They—"

"No," Gregor said, with a gentle finality that was no less effective for not being a shouted command. He reached out his good hand, and Ivan grasped it with both his, kissing the old man's fingers in supplication. "You tortured him, and then you took what he stole for yourself."

Gregor raised his head and looked straight into my eyes with tears gathering in his own.

"You once gave me back my son," he said in a voice like rusted metal graunching over rock. "But now you have taken him away from me again."

"If he gets treatment—"

"No." Gregor cut me off with a shake of his head. "By exposing his . . . treachery."

There was nothing I could say to that, so I said nothing. Silence was becoming my catchphrase.

Gregor looked down at where Ivan still clutched at his hand, head bowed, and met my eyes again. The tears loosed and ran now.

"Please . . ." was all he said.

I knew what he was asking for—an execution.

I couldn't do it.

I don't know how long I stood there, frozen. It could have been a couple of seconds or even a minute.

Then Parris gave a gusty sigh. "That's the trouble with sending a girl to do a man's job," he said. "They simply haven't got the balls for it."

As he spoke, he raised his weapon to shoulder height. From where I was standing, I couldn't tell if he was aiming for Gregor or Ivan, but I wasn't about to take a chance either way.

Neither, it seemed, were Sean or Ushakov.

The three of us fired almost simultaneously, so that it was impossible to say which of the rounds struck Parris first. His body danced from the impact, limbs splaying as he went backward and down. The Shipka dropped from his nerveless fingers and bounced off the carpet in an end-over-end cartwheel that made me hold my breath. Anything that operated on an open-bolt blowback system was far more likely to discharge under such abuse.

For once we were lucky. The weapon spun under a chair and stilled before Parris himself finished falling.

He lay on his back, one leg twitching. As my hearing cleared, I just had a chance to hear him rasp in his last breath as his lungs flooded and his heart gave out.

Hackett, who'd jumped for cover, rose with a shaky breath. *"Fuck."*

Ushakov crossed to the body with care, the AS Val at the ready, but Parris had already gone. Ushakov kicked him, just to be sure, then spat on the corpse.

"Ublyudok," he said.

I didn't know what that meant, but I could make a pretty good guess.

I stepped closer to Ivan, who had not raised his head or reacted to the gunfire. Carefully, I reached down and loosened the tourniquet on Ivan's leg, slipped it off, and placed it on the couch next to Gregor.

He nodded, just once, eyes closing briefly.

"Go," he said.

I listened, and despite the sound insulation inside the room, I could still hear occasional bouts of distant gunfire.

"That may be easier said than done."

Gregor raised tired eyes to Ushakov. "Show them."

Ushakov jerked his head, and we followed him toward another steel door at the far end of the room, where he punched in a code to an electronic lock.

As the door closed behind us, the last glimpse I had of Gregor Venko was of him cradling his dying son.

SEVENTY-THREE

BEYOND THE DOOR USHAKOV OPENED WAS A CORRIDOR LEADING TO a stone stairwell. Instead of flickering torches, the way down was illuminated by floor lighting—the type that shows you the way to the emergency exits on a passenger flight. A cold breeze whistled up the curved steps like a chimney stack.

"Where does this go?" Sean asked.

"Outside. Further down the mountain," Ushakov said. "The tsars used it to smuggle in local girls."

I began to wish I'd kept hold of my stolen coat. As it was, I'd already begun to shiver.

"I hope you've got a phone on you," I said to Sean, "or we'll have frozen to death before we get down to Borovets."

Ushakov reached into his pocket and pulled out a smart-phone, tossed it to me. I only just caught it, one-handed, glanced down, and realized it was the one Parris took from me when I arrived.

"You didn't chuck it away," I said, surprised.

"Was going to sell instead," he admitted morosely. "Would have fetched good price on eBay."

"Thank you," I said. "And take good care of Gregor."

He nodded and gave Sean a vague salute, then turned away without any further good-byes. Hackett, I noticed, he ignored altogether.

I couldn't blame him for that.

I switched the phone on as we began to descend. It seemed to take a long time to go through its start-up routine, but it showed no signal at the end of it.

"I think we need to wait until we're above ground, at least," I said.

"We should have asked him how far it was," Hackett complained. "I'm bloody freezing."

"Don't worry, we'll be outside soon enough, and then it really *will* be cold," Sean told him. "Christ, I never thought I'd miss the heat of Iraq."

"Sean . . ." I began, but wasn't sure how to continue.

He paused on the stairs, looked back at me. With the light at floor level, it was hard to judge his expression—or his mood. "What?"

"What happened—when you found Clay? What did he tell you, exactly?"

He shrugged, began to descend again. When he spoke it was over his shoulder, and I think we were both aware of Hackett, dogging our steps, listening in.

"He was almost gone by the time I got there. Ivan had made a hell of a mess of him. Some of what he said didn't make much sense—about stolen treasures and Parris making him do it, and how sorry he was about the girl." He paused. "I thought he meant you."

"He might have—partly. But I wasn't the last for Clay. He'd acquired a taste for it." And I told him, briefly, about Najida.

About what had been done to her, both by Clay and by her family. At the end of it Sean swore under his breath. Hackett said nothing.

"He kept coming back to Parris, and I couldn't work out if he meant Parris was behind the theft, or the rape. I didn't find out until later that he meant both."

"So why did you go to Karbala?"

"Moe," Sean said. "The kid I hired as my local fixer-cum-guide. I asked him what he knew about stolen antiquities, and he said nothing, but he had an uncle—"

"—in Zubayr," I finished for him. "Yes, he took me there, too."

"You met Moe?" There was animation in his voice. "Great kid, isn't he?"

Yes, he was . . .

The stairs eventually leveled out into a passageway with an arched stone roof like an old wine cellar. The lighting continued in pinpoint LEDs along either wall.

The temperature was dropping constantly. By the time we reached the limit of the tunnel—maybe three hundred meters of gentle downward slope—it was bitter.

At the end of the tunnel was a wooden door with a huge iron key still in the lock. Sean turned it, not without effort, and we stepped out into a one-room hut on the other side. I moved to the window, which was partially covered with snow on the outside.

"Any idea where we are?" Sean asked.

"None, but there's a ski-lift or cable-car pylon just visible, so if they follow those, they should be able to find us."

I tried my phone again, and this time it was showing a single bar of signal. I did that thing where you hold the phone up above your head at arm's length, as if that was going to make a difference. It didn't.

"I'll try outside."

As soon as I stepped out, I felt naked. I sank into the soft powder snow up to my knees and struggled to go more than half a dozen meters from the doorway. It was enough to produce another bar of signal.

I dialed Madeleine's number with fingers that now throbbed from the cold. When she answered, my face was numb enough that my voice sounded a little slurred.

"Charlie! Where are you?"

I explained. She promised to have someone up to us as soon as she could, and that they would bring warm clothing with them.

"Is Sean . . . all right?"

"He's fine," I said without further explanation. "Who organized the assault team?"

"Hamilton."

"I didn't think she had the manpower."

"She had enough for a diversion."

"Well, tell her to pull her men back. I think Gregor's had enough bloodshed. If she goes in and talks to him, she might get further than she expects."

I rang off and turned back toward the cabin. Before I could move closer, the door burst open and Hackett leaped through. He jumped into the snow, staggered as if he'd landed in deep water, and began to run.

Automatically, purely on a reflex, I raised the Shipka to my shoulder and took a bead on him.

A second later, Sean appeared in the doorway. The muzzle of his weapon was already up, already tracking. I saw the intense concentration in every line of his body. Hunter on prey.

"Sean—!"

He fired at the exact moment as my shout. Even after all the gunfire in Gregor's stronghold, out here the shot seemed louder and more crisply defined. Hackett's head snapped to the side, spraying a pale mist of blood and debris into the freezing air. He pirouetted with an odd grace and then flopped into the snow in a tangle of lifeless limbs like a dancing puppet with all strings sliced through.

The memory of watching Sean go down the same way, to the same injury, sent my heart rate screaming. I threw myself down alongside Hackett, rolled him partially onto his back. That was as much as I needed to do to know he was beyond anything I could do for him—even if I'd wanted to.

Part of his skull had sheared away like a broken egg, leaving jagged shards of bone and a glutinous mush that spilled out obscenely into the snow. All around him were stark pinpricks of color where his fluids had melted through the crust.

A flashback to the day of Sean's shooting came brutally into my mind. The injury that had just killed Hackett, and the one that had come so close to killing Sean, overlaid each other, similar enough to send me reeling.

A shadow fell across the body. I jerked my eyes upward, found Sean standing over the pair of us, staring down. The gun was still up and ready

I slumped onto my backside in the snow, murmured, "I thought . . . you promised to keep him alive."

Sean straightened very slowly, moving like an old man. "Only until we got out. Then all bets were off."

"But . . . why?"

His eyes moved to mine. I searched for something behind them, but found nothing.

"Because now we can part even."

EPILOGUE

THIS TIME, WHEN I ARRIVED AT MADELEINE'S AGENCY HEADQUARTERS in Kings Langley, I was shown into the conference room rather than her office, although by the same Mr. Smooth assistant.

I'd spent six days in Bulgaria, going through endless rounds of red tape with the authorities. The final body count was four dead, and another three injured. The dead included Parris, Hackett, Ivan, and one of the men defending the hunting lodge from the assault. The injured included Gregor and two of Woźniak's guys. One was walking wounded, the other more seriously hurt.

All in all, it could have been much worse.

I think once Gregor had been professionally patched up by the doctors, he'd spread enough largesse to make most of what had occurred up the mountain simply go away. He hadn't picked this as his home ground for nothing. What was going to happen to the three truckloads of Iraqi antiquities was anybody's guess, but I daresay Gregor and Hamilton would come to some . . . arrangement.

As for Sean's killing of Hackett, I looked the investigating officers square in the eye and swore it was self-defense.

I'm not sure if that provoked Sean's gratitude or made him despise me. I might have asked him about that, but before I knew it he was on a plane back to New York. I only found *that* out through Parker.

He congratulated me on clearing Sean, told me to take some time before I came back. Feeling aimless, I flew to the UK and spent a couple of days in the uncomfortable company of my parents in Cheshire, where I retrieved the Honda Fireblade. The one Gregor once gave me as a thank-you for saving Ivan's life that time in Germany. It was still under a sheet in the back of my parents' garage. I dusted it off and then escaped up north to visit friends.

It felt good to be back on a bike again.

I was having breakfast in a café in the Lake District when I got Madeleine's call, but within four and a half hours I was pulling up outside her office—and that included two stops for fuel on the way. One of the joys of riding a motorcycle is you don't get hung up in traffic.

Now, aware of being in my flyblown leathers, and with a very bad case of helmet-hair, I sat drinking coffee at the conference table. I'd asked Mr. Smooth if Luisa Dawson was around, but he would only say that she was "on assignment," so I was left to my own devices.

I was halfway down my third cup when the door finally opened and Madeleine walked in, immaculately dressed as always. Two steps behind her was a guy in a dark suit, with prematurely gray hair and watchful eyes.

"Parker!" I said, rising. "I didn't expect to see you here."

"Just got in on the red-eye this morning," he said, looking as rested and relaxed as only a man who always flies first class can do. He took in my unbusinesslike attire and smiled. "You're looking good, Charlie."

I grimaced. "Well, this was not quite how I had in mind spending my day when I got dressed this morning. Speaking of which, would one of you like to tell me what *is* going on?"

Madeleine, who'd been watching the two of us, smiled also. She was carrying an armful of manila folders, which she put down on the table, together with a slim laptop, flipping open the lid.

"Aubrey Hamilton has been mounting a little side operation in Iraq," she said as she tapped on the keyboard. "Luisa is out there with her right now. Things came to a head this morning, and we thought you'd want to be there, so to speak, to watch the footage."

I glanced at Parker, but from the fact he wasn't asking any questions, I assumed I was the only one still in the dark.

"What kind of side operation?"

"Probably best she reads you in on that herself," Parker said. He took the seat next to mine and reached for the coffeepot. There must have been a proximity sensor on the damn thing, because almost as soon as he'd done so, Mr. Smooth appeared with a recharged pot and extra cups and saucers.

Madeleine pointed a remote at the big flat-screen TV mounted on the wall at one end of the room. While we waited for it to sync with the laptop, she handed out the folders.

I opened mine with a certain caution, unsure what I might find. Whatever I'd been expecting, it wasn't the photo of a woman's scarred face, staring straight and fearless into the lens of the camera.

"But . . . this is Najida," I said. "The woman who—"

"—Clay raped in Basra," Madeleine finished for me. "Yes. Ever since Luisa Dawson first told me about her, the case has bothered me. I wanted to do something about it. Not just for her, but for all women who find themselves in that situation—betrayed and abandoned."

"So where does Hamilton come in?"

"We discussed the situation quite a bit while we were in Borovets and you were . . . otherwise engaged. It turns out that under her rather steely exterior she has something of a heart of gold."

"Too malleable," I said. "Titanium, maybe?"

Madeleine smiled but ignored my comment. "And we agreed that the first course of action was to catch the men responsible, and not only for them to be punished, but for them to be *seen* to be punished."

"If you want to punish Clay any further, you'll need a shovel to dig him up first."

Parker took a sip of his coffee to hide what I suspected might be a grin. Madeleine favored me with a stern look.

"Clay was not acting alone, and there has been a further attack with an identical MO since he was killed. So, his partner, whoever that was, has acquired a new accomplice and is carrying on without him."

"Still no official investigation, I assume?"

She shook her head.

I would have asked more, but the laptop chimed with an incoming feed, and moments later Aubrey Hamilton's face appeared on the flat-screen, considerably larger than life. There were banks of monitors behind her.

"Well, the gang's all here," she said by way of greeting, and toasted my boss with the can of Diet Coke she was holding. "You must be Parker Armstrong. Good to put a face to the voice at last."

Parker nodded. "Likewise, ma'am."

"We received intel that a suspicious vehicle had been seen cruising one of the local markets, so we threw chum in the water and waited for the sharks to start circling, ready to take the bait," Hamilton said, straight to business. "And trust me, you have no idea how much chum we had to throw." Somebody in the room behind her spoke and she gave them a curt nod over her shoulder. "OK people, we've gotten the feed from this morning all set up and ready to roll. Let's go."

The picture changed to a jerky shot of a street scene from what looked like a camera hidden in the front of a bag. It swung gently as the person holding it walked, turning occasionally to face street stalls, or outward across the street to the other side of the market. To one side I could see dark folds of cloth from the *burqa* the figure wore, swaying as they walked.

There was a microphone recording as well, picking up traffic noises, car horns, and the noisy exhaust note of scooters, the babble of voices and calls from the market stallholders.

The figure stopped at one stall and spoke to the stallholder in Arabic. I heard enough of the voice to recognize that it was a woman. When she turned sideways, the bag camera caught a portion of the street behind her. Moving slowly at the curb was a dusty beige van, but I couldn't see any detail of the driver.

Unconsciously, I felt my pulse quicken.

The woman finished her conversation with the stallholder and moved on, apparently oblivious. She stepped down off the curb and turned right into a side street. The sunlight was dimmer there, although I calculated it was midafternoon in Iraq, three hours ahead of the UK. It took the lens a moment to adjust, then I saw parked cars, empty boxes from the stalls, and storefronts with shutters pulled down over the windows.

As an ambush site, it was ideal.

The bag swung suddenly, revealing the beige van was now alongside the woman. She turned, said something I couldn't catch, the first signs of alarm in her voice. The van's side door slid open. A man lurched out and grabbed the woman and the bag. The picture went haywire as she was thrown inside, shrieking and pleading in Arabic.

I heard a man's voice say, "Drive!" and the sound of a gunned engine came clearly over the audio track.

The bag was still clutched under the woman's arm. By accident or design, it pointed the camera up at her attacker, who forced her into a corner of the van and pulled a combat knife from a sheath on his belt. His face was hidden by a wound *keffiyeh*, so that all I could see were his eyes. They were all I needed to see to glean his intention.

Suddenly, the man stumbled and almost lost his balance as the driver braked hard and swore.

I heard voices shouting in American-accented English for him to get out of the van, to throw down any weapons, for him not to be stupid.

And then the man with the knife started to swear, too.

He looked down at his erstwhile "victim" with eyes that were fearful now, quickly turning vicious. He lunged with the knife, but a second later his hands dropped sharply and the blade clattered to the metal floor of the van. A long groan escaped from behind the headscarf and he fell backward from, I guessed, a well-aimed knee to the groin.

The side door shot back and Woźniak's face loomed into the shot, a machine pistol in his grasp.

"You OK, Dawson?"

"Oh, yeah," the woman in the *burqa* said.

The bag camera jostled around again, then settled on her would-be attacker, now lying facedown on the van floor with what looked like Woźniak's knee in his back as his hands were zip-tied behind him. Dawson reached out and yanked the *keffiyeh* away from his face.

"Well, hello, *Dave*," she said to Bailey. "Want to hear the good news, mate? Not only are you going to prison for a *very* long time, but you're going to prison in *Iraq* . . ."

❖

I said my good-byes to Madeleine, and Parker walked me out to the bike.

"Did you know what she was planning—Hamilton, I mean?" I asked.

"I had an idea. She's got a surprisingly strong sense of justice, for a spook."

"Yeah, it's a dying art," I said, sticking my key into the Fireblade's ignition. "So is truth, it seems."

He stuck his hands in his pockets, raised an eyebrow. "Oh?"

I sighed. "You knew what Sean was doing right from the start, didn't you? He wanted to know what really happened back in the army, so he decided to track down and talk to the men involved. But before he did anything, he discussed it with you."

"Did Sean tell you that?"

I swung my leg over the bike and reached for my helmet. "He didn't have to. You were his partner, his friend. He didn't trust me anymore. Of course he'd talk it through with you."

"Maybe he mentioned it," Parker allowed. "But when Clay was killed, I was truly worried that he'd gone off the rails."

"Honestly? Or did you realize what it might look like from the outside, and think it might be a good opportunity to cut your losses? To get someone else—me—to do your wet work for you."

"Charlie, I—"

"Save it. I don't think there's a whole hell of a lot you can say right now that will make this sound any better."

I waited, even so, for a more adamant denial. It didn't come.

I murmured, "I thought not," and pulled on my helmet, flicking the front section up away from my face and buckling the strap.

"You said it yourself, Charlie. Since he came back . . . well, he didn't really ever *come* back, did he?"

"There are easier ways to get rid of employees, Parker. Sooner or later, almost anyone can be persuaded to hand in their resignation." I hit the starter, and the Fireblade's engine growled to life. As I toed the bike into gear and began to let the clutch out, I raised my voice so I'd be heard over the top of it, adding, "And speaking of resignations—take this as mine."

ACKNOWLEDGMENTS

Aubrey Hamilton
Britni Patterson
Claiborne Hancock
Courtney Girton
David Farrer
Derek Harrison
Dina Willner
Don Marple
Emma Yates
Heather Venables

Jane Hudson
Jane Parsons
Jill Harrison
John Lawton
Judy Myers
Jules Farrer
Libby Fischer Hellmann
Pippa White
Thomas Talinski
Toni Goodyear